THE TRADED PRINCE

JL KAYSON

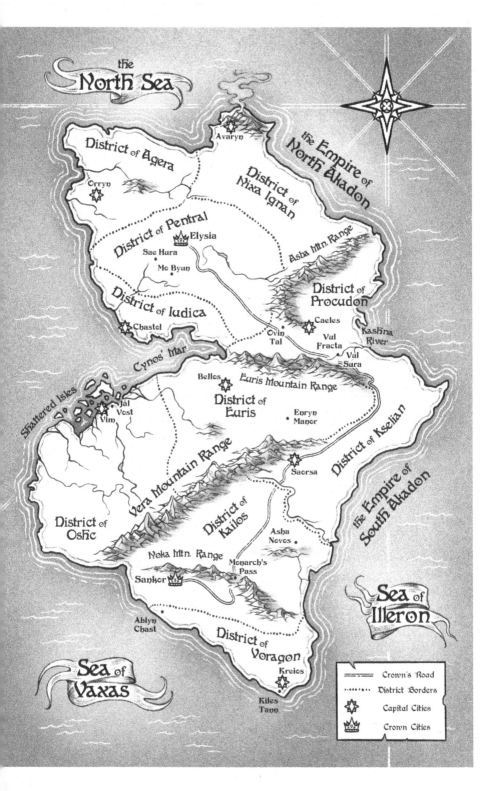

Nymeria Publishing LLC

First published in the United States of America by Nymeria

Publishing LLC, 2023

Nymeria Publishing

PO Box 350747

Jacksonville, Fl 32235

Visit our website at www.nymeriapublishing.com

Print ISBN 979-8-9883332-0-3

Ebook ISBN 979-8-9883332-1-0

1st Edition

Printed in U.S.A

To those who have ever longed to come home

CONTENTS

PART ONE: AN EMPIRE DIVIDED

CHAPTER
ONE

Orryn, Agera District, North Akadon

With the way he was feeling, Ezran didn't think there was a single thing in the Realm that would help ease his hangover. Waking up cradled by a tree in someone's roof garden did nothing to steady his nausea, nor did the sun's cresting soothe his poor, sensitive eyes. The crowd that gathered around him in the vibrant market certainly didn't relieve the shakiness and the incoming fist was hardly a cure for his pounding head.

Ezran hit the side of a sturdy wooden stand, groaning at how exuberantly orange its decorative silks were. The clatter of metal goods came like another blow. His headache now pulsed in time with his surprised heartbeat, disguised as a rhythmic, vicious crown. Each violent ache was a threat to end him then and there, each loud noise another dagger for its use. He put a hand to where his jaw went numb, rubbing out the smart as he fought not to empty his stomach and think properly.

"That was a tad uncalled for..." Ezran said through gritted teeth.

"You deserve it and worse!" came a shouted rebuttal.

Ezran leveraged himself up as he turned just in time to narrowly avoid another fist. Even with the mess he was in, a familiar smile crept onto his face as he raised his hands in peace.

"Now, now, I think we can talk this out, ser."

The man spun, red faced and fuming, taller than Ezran by a significant amount. The autumn stained air made every billowing puff mist as he breathed. He was a bull of a man, one Ezran thought he should have remembered, even as drunk as he'd gotten last night. It was a sobering sight to see this bulk charging right at him.

"No talking! Not after what you did!"

Ezran dodged again, backing up to the perimeter of commoners all gathered for the show. By the looks on their faces, they had no intention of letting him leave, nor calling the city guard. Considering most were farmers, they probably thought it a normal pastime.

"Good ser, I would gladly let you beat me to a pulp if deserved, but the fact of the matter is I have no idea what offense I've given!"

The man bellowed, crashing into another achingly colored market stall when Ezran slipped by him again. His frustration infected his words as he screamed. "You know what you did, Breckhym!"

So Ezran did know the man. Interesting.

"I had a bit too much to drink, ser, I—"

His words turned into a yelp as the man swung. This time, when Ezran dodged to the side, a hand was there to snag his robes and haul him clear off his feet. The man kept him dangling despite his struggle as he walked him back. The crowd had no trouble parting then. Ezran almost cursed them until his attacker captured his attention, bringing their faces close together.

"This is for Brenia," the man snarled through his teeth.

Ezran swallowed, his smile slipping a bit. A hazy memory surfaced of a young woman who tasted of wine and laughter. Dark hair that curled around his pale fingers. Her smile, her lips, her gasping breath, and a bellow from some bull walking in on them.

Next thing he knew the air was failing to catch him. Ezran twisted on instinct just to snag a flash of awaiting cold mud. It splattered over him, his body aching with impact. His head protested sharply at the squealing pigs that ran to the corners of their selling pen, their dropping's scent invading his nose. It made his stomach twist until a gag finally interrupted his groan.

Brenia... his daughter, or his intended? Ezran guessed it didn't really matter as his stomach heaved again, but it might help in navigating the rest of this encounter. After all, the man remained pacing along the pen's safer border.

"Get up, Breckhym. We aren't finished yet."

Ezran sighed, breathing through his mouth as he rose. He swiped a dirty hand across his cheek and tried to fling the filth from his fingers.

"Come now. I think you have gotten more than your share of revenge, haven't you?"

"No!"

Of course not, he thought. *Another part to play, then.*

"Fine, fine," Ezran said as he rose to his feet. His robes were absolutely ruined. Genn was going to kill him. "Look, we can be civilized. How about I give you one good shot and

3

we call it square, yes? Make it good enough to knock me into the shit again and then we can go our separate ways. Satisfactory, friend?"

The bull stopped as Ezran approached the fence. Under all the anger that contorted his features, temptation was working to turn him. Thoughts passed through his light-colored eyes and Ezran could see the exact moment he caved, taking a fortifying breath with it.

"Fine."

A meaty fist rose, cocking back so far that Ezran fully expected to be out cold when it came down. At least it would be some type of relief from his consequences for a while. He screwed up his face, holding his breath, but remained still for the man to aim just right.

"That's enough!"

The man turned with his fist raised, but there was still enough of him that Ezran had to bend to catch his savior. His elation died the second he spotted the dark-skinned man, his muscled arms folded and slightly obscured by an orange half cape. Hazel eyes flicked from the commoner to Ezran, pulling a nervous laugh from the latter.

"Dearest Vyn, how lovely to run into you here!"

"This doesn't concern you," the man snapped.

Vyn strode forward, undaunted by the inch or so the commoner had over him.

"If that idiot is involved, then it does. Whatever grievance you have, you can take it up with me, or be on your way."

The man's eyes scanned Vyn, coming to rest on the weapon strapped to his back, a broad ax with a glowing green edge. His anger wavered, dissipating, and Ezran could almost see the realization that made him hesitate.

Kashadon.

As big as he was, a commoner would have little hope of taking on a trained magic wielding hunter. Even less with Vyn, but there was no way he could figure out his real occupation then.

Instead, he swung around and gave Ezran a withering glare. "We aren't done, Breckhym. I'll find you again. Soon."

Ezran smiled worriedly, giving him a small wave as he stalked off through the crowd. It broke apart as he passed and the people of Orryn finally returned to their bustling morning. The chatter made him wince. He busied himself with climbing out of the pen instead of meeting Vyn's gaze, but that didn't stop him from grabbing the back of Ezran's brown hair and hauling him forward.

"Ow, by Anbast's Judgment, Vyn! Go easy!" Ezran rubbed the back of his head when he was finally released, shooting a dark look that didn't last long once met with those hazel eyes. "Good morning to you, too."

"It wasn't a good morning, actually. I spent all of it searching every crack in this city looking for you. What was that about? Tumble into someone's bed again?"

"Honestly, I have no idea," he said, causing Vyn to take a deep breath. Brave, considering how close he stuck to Ezran's side. "I woke up alone. In a tree on a roof, but alone. He said all that was for a Brenia. Whether that's his daughter or his intended is unclear at this time."

"You're going to lead me to an early grave," Vyn muttered as they cut their way through the commotion.

Once they passed the open stalls of the market, haphazard buildings of white marble and scarlet stone rose to flank them, covered with autumnal silks and atrophying vines. Some greenery still clung on to life and dangled down from the roofs, determined to make it past harvest.

He admired their tenacity. Or maybe he was just looking for a distraction from more consequences.

"That way," Ezran yielded to Vyn's direction, trekking through several poorly planned alleys until they came to a small, tucked away intersection.

A silent, dry fountain made a perfect seat for a well groomed man, luminous teal robes flattering his skin of dark bronze. His black curls glinted with the morning sun as he raised his head, his anger falling away to shock.

It took a moment for him to push past it enough to ask, "What did you do now?"

"What a way to welcome me, Kal. Do we not have proper greetings anymore?" Ezran replied, straightening his robes like it would make any of it better.

A snort answered, and he turned to find a shorter figure tucked away into a corner. "There is absolutely nothing proper about you right now, Master Breckhym. You look atrocious."

"Name me one person who looks good after being tossed into a pigpen, Genn. And how many times must I tell you to call me Ezran?"

"You were tossed into a pigpen?" Kal stood from the fountain's lip, running his grey eyes over his form again. Ezran gave him a flat look.

"How else would I get like this?"

"I don't know. It's you. There are millions of things I wouldn't put past you to end up this way," Kal said.

Ezran had to give him that with an accepting nod.

"As riveting as that story possibly is, we have little time for it," Genn said, stepping up to join them.

His pale lip curled the closer he got to Ezran, while dark brown eyes raked over every inch of his form unkindly. His disgust with dirt seemed to reach a new height and he reflexively fixed his own robes of slate grey. He even went so far as to brush off his shoulders, like any speck of dust might dare tarnish his appearance.

"Just tell me what we have to deal with now," Kal sighed.

Ezran scoffed, "Absolutely nothing, it's all well handled!"

"Some commoner the size of Anbast has a score to settle," Vyn said. Ezran thought invoking imagery of the God of War and Death was unnecessary when dealing with Kal, and shot a look back that conveyed such. Their guard was unperturbed.

"By Aescian's everlasting Sun, Ezran! You are sticking to Vyn, you hear me?"

"Oh, come now, Kal," he said, but all he received was a raised hand that cut him off.

"I will chain you to him, I swear it. Do you understand what Father would do to me if something happened to you?" Kal scolded.

"Right, of course. He wouldn't do a thing to his favorite. There's really no need to worry so much, it doesn't suit you," Ezran responded, scratching at a bit of flaking mud on his cheek.

"Perhaps if you didn't go gallivanting off every chance you can, I wouldn't have to," he shot back. This pushed Ezran on further as he slipped on his best smile and raised a brow.

"You're beginning to sound like Avis." Kal stilled, meeting his gaze and fighting off a grin of his own. It was Kal, though, so he ended up losing.

"It's your fault. Do you see what a wretched thing you turn me into when you do this?"

Ezran rolled his eyes skyward, attempting to sling an

arm around his shoulders. To avoid it Kal backed away quickly. "Leave the propriety nagging to Genn, would you? Anyway, the matter's at rest for now. How about we grab something to eat and get these horrid things off me?"

"As I said before, we have little time. That cultivation seminar you wished to attend begins soon, Kal," Genn said. He stepped up into place beside Vyn as Kal and Ezran took the lead, heading down the furthest alley.

"Really? Another seminar?"

"Not all of us can spend this time drinking our cares away. I came here to learn about the people, and that includes participating in the seminars they so proudly offer," Kal said, which pulled a groan from his hungover counterpart.

"If you really want to get to know the people here, the taverns are the finest of places to begin."

"That may be, but you can't learn of the Miresa innovation through cups," Genn said.

"I do have a terrible headache, Kal, perhaps I can retire—"

"No, Ez. Consider it a punishment for running off. I'm sure you'll find a way to sleep through it regardless," he replied as they turned onto a larger street. Ezran stretched and blew at the strands of his brown hair, which had grown far too long during their time on the road.

"Can we at least have breakfast first?"

Kal gave a loud, annoyed sigh. "Well, before we discovered you had not tumbled into your own bed last night, Genn was going to prepare a rather excellent spread of boiled eggs, spiced potatoes, sweetbread, whipped—"

"I get it," Ezran muttered, his stomach squeezing. "I'm guessing 'there is little time for it'?"

"Indeed," Genn said without rising to the bait. "We can purchase some bread and fish from a street cart, however."

Ezran tried to come up with something, anything, that might help him find an opportunity to get out of this. He glanced down at his robes and grinned. "Well, why waste the coin when we have to go back to our rooms, anyway?"

"We do not have time," Kal said. Ezran lifted a brow and gestured at his state.

"You really want me showing up to a Miresa cultivation seminar looking like this?" Kal's stormy eyes raked up and down. A flicker of give crossed his features. He only needed a bit more of a push and Ezran was sure he could sway him, like he always did eventually.

"They would simply believe you are a regular farmer. Perhaps they might even ask for a demonstration," Genn attempted to jab. There. That would work.

"Exactly." Ezran pointed to him as his normal frown deepened. "What an embarrassment that would be for you, for us! Can you imagine me trying to figure out how to use farm tools and creating a spectacle? You'd be mortified!"

"It wouldn't be the first time," came Vyn's addition, but the sentiment stuck with his brother anyway.

"Fine," said Kal. "We return long enough for you to change and make yourself presentable. Genn can fix something quick to eat on the way, but then *we are all attending the seminar.*"

"Ah, wonderful! I knew you would come to reason." Ezran grinned. Kal shifted their course for the new destination, waving at a few commoners that greeted him.

"If you even attempt to escape this somehow, I will find that chain for you. Do you understand me?"

"Yes, *Avis.*"

Already, Ezran was planning out the details of his

escape. He would fetch new clothes, of course, but he would be sure the divider covered one of the windows in his rooms. Then, it was but a slip out onto the roof and a climb down the side alley's vines toward freedom. It also happened to be how he'd snuck out the previous night. If it worked then, why should he change it?

They came upon their tavern, with Kal receiving a warm welcome and Ezran a rowdy one. Woodsmoke and the scent of freshly seared meat greeted them, just as strong spice and smooth ale added undercurrents to enrich it. Kalin, as always expected of him, had to return each comment in kind. Ezran settled for a few pats on the back and raced up the stairs to execute his plan.

He entered their apartments first, ignoring Genn's call for him to wait, and immediately set about changing his robes. Shutting the door behind him, he only made it a step into the space before stopping short. Standing in the middle of their front room was a group of shining silver guards. Their breastplates glimmered without the slightest imperfection, each adorned with a blazing sun of gold. It wasn't full plate, but the lengths of silver robes underneath were just as immaculate. Despite the fact that none of them should have been this far from the Capital, each guard was pristine in their uniform. They all wore matching looks of disapproval at his barreling entrance and current state.

The Captain of the Northern Royal Guard nodded his head at Ezran, but his light gaze was cold when he looked back up. All the amusement and ease went out of him as he stepped aside, waiting for the rest of his party to hurry along. It was an awkward, tense moment of silence that only grew worse until the others found their way in. The guards knelt when they spotted Kal, who made a rather more collected entrance. The Captain's frosty exterior melted for him, even gaining a slight smile as he dropped to his knee and bent his head. Ezran tried to keep the tightness from his chest. He found it had already threaded through the strings of his heart and pulled them taut.

"Your Imperial Highness," the Captain said. Kal recovered well.

"Captain Talvys. Not that I'm unhappy to see you, but I thought the whole point of this journey was for me to become one of the people. A visit by a legion of royal guards doesn't exactly promote anonymity."

"Apologies, my Prince. Your mother requested that we personally deliver this letter." He rose to his feet again as he pulled free a roll of parchment, sealed with the familiar gold wax and crest of the Nefion house. Ezran couldn't bear to look at it for longer than necessary. He leaned against the wall instead, chewing at the corner of his lip.

Kal broke the seal in a delicate manner, as if any damage would be a slight to the Queen herself. He skimmed the contents as a small smile played on his mouth. "She's already planning a ball for my twenty-first. She wants us in attendance."

"And you're here to be sure we do, in fact, find our way back to the palace," Ezran said. Captain Talvys turned towards him, once again becoming flint.

"I prefer to think of it as protection required for the Prince's rank, but you can choose to see it however you wish, Master Breckhym." Ezran turned away and scowled. *Master Breckhym*, right. From Genn's lips, it never really sounded like an insult, but from the Captain, it was a distinction, a clarity to the divide that separated him and his brother.

"Are you covered in shit?"

"It's a long story," Kal covered and smiled fully,

choosing to ignore the tension that clouded the room. "I assume we will have to leave sooner rather than later, yes?"

The guard warmed once again. "Indeed, Your Imperial Highness. It will be a long journey to the Capital, and the Queen expressed the need for haste."

Genn stepped forward and slipped between the guards like a ghost, most likely to begin packing everything. Ezran followed him, but this time the guards parted like he was some sort of daemon they didn't want touching them. It was the smell, he tried to tell himself, but he knew it for the lie it was. He had almost forgotten that kind of sting. Brushing it off as best he could, he stepped inside his quarters with a cynical grin.

He would have given anything to go to that seminar.

CHAPTER
TWO

Elysia, Pentral District, North Akadon

T he city of Elysia teemed as dusk descended, people flowing like blood through the streets and giving life to the splendor all around them. At the center of this energy lay the city's heart, a shining palace of gold and red. It was made up of arches, spires, and reflective glass that all contended to catch the sun's rays. Now, it burned with the stolen colors of its setting. Night was ascending, but the Sun Palace's resplendence wouldn't be questioned.

Inside, a Prince sat, drinking tea from a golden cup. He flipped through the pages of a book in the quiet as a guard looked on, dressed in the white cloak and silver armor of his station. He stood still as a statue, brown hands folded, and made no sound whatsoever.

"Sol, you really should sit. It must be quite uncomfortable to stand for so long," Prince Avis offered again. Sol blinked once from where he remained, trying to ignore the ache in his back and legs from his full plate.

"It's my duty. Standing isn't so terrible, Your Imperial Highness."

The Prince sipped his tea and shut his book. "Sit."

Sol suppressed a sigh, but moved from the wall all the same. He pulled out a velvet lined chair and sank into it with a few metallic clanks of shifting armor, ignoring the sweet relief that coursed through his muscles. Prince Avis gave him a soft smile as he poured another cup, offering it.

Sol accepted with a nod and brought the drink to his lips. It was a hearty brew with something floral laying over top, most likely to promote energy. The Prince was always trying different herbs and spices in his teas, looking to see which did what and how it helped or hindered him throughout the day. How this hobby came about, Sol didn't know. He'd been experimenting with such things long before he'd joined his personal guard.

"Isn't that better?" he asked as Sol took another sip.

The earthy drink went down easy, leaving a pleasant aftertaste lingering on his tongue. He suspected it might be light jasmine, though he wasn't quite certain.

"Yes, Your Imperial Highness," Sol replied, "though I don't mind standing."

"You can relax with me," Prince Avis chuckled, the sound musical and brilliant even though it was slight. "I believe we've been together long enough."

Sol bent his head as a small smile came to his lips. "I appreciate the offer, my Prince, but one mustn't slack off on the job."

"You are exceedingly self-disciplined, Sol. It's a monotonous job. I doubt that anything will happen to me which you can't defend from that seat, especially within the palace. I really wouldn't mind if you sat, or read, perhaps played cards with some of the others."

"If I slack off now, I will grow used to it, then I will slack off when I shouldn't. It is my job to guard you with diligence. It's my duty and honor to do so," Sol responded almost as a compulsion, his Captain's voice ringing in his ears. The royal shook his head with a smile.

"You are an honorable man," he said. "I will have to appoint you as Captain of the Guard after my coronation."

"If you believe it to be best, Your Imperial Highness. I would accept any position you found for me."

"It would be best, I believe, if you continue improving the way you have. How's your practice coming along? It must be hard to study, exercise, and guard me all at the same time." Prince Avis brought his tea to his lips again and looked out at Sol with grey eyes. A slight blue tint stained the webbing, reminiscent of a storm about to unleash on an ocean. It brought a kind of lively energy to the rest of his tranquil features.

"It's not hard at all. I balance my time equally with all important aspects of my life," Sol said softly and turned away from his gaze, ignoring the heat that crawled up his skin.

"Of course. And your magic? How are you coming along with that?"

Sol swallowed as he studied the bookcases, the tapestries, and the perfection of the carved fireplace. This wasn't a particular conversation that he wanted to have, bordering on a bit too casual in his opinion, but he couldn't exactly say so to his Prince. He settled for as curt a tone as he dared use.

"It comes along as surely as my work with a blade."

"That's good to hear. I apologize if I have overstepped my boundary. I simply don't see you wielding your power as much as the other guards." The Prince gently smiled at him again. The action broke down his discomfort and his tone relaxed.

"Not at all, Your Imperial Highness. Between my gifts, one doesn't lend itself well to idle use, and the other can get out of hand if one isn't careful."

"Of course. You would be one to worry over setting fire to something," Prince Avis sighed as he finished his tea. "You have heard that Kal will be returning, yes?"

"I have, ser. Along with Master Ezran, Master Gennady, and Vyn."

"I hope they both learned much on their journey. It's been too long since I've last seen them, and Ves is quite excited about their return as well. Though, it has been much quieter around here in their absence. I fear I will lose you to Ezran and Kal again," the Prince joked, though Sol knew it could very well be the case.

Master Ezran and Prince Kalin were known to get into whatever trouble they could, beginning from when they were first brought together at six and seven respectively. No matter who was in charge of their guard, from the older members to the fresh young graduates—even to the Captain himself—the boys had been terrors to peace.

Many attributed it to Master Ezran, who was no doubt the more rambunctious of the two. Blamed it on the blood. Sol didn't quite share the same views. He believed it had more to do with temperament, and while the Master certainly started things, he had also known the younger Prince to fan the flame from time to time.

"It will be good to have them all back home," said Sol. He sipped at the tea once more and tilted his head at the brew. It was one of the Prince's finer experiments, went down well. Sol might have to ask for the recipe to help with his exercises and studying.

Before he could gather the courage to do so, a knock sent Sol to his feet. The Prince's amusement at the action came through his tone when he spoke, "Enter."

A guard, which turned out to be Ser Drestas, knelt once he took a step inside the threshold. "Forgive the disturbance, Your Imperial Highness. The King has summoned you and Ser Maisym to the conference room."

Sol raised a brow as his charge rose to his feet. The King wanted to see him as well?

"Thank you, Fenvir," Avis said as he strode past, tapping Drestas' armored shoulder. Sol followed a pace behind with his hand on his sword, his plate giving soft clicks with every step.

The inside of the palace wasn't nearly as luminous as its exterior, but it still couldn't be described as anything less than gilded. White marble veined with iridescent shades of precious stones took the place of glittering metal. Silver and gold trappings lay everywhere the eye could see, covering walls and pillars, stretching in silken bolts from the crystal chandeliers. Paintings of Nefion rulers, of the Gods, the royal family, and their golden crest all ran the length of the halls, spilling down a sprawling staircase. Ornamentations and decor that cost more than Sol would ever personally have filled up the rest, leaving just enough room for admiration as people passed by.

The conference room, however, lacked most of the splendor and wealth of the palace. Inside, there were simple high-backed chairs encircled around a heavy wooden table. An accurate map of Akadon's entirety carved itself onto the wood's face with vibrant summer hues. The walls were bare in comparison, decorated with weapons and shields of previous rulers, whether they be normal or magical in origin. All to avoid distractions from the task at hand. It was a room that hadn't seen proper use in many years, at least in the way intended.

At its head was a frowning King Nefion, bent over the mountains of South Akadon. He worried at a flash of silver metal in his palm with slow, methodical strokes. Even to those entering, the air of the space was thick with aftermath. The Queen stared at her husband with a look that told of their argument, but it quickly fled when she noticed her son had stepped through the doorway.

Prince Avis bowed while Sol knelt. "Father, Mother. You summoned me?"

"Ah, yes. Please rise, Ser Maisym," the King said. He stood, hands folded in front of him, motionless in his silence.

The Prince approached the table and looked on at his father's side, startlingly similar despite the years between them. King Nefion passed on many of his features to his sons and daughter, from their shared shade of deep bronze to their spill of dark curls, but Prince Avis especially took after him. Everything about him seemed to come from his father, except his eyes. Queen Nefion's cutting grey won out over the King's blue with every child of theirs. Her dark blonde locks had perhaps lightened his hair a fraction or two as well, but that was all the victories she gained when it came to her children.

"Planning an invasion?" It was a light joke from the Prince, but the Queen didn't seem to particularly care for it.

"No, nothing like that," the King said. "I have a task for you, Ser Maisym, something that must be confined to this room."

Sol took a step forward. King Nefion looked at him, solemn and stony, then flicked his gaze to his son, and finally let it rest back on the Queen. She arched her brow, keeping a frown fixed in place.

"What is it?" Prince Avis asked as he glanced between them. The King let out a slow breath, something unspoken trading between him and his wife.

"You cannot let this get out. Tell no one, not even Kal when he arrives, and especially not Ezran—" Queen Nefion's cynical chuckle cut him off, but he silenced her with a hard glance. "I wish to be the one to tell them."

"Alright," the Prince said. His concern was written in a line between his brows as he locked his hands behind his back.

"We have received word from King Auberon." He stiffened at the name and set his jaw once, which was the most animosity Sol had ever seen come from Prince Avis. "They have decided to release Kyrith and let him come home."

Sol didn't show it on his face, but the shock hit his stomach like a forceful hammer blow. Prince Avis' mouth parted, and he blinked, staring down at South Akadon's Capital.

"They are letting Kyrith go? Why? Are we to return Ezran?"

"We should," Queen Nefion broke in, "but your father thinks it's best for the empire to keep him here."

"They gave no terms for his release," the King went on smoothly. "They didn't demand Ezran in exchange, or gold, or food. All they wished was to simply return what was ours."

"This... certainly, Father, this is too much of a kindness for them to just hand him over."

"I believe so too, my son." He turned to Sol. "Which is why I will send you, Ser Maisym, to retrieve him, if you will? Captain Talvys assures me that you are the best for the job.

I would have you ride to Sankor and accompany Kyrith back to Elysia under the guise of simple travelers. I wouldn't have the spectacle of the Prince returning, nor do I wish to overwhelm him."

Sol bowed a bit late, his astonishment at his Captain's recommendation and his King's trust catching him off guard. "It would be my honor to go wherever you ordered, Your Imperial Majesty."

"Not an order, but a choice. I understand if you do not wish to undertake this mission. It's highly dangerous. They have assured me of the Prince's safety, but I cannot be entirely sure of your own if you choose to go," King Nefion said.

Sol's gaze dropped to the map, running over the carved mountains of South Akadon to settle on Sankor. The city was home to House Auberon, and was farther than Sol had ever traveled before. Once, the other royal line had been the Nefion's equal, traditionally trading off the Imperial Crown of Akadon every other reign between them. They were also the force Sol's father had died defending the North against in the Fracture War.

Sol nodded once, the decision clear.

"I will do my duty as a royal guard of the Nefion crown to protect all its members, my King, no matter how far or what danger they may face. It will be my honor to go, by your command."

THREE

Sankor, Kailos District, South Akadon

T he city of Sankor whispered as dusk descended, people hiding like shadows in the cracks and corners to watch the darkness fall around them. At the center of this caution lay the city's ever watchful guard, a palace of black and grey. It was made up of pointed edges and a rough finish, with functionality that sought to suit its residents. As the shadows grew in earnest, fires were lit inside, giving every barred window a fiery eye to stare out at the citizens with. Night was ascending, and the Fortress' power would not be questioned.

Inside, a man sat and drank tea from a black cup. He flipped the pages of a book quietly as a black armored guard waited outside to stop any escape. Like Kyrith would try that after all this time. It had been thirteen long years, nearing on another, and he'd since learned that there was no fleeing this place.

He reached for the kettle, managing not to wince as his muscles protested. Pouring himself another cup of simple chamomile, he drank deeply and let out a sigh when he finished its contents. The warm brew settled in his gut like a pleasant salve. Still, his abdomen ached after the training he'd endured that day.

"The core must be strong," Captain Jaxas had snapped, missing no opportunity to test Kyrith with a correcting blow from his staff. *"Strong like stone. Like mountains. Like metal."*

It felt like it had turned to metal and burned with its forging. Still, he pushed on. He always would.

A knock made his grey eyes land on the simple wooden door. The lock was thrown back and a breath later a guard entered, tall and pale and scarred. He didn't kneel. He didn't bow. He stared at Kyrith with hard brown eyes as he spoke with a clipped tone.

"You are summoned before the King."

Nothing was allowed to show on his face as he set his things down on the small table. Kyrith rose and clenched his jaw as the guard escorted him down the cold, shadowed hallways of the Fortress. It was all mountain stone and crude iron, with dark wood to accent in some places. Nothing but black and red banners of the Auberon House decorated the halls, even though the vaulted ceilings had plenty of room for more. Kyrith looked out on the moon-stained city from the barred windows and counted the flying buttresses as he went. It kept his mind and spirit calm. It kept the anticipation and dread at bay. It kept him walking and saved the guard from dragging him forth.

The throne room was a sizable space, big enough for the entirety of the court to fit with comfort, but for now remained empty and dark as Kyrith entered. The vacancy didn't bode well for him. The only people in the room were the guards, flanking with their Prince around two huge grey thrones that held the ruling monarchy of South Akadon. Above them, a monstrous black Sword hung with its blade pointed skyward, eating the light that came off the fires around their dais. The power it gave off was thick in the air, bolstered by shadows and the pregnant night, demanding as much respect as those who sat before it.

Kyrith got as close as he dared before he knelt to the ground, head bowed, leaning forward so his knuckles pressed to the floor. He remained silent as Marek's black-eyed gaze burned into him. The Prince didn't dare move with his father so close.

"Do you know what occasion is nearing?" King Auberon asked. Kyrith closed his eyes—of course he knew. It happened every year, but he still didn't dare to speak. "North Akadon will celebrate Prince Kalin's birthday. It will be splendid, I am sure. Celebrations from the North Sea to Vul Sura. Everything will be just so for the favored Nefion son."

Kyrith kept his breathing even, kept his eyes on the cracks in the stone before him. The King rose from his throne and descended onto the floor with heavy, purposeful steps. He walked in a slow circle around Kyrith's form, a soft threat that was more inevitability than anything else.

"How old will he be?"

Kyrith's lips parted as he took a steadying breath, speaking low. "Twenty-one, Your Imperial Majesty."

"Twenty-one," the King chuckled cruelly. "How splendid. Fortunate of King Thamas Nefion to have his preferred son make it to such an age. I wonder, do you think you even pass through their thoughts on such joyous occasions?"

Silence prevailed again as King Auberon came to a stop before him. Those dark eyes weighed him down, pressed on his shoulders to force him to the stone floor. He didn't dare move.

"How old is my trueborn son now? The one they raised in your place?"

"Nineteen, Your Imperial Majesty."

"Nineteen, yes. I forget, sometimes, you see. I believe he will enjoy himself greatly with the Prince's banquet. It's a pity they've forgotten you." The King began to move again and Kyrith swallowed. He counted the steps, because it kept his thoughts focused, kept his body from shaking. "But we have not."

Kyrith closed his eyes. The King stopped again, this time at his side, and that vicious gaze lashed over him again.

"Bare yourself to me. On your knees."

Kyrith's heart pulsed sharp and quick at the command. He forced his gaze open as he moved his hands to his chest. Undoing the clasps from his black coat, he shrugged it off and hauled his grey undershirt over his head to pile it all next to him. The coolness of the room kissed at his skin as the scrutiny of the King burned it. He didn't kneel again, but placed both knees on the ground and straightened. His head remained bowed, eyes fixed on the cracks, and he counted.

"You scar so easily," King Auberon reprimanded, as if he had some sort of control over the process. A finger trailed over the raised ridges that lined Kyrith's shoulders and back as he stepped behind him. Despite his best efforts to prepare, to distract himself with counting, he flinched at the King's icy touch.

The King paused, then chuckled. He walked around to Kyrith's front again and held his hand out. A guard scurried forward from the shadows to hand him a whip. Once again, he took up his pacing. He never could stay still for long. King Auberon was a predator that stalked his prey instead of lying in wait for it.

"I have a gift for you," he said into the silence.

The crackle of fire was the only other sound. No one dared to make any sort of noise as they watched the scene, most with delight or resignation, one with nervous energy.

"But I can't decide how much of it to give. Should I give you twenty-one lashes, for making it this far? Should I give you nineteen, since you are to be my son's pathetic replacement? Or forty, for the lot of it?"

Kyrith counted the steps, counted the cracks he could see over and over, counted the number of times his pulse throbbed in his throat.

"I think forty would do nicely, Father," the Prince said from the thrones. King Auberon huffed a laugh.

"Marek," Queen Endri reprimanded, and Kyrith closed his eyes at the sound of her soft voice. "Nineteen or twenty-one would be sufficient, my King. You do not wish him dead."

Bless her, he thought.

"Hear how benevolent my Queen is for the unwanted stray. She trembles for you, Nefion. Look. Look and see."

The King knelt with surprising speed for his age and gripped Kyrith's jaw tightly. Forcing his gaze up, he took in Queen Endri on her giant throne. She seemed frailer than when he'd last seen her. Pale around her lips, bruised around her brown eyes. Equally dark hair fell in loose, straight strands around her face and sunken cheeks. Yet, despite the fragility of her appearance, her body was alight with nerves. She clutched the sides of her throne so hard that Kyrith worried her fingers might break. His chest tightened, but he didn't look away.

The King loosened his grip and rose to his feet. Kyrith dropped his eyes to the cracks again, taking in a shaking breath. "Perhaps I should be benevolent as well. Perhaps I should be cruel. On the rack."

Kyrith lifted his form from the floor and braced against the heavy iron rack that King Auberon kept as a permanent fixture. He counted the seconds in his breath. The seconds in the silence. There was a moment when his heart became the only thing he could hear, until the whip snapped, causing his back to seize with burning pain.

No whimper came, no wince, no sound at all. Even so, he made sure not to bite down on anything but teeth. That mistake had come and gone.

He made it to the seventh lash before a gasp finally escaped his throat. Marek's laugh came at the sound. The next he choked down, but on the ninth crack, it clawed itself free. From then on, each strike from the whip came paired with a gasp, a groan, a brief scream. He made it to twenty-eight before his knees gave out and he had to lean against the rack.

Forty. He counted forty, before the whip stopped.

"Rise, kneel, if you can. Cover yourself."

Kyrith's back screamed in protest when he moved, but he pushed himself to unsteady feet. Finding his way to his clothes, he lifted his shirt over his head and slipped on his coat, but left it unfastened. He knelt again and took a shaking breath. The lashes hurt, burning and ragged and raw, but it wasn't the worst he'd endured. At least now he wouldn't have it hanging over his head through the month, waiting for the King to bestow his present. Blood wept in warm, steady rivulets down his back. They clung to his shirt, its fabric searing his inflamed skin.

King Auberon returned to his throne and sat down with

a sigh of cloth. Gazes trained on Kyrith—weighted, concerned, delighted. Kyrith closed his own. It was over with. Now, he simply had to wait out the rest, till the King grew bored.

"I have another gift for you."

Kyrith's stomach turned to ice, but he forced himself to remain still on the outside. Nothing but careful indifference molded his features, even though it was turned down and covered with his curtain of dark curls.

What gift could he possibly have after that? Was he not satiated?

Kyrith wracked his mind for a rule he'd broken or some form of displeasure he had brought the King. He could think of nothing, and besides, the throne room was empty of spectators. Not as though making up some infraction was beneath King Auberon, but why would he need an excuse to hurt him more when Prince Kalin's birthday was sufficient?

"I have sent word to the thief King Thamas. You will be returning to North Akadon before the celebrations can begin."

Despite his best efforts, Kyrith's mouth parted slightly. He swallowed against the pounding in his throat as blood rushed to fill his ears. His head spun. How long had he waited to hear those words? But why, now, did they sound so much like a threat?

"Are you not thankful to my father, *sunshine prince?*" Marek's sneering tones cut through the air and lanced into his shock.

"Thank you, Your Imperial Majesty," Kyrith said. Questions stained his lips, but he refused to give them voice. It was not his place.

"Naturally. You have spent more years here with us

than you have with your trueborn family. I suspect that my own son remembers nothing of his homeland. I would wager the Northerners have made him soft. Their extravagance, excessiveness... Their weakness in magic and dealing with shades... He will be like a soft pile of dough, should he ever return to us."

Kyrith flicked his gaze up as much as he dared. Was he not asking for their Prince back? Was he letting him go without demands or equal exchange?

"But I will send a knife back to them. A crude, dull knife, but one that can cut all the same when enough pressure is applied. There's something I want you to remember on your journey back to Elysia. It is we who raised you, Nefion. We who have taught you strength, taught you our ways. You will never be one of them. You are, after all, the forgotten son. The one they didn't care to lose. They didn't even fight for you when the Ralith came to take you away. We embraced you. We built you. You owe me your life, boy, and one day I intend to collect on such a debt. Never forget where you came from."

The words wrapped around Kyrith's body like chains, weighing him down further into the floor, into the Fortress, into the land.

He swallowed again. "Of course, Your Imperial Majesty."

Everyone's eyes held onto him in the silence. The walls were pressing in. The ceiling was caving. The edges were all staining darker and darker as he waited for the next move.

"Rise. Get out of my sight."

Despite the weight, the darkness leaching in, Kyrith rose to his feet and forced himself not to sway. He bowed as deep as he could. Forced his shoulders straight though his back was aflame. He took a step, and then another, and another, until he was striding out of the throne room with their gazes spearing into him. He pushed himself on, like always.

It wasn't until he reached the hallway, flanked by two guards, that it didn't matter how much he willed himself to take a step. Blood was spilling too heavily down his back. Shadows threatened his eyesight. Reaching out a hand to steady himself, his body lurched against the wall. He shook with the force of trying to keep himself upright.

He took another step. Then another. And another. Because he was going back to Elysia. He was leaving this place and he would have the strength to make it there, no matter the cost.

FOUR

Sankor, Kailos District, South Akadon

T he whistle of blades was the only thing that clued Arra into the knives' positions a second before they landed. She spun away and deflected one of them, hearing both land with a clatter on the floor.

It was one thing for her to avoid them, but it was another to curl her free hand upwards and lift the knives from where they fell. Sweat broke out over her brow as she turned them with a flick of her fingers, sending them soaring back home.

The guards dodged just in time for them to ricochet off the walls, tumbling to the ground once more. Arra took a deep breath in as the exhaustion of using her gift to such an extent settled over her. She knew she was pushing it. They'd been going for hours.

But she had to get faster.

Better.

Stronger.

"Again," she said. After lowering her own blade, a plain

saber without a name, she blew a stray piece of her white blonde hair aside as she wiped at her temple.

"My Lady..." began one guard, shifting from foot to foot. "You have been at this for a while now. Perhaps one should rest..."

Arra caught her breath and blinked at the ground. Should she stop? Perhaps. Would she? Not a chance.

"Again," she said, softer this time. The guards traded glances, shrugging at each other. Arra's vehement practice wasn't something entirely new, and besides, the royals in the Fortress had stranger rituals.

She took up her position in the middle of the training room, the heat of the hearth fire warming her back. The guards crept farther into the shadows, watching, waiting. Arra's dark amber gaze slid closed.

She steadied her pulse. Once it was quiet enough, she focused on the sounds in the room. The warm crackle of fire. Soft footfalls of the guards as they moved. Brushes of their red half cloaks catching on the walls. The unbearable silence of the Fortress itself.

A whistle of a blade.

She spun, carving her saber out in an arc. The knife caught its edge and changed course, but Arra reached out with her hand to halt its movement. The force of ceasing kinetic energy after hours of this made her teeth clench, but she held it and willed it to shift direction.

The first blade went shooting back towards the guard that threw it and the second came whistling forward a breath after. Arra spun, but not fast enough. The knife caught the sleeve of her white tunic and tore through, nicking skin, before colliding with the ground.

The silence grew thick as Arra glanced down at her arm. Blood welled, then spilled over pale skin, leaving a trail of deep scarlet in its wake. She pressed her lips together and bent to pick up the guard's knife.

"Lady Enryn, please, forgive me. I—I didn't mean..." Sera Xan was already on her knees when she approached, pressing knuckles to the ground and bowing her head. Flipping the cool metal between her fingers, Arra held the blade out hilt first and knelt.

"It's practice," she said. "People get injured."

The guard took the knife with a shaking hand. Her brown eyes glittered with panic, but Arra knew it wasn't born of her. Sera Xan visibly swallowed, remaining on her knees, as Arra rose to her feet and sheathed the saber.

"Go. Before the Prince gets wind of it."

Both guards scurried towards anonymity and the protection it brought. Catching her breath, Arra pulled a kerchief from her belts and swiped the blood off of her arm as best she could. Anger stirred in her, brief as it was. She wasn't a fragile doll. She hated how they reacted to any slight wound on her, but she also understood.

No doubt, if Arra had been in their place, she would've been terrified, too.

She set the saber back along the wall, joining the rest of the brilliant and varied array of beautiful swords, pikes, spears, lances, daggers, maces, hammers—anything a Kashadon or soldier could wish to practice with. They all called to her through her element, the metal that bound them together in a way few could understand. A rare Kashadon talent, even in the South, one she inherited along with her family name.

Arra left the training room and slipped through the bare, echoing hallways of the Fortress. Down here, in the belly of the beast, there were no windows. Torches lit the way, but only in long intervals, making half the walk one in shadow. When the gleaming orange firelight did illuminate the scene, there was nothing much to look at besides grey stone walls, Auberon banners, and the fresh, bloody sigils that stained the polished floor. To keep the dead at peace, the restless settled, the resentful occupied. Yet, they did nothing for the living with the same qualms.

Arra heard them long before they arrived. The echo of guards' boots came closer as she slipped under a banner and made herself flat against the wall. They rounded the corner right as the fabric settled back into place, leaving nothing suspicious for them to investigate.

"Heard the King finally summoned the Nefion bastard up to the throne room. Think he's going to tell him?"

Kyrith, she thought.

"Probably. I still think it's risky myself, but who am I to question his decisions? It will be a clever plan if he pulls it off."

"Indeed. Better keep up our practice, or else." They laughed together as they slipped far enough away for Arra to come out from hiding. She didn't follow them, though her interest piqued. Kyrith needed her. She had to find him quickly, and knew just where to start her search.

Her steps were sure and silent as she wound through the maze of the Fortress' structure. She travelled up what felt like an endless number of stairs, through several halls, dashed this way and that until she found herself outside the throne room's heavy black doors. Sure enough, a tall figure slumped against the stone there, black curls falling to obscure his face. Arra didn't make a sound to announce herself, but he looked up all the same with eyes of determined, enduring iron.

"Hello, little ghost."

She pressed her lips together as she came out of the

shadows. He always knew when she was near, no matter how silent or careful she'd been. Others may have let her blend into the background, but never Kyrith. Arra came to his side and pulled his arm over her shoulder.

"I can walk on my own."

"Clearly," she said.

Despite her own exhaustion, she helped Kyr from the wall, walking him towards his chambers. The guards didn't move to help, but flanked them silently, as always.

"What did he do?" she asked softly, wary of their escorts.

"Gave me Prince Kalin's birthday present," Kyr replied through clenched teeth.

Arra wanted to shake her head, but settled for a knitted brow. She hated how he said it. *Prince Kalin's birthday,* as if it wasn't also his. They had taken that from him.

"How many?"

"Forty," he replied. A sigh escaped from her lips.

She allowed them to ease into silence as they shuffled down the halls together. This time, the barred windows of the Fortress accompanied them. The Southern Capital of Sankor spread out from thick palace walls, crushed against the distant Noka Mountains. The city grew so dark at night that it was hard to tell it was a city at all. But tonight, it seemed a ward had fallen in the lower east, and a fire was burning brightly as it tore through the homes there.

May the Gods keep them, Arra prayed. They didn't need any more resentful or malevolent shades in South Akadon, much less its crown city. Turning from the window as they continued down the hall, she put the horrors of others' misfortune out of her mind to tend to the one closer at hand.

Pushing open the door to Kyrith's chamber revealed a

space that was plain and functional, more like a servant's quarters than anything else. He sank onto the ground in front of his hearth, moving slowly to shrug off his coat. Beneath it, his shirt was stained through in dark patches of deep vermilion. Arra gathered a washbasin filled with water, along with a cloth, and set them down beside him as he hauled off his shirt.

His back was a mess of wounds and memories of them, but Arra couldn't remember a time when it wasn't. Like everyone in South Akadon, Kyrith had scars of protection and cleansing sigils, along with ones for strength, clarity, power, and whatever else he needed or was forced to bear. However, unlike everyone else, he bore more from countless whippings, beatings, and a thousand nameless things that only the Gods knew. She was certain they stretched from the prominent scars on his face, all the way down to the soles of his feet.

He had been like this since Arra came here, when she was nine and he was eleven. He had even been tying off a wound, in fact, when she peered out from behind a corner to look at him. Kyrith was frightening. The son of the King who killed so many of her people, who took her father off to war. The same King governesses and tutors warned would lock up children in golden cages if they misbehaved. Kyrith had lifted those light eyes to her, and all he said then was, *"Hello, little ghost."*

Arra knelt behind him, examining the wounds. One or two raised his skin in angry welts, but the rest had been hard enough to split open. They were bleeding steadily, coating his back in red.

"Here," he said in his low, quiet tone.

Arra looked up to see him holding the hilt of a small knife out for her. She took it in a delicate grip. The athame

35

was simple, functional, like everything else in South Akadon, but it held a sort of elegance that sang of Kyrith's energy. She pulled it free from its sheath and examined his back, looking for a clean place among the mess.

"There's no room."

He sighed and crossed his arms over his knees. "Nape, then, or shoulder. Carver's choice."

Arra pressed her lips together as she moved to his left. Kyrith kept his eyes trained forward, completely emotionless as usual. Even when she began to cut the sigil into his skin, he seemed indifferent.

The sigil wasn't a large one or particularly complicated. Arra carved it so many times before that the action was a memory in her bones. Still, it was powerful, and it took a lot of what was left of her energy to make. The fresh symbol was nearly singing when she rocked back to inspect it, its power repelling negative energies from entering the weakened body.

Kyrith accepted the athame with a twitch of a smile, which was the most she ever really got from him. "Thank you."

She shook her head, blowing a piece of her hair out of her eyes as she returned to his back. Arra began to clean him up, trying her best to be delicate. That was an area she never really mastered, however. She was too sharp for such things, made of metal in her spirit and body. It was no wonder why Nakre blessed her with control of the element.

"He's letting me go."

Arra faltered, dropping the wet cloth on the ground and cursing herself as she did. She replaced it with a fresh one as her mind swam, clouded with fears, thoughts, a selfish *no*. She didn't want him to leave. She didn't want to be alone here, not without Kyrith, who understood, who saw, who *knew*. She couldn't be left here alone with Marek.

"Arra," Kyrith began, but he didn't get to finish.

She should have known not to think of him. Her father taught her better when he came back from the war, even up until the day she left for the Capital. *Don't think of the daemons, my iron girl, lest they appear before you. They listen. They come when called.*

"Well, isn't this a cozy scene?"

Arra never did have Kyrith's control. He didn't seem caught off guard in the slightest, but she jumped, placing her shaking hands behind her as she turned to face the Prince. Kyr shifted into a kneel as quick as he could manage, head bowed with knuckles pressed to the ground.

"Your Imperial Highness," Kyrith said.

Marek spared no attention toward him as he strode into the room. His gaze remained solely on Arra, who rose to her feet. She curtseyed, as was proper. Whispered the title under her breath, which came shorter to her with him in this cramped space.

"Arra, I must say, your empathy for the bastard is quite endearing, but you mustn't dirty your hands with tainted blood." Marek came to a stop before Kyrith, who did not move or flinch. "And you're far too familiar with your superiors."

Marek ran his night black gaze over his father's handiwork and then looked at her. She glanced away, fixing her eyes lower. Arra never could look upon him for more than a few moments before feeling the need to run.

"My Lady, who hurt you?"

Her heart stuttered as she covered her graze with her palm. "This? My fault, my Prince, I scraped a nail somewhere in the palace."

It wasn't a good lie, but it was all she could come up with on the spot while his eyes gouged into her. The cut was too clean for a nail, too deep. Marek approached slowly. He towered over her, closer than she cared for, and took her chin in his hand. As he forced her to look up, she saw Kyrith tense.

Amber eyes met black ones. Marek's grip shifted from her chin to her jaw, going from delicate to bruising. She winced as he came forward a fraction, overwhelming her with his scent of pine, blood, and air that cut through dead trees.

"I told you. I will have no scars besides the sigils," Marek said, deceptively calm.

Arra's pulse beat so hard in her throat, she worried her veins would burst. Marek released her as he stepped away. His violence slipped back beneath a cool demeanor, a slick smile spilling across his features in a practiced way.

Marek nodded to her. "My father wishes to speak with you."

Her luck seemed to be unfathomably drained that day. She curtseyed again, then skirted around the Prince, refusing to glance toward Kyrith's still bent form. Even so, she heard Marek's fist connecting solidly somewhere on him and Kyr's choked down cry. Arra wasn't fast enough to stop the wince from slicing across her features.

"If I ever hear her name part from your lips like that again, *sunshine prince*, I will have them cut from you."

Arra squeezed her eyes closed briefly, but kept her feet moving forward. Giving him favor or trying to intervene would be fruitless. Things would end up worse for Kyrith and increase Marek's jealousy. After all, Marek only bothered with her when he thought someone else was interested. She was simply another possession.

Wandering back through the halls, she found herself alone once again. Marek didn't follow, which meant he wasn't done with Kyrith. Arra sent a quick prayer to the Gods and willed them to lend him strength. She knew much better than to pray for their mercy. They had none to give, at least not in this place. Yet, it was best to go through the motions in case one decided to amuse themselves with an answer.

She entered the throne room and walked up the echoing chamber with light steps. Several moments passed before anyone really noticed that she was there. Arra kept the smile from her face as a few guards jumped, and the King himself sucked in breath as she curtseyed low.

"Your Imperial Majesty," she said.

"Rise, Lady Enryn. Are you injured?"

She straightened and found the kind eyes of the Queen first, even though she hadn't spoken yet. Queen Endri smiled, though it faltered, glancing towards her husband as it fled. Despite the black eyes studying Arra, so much like his son's and only a shade less intimidating, she relaxed in the Queen's presence. The woman was like a vibrant flower brave enough to grow between the cracks of dirtied cobblestones, daring to remain delicate, unlike the hardened people in this haunted city. Time and experience hadn't yet taken the warmth from her.

Dragging her gaze to the other monarch, Arra shook her head. "Just a scratch, my King. Nothing that won't heal."

"Excellent. I presume it comes from your practice, yes?"

Arra swallowed. She dared lie to Marek, but the King, who's gaze grew as dark as Odeion's Sword eating light behind him, well... he would know it. He always seemed to. And it wouldn't be a simple matter if she did.

"Yes."

King Auberon nodded. "I have a task for you. Call it an exercise in your practice."

Arra flicked her gaze back to Queen Endri, who paled. It appeared she was quite ill with whatever was about to come out of the King's mouth.

"I am sending the Nefion son back to his soft people in time for the Prince's birthday. I want you to accompany him." Arra fought hard to keep the joy off of her face, despite the prickle that circled the back of her mind.

The King's eyes sparked with a cruel shade of delight and the corner of his mouth turned up. Her relief fled quickly.

"I cannot send guards or Marek, obviously, but you can pose as a genuine diplomatic effort. Thus, you will be safe and able to carry out my will. When you arrive, I want you to secure a way in and out of their palace. You will have two months to do this from the time you enter Elysia. Then, I'll send a small party to retrieve you, my trueborn son, and the Nefion boy once again. On that night, I want you to kill the Northern King."

PART TWO: A JOURNEY HOME

CHAPTER
FIVE

Agera District, North Akadon

E zran ached from so many hours in the saddle. Worse, their progress slowed to accommodate the parade and spectacle, which plunged him further into a darkened mood. As if the procession wasn't enough, the guards stayed in their shining regalia and held aloft the burning silver sun banner of the Nefion, proclaiming the presence of royalty for all to see. People gathered on the sides of the road just to catch a glimpse. Some waved, others shouted blessings, which only slowed their pace to what Ezran felt was a crawl.

Kal, dressed in garb appropriate for a Prince, waved and smiled from the front. Ezran, however, rode behind him alongside a silent Genn. Though he was supposed to be posing as a respected royal servant of some kind, he still refused to wear the violet and silver livery of the Nefion House which the retainer loyally donned. He compromised with a nice black and white coat accented by grey, along with black riding pants and boots which had seen better days. At least he wasn't like Vyn, who seemed displeased at best about being shoved back into his guard's silver. The man never did like to stand out, and it was hard not to in such glimmering attire.

The only good thing about being in such an obnoxious and uniform procession was the fact that all of them could finally carry their Kashadon weapons again. Ezran's great black and silver claymore, *Atka*, rested at his hip, humming in perfect harmony with his spirit. The sword was full to the brim with energy from not being used in so long.

Likewise, golden light radiated from Kal's double-sided glaive, a powerful and temperamental arm by the name of *Sion*, from where it crossed his back. Genn's wooden bow, *Koa*, and Vyn's ax, *Fior*, both had enough magic stored to color their edges as well. It made them all stand out amongst the rest of the Kashadon, who weren't forced into a circumstantial lapse from duties. It had been far too long since their last proper hunt.

Yet, Ezran expected as much when their long journey began to take them north. It wasn't like there was much prey for their kind in Agera or Nixa Ignan. If an unsettled shade stirred up trouble in the upper Districts of the empire, it was most likely a low threat that could be taken care of by local young Kashadon as practice. It wouldn't require someone with the caliber of magic as the Nefion House.

The calm balance of *Atka's* spirit was Ezran's singular comfort as they made their plodding way toward the Capital. Brightly clothed figures ran to further clot along the sides of the road. Sighing, he scanned the crowd as they vied for their beloved Prince's attention. Those devoted gazes turned when met with his own, wariness creeping in.

Neither Genn nor Ezran were much of typical Northerners in looks, with pale skin and dark eyes. Especially the retainer, who was gifted with prominent features of those found in the riverlands of South Akadon. But this crowd didn't know who they were for certain. Maybe some of them guessed through the years. Rumors spread like wildfire despite King Thamas' attempts to keep it quiet. Yet, how could he? One of them had to be that Southern son. It was only a matter of which.

"I'll tell you, Genn, I could get off this horse and walk faster than we're going."

"I would advise against it, Master Ezran. We still have more than two weeks' ride to the palace. You may be sore from riding, but you will be infinitely more so from tramping on foot."

Master Ezran. He let out a long breath as he inspected the hearty trees offering shade from the mid-autumn sun. Almost ten years they had known each other, with just about every waking moment spent together, and yet Genn still refused to drop the title from his name.

"What do you think the guards would do if I took off?" Ezran turned to smile at him while his fingers tapped quick beats across his saddle's pommel.

"I'm sure they would be very displeased with having to chase you down. It would make traveling the rest of the way with them a tad more uncomfortable than it already is," he said.

Ezran's chestnut gelding snorted under him, as if in agreement. He ran his fingers through Taevis' rich mane absently. One good spur to the side and he would take off like a shot from Genn's bow, galloping towards freedom...

"I'm sure they would just send Vyn out. I think I could convince him to chase me all the way back to the palace and leave you all to catch up."

"I think you overestimate your ability of persuasion."

Ezran laughed. "Probably, when it comes to Vyn, at least." He rode in silence for a moment, his thoughts beginning to drift again. When the smile faded from his lips, he turned back to the retainer and studied Genn's perfect form on his grey horse. "Are you happy to go back?"

"I am happy to follow wherever the Prince leads," Genn said. His brown eyes stayed forward, as unrelenting as his posture, which made Ezran turn back himself. He hadn't really expected any other answer from him. "You don't seem fond of returning."

Ezran flicked a flat gaze to the sun banners ahead, decorated with the Nefion crest. "I can't say I am."

"I thought you would be pleased to be back with Prince Avis and Princess Veslyn. Not to mention you'll have access to proper training equipment once more. Or is it no longer your dream to become a famous Kashadon?"

He couldn't help the energy that escaped him as his hand danced to *Atka's* hilt. "Oh, that is still very much the goal, my dear Master Gennady. But returning to them means returning to the Queen and her scrutiny as well."

"The terrible sacrifices one must make for glory. What was it you said again? Something blasphemous about your sword rising to the prowess of a God's Weapon?"

Ezran grinned. In his bones, he knew he was born to leave his mark on history as an acclaimed hunter. *Atka* would rise with his great feats and together they would become legendary, he was sure.

"How can you accomplish such a thing if you are scared off by Her Imperial Majesty? Busy yourself in Sae Hyura or some of the old battlefields. Take to the hunting grounds, even, or simply stay hidden in the training room. It will save you from the Queen."

It wasn't a half bad idea. Sae Hyura was always good to him when he hunted within its borders. Ezran could travel to the lower Procudon District for larger prey, perhaps even scoring a daemon if he was lucky. The peaks of the mountain range there were the only places in North Akadon that such horrid beasts rose to torment, besides occasional skirmishes on the border. If one wanted to hunt the beasts properly, they had to travel south.

"Kal already promised we would hunt Sae Hyura together on our return and I intend to hold him to it. After that, I doubt I'll be allowed anywhere. With the celebrations there will be no pulling the Princes away for a hunt. " Ezran stretched in his saddle.

"You could go alone, if you wished. The King would surely grant such a request and spare a few guards to accompany you if you mentioned it was for your practice," Genn replied.

The suggestion struck him as he settled back down, his mind storming with dark intrusions. His hands danced as they became infected with it. Over his sword's hilt, his belts, his horse's shining mane and muscled neck. Could he ask King Thamas such a favor, and would he really let him go? Especially towards the South? Did he even dare to go near the border?

A chill shivered through his veins. He even thought to name it fear, sharp and sour as it settled on his spine.

These troubles weren't strangers to him. Often, the little questions led to bigger ones, until he was faced with those that were far too painful to acknowledge. What was he doing here? Why didn't he leave? Would the King really let him go if he asked? Did he want to ask?

He didn't know if it scared him, made him apprehensive, or simply boiled down to his attachment to his adoptive siblings. Something kept him barred there. Maybe it was the question itself, whose answer would shatter his perception completely if it was denied.

He shook his head free of the spiraling thoughts before they could sink too deep. Kal turned on his horse, casting a look back and pairing it with a smile. Ezran grinned himself before the charismatic Prince returned to his people, waving and giving blessings out as he went.

The easy nature dimmed for Ezran without his brother's eyes. "The King might grant such a request, but the Queen wouldn't. I won't be the cause of another fight between them just to get the backlash of it from her."

"If you gave her less reason to hold you accountable for your woeful decisions, Master Ezran, you might find her to be more agreeable."

"You know it goes beyond that," he said, casting a dark look towards Genn. "I always seem to irritate her beyond reason by merely breathing."

"You do plenty to bring it on yourself and you know it. Your escapade yesterday is proof enough. Perhaps, if you behaved for once in your life, you would not catch her ire."

"It's different with me, Genn. Surely you know this by now. She may tolerate you, but I have always been..." Ezran shook his head as he said, "someone else to her."

"Then stay busy with your craft. Improve yourself and keep out of her way, at least until the celebrations are over and we return to Kal's educational efforts. Perhaps we can head to Procudon and let you content yourself with hunting instead of mischief. By Vaxas' Seas, it would be better on Vyn and I if you did."

A smile came at the thought, chasing the dark away. "We could blend in better down there, too. Not so many stares for us, huh?"

The retainer went quiet and set his jaw in a way that let Ezran know he said something stupid. Wandered too close to a vulnerability for Genn, and now the walls were back in their proper place between them. Biting his lip, he tried to fight against the ache that rocked in his chest.

CHAPTER
SIX

Agera District, North Akadon

W hen Aescian's burning Sun took its vibrant leave of the sky that day, they stopped along the road at a large tavern all too happy to host them. Everything was getting to Ezran—the spectacle, the hostess and staff falling over themselves to accommodate them, the people, the court manners and expectations suddenly thrust back upon him. He couldn't take another second of the pomp and circumstance.

Not without a drink.

The guards had taken over the tavern's floor, laughing and relaxing as much as they dared while still technically on duty. Drinks weren't stronger than warm beer and their Captain sat lording over it all, waiting for one of his underlings to make a mistake. His icy glare followed Ezran as he ordered something with a bit more bite from a pretty barmaid and flashed her a smile.

"So, who are you among this group?" she asked, sliding over a cup.

Ezran admired the flush that came to her cheekbones and the way her dark hair fell off her shoulder as he took a drink. "Would you believe me if I told you I was the Prince?"

He leaned against the bar as she shook her head, matching his grin with one of her own.

"I'm afraid the Prince has a different visage than you, good ser."

"Ah, well. That is true," he said. "What if I said I was the King?"

"You're quite young to have two sons grown and a daughter nearing a decade, Your Imperial Majesty," she laughed. Ah, and what a laugh it was. It spread all the way to her eyes, which were a warm honeyed gold.

"You're no guard, either. So, what high position do you fill?"

"Who says I'm not a guard? You think I don't have the capabilities?" Ezran sipped at his drink while her gaze trailed over him, still in the clothes he rode in.

"I dare not say that, ser," she said as she raised a hand to hide her smiling mouth. "You seem very capable. But you lack a certain... shine."

Ezran toasted to that. "Alright. I'm a very important son of a Procudon Lord and have been given, oh so graciously, to the royals as a companion for the young Prince. Believe me?"

"I would believe that," she spoke with a giggle and leaned over the bar.

"And you, my fair sera? What part do you play in this fine establishment?"

"A barkeep's daughter. Barmaid. Whatever it pleases

you for me to play," she replied, letting her tone drop significantly as she cast her gaze over him again.

Ezran finished his drink and tilted his head with a smirk.

However, just when he was about to respond, he caught movement in his periphery. He glanced to the side to find Vyn making his way toward them, with the Captain's glare accompanying. Ezran let out a sigh and leaned back from the bar.

"I believe barmaid is the only thing we'll be allowed tonight," he said.

Vyn came to his side and nodded once at each of them. "I'm afraid there are some tables that require your attention, sera," he muttered.

The woman walked away, casting a last lingering look over her shoulder. Ezran played with his empty cup as his facade dropped into his actual stony mood.

"Let me guess, the good Ser Captain Talvys is simply looking out for my welfare, making sure I don't leave a string of problematic bastards in my wake, yes?"

"No. I believe he said something about propriety and honor and a very lengthy monologue about how you don't take your duties seriously, though I have no idea why he feels the need to share it with me. I'm the one who's been chasing you around the Districts for roughly a year now." Vyn took a heavy drink from his mug and set it down with an exhale. "I came over to say you should take a break. You spent your last night on a roof, after all."

"Tree, technically, and not the worst thing I've woken up on." Vyn didn't smile at the crack, though it was hardly a surprise. He never smiled. "Surprisingly comfortable, too, if you can position yourself right—"

"I know you aren't happy to return." Ezran clenched his

jaw and glanced down at his cup again. "I understand it. I do. But it'll only be worse for you if you continue to act thus."

"What act? Surely you know this is simply my nature by now, Vyn," he said as he turned, catching the flat look the guard threw him along the way. Ezran leaned his back against the bar, folding his arms across his chest. "How else am I supposed to act, then?"

"Perhaps by behaving yourself. Don't give a reason for the Captain, the Prince, or Genn to send me after you. Go meditate, or read, or... something other than cause trouble."

"That sounds absolutely boring." Ezran shook his head. "Why is having a bit of private fun such a bad thing? Why am I held to such a high podium? I bet the Captain wouldn't be sending you over if it were Kal."

"No, he would send Genn. It's his job to keep Kal straight. You, however, don't listen to anyone that couldn't seriously harm you in some way." Ezran huffed and slid his gaze over the weathered war hero.

"Don't flatter yourself too much," he said. It earned him a look that had him playing off the words as a joke. "Fine, fine. I won't do anything scandalous while in this tavern."

"On the entire way to the palace," Vyn corrected. "Say it."

"I will behave myself until we reach the palace, I swear," he said, rolling his eyes. The guard seemed satisfied enough and moved off the bar without another word. Ezran tapped his fingers against his arms and decided to turn in, seeing as he could do nothing else.

He climbed the stairs with a hand on *Atka's* hilt, leaving behind the judgment and watchful eyes to enter into the largest of the tavern's rooms. Kal and Ezran were put up in them, along with Genn and a shifting rotation of guards.

Inside, he could find no sign of his brother.

Probably having a go somewhere and nobody stopped him, he thought bitterly as he stripped *Atka* from his belts. He leaned it against his bed and groaned at the boredom creeping in already. Opening the shutters of a window, he examined the street below him. Deserted, for the most part, emptiness soaked in silver moonlight and darkness. Satisfied with the lack of eyes and guards, he turned his face upward, seeking a handhold. He easily hoisted himself onto the shingled roof, letting his legs dangle free over the edge.

"And just how did I know you would come up here eventually?" a rich tone asked, startling Ezran. He turned to see Kal grinning at him while holding out a jar of liquor.

"Because you know Talvys has a thorn in his ass for me." Ezran smiled and accepted the drink with a grateful tilt. He took a gulping sip as Kal joined him on the edge, staring up at Odeion's Moon and the shards of stars that accompanied it. "How long have you been waiting?"

"Not long," he said. "I needed a break, anyway."

"You needed a break?" Ezran sputtered, handing over the jar. He couldn't remember the last time Kal hadn't soaked up every bit of attention he could.

"You know, I don't like being surrounded with people all the time." Kal tipped the drink back and grimaced when he swallowed. He never did develop the taste for strong liquors like Ezran had. His voice was colored with it as he continued, "Especially when they keep saying the same things or asking the same questions. And there are far too many eyes to drink this."

"That is true." Ezran looked up at the stars and leaned back on his elbows to properly admire them. "What's on your mind, then, that's making you so unsocial?"

"The ball," Kal sighed. Ezran glanced at his brother with

a knowing look. Every birthday was shadowed for him, along with the rest of his family. Still, Kal never wanted to admit it out loud.

"I'm sure it will be spectacular. The Queen always did know how to put on a good ball. You'll have fun once it begins, especially when you start talking with some pretty Ladies of court."

"That was always more your specialty, Ez. You know I have little care for such things."

"And yet you're exceptional at it. It isn't fair, I tell you. You squander such talents!"

This earned Ezran a smile, which was all he sought in the first place. Kal leaned back like him and handed over the liquor.

Ezran studied his strange return to solemnity while taking the jar. Yet, there was still crafted perfection there with Kal's short dark curls fixed to be just wild enough and his robes neat even as he reclined on a roof. He would be a good noble, Ezran was sure. The strong Northern royal House would certainly keep the public opinion, something King Nefion instilled and cultivated carefully in his children. Avis was a perfect heir to succeed his father. And Veslyn, well. Who could not adore the wild Princess? Already, she had the people's heart.

Kal especially would be admired by the commoners. After all, for reasons unfathomable to Ezran, he was far more invested in the practical side of helping people than the spiritual. Being a Kashadon was more of a side hobby in comparison. He learned, of course, like every noble family did on both sides of the fractured Empire. It was a gift that was not to be squandered. Their duty was to learn to wield their gifts of weapons and magic, as well as pass them on eventually and increase the number of Kashadon. By now, both Nefion Princes had made a name for themselves among the hunters, and Ves surely would once she began her training.

That just left Kyrith, wherever the Auberon had him cooped up. The mysterious Prince who many thought to be dead. The one Ezran took the place of, and vice versa. He was always a looming absence at celebrations, but it doubled on that particular day they were returning for.

They sat in silence for a moment, the weight of Kal's missing twin settling over both of them. Even after all this time, Ezran still didn't know what was appropriate to say about it. So, he did what he did best, changing the subject instead.

"What do you think will happen to us in the future?" he asked. "What will be our lots?"

Kal let out a small breath of contemplation. "I will be an advisor to my brother, probably work among the people for a few years to improve things. And you... I always assumed you would strike out on your own and come visit us from time to time."

"You know what I think we should do?"

"Please tell me it doesn't result in burning down half the empire," he joked. Ezran tapped him with the jar, causing the liquid to slosh inside.

"We should strike out on our own for a while. Build ourselves up as Kashadon before Avis takes the throne."

"We were on our own for almost a year, remember?"

Ezran took another drink and made an affirmative noise in his throat. "Indeed, but you were dead set on learning about the people. We hardly hunted, and now we're being called back like lap dogs. I mean really striking out on our own. Taking Vyn and Genn and traveling down to the hunt sites by the border, not telling a soul where we've gone."

"*Sion* is too conspicuous, and *Fior* too. It's not like we'd be surrounded by commoners at the border. You and Genn could probably get away with some anonymous hunting, but the Kashadon would know Vyn and I on sight," Kal said as he took the drink from him.

"And? They wouldn't do anything but beg to hunt with you. We would be our own masters, Kal." He stared up at the sky and smiled at the images that came to mind like they were painted above. "It would be a great way to get to know the Kashadon and spiritual problems your people are facing out there."

Kal let out a breath of amusement and took another swig from the jar before he answered. The town was quiet beyond the muffled merriment of the tavern below. Only the rustle of fiery, thick Northern oaks dared to compete with it.

"You could talk me into walking off a cliff and make the drop sound pleasant."

"Well, I've always heard that birds have no problem with it. Why should we?"

"Why should we," said Kal. Unusual silence spilled between them again as the Prince looked away from the sky. He studied the jar, rolling it to reveal the entirety of its painted sides. His other hand came up and rubbed the back of his shoulder as he pressed his lips together. Ezran cocked his head at the action.

"Sore again?"

"I always get sore around my birthday," Kal said, like he had to remind him. "I swear it's my mother's doing. She stresses so much that it infects everyone in the palace and beyond. I can feel it from here."

"She just wants what is best for you," Ezran replied,

practically forcing the words through his teeth, though they were true. "Maybe it's from riding."

"Maybe." The Prince took a drink and passed it off. He leaned back again and tilted his head up, starlight painting itself across his face. "You don't want to go back."

Ezran paused in bringing the jar to his lips. He flicked a glance at him and continued, drinking a little more than he should have.

"What makes you say that?"

"I know you, Ez. We've been inseparable since we met. I know when you are upset about something."

"It doesn't matter, Kal. I would follow wherever you led. And it's not only because your pretty legion of guards would drag me back by my ankles if I didn't."

"It's not?" he laughed.

Ezran passed him back the liquor with a smile. "I'm obligated to say it isn't."

Kal shook his head, but turned back to face him with a solemn hint to his features.

"Will you promise me something?"

Ezran lifted a brow at Kal's sudden seriousness. "Promise what?"

"You will always tell me the truth. No matter if it hurts, or if it's hard, or you think it's better if I don't know it. Even if you're obligated otherwise."

Ezran furrowed his brow as Kal dropped his gaze. He knew this was important to him, though he didn't exactly know what brought it on. His brother was definitely off tonight.

"I promise."

CHAPTER
SEVEN

The Crown's Road, Procudon District, North Akadon

The horse Sol rode was a solid black mount, reliable and fast for its size. He made good time so far through North Akadon, traveling on the Crown's Road. Even after the war, the path cut south from Elysia to Sankor, connecting the two halves of the Empire's royals. From Elysia, it would be an easy and mostly straight path to the border, curving only to accommodate the foothills of the Asba Mountains, which he found himself at the base of now. He swung wide off the path to avoid a certain pass on its slopes, but returned to the Road to follow it the rest of the way. On the other side, in South Akadon, the route wouldn't be nearly as forgiving.

Still, it was a day's ride at least to Vul Fracta. Solris passed through much of North Akadon's forests and farmland, cutting through towns and small villages on the way. Many of the old trading posts had since dwindled. Some remained open, but were now shadows of what they once were. Other strategic locations had been transformed into garrisons during the Fracture War and now sat as ghostly reminders. People were too afraid to rebuild in such places. The shades were too unsettled, fed by too much violence. They continued to be a constant problem despite how many were put to rest by Kashadon.

Despite the empty garrisons and barricades, the Crown's Road was a rather pleasant ride around autumn. The forests were a riot of color. Golds, reds, and fiery oranges painted the leaves, which littered the ground in a bright carpet and filled the air with their crisp scent. North Akadon's rolling hills gave a gentle sort of curve to everything, dotted with the sprawling farmlands and quaint villages of the all too friendly locals. Many were pleased to accommodate him, though he was dressed as only a simple traveler. It was a far better ride than what he remembered, but then again, he'd been going for border training in the dead of winter at the time. That dread tended to cloud the scenery, even in his memory after.

Sol remembered the brilliant hospitality they enjoyed on their way down. It hadn't faded in the years since. Perhaps it was due to his Kashadon weapon at his side. The white and gold greatsword wasn't exactly the most inconspicuous of spiritual weapons. *Chylus* never cared for blending in. It hummed with fiery energy at all times, ready in a moment to burn through enemies it found itself faced with. Its spirit tapped into Sol's affinities, like all Kashadon weaponry, yet its temperament was very much the opposite of its wielder. The balance of blood and fire magic roiled together to banish every foe with a vengeance.

Why a blade as volatile as this had chosen someone like him, at the tender age of fourteen no less, Sol couldn't say. Blessed, people said, when a weapon chose Kashadon to wield them at such ages. A sign the Gods favored them and

Nakre gifted them with strong magic. It left them paired together for life. Perhaps chained was a better term, as Sol was continuously having to calm *Chylus* and meditate to keep his own spirit in check. Any flicker from him, any slight disturbance, and the blade could react whether or not he wanted it to.

The closer he got to the border, the more unsettled the weapon became. It thrummed with nervous energy, pulsing in its connection to his own spirit. *Chylus* wanted to be used. It sensed shades around them at increasing intervals, and something else. Something Sol had no field experience with, but called all the same as he kept on toward South Akadon.

The change affected the people, too, in some aspects. The general contentment in common life began a slow turn to somber as he traveled further south. Not that the North-erners weren't friendly; they were happy to receive him like their culture demanded, but there was a heaviness to the air. The weather kept up a steady trend of growing colder. Farms disappeared as the ground grew rocky and unsuit-able. Villages turned to towns filled more with miners, smiths, and hunters of all kinds. Kashadon only grew in number as he left the Pentral District for the Procudon, run by the great Ferron House under the crown.

He stopped his horse by a well on the side of the Crown's Road to give it a minute of rest. The gelding drank with greed from a bucket Sol pulled up, so he took the opportunity to stretch his sore muscles from the hard ride. The natural splendor of his country surrounded him, yet held a sort of desolate quality without the bustle and noise of the Capital. This was furthered by the fact that Sol trav-eled without a group of fellow guards. Lonesome, yet peaceful.

Chylus pulsed, insistent and sudden, which pulled a sigh from Sol's lips. The weapon rattled in its scabbard, begging to be used. He pulled it from his belts to study it. *Chylus'* gold burned white, thick with power. Something was near.

Sol secured his horse to the well before he situated himself on a nearby rock, his sword complaining all the while. He placed his boots firmly on the ground and held up the weapon. It rocked in his grip, but he paid no mind, letting his green eyes slide closed.

Focusing first on his feet, he ignored *Chylus'* obnoxious pulsing against his spirit. He drew on the ground's strength under him, a steadying thrum of energy. Deep, deep in the earth, a fire lurked within, hot enough to turn rock to liquid. He pulled from it, energy shifting as it rose and cooled. He let the calmness of the earth and its blood rise in his being, entering his core. The sword in his hands grew temperamental at his attempt to subdue it. It shook in its scabbard like a child throwing a tantrum, but Sol didn't allow it to pull his focus.

Instead, he drew on the light, calm force of the surrounding air. The slight breeze was woven through with the scent of autumn and the wheat fields around them, chilled by the promise of coming winter. He allowed it to enter his core with every breath he took.

Chylus finally settled in his palms, though he could still feel its tenacity brimming beneath the surface of its spirit. It was simply pouting, in a way, only calmed because Sol asked it to. He slid his gaze open after he was sure both their spirits were settled enough and smiled down at the sword.

"There will be time for us to hunt," he promised, matching the quiet around them. "Just not now."

He fixed the blade back into place and stood. The horse became intent on him, lifting its shapely head as it chewed on grass. It snorted and pinned its ears with a sharp motion, jerking back hard enough to snap the reins and fill them with tension. The whites of its eyes flashed as it danced, caught with nowhere to go.

Solris cocked his head to the side at the animal's reaction. It was still a guard mount, despite their willingness to get rid of it, selected from birth and trained to be safe to bring into any situation. They weren't normally so temperamental or scared so easily.

A hum came from the surrounding forest, carried by a sudden fierce wind. Sol whirled to examine the trees. Nothing peered at him from the shadowed undergrowth.

Humming turned into what seemed to be singing. It wasn't a solid voice. The melody faded in and out, almost as if the mountain sent it tumbling down the slopes. It was far too close for that, however. Close enough that Sol should have spotted the owner, had it been a solid being.

Chylus rattled in its scabbard and pulsed an impressive amount for just being calmed. Sol pulled it free, holding the blade out in front of him with two secure hands. He drew strength from it as the entrancing melody lapped around him again. If he weren't a trained Kashadon, it would have enticed him into stepping within the forest's boundary. The ordinary commonfolk wouldn't be able to fight against it.

He saw it then. A wisp of white drifted in the breeze between tree trunks, and with it came another refrain of song. A shade flashed here and there, disappearing only to reappear moments later several feet away, or closer. Sol stepped forward, keeping a hard grip on *Chylus* to remain grounded. The sword shuddered. Its blade flared a heated white.

The shade led him deep enough into the forest that the Crown's Road disappeared from behind him. It slipped behind the trunk of one tree to come out the side of another, close enough for him to make out the details of a face. She appeared as a woman, dressed in fine clothes that told of her high status among the commonfolk. She was quite beautiful too, though her skin had gone as white as *Chylus'* blade. Her hair swept down in wisps of tangled black, drifting like ash on the wind. Pale red lips opened wider than should have been possible as she sang again. Her eyes of endless black pools cried tears of scarlet down her defined features.

She probably didn't realize what she was doing when she lured commonfolk out here to die. With a type of shade like this, she most likely wanted something to alleviate her pain, whatever it was. She could have been searching for a specific person, or perhaps trying to fend off her own loneliness. The reasoning didn't matter. The threat level was too high for locals or travelers. She most likely had drifted down from the mountain or wandered from one of the garrisons in search of new prey.

The woman's mouth split open, unhinging like a snake's jaw. Blood poured from ripped skin. Her song turned to screech as she rushed forward. A flash like wildfire, striking out toward him with extended hands, poised to tear his flesh.

Sol slashed out when *Chylus* vibrated, trusting the blade more than reflex. A wide arc of rushing flame sprang forward. Slammed into shade and tree alike. The woman gave an eerie scream as the fire burned hotter than any ordinary kind. It blazed through the layered trunks of several trees in mere seconds, before Sol could raise and clench a fist to stifle it.

The shade rolled onto the ground and cried, folding in on herself several times before she rose in a smoking blend of wisp and half formed body. She glared at Sol and roared with the fury of her pain. Her bloody tears streamed down her face, mixing with the stains left from her mouth splitting wide.

She rushed forward again, and this time Sol moved when *Chylus* thrummed. He dodged out of the way as her clawed hand came down. Before she could turn and attack again, the blade slid through where her ribs would have been if she were still human.

The fire burned within her, spewing out of her split jaw and turning wisp to ash. She tried to scream, to howl again. Nothing but cracking flames poured out of her. In a flash as bright as the sun's first piercing rays, she faded, taking her song with her.

Chylus settled, satisfied with its use. Sol breathed out slowly and put the blade away as he sent a prayer to the Gods for her to find peace at last. He made his way back to his horse, leaving nothing but the smell of charred wood in his wake.

EIGHT

Sankor, Kailos District, South Akadon

"Did I say stop?"

Marek's cool voice cut through Kyrith's consciousness as he sucked in a breath of charged air. The cold stones of the floor were the only anchors that kept him from slipping into Nakre's Realm. Even so, he forced himself to push off of them and get back onto his unsteady feet. Sweat blurred his vision, but he didn't dare wipe it away. He had to concentrate.

The guards didn't hesitate further. One of them tried to land a high kick that he dodged as another came from the left. Kyrith landed an elbow but took a blow to the side. The air in his lungs left in a hiss. Another blow came, meant for his stomach but deflected, then another for his thigh, his arm, his knee, and he couldn't keep up with the onslaught. A punch cracked across his cheek and he dropped. They followed orders, as they always had, and Kyrith couldn't even bring himself to blame them.

They didn't stop this time. Over, and over, and over,

they struck him for his lack of endurance. A lesson, he knew, as another knelt to give him a blow. His head spun as he spat blood. Still, they beat him, with the callous gaze of their Prince watching closely.

Two weeks healed Kyrith's back in part, but there was still more work to be done. Each twist of his body tugged at raw skin and every stray blow doubled his pain. By now, some of the worst of it had split open once more. Fresh blood slicked down his back and stained his shirt, though lacking the original passion it had in the throne room.

"Stop."

Kyrith gasped in air as the guards backed away. The taste of copper filled his mouth, accompanied by throbbing bruises, the sting of reopened wounds, and a split lip. His body ached, wishing for him to curl up, but he couldn't. He forced himself to tuck his knees under him and staggered to his feet. As sloppy as it was, he fell back into a swaying stance and narrowed in on the guard in front of him. The rest he could feel, gathered about him with shadows linking their cores together. All infected with the same streak of malice as their Prince. A pack urged on by its head.

Marek's laugh seared with its cruelty. "I will miss this, *sunshine prince*. We really have made you into an obedient dog, now, haven't we?"

Marek rose from his seat in the training room and approached the circle of guards. They parted for him as Kyrith dropped into a kneel. Fighting himself to remain calm, he willed his form not to tremble. It would be worse for him if he did. The Prince bent down and grabbed a fistful of black hair. Marek tugged Kyrith's head up, but he didn't look at anything but the grey stone wall. Marek studied him in his periphery. That obsidian gaze, rimmed by a freshly gifted bruise on one side, was trying to find anything, any crack at all.

Kyrith didn't give him one.

"I want you to remember something," Marek whispered, so close that Kyrith could feel his words wash over his skin. Kyrith swallowed, but kept everything else locked inside, even as the grip tightened on his hair. "It doesn't matter if you go back to that place. You will never be one of them, and you will never be rid of us. I can reach you wherever you are, understand? And I will know every move you make. Do not touch Arra."

So that was what this was about? He was pushing Kyrith so hard with training because of Arra? He almost wanted to laugh. It seemed the Prince's conversation with King Auberon on the subject ended badly, and thus, he had come to take out his frustration on his favorite target.

"Yes, Your Imperial Highness," Kyrith whispered, voice low and thick from his lip.

Marek stared a bit longer, searching, before releasing him with a sigh. He walked away, folding his hands behind him, and turned that calculating gaze to the walls of weapons.

"Do you think your family will welcome you back?" Marek snapped.

Kyrith stayed silent and focused on the ground. Unlike the King, the Prince wasn't as routine with his terror. Marek's violence fed on other's pain like a starving daemon did balanced spirits. The level of hunger was the determiner, and altercations with King Auberon served to rile it into a gluttonous beast.

Kyrith counted the cracks to stay calm. The steps. The pulse of his rapid heart. He kept his spirit calm and the fear from reaching the magic within him. In all these years with the Auberons, he had learned quite a bit of control.

"We all know they tossed you away without a care in the Realm. After all, you weren't the precious heir or the golden boy. You were the disposable one."

Kyrith heard those words so often that the bones of his ribcage had long since dulled their blades. Some years before, he had accepted these facts and made peace with them. Still, the King and his son never failed to remind him every chance they could.

"I bet when you return to them, they won't even recognize you. You'll be too much of a Southerner for them. You'll be crawling back here to us soon enough." Marek laughed as he raised a knife from a table. Admiring its hilt with the fondness of a lover, he turned to Kyrith's bent form. He came close to him, kneeling to raise his chin with the blade. Kyrith swallowed against the cool, sharp metal.

"I will always have a place for you, *sunshine prince*," Marek promised, in a way that almost sounded like compassion. "You can always return to me."

Kyrith's stomach curled like a snake on the defense. Still, he remained outwardly calm. Focusing on the Prince's bruise made his own throb in time with his rapid heartbeat. Boredom spread over pale features without a reaction. Marek released him and stood, handing off the knife to one of the guards.

"Again."

Marek slipped past the line as Kyrith rose to his feet. Forced his hands up. Fought until it hurt, fought until it burned, fought until he couldn't and kept on past that point, somehow. His fall was inevitable, but late.

The guards descended and within moments, Kyrith was laying back on the floor, curling in on himself as their blows fell like large hailstones from the mountains. Something in him longed to stretch out. It wanted to reach deep within the guards and the Prince, tug on the strings of their hearts, rip what made them special and blessed out from their cores.

Kyrith clamped down on the feeling as soon as it rose, pushing it as far down as he could. They could strike him a thousand more times. He wouldn't let that urge influence him.

"Stop."

They backed off instantly at the bored tone. Kyrith forced air through gritted teeth and turned onto his stomach. There was no way he was going to make it to his feet yet, not without Nakre taking him. Instead, in a wordless admission of weakness, he came up into a kneel and remained still.

Marek scoffed. Without another word, he left, guards flanking him on either side. Only one remained by the door to watch him, to be sure he did nothing the King didn't want him to. Kyrith let his head drop onto his knee. His breath came ragged, his pulse erratic, but it was over. He made it through another encounter with the Prince. That was all he could ask for.

He sensed her before he saw her. Naturally. She wouldn't let herself be seen unless she wanted it, but her spirit was a strong one. Sturdy and sharp and unfailing, like iron.

"Hello, little ghost," Kyrith rasped. Arra padded forward from the doorway, her steps as quiet as a cat's. He couldn't raise his head to look at her.

"Here," she said. Slipping a hand over his shoulder, Arra helped him slide back against the wall. Kyrith rested his head against the stone as she looked over his face, her dark amber gaze searching him as much as Marek had. Where his study sought out pain to derive his own kind of pleasure, hers was driven more in caring and assessment, though neither would be able to find what they were looking for. "What was it today?"

"Doesn't matter," he whispered. Arra set her mouth in a thin line, then brought over a pitcher of water and a rag.

She wasn't in skirts. Instead, a loose blue tunic draped over a pair of fitted trousers, providing enough room to move unhindered. She probably came to train and found Marek. He hoped she hadn't heard everything that he said. Kyrith didn't need her knowing part of it had been a warning to stay away from her. Arra would never admit to it, but it affected her all the same. Her spirit would betray her, darken a fraction, and a look would cross her face for the briefest moment. Sparing her that hurt was worth whatever it cost.

Kyrith focused on her instead of his own pain as she wiped the blood from his face. She was defined, nothing subtle or gentle about the matter. An intricate braid kept her white hair back, only a few loose, straight strands escaping to frame that focused expression. Her features were made up of thin lines and precise angles, as if cut by some masterful blade. Arra was pretty in a way that was challenging, even daring, but severe. She definitely wasn't Marek's preferred type of dainty, soft things.

"Here." Kyrith pulled his athame free from his belts. Looking at it, Arra sighed and raised a brow at him.

"Are you sure? You're hurt enough as it is, Kyr—"

"My back started bleeding again. I need it. Go over the one you made if you have to," he said.

Gritting his teeth and trembling as he went, Kyrith pulled his shirt down far enough for her. The doubt never left her face, but she unsheathed it all the same. He fought a grimace as she began to carve the sigil once more.

He never did have to tell her why he needed these so much more than others. Arra would always accept it, which he was grateful for. Any weakness in him, whether it be spiritual, bodily, or otherwise... it would put him in a particularly vulnerable spot he didn't care to be in. Not here, at least.

After she finished, she handed the athame back and forced him to shift further. She pulled up his shirt to tend to his back, which he had no doubt was a healing mess itself. His lips pressed together as her washing tugged on his wounds.

"How much longer?" Arra asked in the oppressive quiet.

Kyrith swallowed and took a moment to respond, breathing through his pain so his voice wouldn't betray him. "A few weeks. You probably know more than I."

Arra remained quiet as she lost herself in her task. Closing his eyes, Kyrith rested his pounding head against the cool wall. Something wasn't right. There was a cloud to her spirit, darkening and dampening it, and he doubted the shift formed from just another one of Marek's bouts. He glanced over his shoulder at her, ignoring the ache in his body at doing so. She didn't look up at him.

"Arra," he said, as loud as he dared to. She jerked then met his gaze with wide, unassuming eyes. "What's wrong?"

A smile flashed at him, brief and false, one she long since pulled whenever Kyrith or the Queen noticed the bruises on her arms. "Nothing. Traveling so far makes me nervous, is all."

He exhaled, doubting any place could be too far from

here for either of them. "Don't hide from me. Did he do something?" Kyrith flicked a glance to the guard by the door, but their mutterings were too quiet to make out from there. Her hand stilled on his back.

"No," Arra replied. "Not him."

"The King?" Kyrith raised his brow, lowering his voice a fraction more. King Auberon never had shown any violence toward her before, but he couldn't exactly put it past his character, either. After all, Marek learned his cruelty somewhere. Particularly in finding an outlet for his anger through his intended.

"No." She let his shirt fall and Kyrith leaned back against the stone again. Looking her over, he tried to puzzle out the culprit himself. If it wasn't the King, and it wasn't Marek, then who could it be? Or what? He doubted anyone else was brave enough to try something with her. If her own knives didn't cut them first, Marek's surely would.

"I know something is bothering you."

Arra sat down properly, crossing her legs and glancing at everything but him.

"Honestly, it's just traveling," she said. Tucking a stray piece of hair behind her ear, her bright eyes trailed to the weapons' wall as her teeth caught her lip. "The Northern King... he's the one my father fought against the most. I'm afraid he will do something after finding out who I am."

"The King wouldn't send you if he thought you would be seriously injured. King Nefion..." Kyrith trailed off and looked to the side. He wanted to say that King Nefion was a kinder soul than his Southern equivalent, but he couldn't be quite sure. His own memories of the man were hazy at best. By the time he was nearing eight, he had left Elysia. What he remembered was stained with a child's bias and weathered down by the years spent away.

However, he did trust King Auberon's greed and Marek's possessive qualities. They wouldn't allow the legendary General's daughter to fall into the wrong hands. It wouldn't be a risk they would take without good reason.

As for what that reason was, Kyrith hadn't figured it out yet. The lines about improving diplomatic relations were thin at best, if only because he knew those behind it. No obvious answer came to mind, however. It set him on edge.

Arra glanced up at him with his momentary lapse. Kyrith rested his head back and leveled his gaze with hers. That was a question for a time when he had the freedom to think about it. "Everything will be fine. We'll be together. Between the two of us, they can't harm you."

Arra smiled in a way that wasn't quite reassuring. Clearly, he couldn't do anything to settle her mind, which was probably why she had come here in the first place. Resigning himself to his failure, Kyrith nodded once, took a fortifying breath, and hauled himself onto his shaking legs. Arra was by his side in a heartbeat, but he waved her off.

"I can walk on my own."

Doubt clouded her features, but he made it to the door without falling over. The wordless guard turned to follow, ever the constant threatening shadow as Kyrith wandered into the hallway.

He didn't allow himself to think of anything but climbing the ebony stairs. It wouldn't help him to focus on Arra or Marek in this moment, so he pushed them from his mind and focused on moving forward with every step. It seemed like an eternity before he made it to the top. The rest of the journey to his room was a drifting, stumbling battle. The guard remained outside, which allowed him to shut the door and finally let everything go. His hands shook as they pressed against the wood, shuddering with the lock being turned, and his breath trembled as it left him. The raw ache of his skin beat in time with his heart and head, but he could still force in air to fill his stuttering lungs.

It was enough.

Kyrith sank before the cold hearth. Blankets and cushions remained piled there from his nights spent on the floor, preferring it to bleeding over his sheets and straw mattress. Testing his arm, he winced and rolled his shoulder when pain shot through his back. The guards always went harder on him with the Prince present rather than Captain Jaxas. They had been good, loyal dogs to Marek today.

He held out his hand towards the logs and released that tight hold he kept on his spirit. Magic came easily to Kyrith. It thrummed just below his skin, rushing through his veins and core from the suppression. Heat flared over his body as the hearth sprang to life within a breath. His muscles uncoiled and released the tension they kept. Sinking down into his blankets, he allowed himself to think at last.

How many more days?

It didn't matter. He would make it, whether it be a thousand nights or a single one. Kyrith would be free of this place, somehow, some way. It was as close to a prayer as he'd ever come, repeating it over and over and over as he stared into the flickering fire.

CHAPTER
NINE

Vul Fracta, Procudon District, North Akadon

Vul Fracta was a unique place, even for the North. From the rolling rise Sol came up on to enter it, he found it had not shed its marvel in the years since he'd last walked its streets. He stopped there to admire the cityscape for the brief moment he could allow himself to. The ancient marble wall that welcomed him was magnificent, gleaming as it split the once whole city straight from Mount Euris' slopes to the shores of the mystic river Kashna. Known as the Birthplace of All Life, the dark estuary lived up to its name with the number of boats and birds about. People teemed along the docks to spill into the streets, deterred only by that great wall. Though Sol had seen it before, he couldn't help but be awed yet again by its length and size. Many of its attributes were worthy of its prominence, but the one that struck him the most was the fact the thing had stood since the Age of Fading.

As he approached, the people and their bustle became

clearer, keeping the city alive like thick pulses of blood. The buildings surrounding them were artful, daring masses of copper, marble, grand stonework, and gabled roofs. Painted wards became through lines of the streets, meant to fend off negative shades and daemons. Their chemical scent carried sharply on the air, along with salt from the river and earthy winds of the mountains. From those slopes, Kashadon wandered about in impressive numbers, almost competing with the populace of commonfolk. Weapons were toted for all to see as they maneuvered in larger hunting parties. The lower classes they served were boisterous, never resting. Vul Fracta certainly gave Elysia much to contend with.

Even with the clamor and life, the closer he got to South Akadon, the more tension threaded through like an engaged muscle under skin. *Chylus* rattled in its scabbard, sensing what lay beyond. Commonfolk deserted the area right outside the ancient wall. Only Kashadon seemed to brave it, acknowledging him as he passed on horseback. He thanked *Chylus'* lack of subtlety for the attention.

Even so, he made good time through the Fractured City's lower streets. Kashadon dwindled the closer he got to the wall, until the buildings themselves halted and left a yawning gap that would take an entire marching army to fill. He approached the enormous iron gates that defined the separation of one empire from another. In a time before Emperor Regis the Conqueror of the Nefion and Queen Talvinia the Bloodborne of the Auberon set out to unite Akadon under one rule respectively, the gates had separated the kingdoms of Procudon and Euris. They hung open when the Empire was born under the two rulers with a truce, but were closed and reinforced during the Fracture War, only to remain so when there was no victor. Now, the archaic things loomed up in front of him like warnings, molded from end to end with sigils of banishment, suppression, cleansing, and all sorts of other protections. He would have loved to stop and sketch them if he had the time. It would certainly be a fitting challenge to replicate on a round pendant.

Guards flanked the towering, circular iron on either side, dressed in the full armor of shining gold plate. The suns imprinted on their chests were silver. Other than the color scheme, the singular difference between them and the royal guard were the metal helms they donned, which the latter had long since discontinued. They seemed as ancient as the gates they protected while tracking Sol's approach through obscuring chain masks.

"Halt there," one commanded. Sol stopped his horse, ever obedient to those with such an authoritative tone, and waited while the guard approached. Her armor made a familiar soft clink as she moved, and Sol tried to take comfort in it as he stared at the gates again. "What business do you have?"

"Royal orders," he said. Handing over the King's parchment, he shifted in his saddle as she read it over.

"So, we're sending couriers through now?" the border guard replied, softening her tone once she realized Sol's profession.

"No, just royal guards. It's a singular trip, I assure you."

She handed back the orders with what might have been a smile, though it remained hidden under gold links. "Good luck on your endeavors then, friend. I hope you make it back."

Sol took a breath at that and nudged his horse forward. The black gelding snorted as it moved through the columns of guards, flicking an ear toward the iron gates as they creaked open. Sol's heart picked up enough to make *Chylus* voice its irritation. A shout even startled him as it came from the Northern side, alerting when the horse stepped through the tunnel. The sable gates before him opened with a slow hiss and the South spread out in all its glory.

The other half of Vul Fracta, known as Vul Sura to the Southerners, almost froze him in place. If the Northern side was a vibrant fire, the Southern was the ash that remained after. Mountain stone and dark wood formed most of the buildings into blocky, identical rows. If a house was rich enough, it might have polished onyx accents, but those were few and far between. Sigils there were not painted, but carved deep into the wood or stone and stained with what could only be blood. Its metallic scent was heavy on the wind and called to his spirit through his blessed gift. Each one thrummed with powerful energy, stronger than any Northern sigil he'd ever seen. These were meant to keep away things much larger and more evil than a few simple corrupted shades.

Metal chimes created a macabre melody that carried throughout the streets. People moved with eyes lowered and donned simple, functional dress, no matter their class or profession. The only exceptions were a group of black clad guards mounting powerful warhorses, eyeing Sol like he was some kind of invading rodent.

"You must be the Northern guard," one of them called out, a thick Southern accent on his tongue. His dark gaze drifted down Sol's form as his lip curled upward. "We expected something much more... flashy."

Sol clenched his jaw as the gates closed with a groan behind him. He stopped his horse a few feet from them, realizing how much he truly did stand out among these people. Even his simple traveler's clothes of a tan coat and grey breeches seemed too loud, too colorful around their muted neutral tones. His skin was far darker than their pale complexions, his eyes lighter, and his tight ringlets a stark black where they favored straight, bright hair. He was thankful for his hood, but it could only do so much.

"Traveling in armor would be impractical," he said.

The Southerner *tsk*ed and cut his glance to the rest of his party. Most of them seemed as enthusiastic as their leader to be accompanying Sol through the country. Still, they swung their huge mounts around and began to move steadily through the streets.

"Keep up. I would hate to lose you and have to drag some half dead guard before the King."

Sol didn't comment further, not that any of them seemed to mind. They chattered amongst themselves, content to ignore him. Sol was content to be ignored. He only had one mission.

The people here were quieter than those on the other side of the wall. They were thinner, too, and many had scars marring their features or limbs in some fashion. Some seemed intentional, such as sigils carved into the skin, but others gave the distinct impression of accidents or fights with blades. All were quick to glance away from the traveling group, giving healthy space as if they were afraid of a horse's kick.

Though the Kashadon were wary of them as well, they still walked with a kind of superior arrogance among the commonfolk. Each was tall and proud in their stride, eyes raised, showing off the weapon on their person in conspicuous manners. None of them looked approachable at all. How could people come to them with their troubles? Did they really have such an abundance of hunts that they could afford to be so arrogant?

"We plan to make for Saorsa and not stop until nightfall, Northerner. We'll have to move quickly to make it to the outposts in time. It will only become a harder ride the closer we get to Sankor. Think you can last?" one of his new companions asked.

Sol set his jaw once and adjusted his reins. "I can manage," he said. *Chylus* pulsed and he slid his eyes closed for a moment. The sword was already irate—he had to be careful.

Sol was hopeful that as they went the city might liven up, but the opposite seemed to be true. There were more people, that was certain, but they didn't seem any happier than those he passed before. The shops all sold functional things like dishware, tools, and weapons. Few held items of expense or luxury. Those that did had hefty prices for things most in North Akadon could regularly afford and defended such commodities with armed guards on either flank of their stalls. Most weren't Kashadon, but the wicked looking blades at their hips were enough of a threat.

Taverns, tea shops, and other such businesses seemed to cater to the Kashadon or higher class alone. It shocked Sol to find they also coexisted right beside brothels, dens, and other unsavory places without any separation.

This was all very different from his home.

And Prince Kyrith grew up here?

Shifting in his saddle, Sol centered himself as his horse moved under him. This was only Vul Sura. He couldn't chalk the entire empire up to one city, especially one so close to the North. They were the most affected by the war. Of course it would have a melancholy atmosphere. The shades within it must have outnumbered the living after it all ended. If the Kashna and the border hadn't been such a draw, people would have abandoned it.

It was one simple journey. His duty to make, for his Prince, King, and country.

The ride to Saorsa was indeed hard.

While North Akadon had hills, South Akadon had mountain ranges. The Crown's Road cut the edge of Mount Euris, but not its foothills, and as it went on, it seemed like they were trying to clamber up its sides. Beyond that, the path was rocky and uneven, filled with ruts, and often rose or fell in steep intervals. The poor Northern gelding tried its best not to slip or lose its footing along the way. Sol was sore not from their pace, but from clinging to the horse every time it stumbled.

The great warhorses, despite their size, had no problem making their way on the Crown's Road. Even when the Euris foothills gave way to the Vera Mountains to add even more drop and rise to the path, they trudged on ahead like they'd been making the journey since foalhood. Perhaps they had, in order to get used to the terrain.

On the way there, the towns and villages they passed were nothing like the quaint communities back home. The people were distrusting and inimical as they went by. No one offered a place of rest, even when the group stopped to water their horses. They watched like hawks until they were back on the Crown's Road and traveling away.

Sol also noted the lack of farms. There were some, but not nearly as many as in North Akadon. Mainly, there were mines, forges, among other indecipherable places. The singular thing that linked any of these towns and villages to each other was the presence of Kashadon.

There were a handful of hunting parties in every outpost they passed or stopped in. The closer they went to the mountain peaks, the more of them appeared. They were as unfriendly as the commonfolk, even to their own kind, but said nothing to the traveling group. They seemed to settle with glaring, with increasing frequency toward him.

Once, though, as they passed on the other side of the Vera Mountains and approached Saorsa, they did encounter a beautiful sight. Sol could only make out the boldest distinctions, as it sat high on the mountainside and the light was slipping already, but it was a thing to behold. Mountain fog obscured the bottom of an obsidian temple, making it seem as if it were flying with its curved eaves and masterful carvings. Two black pillars stood guard for the steep path up to it, adorned with powerful and fresh bloodied sigils. A weathered grey sign hung down under an archway and declared the ethereal building to be the Temple of Kselia. Fitting, Sol thought. A sanctuary for Kashadon and those gifted with air magic, along with commonfolk that worshipped the Goddess of Winds and Skies.

The temple was an anomaly of beauty in the South. It reflected nothing about Saorsa at all. In fact, Sol wasn't sure they hadn't turned around somewhere on their journey and stumbled back to Vul Sura. The functional, dark buildings were all the same. The sigils, metal chimes, Kashadon— there was no clear separation between them. Saorsa's defining features were the temples dedicated to Kselia and pathways that wound through the disjointed city. They were lighter than the grey stone of Vul Sura, perhaps once even white before time aged their pristine qualities. Now, though, the color peeked through a covering of debris on rare occasions alone.

They stopped at a seedy looking tavern positioned beside a brothel. Sol was grateful to retire in his room while his companions went to please themselves, leaving him be for the first time since dawn. He settled in the cramped quarters, but didn't complain. Instead, he sent up a prayer of thanks for the privacy and settled *Chylus* on his palms.

The sword was close to dancing with its energy. It rattled nonstop, pulsing with every little sense of shades or daemons. It wanted to be unleashed. It wanted to banish something, burn through more corruption. Magic thrummed over its white blade and flared at the clean edges. Even flickered inside the sigils that tumbled down the smooth metal in artful work that Sol could never hope to replicate.

He centered himself and closed his eyes. If his spirit was calm, *Chylus* would soon follow.

CHAPTER

TEN

Sankor, Kailos District, South Akadon

Arra turned before the mirror, trying to find any faults in the light grey robes and skirts she wore. The belts at her waist were stark in comparison, crimson and midnight black to acknowledge her ties to the Auberon House. With her hair braided properly, she couldn't find an outward issue with her attire, yet something was amiss. She looked so ordinary standing there with no Kashadon weapon to mark her out. She settled with a few knives and a saber that was as common as could be. Expensive, worth its service to the crown, but lifeless by her side. Its metal sang to Arra in a way she'd heard a thousand times before.

Now, the tune was tiresome.

Knowing she couldn't fix it at the moment, she turned from her reflection. It was best to get this day started, beginning with a standard blessing and ending with an Auberon dinner that Arra already dreaded. Avoidance would only make her late and anger Marek. With his mood remaining in a constantly terrible state since the King denied his request to send someone else to the North, it was best not to add to it. She smoothed her skirts one last time before heading for the door.

Arra cautiously opened it to reveal the hall of the east tower with its lined rows of noble bedchamber doors. While Kyrith was holed up on the opposite side of the palace, she had the *luxury* of spending her time near Marek. Even though she would be forced to accompany him later, she still peered out of the threshold to be sure she was alone. It would only be a brief reprieve, perhaps a minute or two, but any chance to avoid him was one she was willing to take.

Her father's words on daemons proved true again. The Prince stood out in the hallway, his shirtless back to her. Sigils spread over his otherwise unmarred skin in a pale webbing of scarred knotwork, almost like a living Kashadon weapon. Arra ducked back into her room, slowing her door as it closed, all without even a fabric's whisper to alert of her presence. Yet, laughter broke in through the crack at the last moment. High and feminine. Definitely not Marek's cruel tones.

She dared to peek out, though caution wove tight into her muscles. Marek was in the same place as before, but this time Arra took in the woman with him. She was a maid Arra had seen around the palace—Rian, she thought her name was. Her light blonde hair was pulled back in a fashionable braid, with a few spare strands framing her delicate face and dark eyes. Marek's hands traced her curvy figure. His gaze skated her chest, the black stain of a sigil painted there. Arra pressed her lips together when he kissed her, claiming her mouth like a conqueror as he pinned her to the wall.

Marek's hand was far lower than it needed to be in the middle of the hallway, but a second later Rian pulled away with another giggle. She backed down the corridor without looking away from him, fixing her robes with a sly smile. Marek leaned against the wall as he returned it.

Rian disappeared as she passed Arra's door, finally escaping down the servant's route. Marek leaned his head back against the stones. His smile faded. Sighing, he swiped his forehead with the back of his hand and disappeared inside his chambers.

Once they were gone for good, Arra crept into the hallway. She smiled as she reached his door. By Kanah's Fire, she might have to bed the maid herself, in thanks for keeping her intended's attention off of her for what had to be a good few hours. She didn't have to sneak the rest of the way, though her steps remained light by nature as she slipped down blackened stairs and through dark halls.

The Fortress' courtyard, though plain and rather barren, was alive with energy when compared to its usual state. Its walls penned the gathered in, making Arra see the black clad guards more as sheep as they moved about in herds. Captain Jaxas acted as the stock dog, preparing them in a timely manner. All the while their shepherd, King Auberon, remained still at the center, dressed regally in robes of muted scarlet and black, his dual blades sheathed at his side. He looked to the sky, where snow was falling in fat, meandering flakes. Not yet enough to stick, but a threat all the same.

Arra approached, then dipped into a proper curtsey. Even the King's attention dropping to her couldn't stop the warmth from spreading through her chest at seeing the Queen beside him. As tired as she looked, swallowed in her skirts of dark blue, she managed to spare a smile for Arra when she rose.

"You look lovely, Arra. My King, would you permit us a moment?"

Arra almost startled as Queen Endri turned to her husband. He narrowed his gaze a fraction, and for a moment, Arra could see his mind working in his fathomless eyes. He sniffed and jerked his chin, to which his wife curt-seyed low in a sign of respect. She led Arra away, though with the guards and bustle, they were hardly alone.

"I wanted to warn you, my dear," she began, folding her hands in front of her as they walked. Arra couldn't help but note the bones of her fingers, her pale wrist far too small, and she swallowed against the ache it brought. "Surely you heard of the lower quarter fire?"

"I saw it," Arra said. "Unfortunate. I thought they replaced the wards a few days ago. They must've missed that one."

"Oh, no, the ward didn't fall, by the Gods' mercy," the Queen replied, though the warmth in her tone dropped at the end. Arra couldn't blame her. What were Gods to them in this place? "It was a terrible tragedy, actually. It seems some lower class Kashadon stumbled on a corrupted spirit user and killed them before they could escape."

A slash of fear carved through Arra until it broke against her defense. Fear had no place in her. Especially when she was surrounded by people who could sense it like daemons their prey.

Still, the thought of a spirit user, corrupted by chaos, being in the low quarters of Sankor made Arra squirm a little. Out of all the Kashadon and their incredible talents, they were a sect all their own. Her fears were shared by many, if not all. Commoner, Kashadon—it didn't matter what class or rank. How could they not, raised on stories like Benras the Cruel, who could drain someone of magic and free a spirit from its body with a simple brush of his fingers?

Of course, there were those like Master Lyrana, who spent her years studying daemons and how to kill them. Without her, the entire populace would still be in the terror and vulnerability of the Age of Fading, yet fear of her kind remained. It was impossible to shake. Having the power to take magic from Kashadon, turning them into a commoner, was a nightmare even Nakre shied from. Arra would rather experience the most violent death than be rendered powerless so easily. And with them being naturally susceptible to a daemon's influence, along with chaotic magic within their reach, it was almost inevitable that they would turn against their fellow Kashadon if they weren't secluded in the Temple of Odeion.

"What were they doing in Sankor?" Arra asked.

The Queen pressed her lips together and flicked her brown gaze around the commotion surrounding them.

"It's not quite clear. Perhaps they were trying to make it to the Temple for help, but the chaos in them was too great. They killed some commoners and drained a few Kashadon before they were stopped, though thankfully only one seems to have lost their magic permanently. The lower class hunters trapped them and burned the structure. Everything seems to have gotten out of hand too quickly. The guard didn't even have time to intervene or collect the remains before they were stolen." Arra swallowed, trying to process the images her mind came up with. "That's not what I wanted to discuss, however. I wanted you to be aware that there might be some unrest when you visit the

Temple today. Tensions strain between classes when something like this happens."

Arra's brow knitted together, unsure why Queen Endri was saying such things. She knew that tensions would grow. Sankor and the South in general was an iron cloud of pressure, ready to break into a storm at the slightest tilt of its precarious balance. It was why King Auberon was so ruthless. As much as that cruelty could be turned toward Kyrith, it was necessary to keep the empire from dissolving into chaos. Fear meant order, and order was survival.

Seeing her reaction, Queen Endri stopped and turned to her. She grabbed her hands and Arra stilled. "I couldn't bear anything to happen to you, dear Arra. You will be my family by law soon, but you have always been a daughter to me. Promise me you will take care of yourself out there."

Despite how weak her hands looked, the Queen's grip was strong enough to make the hard fold of parchment bite into Arra's skin as she pressed it into her palm. She managed to keep the surprise hidden with a soothing smile.

"Of course, Your Imperial Majesty. Please don't worry yourself for my sake." Arra folded her hands as she retracted them, pretending to smooth her skirts as she slipped the parchment into her belts. Curiosity burned within her, but the eyes of the careful watchers all around were only growing on them. Arra could feel them studying, waiting for the smallest break.

"I always will, but I have faith in your strength. You must find it too," Queen Endri said, giving her one final look, a lasting one with too many stories to tell. She bowed her head in a slow, careful motion. "You must excuse me, Arra. I wished to see you off, but I haven't been feeling well. Please, forgive my leave."

Arra's chest tightened as she dipped into a curtsey. "Of course, my Queen."

As she walked away, exhaustion weighed on her shoulders. Her stride was short and slow, her path direct as she headed toward the Fortress' doors. Clearly, it was not a good day for the monarch. Queen Endri must've battled to get out of bed and see her, all for the chance at slipping her a message.

Concern turned sour as the Queen stopped, letting her son pass her by with a few exchanged words and a hand on his shoulder. Arra fought to keep her spine still as she took in his now put together figure, dressed in robes of dark wine. The vibrant red slash of his cloth belt brought the eye to his black whip, *Athak*, and the way its many hooks clinked against each other as he walked toward her. All she had was a moment to prepare and curtsey.

"You wore those?" he snarked. She glanced down to figure out what displeased him about her appearance. Last she remembered, these robes were fine to him.

"Yes," she replied carefully. "Is there something wrong, Marek?"

His eyes cut into every aspect of her as he raked them down again. Under such scrutiny, her body seemed to shrink, compacting into something small, yet unable to hide.

Marek slid his tongue over his teeth and held out his hand. "Not at all, if you want every commoner and Kashadon alive looking at you."

Arra swallowed as her face heated, but she took his arm all the same. As much as she fought, she couldn't hide the blunt edge from her words as she spoke, "If you wish, I will put on something more suitable to you."

"There's no time," he sighed. "Don't let it happen again. I'm marrying a noble. A lesser one, true, but not a whore."

She struggled with everything in her not to clench the hand he held. Whether it was the insult or the reminder that made her burn, she couldn't tell. It was the Queen's doing alone that was delaying the inevitable, but she couldn't interfere forever. Arra was already nineteen to Marek's twenty-four. She couldn't imagine the King waiting much longer, or her intended for that matter. He might have flings with maids and others, but eventually...

Arra forced it from her mind as Marek led her forward, grateful that was the end of it. With the last of their party prepared, the guards took their final place as a shielding ring.

Shrieking gates announced their leave as Sankor opened up before them, its people as on edge as she was. They glared from alleyways and cracks they had tucked themselves into, peering out darkened windows and stoops. Still, the cramped streets were clear, no one daring to come too close. As a snapping breeze cut through them all, Arra swore it smelled of ash and cold copper.

"Still angry, then," Marek muttered.

Arra paused, unsure if he was speaking to himself or actually acknowledging her for once.

"It's understandable," she said with caution. "A spirit user wandering free is never a good thing."

"A waste."

Arra didn't know if he meant the spirit user themselves, their death, or the anger of the people. Turning to him, she settled with asking, "Of a Kashadon?"

Marek seemed bored, flicking his gaze over the people like they weren't even there. "Of magic."

She didn't see the difference between their answers, but

wasn't quite curious enough to push further. He was in one of those particular moods that was difficult to navigate. A single misstep and she could bring out that violence which lurked just below the surface.

Instead, they remained quiet for the rest of the walk to the Temple of Odeion. Great obsidian walls were skirted by glimmering weapons, laid out along the dying gardens like stars in the sky. Power thrummed through each and every one of them, from daggers to swords, polearms to bows, along with a scattering of a few unique weapons here and there. The metals sang sweetly to her in a tune she preferred much more than the saber at her hip. And yet, as with every other Kashadon weapon she had ever come across, Arra knew that all of these were off limits to her.

It wasn't unusual that a weapon hadn't chosen her, considering her age and social class, but it solidified her thought that she needed to forge her own. She was, after all, gifted with control of metal. Kyrith offered to lend his help, with his blessings of fire and knowledge. Since then, it had become something of an obsession. It was a lot more work than she initially thought when she first began. Arra had to choose a proper metal, one that could bear the power of a Kashadon weapon and hold a spirit of its own. It had to be strong enough to withstand the powerful sigils, but also be malleable enough to forge.

Not just anyone could make it a Kashadon weapon either. She had to find someone gifted with spirit itself to bind magic to its core, in order to make it capable for their type of hunting. Involving one of them, however, wasn't the most pleasant idea to her. It would be easy, living at the Fortress with the Temple so close. Lucky spirit users spent their lives making weapons there, after all, so it wouldn't be such an outlandish request. But being close enough for one of them to touch her, drain her magic or take it for their own...

Arra flicked her gaze over to the line of spirit users looking on a safe distance away at the temple's covered walkways. Their expressions varied from stoic to bored, none of them too outwardly different or dangerous looking. Yet, every one of them had a potential for chaos.

Arra turned her thoughts from them as the priest stepped into the courtyard, followed by the familiar ritual items. She prepared herself to stand there through the long winded prayers and blessings until her legs cramped. At least it was a sure period of time where Marek would have to keep himself in line.

Yet, before anything could begin, a commotion tore Arra's attention from the blessing to the back of their procession. Guards descended, slinging magic and metal around while terrified screams cut through the air. Bystanders were fleeing, people dashing back into their homes or the narrow alleyways so as not to be implicated. Marek let her go and she found her saber's hilt, only to freeze before she could unsheath it. A group of guards dashed off after some unseen opponent in the exiting crowd. Few remained, gathered around something with stony faces.

"What is it?" King Auberon snapped. One guard bent to retrieve something as the others moved out of the way.

Arra froze with her tense disbelief. A body lay in the middle of them, burnt and headless, limbs strewn as if it had been thrown. She swallowed against her revulsion as the guard stretched out a banner, letting them all see the handprint symbol and red paint.

They do not protect. They do not provide.

Marek sighed, looking disinterested in a way that sickened her. "Ah, Hallow. Always a tad dramatic, don't you think?"

Arra set her teeth at the name and turned away. A thief like Romulan Hallow, who thought himself a revolutionary, didn't concern her. However, that same commoner having the gall to throw a Kashadon's body at a royal procession, corrupted spirit user or not, did. If things were getting that bad, she understood why the King would be so desperate as to turn to assassination.

"Have the culprits found and cut out their tongues before they can claim Kven Endelio. Hang them for all to see. I won't waste my time with this foolishness further," King Auberon said, turning back to the Temple.

Yet, his knuckles turned white from how they clenched, and Arra pretended she didn't see the look he gave her.

ELEVEN

Elysia, Pentral District, North Akadon

E zran was content to stay in Elysia. He loved the Capital, as long as he stayed anonymous among its citizens. It was an elegant city full of elegant people, crowned with the resplendent Sun Palace at its core. Always brimming with energy, just like an unused Kashadon sword and Ezran himself. He loved everything about it, from the food, to the slums, to the architecture. He'd grown up on these streets, chasing after Kal as soon as they discovered a way out. He would always feel at home here.

But now, home was a little uncomfortable with its welcoming.

Their parade tripled in size due to the increase of guards. The entire city seemed to spill out to participate in Kal's homecoming, seeing as he had been away so long. He played the part of their darling Prince perfectly. They threw fragrant dried flowers and colored scarves out for him.

Cheers went up as he waved, smiled, and blessed them. Ezran, however, was barely able to keep from scowling

"Master Ezran, you look like a prisoner being hauled back to his cell. Perhaps a smile and a wave?" Genn jabbed as he nodded to a few giggling girls. Ezran's frown deepened.

"I feel as if I *am* a prisoner, Genn," he said, "and I'm late for a meeting with the judge."

They marched through the streets straight into the arms of the palace, dismounting once the gilded gates clanged shut behind them. Ezran handed off his tired chestnut to a stableboy as he let his gaze travel up the ignited spires of the palace. He could already feel the Queen's skewering gaze from his place.

"Stop looking miserable," Vyn said. He put a hand on Ezran's shoulder and maneuvered him forward toward Kal.

The guards of their company began to group up, taking off to do other important matters. Ezran had half a mind to slip away and join them, but Vyn's secure grip kept him from acting on such a dream.

"Kal! Ez!"

His dark eyes sifted through the crowd to find the voice's owner. A bolt of lilac silk came flying through the ranks of armed guards faster than they could get out of the way or kneel. The finely dressed force hurled itself at Kal, smothering him in a cloud of unruly black curls.

Kal laughed and swung the lithe figure around once before setting her down. He brushed the wild tangles from her face and smiled. "Little spider! You have grown a foot."

"I have not. You've gotten smaller!"

She wriggled out of his grasp and threw herself at Ezran in a similar fashion. He caught her with ease, though Kal was right about her gain in height.

"Veslyn Nefion, I think I've missed you the most," Ezran said. She beamed as he set her down and ruffled her hair even more, as if it needed such treatment.

"I won't tell Avis," she giggled, giving him a bright, gap-toothed smile.

"Won't tell Avis what?"

Ezran glanced up from Ves with a grin. The eldest of the Nefion brood made his way through the guards in a much calmer manner than their sister. He kept his hands clasped behind his back as he walked, nodding with a small smile to every guard that knelt.

"Nothing! It's Ez and my's secret!" Ves said. Avis shook his head, turning with a proper grin and embrace for Kal. Ezran bent next to the Princess and slipped something out of his sleeve, presenting it in front of her.

"For your secrecy," he murmured. She took the pale jade pendant from his grasp and admired it with wide, silver eyes. Carved with delicate care, a sun gleamed with gold to set the rays, and a silk ribbon to secure it in place.

"You spoil her," Avis said, but amusement laced through his tone. Ezran straightened and brought his brother into a fierce hug.

"But of course. Who else could I spoil? You?" he tossed back, already pulling something from his coin pouch and lifting it for inspection. Avis smiled wider as he took in the pendant.

"You shouldn't have," he said, taking the jade from his hand. Its soft blue matched the robes he wore. A protection sigil formed its face, ringed around a rendition of Aescian in his lion form. Avis studied it, then looked back at Ezran with warmth.

"I had to. The Nefion patron God and sun crest? How could they not be yours?" Ezran grinned. Someone hit his shoulder and he turned to find Kal the culprit, raising his eyebrows expectantly.

"And me? Where's my present?"

"I was your present. My company while you 'learned about the people' was your present, Your Imperial Highness." Ezran pushed back. Kal voiced his offense loudly and rubbed his shoulder like he actually hurt him.

"Can I return it?"

Ezran tackled him into a headlock and ruffled his hair as punishment. Kal laughed as he struggled free, dashing out of reach as the group began to meander towards the palace.

"Can you two behave for at least a few seconds, seeing as you've been away for so long?" Avis asked, speaking with the confidence of a someday King. He took up his place as leader of their herd, letting the rest fall in line behind him.

"No," the two responded in unison. Ves giggled as she dashed up to Kal's side, claiming his hand.

"Why didn't you get me something, Kal?" she asked.

"You see what you do?" Kal shot at Ezran, who gave a simple shrug in return. "I do have something for you, but it's packed away with my things. I will have to go dig it out for you."

Ves skipped in excitement. "I've missed you two! It's been so boring here. I was worried, too. You both barely wrote!"

"We wrote when we could," Kal said. He left out the fact that most of the time spent not writing was nursing hangovers, among other degenerate businesses. Ezran was hardly one to give up his secret.

"I hope you learned something out there," Avis cut in as they began to ascend the white marble steps.

"I learned plenty," replied Kal.

"I did as well," Ezran said, though his eldest brother couldn't see the grin on his face.

Kal betrayed him with a snort. "He certainly learned about many of our people intimately."

Avis cast a disapproving glance over his shoulder, which made the betrayer and Ves both crack into laughter. Ezran sheepishly rubbed the back of his head and feigned embarrassment. He was still sure he had learned more about the people than Kal did in all his fancy seminars.

"I hope they weren't too much of a hassle on Master Gennady and you, Vyn," Avis said. He led them through the massive front doors, gilded like the rest of the palace. The familiar emblazon of the sun crest reflected over them all the while, slicing sunlight over the walls when they shut.

"Nothing we couldn't handle," the guard remarked, gruff and low. Genn remained silent, walking a step behind Kal with folded hands. Ezran blinked as his eyes adjusted from the brilliant light of day to the richness of the palace depths. He breathed in deep, smiling at the familiar scents of hearth fires, autumn winds, and polish.

Now, all he wanted to do was steal a good jar of liquor from the kitchens, then collapse onto his own bed. He was already plotting out his events for the week. After he recovered from the ride, he would definitely return to his favorite taverns in Elysia. He had been away from his old haunts for too long, and it was also an excellent way to avoid the Queen, at least until he could hunt.

Avis turned to face them as if he heard his thoughts, which put an instant damper on his planning. His spirits dropped before a word was out of his mouth.

"I know you've just returned, but I'm afraid we must go see Father as soon as possible. There's news he has for both of you." Ezran didn't like the sound of that at all. Was Avis finally getting married? Or were they picking an intended for Kal after his years of blatant disinterest? He doubted it. His brother wouldn't look so solemn if that were the case.

This was something serious.

"Alright. We should freshen up first, right, Ez?" Kal prompted. He turned his gaze to him and saw the confusion mirrored in his brother's. Nodding, he returned to Avis.

"We'll head to the throne room after," Ezran said. Avis accepted the answer with a brief smile, but it didn't reach his eyes.

The two returning men made their way up the stairs of the palace to their respective chambers. Ezran's was exactly the way he had left it, though it was cleaned every day. His canopy bed and black blankets beckoned seductively, and his weary muscles almost collapsed at the sight. It was a battle to resist them. Instead, he chucked his used riding clothes, then pulled fresh trousers and a decent embroidered tunic from the recesses of his closet. Satisfied with his appearance that the Queen would definitely not be, he headed out of his chambers and met Kal in the hallway.

"Did we do something before we left that would anger him?" Kal asked as they hurried down the steps.

Ezran furrowed his brow as he tried to think back.

"No? I don't recall anything. Besides, Avis would have told us if it were just something we had done... right?"

"Right," Kal repeated, though he didn't sound convinced.

Avis waited with their sister outside the doors to the throne room. He nodded once, then moved to enter before they could even begin to pester him. Ves flounced in behind him without a care in the world.

Ezran always felt odd being received in the throne room. It reminded him of his first time coming to the palace, when everything terrified him. The gold, the splendor, the kindness. He didn't remember much, but he did know that he feared people being tender towards him.

The room was like everything else in the Sun Palace: gold and extravagant. Two decent sized thrones of gilded marble ruled under a white, blazing Shield. It radiated light much like Aescian's Sun, bathing everything in its glow and nixing the need for torches. The space was close, comfortable, with a sense of ease for those inside. Still, it was hard not to be in awe of the precious stones trickling through the marble walls, the pristine gold furnishings, the white velvet accents.

Ezran bowed to the King and Queen, who sat above in a regal manner. King Thamas beamed at them, warmth in his vibrant blue gaze. Queen Nefion smiled at her son, then cast a frosted glance over him. He shuffled a bit under its weight.

"Veslyn," she addressed first as the air grew thick in the room. Her silver eyes only moved from Ezran after she was sure to skewer him in place. "You look an absolute mess."

The Princess flounced once and raced up to her mother's throne. At the action, the woman melted for her youngest child. Ves held out her necklace for her to inspect, which made Ezran look away and shift his weight. He caught Kal daring a glance at him from the corner of his eye.

"I know! I was in the gardens trying to catch spiders. Look what Ezran gave me!"

The Queen studied it and huffed, "Well, what did this cost you, Master Breckhym? Looks real. It was paid for, right?"

"Illynthia," the King said. He softened when Ves looked toward him and held out his hand. She went to her father, letting him inspect the pendant. "I hope your trip went well, and that you both learned much."

"We did, Father."

"I hope you put it to good use, Kalin," Queen Nefion said, though her gaze shot to Ezran. He shifted his own to the floor, biting at his cheek.

"Naturally, Mother. I would love to tell you all about it, but Avis said that you have something to tell us. It seemed more important than our trip," Kal replied.

The Queen's mouth hardened further as she sat back on her throne. King Thamas cast a resigned gaze toward her and cleared his throat.

"Yes," he said. "It is rather important. I think you'll be happy to hear it. We received word from King Auberon, and he's releasing Kyrith to us. As we speak, a guard is making his way to Sankor to accompany him home."

Ezran blinked as his mouth parted, and his gut ached like the King hit him. He ripped his gaze from the monarch to Avis to Kal and back again. Their eldest brother seemed serene as always. But Kal...

He looked as if he had been struck as well. His bronze shades went ashen, to the point Ezran was almost worried he was going to faint. He tugged at his collar with absent fingers and swallowed. Ves' brow knitted as she played with her necklace in the silence.

"Kyrith..."

"What..." Kal tried to begin, but his tone was hoarse and flat. "What of Ezran?"

Queen Nefion's eyes shot ice toward the King. Ezran's heart leapt to his throat at the thought of going back to South Akadon. He couldn't leave. This was his family. All he had ever known.

"King Auberon demanded nothing. He simply wanted

to return what is ours, in his words. Ezran can stay on if he wishes, or return to South Akadon, though it would deeply pain us all to part. It's his choice. One he must make alone, just as the journey will be if he decides to leave us."

Every pair of eyes in the room centered on Ezran. It was his turn to swallow this time. He made sure to avoid the Queen's gaze as he shook his head, unable to trust his voice. He didn't know what to feel. Grateful, of course, to King Thamas and having the chance to stay, but his own father hadn't asked for him back?

King Auberon didn't exactly seem like the giving type. Not when it came to the Nefion. Ezran's stomach twisted sharply. Something wasn't right.

And by the look on Kal's face... his brother agreed.

CHAPTER
TWELVE

Sankor, Kailos District, South Akadon

Arra was on borrowed time.

It seemed that the Queen's venture to sneak a letter to her had drained her far too much, and it left Arra facing down both Marek and his father alone. She kept her eyes lowered on the small, bland plate in front of her. She didn't eat anything off of it. Her stomach was tearing itself apart, especially since Marek was getting tenser beside her. Something was about to break. Arra's skin prickled... she needed to disappear.

"Are we agreed, then? On all you're expected of in the North?" the King asked, taking a deep drink from his cup. Marek was motionless beside her, knife in hand, resting right beside his plate. Arra ripped her gaze away from its blade.

"Yes, ser."

"Good," he said, setting his cup back down. He surveyed the thin, transparent bones left over from his fish before letting his eyes skitter up to her. "Make your father proud, then. You have much to live up to, but if you have a drop of him in your spirit, you'll do right by the South."

Marek's empty hand, the one closest to her, curled into a fist.

Arra's heart picked up in pace. "Of course, ser. It is my honor."

"It's more than that," the King said, letting his jerking gaze flit around the room again. It allowed Arra to spare a brief glance up to her intended's face, where his carefully indifferent expression only served her urge to run. "We will settle this at last, then."

"If preparations are finished, you should retire, Father. You seem tired," Marek interjected.

Arra's attention snapped to the monarch, desperate for him to stay. At least with him there Marek had to stay calm. Yet, the weariness was in the King's dark eyes and sagging frame. Even the drink born flush couldn't hide all of the weighted exhaustion in him, laying in circled shadows under his eyes. The King remained for one more moment, gaze flicking about the table as if it held all the details of their plots. He seemed satisfied with what he found.

King Auberon rose from his chair, dragging Arra and Marek up as well. Her lungs couldn't get enough breath as she followed them around the table, then curtseyed next to her intended. A step away and behind, naturally, like that would serve to protect her from what was coming. There was a clacking snap as the guards around them stiffened into attention. They turned, following their monarch out of the doors to leave them alone.

The door hadn't even shut properly before Marek closed a hand on the back of her neck. Arra barely had time to prepare herself for the impact before she was hauled over and thrown against the nearest wall. Her shoulder took the brunt of it, aching in a demanding way she was forced to ignore. All her attention was on Marek's hands as he came close, pinning her there.

"Can you do it?" he snapped. Arra flinched a little despite herself, her heart galloping in her chest. Still, she kept her voice as placid as she could.

"The King ordered me to. I'll see it done."

Arra flinched again when Marek's hand slapped against the stone right by her head. "That's not what I asked you. *Can you do it?*"

Arra flicked her gaze up as briefly as she could manage. Even so, meeting those dark, focused eyes seared a bolt of fear through her core. She could only make herself nod. Marek let out a scoffing breath as he pushed off the wall. It was just a little more space between them, but Arra found gratitude for every inch gained.

"This isn't some game, Arra. Nor is it a simple hunt where you kill a shade or daemon. You realize that? You'll be cutting the throat of the precious bastard's father. Do you honestly have it in you?"

Arra hated how small her voice came out when she made herself speak, "He's the thief King. He broke Akadon for greed and took my father off to war. He deserves what's coming for him."

"Oh, yes, I'm sure you're as patriotic as the rest of us when it comes to that. Him choosing that common whore over my long dead aunt and defying the Gods' wish for my father to be Emperor decades ago must be gravely suffered wounds for you. Don't act dull, darling. You know what I'm asking."

Of course Arra did, but answering him would be like trying to forge ahead on a thinly iced river. Acknowledging Kyrith was never a good thing around Marek.

Especially if that meant admitting she cared for him in any capacity.

And his question—would she be able to hurt Kyrith in such a way? Arra didn't know. She wasn't even sure the loss would pain Kyrith. He'd been gone for so long...

Arra couldn't keep up that delusion for long. Of course it would. He was his father, no matter the years they spent apart. He had a twin, someone who came into this Realm with him. A mother and two more siblings. They mattered, even separated, like Arra was from her own parents. She didn't know if he would be able to forgive her for the hand she played in their deaths.

Yet, there was no way to refuse. People were starving already. Rebelling thanks to the likes of Romulan Hallow. The civil unrest would only grow worse as winter came, with death rising. Besides, she'd been ordered to. King Auberon wasn't someone to cross. He once took the eyes and tongue of his prisoners during the war, then hunted them through the mountains to boost morale in his ranks. He wasn't a man one said no to. Not when he could so easily reach their family.

Not when he could so easily reach her as well.

"I'll do what I have to," Arra said at last. Marek's smirk was humorless as he leaned in close, sliding his hands over her shoulders.

"Good. Because the only way the *sunshine prince* comes back here alive is if you do. You'll do everything perfectly, just the way my father wants. One bit of this plan going awry means Father will take it out on not only you, but him, too. Fuck up enough and he might take one of the other Nefion bastards instead to hold the North over. Do you understand? You'll do it right. There's no other option."

His fingers squeezed hard enough to leave bruises on

her arms. It took everything for her to keep herself outwardly calm despite the fear that coursed through her veins. Raising one gentle hand, she held his wrist and kept her voice soft. "Marek. Please. I'll carry out the orders as they've been given."

Marek's eyes remained unfathomably cold, the dark in them unknowable. His grip never lessened. He took a breath as if to speak, but was cut off by the loud metallic echo of hinges as a far door opened. Marek backed away from her quickly as Arra straightened herself off the wall. She studied the worn stone at his feet as her entire body burned.

"My apologies... for the interruption, my Prince, my Lady," a quiet voice said. Arra flicked a glance up to catch Rian by the door, hesitating. Marek inclined his head, fixing his robes as his deceptive smile came back to his lips.

"No need. My intended and I are just finishing up."

Arra knew he was staring at her again, her skin heating with it, but she couldn't meet his gaze.

After a weighted pause, he turned, striding toward the door until he came to a stop before the maid. "I have some work for you. Come to my chambers when you're done here."

"Yes, Prince Marek," Rian said, bowing her head, but Marek didn't stay to hear it. Arra's air finally left her lungs in a shudder once the Fortress' shadowed halls swallowed him whole. It was a battle for her not to hunch in on herself, especially with her heart beating hard in her throat. Her fists clenched at her side as she forced herself to take in a stronger, calmer breath. She couldn't break. Not here, and not with Rian looking on.

Arra met the other woman's eyes briefly. Rian hadn't budged from the door, and turned her head to the side at her stare. Arra moved, then, taking another door out to find her own way through the Fortress' dark.

She was too pent up to go to her chambers, as well as too sure that Marek might want to finish their conversation if he caught her there. It left her pacing the halls of the Fortress, remaining as unseen as a ghost. Arra had long since figured out how to come and go without being spotted, if anyone even cared to notice. It was a giant place, after all, with few occupying it and little to do inside. Arra used to entertain herself by getting lost, then finding her way back again. Now it was more of a necessity to buy herself precious moments away from Marek. It was relatively effective with how many parts of the Fortress were abandoned, lost to the centuries. They heaved their last breath after the army stopped using it, once King Auberon made his truce and the Ralith charged him with inciting war.

Of course, for appearances' sake, they also charged the thief King. They had taken her second Prince then, though she hardly remembered such a thing. She had been six at the time, the same as Prince Ezran, and could only recall her father coming home. The family had been reunited and that was all that mattered, even though the war never really left the returning General. That was an entire lifetime ago, however, and one Arra sometimes forgot belonged to her. Especially when she walked the shadowed halls, alone with nothing but the thudding of panic in her veins.

By the time that faded to a more manageable beast, Arra found herself in the familiar torch-lit depths by the training room. It was only there that her hands lost enough of their shake to pull out the note Queen Endri had slipped her. After a cautious glance around, Arra unfolded the parchment in the firelight.

Something fluttered free from the paper, which turned out to be another folded over note when Arra snatched it up from the floor. Turning it over, all she was faced with was the curling cursive forming *Ezran Auberon*.

Arra's brow smoothed out as she exhaled slowly. After pressing her lips together, she carefully placed the smaller parchment back into her belts and returned to the original one. It was a simple line, written hastily.

I know you'll make the right choice.

Arra stared at the words, guilt clawing its way up her throat until it was tight and swollen. What choice was there?

She fed the first note to the torch above her, watching until it was gone and the flames danced black in her gaze. The least she could do for Queen Endri was get the note to her son, but that didn't get Arra's mind away from the rest of it. She needed something more pressing.

She made her way into the training room, scouting out to see if any guards lurked nearby. Finding none, she trailed to the back corner where the blunted children's blades were, coated in a fine layer of disrepair after going so many years neglected. Still, they made a fine and innocuous hiding place. If he had finished with it, that was.

Pushing some of the blades aside, Arra shoved her hand under the rack and sought out a familiar leather bound shape from its depths. To her delight, her fingers hit pages, and a moment later, she freed a rather ordinary book.

How they officially started this, she couldn't remember. It might have been when Kyrith left a tome or two behind somewhere, and Arra returned it with a note slipped inside. Since then, they'd communicated like so, passing books back and forth with hidden messages waiting in the bound pages. Kyr's penmanship was equivalent to smeared scratches, but she had long since been able to decipher it. She had to, if she ever wanted to be sure their conversations were truly private and wouldn't be reported right back to Marek.

These notes, however, were particular ones they'd been trading for weeks, and sent warmth spreading through her as she flipped the cover open. Both his messy handwriting and her curling cursive were side by side, comparing and adding to each idea, flowing in and out together. Rough sketches of a Kashadon saber decorated the paper, mirrored in a perfected version to the right. There were also renditions of different hilts, blades, and sheaths, along with sigils stamped in ink without any spiritual power to give them capability. Beside each, Kyrith's scrawl denoted attributes and hindrances that would come with each.

Somehow, he seemed much more knowledgeable about all of this than her. She chalked it up to him spending so much time reading, but then, she had, too. At least on this subject. Whatever the reason, Arra was thankful for his invaluable aid with both the design and the promise to help her forge it. He had struck down several of her suggestions and made some adjustments to her sketches with crude slashes of smeared black ink. He had even marked in some numbers and equations on the side, going into the science of the speed of the blade versus its weight. Arra accepted his numbers without checking them, on the whole because she wouldn't trust her attempted answer in the first place.

She bit at her lip as she flipped through the book instead of only the notes he sent back. A metalworking tome. New sections were marked out for her to read with slips of parchment. Closing it with a snap and tucking it under her arm, she knew that she finally found a suitable enough thing to keep her occupied.

CHAPTER
THIRTEEN

Sankor, Kailos District, South Akadon

S ol thought the Crown's Road couldn't grow any more difficult. Then, they cut through the Noka Mountains in their last push to reach Sankor. The Monarch's Pass seemed more like a dip where Cynos rested his Ax while shaping the rest of the land. Hardly what he would classify as a pass. After the weeks on end of traveling through endless mountains and thick forest, they had battled through the worst of it. Exhaustion wore heavy on Sol as they finally spotted their destination.

Sankor lay below, bathed in light as Aescian's Sun climbed toward the west.

Along the way, they stopped only when Odeion claimed the sky from her lover and they reached proper outposts to halt in. They never did camp out under the stars. Each day, they woke to keep moving at dawn, barely stopping as they rode hard for the Southern Capital. The Crown's Road didn't lessen as they went further south. Its steep, rocky footing continued to worsen in the rural stretch between

Saorsa and Sankor. The mountain views were decent, but South Akadon's trees weren't the fiery blanket of color Sol was used to. Instead, he met trees already stripped down to blackened bark, or evergreens with needles piercing in jagged directions. Blank snow even capped the distant peaks, though Vaxas and Kselia weren't to bring winter for a good few months. That didn't stop the cold from accompanying them, though, or increasing day by day.

Everything was isolated. From one city to the next, there seemed to be almost no one. The towns, villages, and outposts were sparse at best and far too spread out. He was sure at some points the Southerners were purposefully leading him astray. *Chylus* would rattle in its scabbard at the thought, reminding him to keep settled.

His companions were disagreeable to say the least, but they left him to his own, as long as he did the same. Sol never asked for a break or bothered them, which seemed to at least earn him the same courtesy. They moved fast through long, unforgiving stretches. When they did stop, they kept their guard up. It took him only a few instances to understand why.

When they encountered the most unmaintained parts of the Crown's Road, they would send a rider forward, waiting in silence until a shout came that the path was clear. Other times, these hardened Southern guards would flinch or spook from any slight rustling that emanated a little too close from the woods. They were wary of daemons. At one point, they even heard the distant roar of one, and the leader of the group forced them into a gallop for a decent stretch. Their caution never lessened, even when they clambered over the Monarch's Pass. The glimpse of Sankor appeared less like a welcoming home and more as an acceptable reprieve to the Southerners.

Not that Sol could blame them. The city was grim. Like Saorsa and Vul Sura before it, the buildings were made of dark wood and dull stone, with little regard for architectural design beyond functionality. They were thin and tall, more so than the previous cities, and maximized its space as best it could. The Capital was a sprawling thing. Easily twice the size of the ones that came before. It hugged the side of the mountain like a shield, crushed up against it in defense of some unseen challenger. Charred remains of houses climbed up one side from where a fire had eaten through a packed quarter. Towering black pillars rose on the outskirts, carved and stained red with powerful blood sigils. The frosted wind was coated with copper and an echo of smoke. The city itself seemed to hold an inimical disposition, threatening those that approached it.

The narrow streets were black stone, rough and set long ago, Ages wearing them to task like a broken down workhorse. Sol's own tired gelding seemed thankful for the flat and somewhat even ground. People around them stared at the group of guards and a clearly foreign traveler with hostile curiosity.

Sol was sure he could have made it to the palace himself, if it could even qualify as such. The monstrous thing loomed up over everything else, pinning the city between it and the mountains, as if it were the body and the rest of the city the shield arm. Erected in clean lines and sharp corners, with massive wings of flying buttresses to support the height, pride radiated from its structure. It was the largest thing Sol had seen since crossing through the Northern gates.

The group flanked him as they approached, and the easy conversation between them died. Sankor was so much quieter than Elysia. It had a unique, unsettling melody of metal chimes and the normal dull roar of a crowd, but it was nothing like the chaotic merriment of his home. Everything was hushed, as if scared of drawing something out from the surrounding mountains with too much noise.

It only grew into melancholy silence when he rode through the black gates of the palace. A legion of guards waited there, all in shining black armor with accents of scarlet. One stepped forward, thick red crossbelts rioting across his breastplate as a tell of his rank.

"Welcome to Sankor. His Imperial Majesty has instructed me to escort you personally to the throne room, ser...?"

"Maisym," Sol replied in a clipped tone as he dismounted. He looked over the amount of people with weapons around him and set his jaw. Their gazes sharpened into daggers at his name, air growing heavy with the tense weight it carried.

Despite Sol's best efforts, apprehension laced through his muscles and made his heart pick up in his chest. *Chylus* rattled once and he put a hand to its hilt to silence it, forcing in a calming breath. The last thing he needed was to give them an excuse to separate him from his sword.

"This way, then, ser," the Captain said, gesturing widely to lead him through the ranks.

Sol took in the guards on either side of him, sure that this show of personnel wasn't a simple welcoming party. No one turned to look at him. They stood in rigid formation, perfect in their lines. He was almost flattered at the turnout for a single escorting guard.

The interior of the palace was certainly... sparse. If it weren't for the black moon and red sigil crest of House Auberon flying from banners, he wouldn't have been sure a royal family really inhabited the place. They led him further through twisting hallways and stairs, but there still was nothing for decorum.

The throne room was just as massive as the palace. It seemed as if its designers wished for the entirety of the Capital to be housed within it. Two towering grey thrones sat around fire pits, but it was the regal weapon above them that seemed to be the centerpiece of the room. It pulled the flames' light into itself, eating the surrounding brightness with its shadowy blade.

The Sword of Odeion, Goddess of the Moon and Night. Patroness of House Auberon. Partner to Aescian. Sol heard of the Sword, naturally, but it was even larger than he imagined. Oppressive, too. Something about it made him cautious, as if it threatened him in some way. He sent up a quick prayer of peace to its first wielder.

"Ser Maisym," a croaking voice called, drawing his gaze down at last. It came paired with endless dark eyes and a head of brown hair that was just beginning to lose the battle to grey. Still, the King looked capable of swinging the Sword behind him. He held his black crowned head high as the Northern guard stopped and bowed.

He did not kneel. He would not kneel before anyone but the Nefion.

"Your Imperial Majesty," he said. His voice sounded too loud to him, echoing its baritone off the empty space and stone walls.

"Your father was a General, no?"

Sol paused, keeping his face neutral. There was no doubt the King knew of his father and remembered him in perfect clarity. After all, General Maisym had been the final blow for his campaign. "My father was Captain of the Guard during the war, ser."

"Yes." The King smiled and it sent a tremor down his

spine. "I remember. Yes. He was an excellent strategist. Pity about his end."

Sol took a deep breath before his sword could voice his unease and stabbing anger. He took the opportunity to glance at the Queen and almost raised his brows in surprise. She was a frail thing. Thin in a painful way, but there was still something kind about her face.

Everything about her reminded him of Master Ezran. Their features were similar, with her high cheekbones, thin nose, full lips, and pale skin. Even her brunette locks matched his to the exact shade. The only things he seemed to get from his father were his black eyes and squared jaw.

She smiled at him, as if the action took much of her energy. "Thank you for coming all this way, Ser Maisym. I hope the ride wasn't too rough. The Crown's Road can be treacherous on this side of the border."

"It was a decent ride, Your Imperial Majesty. Thank you for receiving me," he said, finding his voice softened a considerable amount to address her. She smiled again, but her gaze flicked to her husband and the action dropped just as quickly.

Sol was almost sad to see it go.

"This is my son, Prince Marek Auberon." The King's introduction was jarring, pulling Sol's focus to a tall mass of muscle at his side.

Prince Auberon had similar features to his brother, but there was something different about him. His gaze was too dark and his smile was a twisted form of Master Ezran's smirk. Not only that, but he had a good few inches on him and a few pounds of muscle, too, if Sol was remembering correctly. He bowed appropriately, but said nothing to the Southern Prince.

"So, have you encountered my other son at all? The one sent to your King against his will?"

Sol flicked his gaze back to the monarch, feeling as if he were on trial. "Yes. Prince Ezran was given every opportunity the Northern Princes were and was raised among them."

The King chuckled. Sol let the rest of the report King Nefion instructed him to give die on his tongue. Instead, he shifted his gaze from one Auberon to the next, trying to keep his nerves in check despite feeling surrounded.

"I have no doubt my son was raised in extravagant comfort. I expect his softness would be the death of him if he were to return home."

Sol's brows came together. He never would have imagined the King talking about his son in such a way. Did he truly care so little for his own blood?

King Auberon raised a pale hand to the guards at the far side of the room. "If you have made my son such a Northerner, then I give you my best attempt to do the same. Bring the boy."

Sol turned away to watch as the doors opened. Two figures walked forward in shadow, their steps surprisingly light in the room's quiet. They came closer until they stopped in front of the thrones. Sol had to press his lips together to keep them from parting.

There was his Prince.

A Prince that resembled Prince Kalin and yet didn't at the same time.

A Prince that sported healing bruises and a split lip, along with three jagged scars lining his face.

A Prince who was *kneeling*.

He was muscular. Far more than any of his brothers. Tall, too, when his form wasn't bent and pressed to the ground. He had the same thick black curls, the same lightened bronze skin, and a face that resembled his father's.

"Rise," King Auberon commanded. His Prince did. He folded his hands behind his back and didn't lift his grey eyes from the ground. Sol was too shocked to do anything. He knew he should've dropped as soon as he entered, but...

Prince Kyrith *knelt*.

He was so stunned that he didn't even take in his fair companion. She almost faded into the background as he took in the scene.

"Are you happy to part from us?" the King asked.

Prince Kyrith took a moment to answer, parting his full mouth. Sol took in the split of his lip again. Who had struck his Prince? No, not just struck, but beat him? Who dared to lay a hand on someone of such rank? And why did no one see to his injuries?

"I leave knowing I carry all your lessons with me, Your Imperial Majesty," Prince Kyrith said, his voice thick and low, lower than Prince Kalin's, lower even than Sol's. Threaded with the sharp Southern accent that surrounded him since he crossed the border.

King Auberon's laugh tore his gaze away from him at last. Sol glanced back up at the King with a furrowed brow and a frown tugging at the corners of his mouth. Prince Auberon's hard gaze studied him, as a smile twisted his lips into a cruel grin.

"You certainly will," he said. "Oh, and how fortunate the escort was you, Ser Maisym, if a bit expected on your King's part. This is Lady Arra Enryn. I'm sure you know of her prestigious family line. She will be accompanying you back to Elysia, to be sure the boy settles in well, and so we might... improve our relationship, from crown to crown."

His chest tightened. Sol turned, registering the specter

by his Prince's side properly. *Enryn*. It had to be Enryn. She curtseyed and he forced himself to bow to her as King Auberon rose from his throne. The guards all snapped to attention, but Sol caught the tremor that shot through Prince Kyrith, even though he was exceptional at covering it up.

"I entreat Kselia to bless you with fair winds on your journey and Vaxas to grant you smooth seas, so you may arrive back North as swiftly as possible. My guard will take you to the coast and see you off to Chastol. I hope you and your King enjoy my kindness, Ser Maisym. I did what I could to make the boy realize his place in the Realm. It will be up to you to judge if I succeeded."

CHAPTER
FOURTEEN

Elysia, Pentral District, North Akadon

"Come on!"

Ezran ran through the streets, tugging along not one, but two lagging Princes by their wrists. The oldest of them was simply calm, in no need of such a hurry, but the other seemed dejected. Even with Ezran's direction, he almost toppled into several Elysian citizens, which made him shout apologies over his shoulder. Even so, Ezran barreled on through the wide, confusing streets of the city like he'd been born to them. He was sure he could have found his way on a moonless night, drunk and blindfolded. Even Kal and Vyn weren't as skilled as him in navigating the Capital, and especially not in such a quick fashion.

"Perhaps it would be better if we walked to our destination," Avis suggested.

Ezran shook his head. Walking was mundane, boring. It wouldn't get Kal out of his own thoughts. Finally, they reached the stretch of streets that Ezran was so eager to get to. He slowed their pace, releasing his grip from both his brothers with a smile.

"I thought the whole point of going out with just Vyn was keeping a low profile," Kal said. "We can't exactly hide in the Kashadon quarter."

Blacksmith shops and trinket sellers lined either side of the street, packed to the brim with off duty royal guards and Kashadon. Tailor shops sold high quality robes and tunics for hunting, bordered by jewelry stalls with sigils for everything one could need, and popular mystic stands harking spirit enhancing items. It reeked of tightly packed sweat, downtrodden dirt, and heated forges. It ignited something familiar and soothing in him. Nothing had drastically changed. Ezran grinned as Genn and Vyn managed to catch up.

"Live a little, Kal. I've missed this and you needed to get out of your room."

"It is nice to get some fresh air," Avis concurred. He strolled through the ruckus on the street, as casual as he could be with *Ceto's* golden hilt gleaming at his side.

Ezran always admired the rapier, with its shared affinities of earth and water. If his brother pulled it, which was a rare occasion indeed, one would find a blade that mimicked icy, frosted glass. It looked like such a fragile piece paired with the winding, gilded vines, which flowed into sigils along the blade's base and hilt. Ezran had seen it cut through enough things to know it was stronger than most regular iron weapons.

"Come on," Ezran said, pulling Kal along again.

Vyn and Genn wandered a step or two behind, sure to always have an eye on the Princes. Each member of their party had their weapon strapped to them in some fashion, on part of Ezran's insistence. He wanted people to see them. He hoped some desperate being would find them, eager to gain favor with the crown, and tell them of a hunt nearby.

Alas, none of the Kashadon seemed to have that goal in mind. They bowed and greeted their Princes, to which Avis conversed for a few moments with each. Ezran shook his head. Both his brothers were usually naturals when it came to polite socializing—it almost made him jealous. Kal, however, still wasn't his usual self. Ezran studied him out of the corner of his eye, head lowered, grey eyes fixed to nothing in particular, remaining silent...

This wasn't helping at all.

Ezran lifted his dark gaze, glancing about the street. A solution came to his eye as they rounded a bend, and a smile lit up his face so quickly that it caused Vyn to sigh.

"Perfect!"

He raced forward, grabbing his sociable brother by the wrist once more. It took a surprising amount of energy to hurry them both along, but he did it, until they were charging up steps of dark wood and entering into a dim tavern. Patrons were everywhere, already into their cups though it was only midafternoon. Avis shot him a look, but Kal finally seemed to perk up a bit.

"You are not getting drunk at this hour," Vyn said from behind them. A round of cheers filled the space as the crowd recognized the newcomers, lifting their cups for the Princes and the war hero guarding them.

"Of course not, dear Vyn. Who hunts in such a state? That's just asking for Anbast to come claim you. But that doesn't mean there isn't a good tip to pull out of these inebriated hunters that would otherwise be kept to themselves for later."

"It's midafternoon, Master Breckhym. I highly doubt

many beyond you use this time to become so inebriated," Genn said. Ezran turned back to both of them as Avis and Kal passed by, making for a table at the far end of the place.

"Why must you two always crush my spirit in the most thorough, personal ways? It hurts, you know. Deeply."

"Hurt deeply over there, then," Vyn said, pushing him along to follow the rest. He went as directed at first, but ducked out of reach right as they passed by the bar.

"Don't you even—"

He shot a smile over his shoulder and held his hands up in false innocence. "I'm getting tea, Genn! Relax, would you?"

The retainer let him go with an eye roll and some muttered insult to Vyn, but they let him slink up to the bar all the same. Ezran ordered tea, of course, and also snagged a jar of some mild liquor for his further exploits. Most days, Vyn's warning was a necessary one, but today Ezran had a goal in mind. He would give Kal a distraction even if he had to dress up like a shade himself and dash about Elysia, causing a ruckus in his wake. But, seeing as that took a lot more effort than hunting, he wanted to try this first.

While Avis and Kal might be amiable among the citizenry as a whole, Ezran knew his people. He was gifted with the ability to make fast friends of the nefarious sort, the kind that seemed to live in taverns more than their own homes. He spoke the language of drunks and degenerates, which was something the perfect Northern Princes never did truly master. It wouldn't take him long to get the information he needed. All that was required were the proper conditions, and sadly, Ezran had to admit Genn was right. None of the patrons around them seemed enough into their cups to give away a hunt that would be worthwhile. They'd want the coin and glory for themselves, and Ezran's troop had far too much magic to waste on something insignificant. It wouldn't help Kal, either, unless it was something good.

So, he returned to his table trying to cycle through talking points that would keep Kal out of his head and Ezran's own mind off the ever looming topic of future events. Plunking down next to him with the spoils of a kettle and the precious jar, Ezran didn't even get to suck in a breath before Genn was speaking.

"How perplexing that tea seems to take the form of a liquor jar here. I don't recall that being so the last time we indulged this place."

"I did get tea. I never said it would be unaccompanied, however." Ezran swiveled to his somber brother, clapping and rubbing his hands together in a way that caught his attention. "Kalin! What birthday activities are piquing your interest? We only have so much time before your mother ropes us all in for preparations, so we should spend it wisely. Want to take that hunting trip?"

Avis took the kettle while Ezran plucked up two cups, filling them both with liquor before holding one out. Kal accepted it with a sigh. "We just got back, Ez. I don't want to ride out anywhere now. As for other activities, I think we should just... Honestly, I haven't thought that far this year. I don't have anything in mind."

"You always use your birthday as an excuse to get us to do what you want," Avis said, a small line coming between his brows despite his smile. Ezran finished his drink in one go, wishing it was stronger. "Is there really nothing you'd like to do?"

Kal looked down at his cup, frowning in a way that made Ezran's knee begin to bounce. "Seems so."

"What about the arts quarter? There's not some play on

that you'd like? Even if we've seen it before, it might be nice to see the Elysian actors again."

"The play they're putting on is about Nirat and Aonai."

Ezran almost flinched outright, but instead settled with a hard bite to his cheek. He should've checked himself before saying anything. Of course they would be putting that on around Kal's birthday. What was more fitting than the myth of the first twins, beloved by the Gods?

Ezran's mind spun to find a way out and let his first thoughts come tumbling free from his mouth. "Well, easy solution. I put on a better play for you. Anything you want. I'll act out all the parts, make all the costumes, it'll be fantastic."

Genn snorted. "Yes, because those who bring ancient, sacred stories to life through dedication and craft have nothing on you, Master Breckhym."

"I didn't say that. But tell me, what's more entertaining —some person who can memorize some archaic lines out of a dusty tome or someone who makes it up based on memory? I can tell you what's more impressive to me," Ezran said, leaning back and slinging his hands behind his head. He even went so far as to put his boots on the table, but Vyn caught his heel. He lifted it higher until Ezran's chair almost toppled over. "Hey!"

Vyn let him go, allowing Ezran to right himself just in time. The chair slammed back onto all four of its legs as its occupant caught himself on the table. He gave a glare to the guard.

"Uncalled for!"

"Is this table yours?" Vyn challenged, and when Ezran only narrowed his gaze, he swept an indifferent look back around the room. "Then respect it."

Ezran scoffed, turning to Kal again. "Why am I always treated so? It's unfair."

"You bring it on yourself," Kal said, but there was a hinting smile about his mouth. That was enough for Ezran, at least. He was trying to figure out a way to further bring it about when Avis beat him to speaking.

"Well, if there's nothing you can think of doing now, why don't you tell me more about your travels? It sounds like it was quite enlightening."

"It was, in some ways," Kal replied. Ezran took the opportunity to refill their drinks while Avis sipped on his own. "I learned much about the individual cities we visited, at least, but I'm still interested in the smaller areas, like the villages and outposts, and how they impact things all over the empire. They don't exactly turn out bountiful seminars on that way of common life, however. I enjoyed learning more about the people."

"And your training? You must have had plenty of opportunities to hunt along the way, yes?"

Ezran downed his cup again and settled with the mild burn before saying, "Not as much as you think. We stayed more northward than anything so we had to satisfy ourselves with Vyn's form of training, mostly."

"Oh, and how was that?" Avis asked with humor. Ezran grimaced with the memories of sore muscles and Vyn's uncanny ability to sense the slightest bit of faltering attention. He reached for the jar again, but his hand was slapped away by Genn.

"It was alright, nothing too bad. And it was the only thing that Ezran actually participated in," Kal said.

"Hey, now." Ezran shifted closer to his brother. "I took part in many things. They simply didn't happen to be your seminars, lectures, or other boring activities."

"Right, because it's not as if our entire trip was so we could do all those so-called 'boring activities.'"

Ezran rested his arm on Kal's shoulder and raised a brow. "It was? Hm. That wasn't brought to my attention."

Kal elbowed his ribs and grabbed him in a headlock. Ezran laughed as he fought his way out of it, shoving his attacker aside.

"Alright you two," Avis laughed. "Let's not make a ruckus in such a fine establishment."

They did settle down, and in a much too quick way for Ezran's liking. Barely a breath seemed to pass before that hard earned smirk fell from Kal, and he was lost again in thought. Ezran's mind worked to find something else, anything, that might get him out of it. His own thoughts betrayed him this go around, getting stuck on Kal's returning twin as much as he sought to avoid the subject. His knee bounced faster as he bit at his cheek. Well, fine, then, if the topic was unavoidable.

Time for a different tactic.

"What's bothering you?"

The question seemed to startle everyone in the group from the silence that had come over them. Kal lifted a wide-eyed gaze to him and shook his head. A smile broke out over his lips with just a bit too much brilliance.

"Nothing! I'm well."

"There's something troubling you. You've been distracted all day," Ezran said and Kal glanced away. "Is it Kyrith?"

He caved after only a moment of deliberation. "Of course it's Kyrith." Avis turned toward his brother, his features knitted in worry. "I... I am happy. I'm thinking too much, that's all, and I am far too sore."

"We did ride a fair amount," Genn added. Kal shook his head and rubbed the back of his shoulders.

"Yes, but it isn't just the riding. My back has been aching for a few days now, but it's spread everywhere. Even my face," Kal said. Ezran mirrored Avis' look. It happened, from time to time. Kal suffered a strange soreness, with no real discernible cause, and it would fade every couple of days. Most chalked it up to stress, but it still made Ezran concerned.

If he was this worked up about his brother returning...

"What are you overthinking?" he asked.

Kal shrugged and lowered his hand.

"I've been worried about it too," Avis said. "I don't know what he will be like, or what will happen... I can only perceive that it's worse for you."

"Will he even remember me?"

The question hit Ezran's chest hard. He pressed his lips together as he glanced down, unsure of what to say. Lucky enough for him, Avis was more well suited for this.

"Do you remember him?"

Kal tilted his head in thought. "I do, in a way. More the feeling of him than anything specific. He was always with me. And I felt safe with him around. It was like I wasn't complete without him there... but I don't know if it will be the same now."

Ezran hated feeling at a loss like this, but he didn't know what he could say. After all, he came to Elysia because Kyrith left. It wasn't his fault he was gone, but at the same time, he seemed like a cheap replacement for Kal's twin. At least, in his own opinion, and one shared by the Queen.

"Then I'm sure he remembers the same," Avis said, and Ezran glanced at him. "We mustn't dwell on possibilities. It will only set us up with expectations of him before he can even arrive, which isn't fair to either him or us. He is our brother, and that's all we need to know. Everything will work out once things settle."

Kal flashed a reassuring look that Ezran knew too well. He didn't believe them. Worry would still plague him, and it was hopeless to get it to stop now. They would simply have to ride out his mood until Kyrith arrived.

Ezran thought himself selfish for almost dreading it.

He glanced at the jar Genn was guarding diligently, trying to figure out a way to snag it back. Threads of an idea were just beginning to tangle together when a table laughed nearby, a sound that was just a bit too boisterous. Ezran shot a look back toward the gathered hunters, their robes worn and faces flushed. He grinned.

"Ten escs says I have a hunt for us within the hour," Ezran said, turning back to his table. Kal rolled his eyes as Avis' brow raised.

"Fifteen says you don't," Avis challenged. Ezran stood with that, making his careful way over to Genn.

"Twenty says he has it in half the time," Kal joined in.

Ezran took that bet by snapping and pointing at his brother before snagging the jar from Genn. The retainer made a grab for it, but he was already too far out of reach. Ezran danced away with a grin, Genn's glare doing nothing to dampen his mood as he made his way over to the hunters' table.

Within the half hour, he had the information he needed, and it only took him one drink to do it. He finished it, leaving the jar and flashing a smile to his new friends before he returned to his party. Kal held out his hand to Avis, who begrudgingly handed over the allotted escs.

"Gentlemen, and Vyn, we have a hunt."

CHAPTER
FIFTEEN

Chastol, Iudica District, North Akadon

When he stepped off the boat that had taken them from the small port town of Ablyn Chast back to the familiar North, Sol couldn't help himself. He sucked in deep measures of air, settling himself with the differences—the warmth of it, the lack of an iron tang and bitter ice. He was met with dying leaves instead, no more salt and fishy sea. As different a city as it was from Elysia or Avaryn, the more uniform, practical architecture of Chastol still lent some comfort, if only for the accompanying lively row of its citizens. The riskiest part of the journey was over. Sol had fulfilled the first part of his duty to return his Prince safely to the North.

An unadorned carriage waited for them close by the docks. Sol glanced back to his charges, both of which he hadn't seen since boarding. They'd holed up in their respective rooms throughout the journey and, to his knowledge, had not once braved leaving them. Not even the great, historic sites like the Shattered Isles or the gaping void of Cynos' Mar could tempt them out. To the guard, it seemed like both wished to remain sheltered away with how they were warily glancing toward the city's inner quarters.

"This way, ser, Lady," Sol directed, gesturing with a bow of his head.

He wouldn't kneel, not out in the open like this, at least. Yet, apparently Prince Kyrith hadn't even expected that, as after an awkward pause he returned it with a brief, unsure bow of his own. Sol moved to open the door for him, but stopped when the Prince began to speak.

"You don't..." Prince Kyrith's brows came together slightly, "have to address me as ser, or... anything... Kyrith is fine."

Sol nodded once, opening the door. Without another word the other two clambered in, settling before the guard joined them. He barely had time to lay *Chylus* down securely beside him before the carriage was moving. Just as Chastol's scenery enveloped them outside, a hush did the same within. Normally, Sol wouldn't mind. He had always thought of himself as a quiet person, comfortable in its company. If that were true, however, his Prince was a silent one, and far more at home in its presence.

Prince Kyrith stared out as the grey stone and red brick of Chastol flashed by. If only going by his features, one would think he was bored with sight. His eyes were the only things to attest differently as they shifted in a quick manner to take it all in. The interest wasn't shared by the Lady, however, as when Sol cast his gaze to her, he found her fixated on the greatsword beside him. On defensive reflex he slipped a hand over its hilt, almost as if to shield it from view. It broke her out of her thoughts, making her flush, unable to hide it with her fair complexion.

"What's your weapon's name?" she asked.

Her voice was unexpected. With someone as reserved as she, he thought her voice would have been high and soft. Instead, a tone of solid sharpness came from her lips. More than that, he was surprised to have her speak to him at all.

"*Chylus*, Lady Enryn," he said, unable to keep the tightness from his tone. She pulled her white braid over her shoulder and sat back against the seat.

"It's beautiful," she replied, seeming not to notice the tension.

He nodded his thanks as her gaze drifted to the window. The buildings gave way, revealing the principal attraction of Chastol. A depiction of Endelion right outside the sprawling Ralith Manor, carved so realistically that it seemed the blind God would come to life at any moment to accept the offerings left at his feet. Held aloft in one veined hand was a metal casting of his great Mace, the other grasping a set of balanced scales to his chest. At his shoulder appeared a giant owl with claws outstretched and marble wings flaring out to beat the air.

The Lady paused to admire it before continuing. "This is a lovely city. Will we get to see a lot of North Akadon on our way through?"

"Not much," Sol answered. "Chastol isn't a long ride from the Capital at the pace we will be going. We will pass more farmland and rural towns than anything, your Ladyship."

"Oh," she said. "It will be nice to see all the same."

Sol studied her for a beat longer, eyes narrowing a bit, but she remained focused out of the window. They let silence once again rejoin them as they made their way out of the city. Once the sights were replaced by the unchanging view of a thick Northern forest, his charges began to occupy themselves by passing something back and forth. One would scribble on a pile of notes, using a cover of a book as a hard surface, then hand it to the next. It piqued his curiosity, but he didn't pry. It wasn't his place. He couldn't help but notice that Prince Kyrith's left hand became smeared with ink as they went along. Sol raised his brows at the discovery, knowing his twin brother was right-handed. It was another little difference between the two identical Princes beyond the scars.

They continued on like this for quite some time. The towns came and went, the driver pushing onward without rest. She must've been set on getting as close to the Capital as she could before sunset. The Prince and the Lady before him seemed content to go along as well, neither asking for a break even as the hours passed by.

Sol actually drifted off, caving under his exhaustion of riding and sailing for so many weeks against his better judgement. He didn't even realize he slipped into Nakre's Realm until the carriage jolted to a stop, pulling him back from the Goddess' domain. He grabbed *Chylus*. Nothing came to tear open the doors, even as the Lady peered out the windows.

Sol stepped out to investigate, seeing as they weren't near a town as far as he could tell. The driver knelt on the road, comforting a sobbing woman. Her robes told of her rank as a common villager, torn and frayed, and her mass of dark hair tangled about her head in a hopeless mess.

"Please, please, you must help us. Please. Oh, ser! Oh, you are Kashadon, thank the Gods! Please help us!"

"Take a moment, sera. Explain what's happened." Sol knelt beside them and pulled a kerchief from his coat. She took it and pointed down an offshoot of the main road, shaking with the wild force of her panic.

"The village! It's been wreaking havoc on us in the village! We don't know where it came from. It's already destroyed so much!" Sobbing, she patted at her face without real tact. The commoner gripped the driver after, knuckles turning pale as they bunched her violet sleeve. Her pleading look shifted between the two of them. "It stopped us from going to get the Kashadon. I barely escaped before it slaughtered my animals!"

Sol looked back at the offshoot and put a hand on *Chylus*. The sword rattled in its scabbard as if to confirm her story. Rising to his feet, he looked down at the pair. "Stay here with her and the carriage. I'll take care of this."

He set to move off, but was startled to find the Prince and the Lady standing just a pace away. He hadn't heard either approach, or even the squeal of the carriage doors opening before that.

"May we accompany you?" Lady Enryn asked. Sol flicked his gaze between them, weighing his options. From the sound of it, he could use an extra hand, but he also had to keep the Prince safe. How good of a hunter was he? Could Sol risk even leaving him here?

He had a job to perform for the King, but also an oath to uphold, both as a guard and a Kashadon. His hand clenched on *Chylus* as he quickly tried to run through his different options.

The woman sobbed behind him. He didn't have time to debate.

"If you can handle a hunt," he said. The Prince moved off and disappeared around the back of the carriage. He came back only a moment later with two twin Kashadon swords strapped to his back and a normal saber in his grip.

He tossed it over to the Lady even as Sol raised an eyebrow, both at the Prince's weapons and her own, but he didn't argue.

The three moved off at a quick pace, but it wasn't long before they began to hear the sounds of screams. Sol started running. He led them forward through the underbrush, following the scent of blood. The village opened up before them. Or, at least, its destroyed remains did.

Sol drew out his greatsword as soon as he spotted the threat. A shade, as he assumed, but it was bloated from the living spirits it had taken. So much so that he couldn't tell the gender of it anymore. Veins pulsed a simmering red under its soured, milk white skin. Hair stained as dark as the deep of Odeion's shroud drifted on the wind. It was tossing bodies through homes with its rage, trashing those few that were still standing. Already, it had soared several heads higher than either Sol or Prince Kyrith. They'd have to move quickly if they wanted to save anything.

The guard spun and sent an arc of blinding fire racing toward the bloated shade. It rolled out of the way, catching the edge of flame across its side. The ground shook with the roar it let out.

"Arra, help the villagers. Get them safe before you join," a low voice muttered beside him. Sol flicked a glance over to see the Lady dash away and his Prince pull only one of his swords free. Sol raised a brow again. He had the power to wield both, yet he only settled for one?

The shade roared again and swung its lumbering, smoking body to face them. Sol didn't wait for it to charge. He sent another two arcs of flame toward their target, advancing in hopes to keep it focused on him. It dodged the assault and came stomping in his direction, just as he'd hoped. Red eyes glared at him, the wrath in them clear and vibrant.

Right as it was about to charge, a spurt of red fire caught it full in the face. Sol didn't let the shock of it stall him. He dashed forward and slid *Chylus* across the shade's side, leaving a gaping, charred wound in its wake.

Flanking the creature, another flash of red light came from his Prince's position. He spared a glance toward him, catching a brief image of his sword's blade engulfed in the flame and its wielder, just as charged. Intent on the shade. A hunter in his element.

The shade turned and caught sight of that scarlet blaze, forgetting about Sol. It gave him an opportunity to open another gash on its side. The wounds were wide, *Chylus'* flames burning white deep within, but it wasn't enough. This thing had swallowed too many living spirits and taken all the magic it could from its prey. It wouldn't be a simple matter to bring it down.

Sol ducked out of the way of a wild swipe, rolling his wrist and *Chylus* with it as he waited for another opening. The sword pulsed as he cast another flare up. It caught the shade right where Prince Kyrith's had. The thing stumbled backward and pressed a hand to its smoking face, roaring in pain.

It seemed to compose itself for a moment, but Sol realized that the action was false a little too late. As one hand tore at its face, trying to put out the white fire, its other dug around in the ruins. He saw the beam at the last moment, when the shade heaved it up and chucked it in his direction.

Sol dove out of the way, wood shattering right next to him. Splinters flew around the space with one catching right above his eye, slicing a sting across his brow. He pressed the heel of his palm to the wound and hissed as it came back stained with red.

The shade didn't stop. It hurled whatever it could at them. Corpse, house, animal. Prince Kyrith hid behind a post, his sword lowered at his side. Its blade had a slight bend to it, appearing thin and wickedly sharp. It glimmered a dark vermilion under a black hilt, like the fire it wielded lived inside the metal itself.

The beast roared and ceased its onslaught with a suddenness that startled Sol. He dared to peek around, where he spotted Lady Enryn ducking under its wide swing. She slashed at its wounded side with surprising speed and skill. Of course, the weapon she wielded was a common one, so it wouldn't finish anything. By the Gods, if she wasn't attempting to cut the thing to ribbons anyway. The fact that it was actually working awed him.

Sol stepped out and carved *Chylus* through the air to assist her. The shade roared at him as it lashed out at Lady Enryn, despite his flames eating up its side. She was nimble, ducking and planting five blows to the creature's one. Sol was just about to swing again when a black blur dropped from the sky. He parted his lips in surprise.

At some point, the Prince had clambered up onto what was left of the roofs. The Lady provided the opening, which he took by leaping from his place. His blade swung, quick and precise. The Prince landed a beat later, rolling with the momentum and using it to return to his feet. He turned to face the shade slowly, the same impassive look on his face that he had while riding in the carriage.

The creature folded in on itself as red flames ate the skin of its neck. It grumbled low with its banishment, no longer able to scream. Within moments, the thing that caused so much destruction to this tiny village faded with a simple flare of smoke to send it off.

"Well, nicely handled," Lady Enryn said. She sheathed her saber and meandered toward Sol like they had taken a simple stroll through the woods. "Are you alright, Ser Maisym?"

Her gaze flicked up to his wound and back. Raising his fingers, they came away with blood again. The heat of it dripped down the side of his face, making him sigh. Head wounds always were a pain because of how much they bled, no matter the severity. His Prince strode forward as he pressed the heel of his hand to the cut. The look he trailed over Sol was piercing, inescapable. Never had he been subjected to something so cutting and focused, even by his Captain or the Queen. Paired with the fact that there wasn't a smile to temper it, unlike his brothers, he carried the full weight of such intensity within those grey depths. It took a moment for Sol to find his tongue again.

"I wasn't expecting something that big." Sol searched for his kerchief, only to remember he'd given it away. Prince Kyrith moved closer still and pulled one from his black coat, obscuring the Lady from view.

"Really? These aren't normal for North Akadon?" she asked as Sol watched his Prince. He didn't hand the kerchief over, but glanced over his wound with it in hand.

"Let me. I can see it better," Prince Kyrith muttered. Sol didn't have an opportunity to respond before he wiped away the blood with surprising gentleness. His shock almost made him forget the Lady's comment.

"No, that... that is a rather large shade for the North," he said slowly. Prince Kyrith narrowed his gaze a fraction and lifted his other hand. A sharp, sudden sting made Sol let out a soft hiss.

"My apologies. Splinter," the Prince explained. Flicking his hand, he stepped back and let Sol hold the kerchief to his temple. His gaze returned to the guard's rather than the wound, and Sol almost caved to the need to glance away. "It isn't bad. Head wounds always bleed a lot."

Sol knitted his brow as much as he could, but the Prince was already stepping away.

"Shall we? We best tell those villagers everything is safe now, so they can go over the remains before any of these start to rise as shades," Lady Enryn said, vaguely gesturing toward the corpses spread around the wreckage. Sol nodded and let the pair of them take the lead, pulling away the kerchief as he walked to wipe up what blood he could.

The surviving villagers gathered together on the road in a crying, distraught mess. Lady Enryn took up the job of speaking to them, which allowed Sol to walk over to the side of the carriage instead. Some of the commonfolk were injured. His wounds needed staunching before he could see to them. When he sought out his reflection in the glass, however, he stilled.

He knew head wounds. Sol had been on the receiving end of them before and treated countless others. The scratch that met his gaze would not have caused all the blood that was now drying on the side of his temple. And when he thought about it, he wasn't sure the Prince had tossed away anything when he flicked his hand.

Sol glanced back toward him with a raised brow. The twin swords were a telling sign that he had at least two gifts, yet the guard hadn't expected this. Not only did Prince Kyrith share his affinity for fire, but also the blessing of blood magic, which made them able to heal wounds or stop hearts with a mere brush of a finger.

Yet, he hadn't healed him in full, nor offered his aid

further. Sol didn't understand why he was trying to hide it. Certainly being a blood wielder was contentious with how easily it could turn lethal, but not so much that it warranted being withheld. It had its uses with healing.

So why had his Prince tried to keep his magic secret?

PART THREE: A PRINCE RETURNED

CHAPTER
SIXTEEN

Elysia, Pentral District, North Akadon

A banging woke Ezran up from his nap in such a violent manner that he almost toppled over in his chair. The book he had been reading skittered across the floor with his flailing. He rubbed the heels of his palms against his eyes and stumbled to the door, trying to orient himself along the way.

As he opened it, Ezran found himself blinking up at Vyn's towering form, once again dressed in shining silver plate. "Get ready. Prince Kyrith is arriving soon. Dress well so the Queen doesn't have anything else to worry over."

The guard's words were cold water thrown over Ezran. He didn't even have a retort for it. He simply shut the door and pressed his temple to its cool wood.

By the Gods and all their Realms, this had to be after a disorienting nap.

He stripped himself of his current clothes, throwing

on new ones. Buttoning up his black and white coat, he knew that the Queen didn't *hate* it, which was the best he was going to get when it came to her. His fingers ran through his brown locks to tame them down, then he yanked on his boots, hopping out of his doorway to save time.

As he expected, Kal was not put together at all.

He only had to knock once before the door swung open. Genn stood in the doorframe and gave him a dejected stare as Ezran took in the disaster. Clothes littered the room, as if Kal had plucked every single thing from his closet only to discard it a moment later. The Prince himself, however, remained absent from view.

"Kal?" Ezran called.

"How is it that I have absolutely nothing for such an occasion? I have tunics and robes in damn near every color under the sky and *none of them* are appropriate."

Ezran entered cautiously and glanced down at the array of fine fabrics cluttering the space. From his vantage point, he saw several things worthy of such an event, but he knew it wasn't about clothes.

"Go with green. That one tunic with the gold embroidery always looks good on you," he replied. Genn gave him a look that said it had been proposed and discarded. Kal's exasperated groan confirmed such.

"What if Kyrith wears green? And I wore that to Avis' birthday, what if he knows that? What if he thinks I just threw something on and I don't care in the slightest that he has come home? He will hate me for it."

Ezran turned a disbelieving glance toward Genn, who shrugged in answer.

"Kal, I highly doubt he will remember what you wore to Avis' birthday, even if he was told. You're being worse than the Queen." He picked his way carefully to the closet so as not to tread on any of the lavish silks.

Kal paced back and forth among what remained of his clothes. Only a jade pendant and his birthright of a small golden sun lay on his bare chest, dark trousers slung low on his hips. He pulled at the skin of his lip without even glancing at the fabrics around him.

"It has to be just right. It has to be. He's going to hate me if it isn't. Oh, Gods, I knew I should have planned this out, bought something or had it made—"

"Kal!"

His brother tore his grey gaze up. Braving the mess, Ezran put his hands on his shoulders and shook him.

"It's clothes. Kyrith isn't going to give a shit if you show up in your underwear. It's the Queen we are pleasing with the attire. He will not perceive some slight because you wore green or violet or chartreuse, but you do need to be there to receive him on time. Alright?"

Kal trembled like a Kashadon weapon with too much energy. He nodded and tore at his lip with his teeth, glancing at everything around him, yet settling on nothing.

Ezran sighed. "Genn, find something appropriate. Let's do something with that mop of curls on your head, yes?"

Ezran didn't allow him to answer. He maneuvered Kal by the shoulders and sat him down in a chair. Genn rummaged around in the back, comparing things as he went. While he did comb his curls into somewhat less of a mess, it was only an excuse to get him to remain still. Bouncing his knee all the while, Kal kept a tight grip on his chair as he worked. Ezran patted his shoulder again before he tossed the comb back onto his vanity.

"Take a deep breath. Settle yourself. If *Sion* was in your

hands right now, it would have already cut the palace in half."

Kal met his gaze in the mirror, but he relented. His eyes closed as he took a few deep breaths. Ezran smiled, though Kal couldn't see it, and breathed with him. His shaking didn't stop, but it certainly lessened the more he centered himself.

"Here," Genn said as he offered a dark green tunic.

Stitched with gold thread and interwoven in the silk, the tunic gave off a certain shine with the proper light. Kal slipped it on without questioning it, though his doubts practically swam in his gaze. He accepted the brown leather bracers Genn presented after. Ezran forced him to tug on his boots and dragged him from his chambers before he could begin to spiral once again.

As they walked, Kal took several shallow gasps of breath and descended the stairs with a shaking hand on the rail. Ezran kept a firm grip on his other wrist and tried to exude a calm, strong air for him. Inside, though, his gut turned over and over again, making his unoccupied hand tap out a fast rhythm on his thigh.

Avis met them at the foot of the stairs, dressed in flattering sky blue robes and black trousers. Kal froze in Ezran's grip. Turning on his heel, he attempted to flee back up to his room. "I have to change—"

"Kalin Nefion, you look fine. Get down here," Ezran said and held on tight to his bracer, forcing him to stop. Avis tilted his head at his younger brother before putting a hand on his shoulder when he finally obeyed.

"Calm yourself. Everything is going to be fine," Avis murmured. His words seemed to have a much more profound effect on him than Ezran's. Kal nodded and allowed the two to guide him forward.

Ves waited outside the throne room door, easily the most excited of them without the slightest shadow of nerves. She giggled, bouncing in her favorite lilac robes and skirts, with Ezran's gift dangling free around her neck. Her hair was tamed into a knot of cascading dark waves.

"Can we go in, Avis? I've been waiting so long," she said. "I want to see him!"

"Wait a moment. Father and Mother go first," Avis reminded. Impatience made her huff and cross her arms. "Kyrith isn't in there yet, Ves. He will come after we go in."

"When?" she pestered.

Kal trembled under Ezran's grip. When he turned, he found his brother biting at his lip again.

"You're going to make it raw if you keep doing that," Ezran said as Avis answered their sister. Kal stopped and flicked a glance toward him. They shared a look, the nerves unspoken, but palpable between them. "Everything's going to be fine. I promised I would tell you the truth, remember?" It took a second for Kal to nod, his brow smoothing out as he kept on. "I know it's going to be fine. Just be your usual self."

"Ah, wonderful," a voice called out with a harmony of metallic clinks. Ezran glanced down the hall to find King Thamas escorting his wife, along with a number of the royal guard marching behind. "All of you are here."

"Let me look at you," Queen Nefion said. Each of her children turned to face her, lined up in a practiced manner. She chose robes and skirts of a mesmerizing gold and silver for herself, intending to match the crown on top of her head. Her dark blonde tresses were pinned to perfection beneath it, held with accents of pearl and amethyst. The King, however, wore a simple cream tunic embroidered with gold. He worried at a bit of silver in his palm, the only outward sign of his nerves under his usual warm smile.

Queen Nefion cut her gaze over every single one of them, beginning with Avis. She smiled at him warmly as she fixed the fold of his robes and smoothed out the fabric over his shoulders. She placed her hand on his cheek before moving on to Ves, wrinkling her nose in a playful way as she styled her daughter's curls back into perfection. Next came Kal, where the Queen's gaze turned into a subtle reprimand at the state of his lip, but that left for her assuring smile as soon as she moved to straighten out the pendant he wore. Her warmth faded completely when she got to Ezran. Her lips pursed as she fixed his collar and retracted her hands like he'd burned her.

"It'll do," she said.

Ezran withheld himself from rolling his eyes. It was far better than he hoped for and he didn't need to make it worse.

After they received the approval of their mother, the Nefion brood filed in by rank and age, leaving Ezran to take up the rear after Ves. Still, he made sure to put himself as close as he could to Kal, if only to keep him from bolting. Ezran managed to plaster a somewhat believable smile to his face, though his hands clenched behind his back.

They didn't have to wait long. Yet, to those within the throne room, it was as if Endelion slowed time. Perhaps the blind God of Justice worked alongside the Goddess of Sleep and Madness within his other realm to turn moments into eternities. Ves bounced on her toes with her impatience, while Ezran watched Kal's fists relax and clench in imperfect intervals. Even Avis seemed to have his tells. Every few moments, he would flick his gaze over his family members before returning it to the ground, which was the most unsettled thing Ezran had ever seen him do. His own worry won out as well, making him tap his fingers rhythmically against his legs and each other when he folded them behind his back. The brief wait was dragging uneasiness out from all of them, more and more, until Ezran was close to bursting.

"Presenting Prince Kyrith Nefion, Lady Arra Enryn, and Ser Solris Maisym."

Ezran jerked at the name of the Lady, lifting his gaze to the crown. The ruling monarchs, too, traded a glance, but it soon shifted as three figures entered.

The Lady in question looked around the throne room as if she had never seen anything like it before. Ezran blinked at the sight of her, taking in her sharp features and odd clothes. They weren't exactly something a Lady would wear, in his opinion. The muted grey clothes were nice, but they were plain and cut short in a functional way. It showed off her pale skin and paler braided hair. Dark eyes stood out as the only solid splash of color on her. In fact, her entire air seemed to be shadelike, as if it was on the brink of disappearing right before them all. Her gaze swept over the royal family, but it halted on him. She looked startled at seeing him. It wasn't exactly a pleasant start either. It was almost as if he scared her.

He didn't have time to dwell on it. As soon as the three stopped, Kyrith drew every eye in the room, and not for the obvious reason. He was kneeling, even lower than Sol, with his knuckles pressed to the ground and one knee bent to his chest. The action cut any noise away to leave space for a tense, uncomfortable silence. It pressed against them all, but choked Ezran where he stood.

Some of those eyes that stared at Kyrith in shock eventually shifted toward Ezran. He swallowed against the memory that threatened him, when he had arrived to the palace at six years old, his own knuckles and knee knowing the feel of that polished marble.

"Oh," King Thamas said into the silence. Struggling to find composure, he rose from his throne and approached his son. "You don't have to—"

As soon as his hands moved to grip Kyrith's shoulders, the Prince flinched. The silence thickened as the King froze. Ezran's own energy came to a stop as his pulse throbbed in his neck. Kal's hands returned to a sharp paleness, while Avis' eyes traveled once more. Even Ves ceased her movements.

King Thamas was slow to rest his hands on his son's shoulders and pull him to his feet. Kyrith kept his gaze on the ground. Still, everyone could see the healing bruises. Queen Nefion made a noise and pressed her hand to her mouth, shaking, yet she didn't move from her throne. The King studied his son for a beat, then seemed to remember the rest of the party gathered. He took a step away from Kyrith and cleared his throat.

"Ser Maisym, please rise. Thank you for seeing my son safely home," he said. The guard rose and nodded toward the King.

"It was an honor, Your Imperial Majesty."

"Did you run into some trouble on the road?" Queen Nefion asked, her voice strangled into something high and tight. "Is that why you both are in such shape?"

Ezran winced. Kyrith's wounds were far older than the guard's. On top of it, he had a simple scratch over his temple, while the Prince had clearly taken a beating. Ezran doubted Sol would ever allow his charge to suffer in such a way without sustaining life ending wounds. He certainly wouldn't leave him in such state after if it did manage to happen. The guard's mouth parted slightly, at a loss for words. He glanced from the Prince to his father and back to the Queen.

"We encountered a large shade terrorizing a small village on the way back, my Queen, which was where I acquired this..." His gaze shifted back to the Prince as his hand skated his temple. Kyrith didn't look up from the floor. In fact, he seemed like a statue compared to everyone around him. Ezran wasn't entirely sure he was breathing.

The silence was unbearable. It pressed down on them like some invisible, terrible weight. Now, it was Ezran who wanted to bolt back upstairs, his fingers dancing no matter how much he tried to trap them into stillness.

"Well, I'm glad you all took care of such a terrible misfortune," King Thamas said. He hovered, seeming unsure of whether to climb back up to his throne or stay by his son. His hand worried at the silver ever faster. "And Lady Enryn, was it? I did not receive word that you would be accompanying my son back to our home."

Ezran turned his gaze to her once more. Her mouth was tight as she forced a smile onto her thin lips. A lilting Southern accent spilled forth into the room with nowhere to hide. "Yes, it was a last minute suggestion from King Auberon that I come along. He thought my presence here would improve diplomatic relations between the crowns."

"Why would that be?" Queen Nefion asked, amiable enough, but not so much as to hide the bite of ice behind her words. Lady Enryn turned her sharp gaze to her, the smile she donned growing even thinner. She took a moment to respond, as if she were pulling the words through her teeth.

"I am the intended of Prince Marek Auberon."

Ezran's breath hitched. He didn't remember much

about his brother. But by her expression and tone, it wasn't exactly an arrangement she was happy with.

"This is... a rather interesting step for the King to take." King Thamas chuckled without humor. "Well, if the intent is true, we welcome you to the Sun Palace, Lady Enryn."

"Thank you, Your Imperial Majesty," she said, but everyone's attention had already shifted with the King's. His smile faltered when he looked back at his son, who still hadn't moved at all.

"We welcome you too, Kyrith," he muttered, but the quiet of the room allowed it to reach everyone's ears. The Prince finally lifted his gaze up, if only for a second.

"Welcome home."

King Thamas moved slowly to embrace him. Still, Kyrith looked incredibly awkward and stiff. His brow furrowed the slightest bit. At least it was a reaction. Proof that he was, in fact, a living being among them.

The Queen seemed to reach the end of her self control. She stepped down from her throne and approached him as the King let go. Taking his head in her hands, she lifted his face enough to see him properly. So much like Kal that it hurt to notice those glaring differences. Ezran's stomach twisted at his scars, his wounds, at the way he didn't even smile as his mother grabbed him into a fierce embrace. He didn't lift his hands to return it. In fact, he winced, though it disappeared before Ezran could be sure.

Avis stepped forward after her, cautious and steady. He smiled at Kyrith, calm as ever, and didn't reach out to hug him. The Prince took a moment to study his older brother, like he couldn't quite fit the pieces together.

"Prince Atavis," Kyrith said. His voice was low and rough, like he used it only once every few months. Similar to the Lady, the South stained his accent, and gave his words a sort of cutting twist. His brother nodded once with a small smile.

"Avis is fine. It's good to have you home." Kyrith blinked a few times, like he was memorizing his brother's face. Avis stepped aside and glanced back.

Kal moved forward slowly. Kyrith watched him with the same intensity as he had everyone else in his family, but there was a shift in the edges of his features. Something subtle cracked in his mask.

"Kalin," he said, so quiet that if his lips hadn't moved, Ezran wouldn't have been sure he spoke at all. The twins stared at each other for a beat more, and then Kal threw himself at Kyrith with a force that would have made most stumble backwards. Not him, though. Kyrith stood rigid and rooted in place. He was a perfect, still wall that Kal clung to.

And yet, his hands lifted. They froze in midair, as if he was unsure of the action, and then settled over his brother. It wasn't as fierce as the one holding him, but it was something. Ezran flicked his gaze away. It felt too intimate for him to be witnessing, like he didn't have a place among the gathered.

He watched Queen Nefion instead, swiping at her face as Kal buried his in Kyrith's shoulder. Avis laid a supportive hand on her arm and King Thamas beamed at the scene. His blue eyes shifted to the last Nefion in the room, whose eagerness and usual confident manner seemed to flee from her. She wrung her hands behind her back and looked uncertainly between her parents.

"It's alright," the Queen laughed.

Kal finally released his brother, though he looked like it caused him physical pain to do so. Ezran could see the tears staining his face. Wiping them away, he stepped back and motioned for Ves to approach. Hesitantly, she did.

Ves wasn't the only uncertain one. Ezran caught movement in his periphery. He turned to see Kyrith as he flicked his gaze between his family, colored with his disquiet. The returning Prince swallowed once and glanced back at Lady Enryn, trading something between them that Ezran couldn't decipher.

"Hello," Ves said. Kyrith's lips parted, and he bowed slightly to her, like he couldn't figure out what to do.

"Hello, Princess," he replied. Ezran narrowed his eyes. Didn't he know her name? Surely, King Auberon had told him of the royal birth. Kyrith had to know of his younger sister.

He had told him, hadn't he?

CHAPTER
SEVENTEEN

K yrith was sure he had never been so unsettled in his life. He made so many mistakes. They slammed together one after another, to hang over his head as he waited for the punishment to come crashing down. He couldn't breathe fully until it did.

Yet, they didn't punish him. They embraced him. Welcomed him. Though, they did stare at the scars and state of his face. He'd almost forgotten the bruises. It was so commonplace to him, he was more shocked to find a healed face whenever he passed by a mirror.

On edge wasn't enough to describe the pitch of his stomach. This was more than waiting for the whip to strike or Marek to hit him. Their kindness was its own kind of torment, and Kyrith wondered when it would shatter to the reality underneath.

He didn't mean to flinch, but he hadn't expected the King's hands to appear so suddenly. And when each person hugged him, they brushed against the whip marks of his back, healed but still raw. He tried to keep the pain from his face as much as he could, choking down the need to flinch behind his schooled features and biting his tongue to keep any sound from leaving him. Avis, as he had been told to call him, hadn't touched him though, and he couldn't help but be grateful.

Then came Kalin. He looked young, and pristine, and handsome, compared to what Kyrith saw in himself. They weren't exactly alike, he knew, as some twins were. Mirrored images of each other once before, though less so now that he had returned so different.

Still, they were similar enough for it to hurt.

Kyrith didn't mind being hugged by him, even though his grip was much stronger than the Queen's or King's. He swallowed the discomfort down and reveled in being so close to him again. Something large had always been missing from his life, beyond the fact that he was forced to grow up in another King's court. Now it was before him, and despite the distance between them, something in his spirit was at peace with his presence.

That changed the second the girl stepped forward.

King Auberon had mentioned some years ago that the Queen had another child. He brought it up on occasion to remind him that they had moved on, replaced him. He never gave the child a name, however, or even a gender.

Kyrith looked to Arra for help of any kind, but she seemed as clueless as him. His tongue was thick and swollen in his throat as he stared at the Princess. Clearly, she was a sibling of his, with those eyes and that nose and the jade sun dangling from a silken thread around her neck. Yet, he had absolutely no clue who she was.

"Hello," she greeted.

His mind and body froze. Uncertain, he almost dropped into a kneel again, but then his mind railed against him about how it was incorrect. The gazes of the gathered bore down on him, waiting, watching, condemning.

Without conscious thought, he gave a sort of half bow and floundered for the right words. "Hello, Princess."

His mind screamed. He couldn't think. Couldn't figure out what he was supposed to do. His hands clenched behind his back so hard his nails left half moons in his skin.

"Veslyn," a merciful voice said.

Kyrith snapped his gaze up and his heart stopped. A shorter, thinner version of Marek stepped forward from the edges of the room. Kyrith immediately glanced at the floor, fighting the urge to kneel, and cursed himself for not noticing earlier.

Still, the Auberon Prince went on to clarify. "Princess Veslyn Nefion, Your Imperial Highness."

He battled to stop himself from flinching at the title. Some of the gathered shuffled, murmuring as they realized he didn't know her name. Kyrith shut his eyes for a brief moment, counting his mistakes under his breath, and glanced back down at her. She didn't seem offended. A sheepish, shy smile met him instead.

"I apologize, I thought you knew my name. You did leave before I was born."

"No, it's my fault," he said without thinking, and then froze. His brain had been replaced with a block of ice. The numbing cold was impossible to think beyond. He dropped his gaze to the floor at once and started to count the colored veins in the impressively smooth white marble.

"Father, Mother, perhaps we should retire to the dining hall, where we can all relax a bit more," Avis broke in. Kyrith shut his eyes, grateful for his eldest brother again.

"An excellent suggestion," King Nefion said. He stepped away first, leading the Queen by the elbow with a gentle hand. Kyrith watched the gesture, thinking of a different King and Queen, where the grip had been hard instead of a subtle proposal.

"Kyr," a voice murmured. He shook himself out of his head and glanced up, catching Arra's gaze. She shot it toward the door. He looked around before he realized everyone, including the Auberon Prince, Princess Veslyn, and Arra herself, were waiting on him.

His steps were slow at first as he made his way toward the side door by the thrones, where the royal family had exited. He swallowed at the fact that both of his brothers had waited on him. Everyone had, apparently.

He was messing up. He didn't know. He didn't know what he was supposed to *do*. Or how to act. He was drowning in it all: the mistakes, protocols, forgetting, ignorance. Breathing fully was a fight, as everything overwhelmed him and pressed heavily on his chest.

Stopping short in the hallway, he let Veslyn bounce by him in a flurry of drifting silk. Kyrith tugged at his collar and closed his eyes. He had to get it together.

"Kyrith." He glanced at Arra and tried to smile, but just ended up pressing his lips together. "Take a moment if you need. It's a lot."

"I'm fine," he said. Arra placed a gentle hand on his arm, making him hold her gaze.

"You aren't. I can tell." Sighing, he shook his head. If she could see it, then he was letting his weakness out. He swallowed and tugged at his collar again. They must have noticed his absence by now. "I'm right here, alright? I will be with you the whole time."

He let his gaze wander and found Ser Maisym waiting a few paces away. Was he his new guard? Was he here to make sure he didn't run?

His hands trembled. Clenching them into fists, he forced his legs to move and follow the path his family took.

Kyrith wasn't expecting the dining hall to have food. He didn't eat with the royal family in South Akadon. He ate in his room, if at all, and the meals were always plain and bland. There was an assortment of delicacies piled high on golden platters that he couldn't even begin to name. Nausea twisted in his gut.

Arra's soft touch startled him. She guided him to a seat at the table, next to Kalin, and sat beside him with grace. She wasn't disturbed, at least not outwardly. He envied her calm air, and how she knew what to do without thought, even in an unfamiliar court.

Someone served the food. He stared at everything on his plate as it seemed to shift and blend together. He didn't move to touch anything. He couldn't. If he made a mistake one more time, he was surely going to break apart.

Kyrith forced himself to clamp down on the shifting knot that his stomach had become. He counted softly, keeping his back off the chair and his form rigid. If he could survive the Auberon whip, if he could make it this far, he could get through a Godsforsaken dinner.

"So, Lady Enryn, is this your first time traveling?" the Queen asked, as if she couldn't bear the silence. Kyrith longed for it. It seemed like everyone was speaking too loud, their Northern cadence too foreign and taunting in his ears. Somehow, it seemed to hold echoes of King Auberon's laugh in the subtleties of their tones.

"I have traveled in South Akadon, Your Imperial Majesty, but not beyond," Arra replied as she began to cut her food, keeping up a polite air. Kyrith couldn't raise his hand to do the same since it clenched the seat too hard.

"How exciting," Queen Nefion said. A tension coated

the air as neither went further with the conversation. Finally, Avis once again stepped in, speaking in a manner that soothed the ear.

"Ser Maisym said something about a shade on the way in. I do hope it didn't cause you too much trouble."

"Oh, none at all, really," Arra said. He had never heard her sound so open and amiable before. "It was a pleasant stretch on the way. A rather common shade."

"Common? He said it was large," Kalin joined in beside him.

Arra flashed a polite smile.

"Yes, he did. It was common for South Akadon. I apologize for the confusion, Prince Kalin. We see those kinds of shades everywhere in the mountains."

"And you hunt too, Lady Enryn?" a voice asked, making Kyrith raise his gaze for the briefest moment before glancing away again. Arra's tone took on a reserved quality as she spoke to him.

"I do, Prince Auberon."

The room seemed to pause collectively and Kyrith caught several members of his family trading glances. All of them seemed to end on the Queen, who stilled at Arra's remark. The King even took a deep gulp from the golden goblet by his spread as the Queen gathered herself to speak.

"Ah, Lady Enryn, we didn't let you know, did we?" she began, and though her tone was polite, it was sharp. Kyrith thought he sensed something flicker within her, a shadow almost, and he closed his eyes against it. "He goes by Master Ezran Breckhym here. It's for his own safety. I'm sure Kyrith understands, right?"

Arra traded a glance with him. She pressed her lips together and set her utensils down slowly, cautious as she said, "Not exactly, Queen Nefion."

Something hard and defensive laced through the King's tone. "King Auberon called him by his true name?"

Arra slipped her hands under the table and twisted them together. "The King wouldn't... He..."

"Nefion, if anything, Your Imperial Majesty."

The room became silent again as Kyrith stared at the food on his plate. It was a name. His name. But it came without title, without his first moniker, a threat in the form of dehumanization he'd long grown used to. He was simply Nefion, a target to those who held grudges for the war, their stolen Prince, and their mundane frustrations. It wasn't meant as a courtesy or a kindness.

"He..." The Auberon Prince cleared his throat. "Did he allow you to train as a Kashadon, Prince Kyrith?"

His head jerked a bit at the title, expecting a blow to come from a Prince or King or guards that weren't there. He pressed his lips together, but dared not look at the one who'd spoken. "Yes..." He didn't know the title to address him. It should have been Prince, but it wasn't. Panic froze him yet again.

"From my limited experience on the matter, he was well trained, ser."

It was Ser Maisym who spoke from his place on the wall, bowing for his interruption. Kyrith counted the guards in the room and noticed Ser Maisym's lingering study of him. Did he know how tense he was?

Could he see it?

Could they all see it?

Kyrith couldn't take it anymore. He glanced at Arra, trying to get her help. He couldn't get up without being dismissed, and he didn't have the right to ask. She knitted her brow slightly as she met his look, then flicked her gaze toward the King and Queen. She couldn't ask either. He had to sit there. Wait it out.

Yet, he was too unsettled. His disconcerted spirit rose in him, wrapping tight claws around his throat and choking the breath from his lungs. If he stayed in this room another moment, he would set fire to something.

Or worse.

He'd take the punishment. He had to. The risk of losing control was far greater than his fear of stepping out of line.

"Excuse me." He nearly toppled his chair over in his path to escape.

Bursting out into the hallway, he ran into a decorative table. As the rattle of the lavish decorum pieces filled the air, he ripped his collar free from his neck. He crouched on the floor, sucking in slow breaths, and tried to get the storm inside him to settle. His palms burned with heat. The blood in his veins sang with energy and power. He tried to fight against the shadow that roiled within him to be free. He clamped down on it and counted to keep it subdued, locked away where it belonged.

Kyrith hadn't been this close to losing control in years. Even with the beatings, the rules, the lessons, the endless days and short nights, and unexpected gifts from the King, he had always kept tight control on his magic. He could not risk it breaking loose.

"Are you alright, Kyrith?"

He startled so badly that he ended up on the ground, lifting an arm as a shielding defense of a blow that never came. Instead, Avis lifted his own hands in peace with a worried look on his face.

"I... I apologize. I should have announced myself better. I wanted to be sure you were okay." His brother approached cautiously and, despite his fine robes and the fact he was the heir apparent, sat down on the floor with him. Kyrith lowered his gaze.

"I'm fine, Prince..." He stopped himself, flinching. His brain wouldn't work properly.

"Avis. It's just Avis." A smile came to him easily, soothing and hiding no trace of malice underneath. His gaze was drawn to his brother's, despite the voice in his head that screamed that he was below him and shouldn't even glance in his direction. "I know this must be quite overwhelming for you. I told them we should let you rest, but our parents have missed you greatly."

Kyrith glanced away then. He could hear King Auberon taunting him, laughing...

"Everything is... different," Kyrith managed. Avis tilted his head with a knowing look.

"You mean everything is unfamiliar." Kyrith trained his attention toward him, waiting for the sneered remarks to come, but they didn't. Avis clasped his hands together and kept that same gentleness to his features. "Do you really remember anything about here?"

Kyrith blinked, trying to search back through his memories. "I... Kalin. I followed Kalin around everywhere. And you... I remember, but..."

"It's not specific," Avis finished for him. He nodded. Shifting his gaze away, his brother looked towards the stairs as a gentle smile played on his lips. He gestured to the top of them. "I was about eight, while you and Kal had to barely be four. I got it in my head that it would be a good idea to slide down the stairs in a wooden crate, but naturally I wasn't going to put myself at risk to try it. It's always been easy to get Kal to agree to anything, and you went wherever he led, like his second shadow. I put you both in a crate and launched you off the top of those."

Kyrith spotted where he referenced. The stairs plateaued into a landing to change course, with beautifully curved railings and moldings on either side. He couldn't remember the event he spoke of, but his words brought forth an image painted more by imagination.

"I didn't account for the landing. I figured you all would simply keep sliding. You didn't. The crate toppled on you both, and Kal immediately burst into tears. I rushed down, mostly to quiet him before the governess came running, but you were already there. You weren't even upset, though you were the one with the bleeding cut. You simply comforted Kal and went on about your day as usual." Avis laughed and ran a hand through his short hair in a thoughtless gesture. His smile faded a bit as he turned back to him. "That's what I always remembered about you. You hardly cried and you always comforted everyone else when they were upset. You somehow knew. Even if they tried to hide it."

Kyrith glanced away, though he was considerably calmer and in control now. There was something about hearing Avis speak that soothed him. "I don't remember that."

"I do," Avis said. Kyrith's gaze caught his, and this time he didn't look away. "I know everything seems very out of sorts. We may not show it outwardly, but we are nervous, too. Especially Kal. This is unfamiliar territory for us all, but I'm sure we can figure it out together. You are still our brother. You belong here, Kyrith."

He slid his eyes closed and breathed out. It made sense now. His loss of control, his panic. It wasn't his feelings alone—he had been feeling everyone else's, too.

"I... I'm sorry," he whispered. "It's just going to take some time."

"We can give you time. We can give you anything you

need." Kyrith tried for a smile again and actually got his lip to twitch upwards. Avis got up and held out his hand, which Kyrith took with considerable caution. "I can show you to your room if you want, or we can try the dining hall again. Whichever you prefer."

He cast his gaze back at the doors he'd fled from and his stomach twisted. He didn't even have to say anything. Avis nodded and led the way up the stairs.

EIGHTEEN

Arra had to admit, Kyr was incredibly skilled with a blade. Even more so than she thought. Then again, he had never been able to spar with her before. It wasn't permitted for them back at the Fortress. But since she was the only one that knew South Akadon fighting techniques and training styles here, it was natural that Arra was the only one he could practice with. She also happened to be the sole person he was comfortable enough to ask.

"Are you trying to exhaust me?" Arra asked as she dodged another swipe of his saber and countered the next blow with her own. Kyrith's gaze was nothing but concentrated.

"Not you," he said. Swiping his blade aside, she lunged with her own, but he seemed prepared for that. Their weapons met with a sharp clang as he leaned away, knocking her saber from its course. He could and should have disarmed Arra more than he had already, but he let her get away with things for now.

"Seems like it," she said through clenched teeth. Her

blade wasn't quite fast enough to block, and she caught part of his attack on her side. Lucky for her, this was North Akadon, and they trained like children with blunted blades. Otherwise, she might have had to worry about sporting a scar to Marek.

She winced at the thought of him and her guard dropped, but Kyrith didn't press the advantage. "Did I hurt you?"

"How could you hurt me with these?" Arra said, holding up the saber. "I got caught in my head is all."

Kyr didn't say anything. Instead, he lifted his blade to fend off her attack again. Desperate to keep up her onslaught despite her fatigue, she put him on the defensive for as long as possible. He moved like he'd been born with this particular blade in hand, though Arra knew he preferred the weight and style of his Kashadon swords more. She loved the saber, and yet he was somehow better than her, despite the fact she was the one using a preferred weapon. It made her realize how much more she needed to press her training.

Kyr shifted, and in a fluid motion Arra could barely see, her saber skittered across the ground. She didn't stop, though. One didn't stop in South Akadon. If that kind of formality was practiced in training, it would surely come forth in a proper fight, and that was how someone ended up with their head separated from the rest of them.

Arra ducked under another blow and dove to the floor. Rolling on the stone to put distance between them, she held out her hand as the momentum carried her to her feet again. The saber rattled, stubborn against her call, but it soon came back as her will won out. It brought a smile to her face as she took up her stance once more. Kyrith's features never shifted from his intense concentration.

"Good," he murmured.

Arra circled with him, watching the sun catch on his sweat soaked curls. They had light in the Sun Palace not solely made by hearth fires. It streamed in through iridescent windows, refracting on the gold and white marble, bathing everything it touched. It had nearly blinded them when they first arrived at dawn.

"Again."

She came at him first. He was ready for her. They once again entered into a duel of blows traded in defense and attack, sometimes in the last second before one could land and gift a bruise. She smiled at the sound of metal clanging together over and over again. The vibration of it rang in the bones of her arm. Kyrith looked the same as always, but she entertained the thought that a hint of a smile was forming at the corner of his lips when she stretched out with her magic. Tugging at the saber in his hands, she willed it to betray the one who wielded it.

Kyrith did falter when the hilt slid in his grasp. It was enough for her to finally gain an upper hand, and within three more moves, his saber was hers. She held the blunted blade to his chest, and he stared down at it as if she were threatening him with a wooden spoon.

The fight wasn't over. He ducked in the time it took between heartbeats and knocked the blade aside with the back of his hand. He came close to her, so close that he grabbed her arm when she moved to counter. Careful pressure on her wrist caused her to drop the blade, so she swung the other saber instead. Kyr caught that as well, and within moments, he leveled the playing field once again.

Yet, Arra spun out of his grasp, twisting so he couldn't get a decent hold on her. He deflected a hook she threw, and then another, but she kept trying anyway. Energy ebbed and flowed between them. Never still, never grounded. It was a careful dance of calculation and redirection to fight in the Southern style. While he had height and reach on her, she had speed. Though, even that seemed to barely be true.

Kyrith caught her hand again and used the momentum to pull her forward until they were as close as one could get while fighting. They entered into a deadlock, hands tangled together and muscles straining in opposing goals. The energy settled at last. She blew a tuft of blonde hair from her face and glowered at him.

"What now?" she asked. His lips twitched upward.

"I'm not the one with options," he said. Arra's brow arched as Kyr released her slowly, which probably saved her from spilling in an ungracious heap on the floor. He gestured to the weapons racks around the room. Arra shook her head with a smile.

"I was trying to be fair."

"Fighting is never fair," he replied, echoing the Southern Captain that trained them both with eerie precision.

"I didn't see you pulling your magic." She moved to pick up the sabers, her braid falling over her shoulder.

"I can't exactly *not* burn you with fire," he said with what counted as amusement for him. "You can safely practice yours here and should."

"You want me to get better. I'm flattered." She returned the sabers to their place.

Kyrith leaned against one of the tables, as casual as someone like him could be. He seemed more relaxed now, even more so than when they first began to train. She was happy about it. Never had Arra seen him as wound up as he was yesterday, and it was almost shocking to witness.

"I know how important it is to you," he replied.

Wiping the sweat from her brow, she smiled at him.

Arra hadn't noticed the guard, but her smile faded the moment she did. It was the same man that had accompanied them, the one with an inquisitive gaze and physique that said he could rip a log in half if he wished. Ser Maisym. She'd heard her father mention the name once, or perhaps it had been the King. Either way, she knew the name and the legacy that came with it.

Arra didn't appreciate him studying them like that. Had he been watching the whole time?

She didn't know when he had entered but it had to have been recent, as he was still wrapping up his hands. Kyrith turned to see what froze her and noticed him as well, moving to stand straight again. The guard bowed his head and made to kneel.

"You don't..." Kyr began, his voice dropping and losing its relaxed qualities. The guard stopped halfway and glanced up at his Prince. "You don't have to kneel or bow, Ser Maisym."

The guard gave nothing away on his face. He returned to an upright position and bowed his head all the same. Kyrith looked uncomfortable.

"As you wish, my Prince."

If the action made him uncomfortable, the title seemed to hit him like a physical blow. He glanced away and Arra fought the urge to reach out to him. How long had he spent fearing his own rank?

Marek mocked him with it. King Auberon stripped him of it. If anyone in the Fortress called him "Prince" as a true title, they were lucky to keep their limbs. Kyr himself would be lucky to walk after, due to either the King's whip or Marek's various violent indulgences.

The distinct clink of plated guards echoed from somewhere in the hallway. Kyrith froze. Her own desire to hide sprang through her muscles in a jump, but she forced herself to remain where she was. A moment later, three of the shiny things entered, flanked behind the Queen in her gilded trappings of soft plum. A belt of braided gold caught the eye around her waist, along with a glittering sun at her throat, and pearls in her ears, in her hair... Arra had to rip her gaze away before they noticed she was staring.

She had never, ever seen a woman wear so much jewelry. In fact, she'd never seen a man do so either, until she had seen the thief King and his Princes last night. Everything was so painfully extravagant here. Something sharpened in the pit of her stomach and burned as it cut through her.

Kyr moved to kneel as soon as she entered. Arra grabbed his elbow, stopping him, and curtseyed as proper. A shooting look of gratitude came from him, or what passed for it considering his nature, and he bowed stiffly.

"Your Imperial Majesty," he murmured. Queen Nefion approached, turning her gaze from her son to Arra and back again. There wasn't a lot of warmth spared by the woman. It made her want to disappear into the background with every sweep of those silver eyes, so like her son's and yet so hostile at the same time.

"Kyrith, please, you don't have to be so formal with me. Everyone, rise." Arra straightened and noticed Ser Maisym get to his feet. She wished they could trade places. The Queen hardly gave him a second glance.

Kyrith didn't fidget or shift in any way, but there was tension in his mouth as his mother smiled up at him. She reached out to fix his collar. A muscle jumped in his neck as he fought back a flinch, at least to Arra's attuned observation. The Queen either didn't notice or chose to ignore it altogether.

"I've been looking for you. I wanted to catch you at breakfast, but you must have been here," she said, her voice full of surprising affection. Kyrith remained motionless and blank, like he did every time he came before King Auberon. "I wanted to let you know about the ball. It's in two days. I know it might seem rushed, but I would love for you to be there. I can have the tailors come fit you immediately, so you can wear something nice. They work miracles. Even with a time limit."

"For Prince Kalin?" he asked, then caught himself. "I... The ball is for Prince Kalin's birthday?"

Queen Nefion faltered. She fixed his collar again and left her hand on his shoulder. "And yours." Kyrith shifted his gaze to the floor. She smiled once more, though it wavered the longer she tried to hold it. "I will figure everything out. Don't worry about anything. Lady Enryn is also welcome to come, of course, if she wants."

Arra bowed her head in gratitude, but the Queen didn't wait for her to speak. She stepped away from her son and swiped at her eyes.

"Please excuse me, Kyrith. I have some things to take care of."

Queen Nefion left in a whirl of silk and skirts, taking her armored guards with her. Kyrith looked after her with the same intensity he gave Arra during their fight. "I... haven't ever been..."

Arra empathized. She attended many balls of course, but South Akadon's were quite ceremonial affairs. There were specific steps taken, certain dances in precise orders, along with rituals and other things that Arra doubted the

Northerners participated in. Her Southern experience left her as lost and clueless as him when it came to the North.

"It will be an excellent training exercise," she joked. Kyrith's lip twitched again. It was the best she was going to get out of him at this point.

"I best change and... figure out what I'm supposed to be doing," he said. Arra nodded and he left, walking with a quick pace.

Glancing around, she found Ser Maisym on the floor. He sat cross legged and held his greatsword in his hands, the one that shone like a star with pale light and set arcs of flame out with a simple swipe.

The sight and reminder made her desperate to figure out her own weapon. She decided to leave him to whatever he was doing, chalking it up to some Northern Kashadon technique. Besides, she had another important matter to attend to.

Arra always had a way of figuring out palaces. Of course, the Sun Palace was infinitely more crowded than that of the Fortress. She figured it was simply due to the difference in size. Every bend seemed to have guards or servants bustling about, along with retainers, nobles, or someone of royal birth on a few rare occasions. And here, she didn't seem to fade into the background all that easily.

How could she? Arra was different from them in every aspect, even down to their clothes. Theirs were flowing, long, and so vibrant that they could blind. Few exceptions wandered about. Her robes were meant to blend in, to keep her safe, and yet here they betrayed her. She didn't like it.

Keeping to the shadows as best she could, she traveled down the hallways with the least amount of people. Gifted with her featherlike step and a way of disappearing if she wanted to, and not to mention all the decor around, she had plenty of choices for hiding spaces.

How did they ever feel safe in a place like this? How did the people not rise up to pillage every precious item inside? The Northerners were very odd indeed.

She kept her mind focused on the task, not allowing it to wander to why she was slinking around like a stray cat. Sickness hit her every time she thought of it, and of what she would have to do after. Two months. Arra had two months to prepare and make her peace. Two months to secure a way in and out of this gilded monstrosity. She could do this. She had to. There was no other choice.

CHAPTER
NINETEEN

"Are you sure, Ez? I don't know if it's such a good idea for us to leave," Kal said from his chair. Ezran stared down at a map of the Pentral District on the table, trying to plot the quickest course.

"You said we would do this when we got back. You promised. Tomorrow we will be forced to help with the preparations for your birthday, and after that the Queen won't let us go." Ezran glanced up just enough to catch Kal's doubt as it crossed his face. "She's hovering. The King is wandering the halls just to avoid her himself. You need to blow off some energy, and I definitely need to get away from here before your mother decides to tear me apart limb from limb."

"Don't be so dramatic," Kal replied. Ezran shot him a flat look. "What do you think, Avis? Taking an entire day away?"

Ezran turned to look at the eldest, who was sipping on a steaming cup of tea like a serene priest.

Avis just shrugged. "I think it might be a good idea. You do need something to distract you, Kal. It might be the last chance we have before the frost sets in and duties make it impossible for another year."

"Yes!" declared Ezran with a grin as he faced Kal once more. "You see? It's a good idea. It's bonding! We can all get close after spending so much time apart."

"I don't know," Kal said hesitantly.

Ezran slumped forward and pouted, turning his dark gaze to Genn. Catching his look, the retainer rolled his eyes from his chair a few paces away.

"Genn agrees," Ezran said. "He wants to go."

"I ask that you leave me out of this, Master Ezran."

"See? He's dying to go." The retainer sighed and Ezran smiled as bright as he could manage. "Come on, Kal. It's our last shot at freedom. Who knows what we will find out there! You could slay a giant shade and impress all the people, not to mention save them from a complication when the snows fall. They would be so grateful. Isn't it you who is always going on and on about what the people need?"

"What they need in regards to quality of life, Ez, but I see your point." Kal rubbed his eyes and glanced back at Genn. He lifted a brow, remaining unhelpful to either side. "This is a terrible idea, isn't it?"

"I don't believe the Queen will care for it. Master Ezran and Prince Avis are correct, though. It will most likely be the last chance you have till spring, if your duties don't keep you longer," Genn replied.

Kal let his head fall back with a groan. "Why is it always up to me?"

"Because we won't go without you. You are the rope that ties us all together," Ezran said. "But if we are to leave, we should go now. It will take us at least three hours to get there if we hurry, and then we have to hunt and get back before nightfall."

His brother went quiet again, working his jaw as he stared up at the ceiling. "Alright, you talked me off the cliff. Let's go."

Ezran jumped from his chair with excitement and hauled Kal up. Avis tried to finish his cup of tea first, which led to it being plucked from his fingers before he too was tugged from his seat. Genn rolled his eyes as he rose, joined shortly after by Vyn and another guard by the name of Ser Ryslyn, who followed the Princes into the hall.

"This will be an excellent time!" Ezran said, slinging his arms over both his brothers shoulders. They clambered down the steps together and made it to the front hall before Kal stilled beside him. Ezran turned, his own joy and enthusiasm dampening.

Kyrith stood there like a statue as he gazed up at the portraits on the wall. It was still odd to see him so suddenly, appearing like a shade out of nowhere. His clothes didn't fit in with the splendor. The black breeches, leather boots, and grey undershirt were all practical, plain, and belonged more on a servant than a Prince. It didn't help that he looked as if he had run around the palace grounds for hours on end either.

His gaze flicked between two paintings, and Ezran didn't even have to wonder about which they were. The Queen had one commissioned annually, detailing the growth of the family with precision. Yet, there was a gap of time which disrupted this often dreaded tradition. For five years the King hadn't been present, so the artist used older commissions as models and improvised. In the last of these, a younger King Thamas stood with his regal Queen and one hand on nine year old Avis. Seated before them were the identical visages of Kal and Kyrith. The next was a much aged King, a bit more space allotted between him and his Queen. Fifteen year old Avis stood by a lone Kal, and swaddled in her mother's arms was a newborn Veslyn, crafted with innocence and care.

Ezran bit at the corners of his mouth and shifted in discomfort. It grew over their group, which only moments before had been so merry and excited. He had to do something to fix it, and quickly.

"Hey, Kyrith!"

Walking forward, he tried to be casual as the Prince jerked his gaze around. He turned sharply to face him and almost descended into a kneel, but caught himself somewhere halfway. Freezing there for far too long, Ezran looked away, the awkwardness of it all making him chuckle with his nerves.

"I apologize, Prin—Master..."

"Ezran. Don't worry about a title," he said. "It's okay. I didn't stop kneeling to everyone for an entire year when I first arrived."

Kyrith truly looked at him. Despite himself, Ezran swallowed. He inherited his mother's icy gaze, but he seemed to have chilled it even further, somehow. The scars didn't help, nor did the shadows of still healing bruises. Ezran's stomach twisted hard in their presence.

Is this what he would look like if he had stayed in South Akadon?

He realized they had lapsed into a silence as they studied each other. Trying to cover it, he pulled his smile further onto his face, then gestured back to the group.

"We were about to head out to Sae Hyura. Do you want to join us?"

Kyrith flicked his gaze to the rest of the party. "Sae Hyura?"

"It's a hunting ground." Kal stepped forward like he was scared of chasing his brother away. Ezran couldn't be sure the caution wasn't warranted. "It's the only place that holds big prey for Kashadon this far north, really."

Kyrith lowered his eyes again. Ezran couldn't tell what he was thinking or feeling. It put him slightly on edge. He chewed at his cheek while the other took his time to answer.

"You... wish for me to come?"

"If it pleases you," said Avis. He smiled warmly. "It's alright if you would rather settle in here. You did travel a long way."

Kyrith shifted his gaze to Ezran once again. It took him a minute to realize the question was directed at him, more than it had been for the others. His smile slipped a bit and he struggled to find words, which was a novel experience. One he didn't particularly care for, either.

"It is a decent ride out, but it will be worth it when we get there. It'd be no trouble, really, if you wanted to come along. We always welcome any Kashadon that wishes to hunt alongside us."

Kyrith swallowed and glanced away again. Ezran's face warmed after he did, finally able to take a full breath. "Alright, if it isn't... If you'll have me."

Ezran blinked in surprise, letting another smile break out on his face. "Excellent! We'll head to the stables to saddle up some horses and meet you there."

Nodding once, the Prince waited until Ezran stepped out of his way to move. Kyrith disappeared up the steps, leaving Ezran to the rest. Kal raised a brow, to which he shrugged in answer. The entire exchange had certainly been awkward, but it went better than he expected it to.

***

Ezran wouldn't have thought it possible, but there it was, sitting astride a bay gelding in the flesh. Proof that someone could be quieter than Vyn.

Kyrith hadn't spoken a word as they set out for Sae Hyura. He rode well, with posture both tall and perfect. Dressed in his black coat of Southern make and paired with his twin blades across his back, he was intimidating. That seriousness which remained a permanent fixture about his aspect didn't help the matter.

Ezran hadn't ever seen someone wield two Kashadon weapons. He heard of such occurrences, of course, but it was rare. Exceedingly so. It only happened to those blessed with at least two gifts from the Gods, like Kal's light and earth, and Ezran's own water and fire. It was also a sign of a Kashadon who wielded immense power. Weapons were picky things, and to have two choose someone...

Ezran tried not to sulk as he returned to the conversation with his brothers.

"So anyway, we've only just arrived to Faenas, this decent village maybe seven miles off of Avaryn, and the only thing I wish to do is sleep. We settle in, and I swear, not an hour into it Ez decides he has the energy to go jaunting through the town," Kal said, one hand on his reins and the other moving along with his words. Avis lifted an attentive brow as he cast a look between Ezran and the one speaking. "Dawn comes, and of course he isn't back yet, so Vyn, Genn, and I go in search of him."

"As usual," Avis supplemented, though amusement

lingered somewhere in his tone. Ezran flashed a wide grin, faking sheepishness.

"I swore I was going to call the city guard, Avis," Kal continued. "We found him, what, three villages over?"

"Two," Vyn corrected.

"It wasn't the worst thing," Ezran said, but Kal waved him off.

"We find him in this farmer's field—"

"Technically I don't think it was his."

"And his chained—I mean that literally—to this gigantic donkey."

"She was my friend! We were having a very nice time together until everyone came and ruined it."

Genn sighed from behind them, making Ezran turn to catch his unamused addition. "Ruined, Master Ezran? As I recall you were fortunate with our timely arrival. Another few moments and I believe that farmer's grievances would have taken a decidedly physical turn toward retribution."

"We were just in the middle of discussing things," Ezran said. Vyn cast him a flat glance. "Sure, the farmer was disgruntled, but it wasn't that bad."

"You were two words shy of getting your head knocked off your shoulders," the guard replied.

"As usual," Kal added, matching Ezran's glare with a bright smile. "We managed to talk the farmer down, but you should have *seen* how despondent Ez was. It was like he was giving up *Atka* instead of some animal he'd stolen."

"Stolen!" Ezran slapped a hand to his chest. "How dare you accuse me of such baseless things! We were friends. The best of friends, in fact! And she would never have thrown such falsities at my character, just so you know. She's the worst heartbreak of my life so far."

Vyn rolled his eyes, but Avis laughed, which made Ezran

smile. He swept his gaze over their party, his good nature faltering when met with Kyrith again. It wasn't his reaction to the story, but rather his lack of one. There was no amusement like his brothers, or annoyance like Genn or Vyn. Kyrith was simply blank. Nothing about him had changed. Ezran didn't necessarily know how to work with that utter indifference.

He had so many questions for him, too, but he also didn't know if he wanted to hear the answers. Settling for ignorance instead, he kept on with his brothers and decided to brave such things when he could gather enough courage to do so. Kal had moved on to a more enlightening story of their travels, so Ezran had to wait through it to launch into another much more entertaining experience of his own.

After a decent amount of time in the saddle, they reached their destination. Sae Hyura wasn't exactly marked out. It was a borderless valley situated in a basin between the rolling hills of an unnamed Pentral forest. Signs were nailed to trunks, warning commoners of the dangers that lurked inside. Still, Ezran spotted fresh tracks heading in, most likely from fellow Kashadon.

They tied their horses off near a well right outside the forest's boundary and stretched before heading in. Ezran's excitement came back to him as *Atka* gave a weak flare, warning already.

"This is going to be a good hunt," he whispered to himself. After a traded smile with Kal, he took the lead of the group and stepped into the waiting shadows beyond.

The forest was eerie with its quiet. Nothing stirred in the branches of the trees or the underbrush at all. There were no birds or animals to disturb the hush, even with the crisp carpet of fallen leaves. They added their scent to the wet and heavy air. Ezran kept a hand on his sword as he scanned the area for any signs of movement, but none came.

Yet, *Atka* still flared with increasing frequency as they continued in. He wasn't the only one, it seemed. Vyn had *Fior* in his hands and *Koa* was at the ready in Genn's. Ezran was pretty sure a single bolt from that bow could have burst through a daemon's chest with the amount of energy it held.

Something felt off. They had been to Sae Hyura many times before, and it never took this long to run into something. This forest was like a capital for shades. No one quite knew why, but it drew them like flies to spoiled fruit. So much negative energy resided there that the valley remained covered in a constant layer of thick clouds and fog. The light shifted to clouded dimness the second one stepped foot inside its boundary. It had to be the sight of an ancient epic battle or misfortune, but the origin had been lost to time.

Atka gave out a surge of power so violent that Ezran startled. His blade was normally well tempered, balanced, and would warn him with a kind of politeness that Avis possessed. Now, it was doing so in a way that he could only describe as shouted orders.

"Something's coming," Vyn said. He twisted *Fior* in his grip, and even Ezran could see the ax vibrating with power through the surrounding mist.

A distinctly refined clatter tore Ezran's attention toward Avis, who was already clamping a hand to *Ceto's* hilt to quiet it. Avis' brow furrowed deeply as he searched the forest again. His rapier was normally like *Atka*, balanced and peaceful. Rarely did it feel the need to warn of shades, unless they were so bloated with negative energy that they were practically daemons themselves. As *Sion* joined in with a flash of light, Ezran smiled. Excitement made him shift his weight and readjust his grip on his sword.

"Find cover," a gruff, low tone instructed with such abruptness that Ezran jumped.

Turning toward its owner, he caught Kyrith staring out into the forest like he could cut through the trees with his gaze alone. His hand was on the red hilt of one of his swords, stilling it from making noise, but Ezran could see it vibrating all the same.

Nobody questioned him. Ezran and Kal hunkered down together in some underbrush, while Kyrith pressed his back to a tree beside them. Avis and the rest of their party found hiding spots on their other side, peering out with curiosity.

Ezran, however, kept his eyes on Kyrith. He pulled his blade out with a sort of calm indifference. The thing radiated power, its scarlet hilt of wrapped leather shaking in its wielder's secure grasp. The blade itself was thin, curved ever so slightly, and colored an endless, inky black that almost appeared to be liquid.

Taking out his own weapon, Ezran forced himself to tear his gaze away. He peered out at the forest and found nothing moving out there. Still, *Atka* was insistent, and he trusted his sword more than anything. Someone sucked in a soft gasp, pulling his attention away from searching the mist. Both he and Kal glanced up to Kyrith placing a hand to his temple and wincing.

"Are you alright?" Kal whispered. Kyrith lowered his arm and nodded, pressing his lips together.

"It's here."

Ezran looked out again. He expected to see a huge shade full to the brim with negative energy, but he didn't. No, the thing that meandered toward their position wasn't a shade at all.

That cursed creature didn't even resemble a human or natural animal form. It looked as if Aethra herself had taken a snake, given it thousands of claw-like legs down its sides, and covered its head with red eyes. The scales of its body were the same mottled brown as dying leaves. Rising, it scented the air by splitting its jaws wide in four different directions. Inside, the flesh was a sickening grey. A red tongue served as the only slash of color, as bright as the autumnal stains above it.

Kal almost tumbled backward, but Ezran's hard grip kept him in place as he stared in horror. Snapping around to Avis, he found a similar disturbed intensity as he studied their prey. Ser Ryslyn's mouth remained parted with his own shock, whilst Vyn's concern was layered over by a determined glare. Genn and Kyrith, however, didn't appear affected by the dark surprise. The retainer looked almost angry at the sight of the creature. Kyrith, except for his occasional twinge of pain, looked the same as if he were reading a particularly boring tome.

The thing made a noise so horrid that everyone winced in unison. Kyrith took the opportunity to move, using the trees as cover, his steps silent even with the leaves blanketing the ground.

Ezran tried to think. Daemons were far trickier than shades. A hunter could wound shades, in a technical sense, and it would lead to the eventual banishment or settlement to the Gods' Realm for Judgment. Daemons were physical beings, however, born of Chaos like some of the Gods' themselves. From his brief teachings on the matter, Ezran recalled they were hard to wound and intelligent in varying degrees. Not only that, but to banish them altogether from the Realm, a hunter had to find and strike its heart. Most daemons guarded it close, and depending on the species, it varied about where it was. If the heart wasn't struck, it wouldn't matter how many times the beast was wounded. It would simply heal itself over and over again.

Ezran had never dealt with daemons before. Neither had Avis, Kal, or Ser Ryslyn that he knew of. Vyn had told him a tale of facing a daemon once, during the Fracture War. He hadn't been able to finish it off completely and sported scars for trying. None of them had enough experience to really classify this thing, much less know where to find the heart.

Atka beat at him, enough to spark blue fire along its sharpened blade in preparation. He had to trust it. That was the first thing they taught when a weapon chose a master. *Trust it.*

He lifted his gaze over their cover once again to see the daemon had trailed further into the clearing. He couldn't see Kyrith, but he could see the glow of Genn's shifting lightning flanking it on the opposite side. He was aiming his bow.

The arrow of lightning shot off faster than Ezran could blink. A crack of thunder deafened the valley as it struck home on the daemon's back. It screeched, more out of surprise than pain, seeing as the magic did nothing but dance over its scales and singe them around the edges.

Atka pulsed at him again, making Ezran leap out from his cover. He shot an arc of blue fire at the thing, catching its underbelly as it rose up. Fire fared better than the lightning. The thing seemed to sway as its flesh hissed. It started to screech again, but was cut off by two different bursts of magic. One was an explosion of golden light that crossed over Ezran's fire. The other was a bright green that caught it full in the face. Avis and Kal joined in the fight beside him.

Ezran smiled as the beast snarled. Brackish blood

poured from its eyes, where Avis managed to slash through, as its underbelly sported severe burns by the other two. Yet, the daemon didn't go down.

It swung the back end of its body toward them, and a mass of chaotic magic hurtled in their direction. Ezran tackled Kal to the ground as Vyn caught Avis. The daemon clicked its jaws together a few times before swinging its body in a tactless, wild manner. Magic flew all around the area, breaking the trunks of trees and causing the under-brush to decay rapidly, the sharp smell of rot choking everything else.

A flash of red drew Ezran's eye up. The force slammed into the daemon's back hard enough to send it flying toward them. The thing rolled and dug its clawed legs into the ground, gouging deep wounds into the dark, wet earth. It shook its head when it got up again, slinging black blood. Its tongue flashed out of its split jaws and tasted the air. Avis' blow had been better than he thought.

The daemon was blind for the time being, at least to some capacity.

Ezran got to his feet and attacked once again, this time teamed with Vyn's ax. The guard didn't rely on his magic. Instead, he shot forward and slammed *Fior* down, severing many of the beast's legs with sickening cracks. Ezran's blows cut into the flesh of its back and head, further blinding it before it could heal properly. Blue fire licked at its mottled skin, charring the grey flesh underneath.

The daemon didn't lash out with magic either. Instead, it slammed its writhing body into them, sending both stumbling back with the force of hardened muscle. Ezran's breath was stolen from his chest as he hit the ground and rolled.

Kal sent two more arcs of light from *Sion* to keep it busy

as he came to Ezran's side. Ser Ryslyn helped Vyn up once again while Ezran grabbed Kal's offered hand.

"Try to stay on your feet." Kal grinned at him.

The daemon chattered and began to sling its body around once more. Ser Ryslyn took a burst of magic to the chest and struck a tree hard enough for Ezran to wince. He ripped *Atka* through the air as quickly as he could, countering dark magic with spurts of his own. It was an utter chaotic onslaught and their party soon found themselves forced to give up ground as they tried desperate counters.

This time, Ezran got to see where the red light came from. Kyrith had pulled his second sword at some point and stood with Genn on the other side of the beast. The retainer shot off arrow after arrow at the thing, but it was only meeting magic. Kyrith's arc, however, cut through it.

Not only that, but the blow kept going. It didn't lose momentum or die out in cancellation with the dark powers. Red flames shot forward and hit the beast time after time, no matter what it did to try to block them. The daemon rose up again to its full height, facing the Prince, and screeched.

That's when Kyrith threw his sword.

Now, Ezran thought that keeping your weapon in the middle of a fight was rather important. Granted, Kyrith had one to spare, but still. What really caught his attention was the fact that he hadn't thrown the one engulfed in flame. It was the black bladed one he first pulled which soared through the air.

The daemon, blinded by wounds and blood, still screamed, even as the sword shot towards it. A moment later, the entirety of the thin blade burst out from the back of its throat, having found an opening through its mouth.

The daemon stopped screeching. Its body wavered before it collapsed into a curling heap. A last rattle filled the air, sounding wet from blood that never came leaking free. Kal burst out with a joyous laugh. He grabbed Ezran in his arms and swung him around once before he released him, leaving him to stumble back onto his feet.

"We just killed a daemon! We lived through it!"

Avis knelt by the body and examined it as his younger brother continued to voice his celebration. Vyn wandered over to the fallen Ser Ryslyn and helped him to his feet while brushing away debris, not that any of it diminished his appearance at all. Catching his breath as he surveyed the mist covered scene, Ezran sheathed *Atka* and swiped at the sweat on his brow. Kyrith, however, was as impassive as ever. Did anything ever get through to him?

"Its heart is in the back of its throat?" Avis questioned as the stoic one jerked his weapon free. Not even a single drop of blood dripped from its edge.

Intrigued, Ezran stepped forward as Kyrith answered with, "Rsevna's are. They're common in forests."

"They aren't common here," Ezran muttered while he knelt. It was even more disgusting up close, and smelled horrid. Yet, none of its wounds were leaking at all. Its blood was gone.

He glanced at Kyrith's sword again, studying the black blade in the dim light. It looked the same as it had when he first saw it, like ink poured into the form of a sword. Ezran blinked as it dawned on him.

It wasn't simply dark liquid. It was daemon blood. The sword he held fed on it, and most likely grew in strength with every kill.

Its twin calmed down enough that the flames no longer leapt from it, but they still flickered in the depths of the scarlet blade itself. Ezran gawked at the pair. For Kyrith to be able to use such powerful swords, he had to have been gifted with the magic of fire, and of blood. It was said that twins were always blessed with large amounts of magic, and Kal certainly was, but with Kyrith...

Ezran sat back as Kal came forward, but he didn't catch the comment he made. Instead, he glanced up at the returned Prince, at the bruises and scars on his face. Why had he let them treat him so if he was that powerful?

Kyrith seemed to feel his gaze. He glanced down, then at his swords, and sheathed them with a quick motion. He didn't look at him again, but Ezran followed as he stepped away.

The lost Prince had a few intriguing mysteries locked behind that indifferent mask.

CHAPTER
TWENTY

I f weapons felt emotions, Sol would have chalked *Chylus* up to being irritable. The blade kept rattling at him, even though he calmed it the day before. It should have given him at least one or two more of relief. It was pulsing, though in infrequent bursts, like it sensed something far off and yet still demanded to be used. It called to him while he tried to study, sleep, even relax on his first snippet of leave in a long while. Even trying to concentrate on carving pendants hadn't earned him the courtesy of peace. The blade didn't care.

Sol relented by the time evening came along and found himself back in the small training room, far above where the guards would be running drills in the bowels of the palace. It lacked the presence of Prince Kyrith and Lady Enryn this time around. That had been a sight to see, he had to admit. They both were relentless with their training and didn't hold back whatsoever. By the time he arrived, it was clear by both of their states that they had been going at it for a while, and still continued for a quarter of an hour before they noticed him.

The Prince was exceptionally talented. He was fluid, strong in his moves, quick on his feet, and calculating enough to adapt. The Lady wasn't that far off either. Sol had never seen two people train like they did, or fight like they did for that matter. Southern Kashadon seemed to have a particular style that appeared difficult to learn. The footwork and sheer strength required for some of the moves...

Sol shook the thoughts from his head as he settled on the mat. He couldn't distract himself, especially not with thoughts of fighting while trying to calm his blade. Holding *Chylus* in his palms, it began to dance in his hands as if expecting to be unsheathed. Sol sighed at the sword as his eyes closed. In protest, it swelled against his spirit.

The white marble of the Sun Palace wasn't just a choice of expensive taste. That particular type of stone, laced with endless colorful strains of cleansing gemstones, was hauled from Orryn itself. The Miresa family ruled over the city and the District it resided in with the crown's blessing, along with the same from the Goddess of Life, Aethra. She was said to have struck the ground when she granted the noble family her Lance, opening a mine and revealing the marble to the people. It amplified power and promoted balance, restoring the spirit and magic one wielded to full, calm strength.

Thus, Sol always found peace when he went there to settle *Chylus* down. With small obelisks of marble surrounding the meditation space, carved with Northern concentration sigils, it wouldn't take him long at all. The Princes graced the training room with their presences only on the rare occasion they needed to train indoors. Except for Prince Kyrith's odd interruption, it would remain empty until the Princess came of age and began her lessons to become a proper Kashadon.

Sol pulled cleansing, light energy from the stone and the hearth fire which warmed the air all around him. He allowed it to enter his core and soothe his own spirit first, though his strong, unwavering balance didn't need much. Next, he let it enter his chest, fill his heart, and trace through his veins to his palms. *Chylus* rattled once, but it was no match for this concentrated energy. It wrapped around the blade, lulling it into a calm state within a few slow heartbeats.

Sol still kept the energy flowing through them both, even though the task was done. He took the time to relax and let his mind go blank for a while. It wasn't until he found complete peace, in body, mind, and spirit, that he released the energy and opened his eyes.

He wasn't expecting to find someone there when he did.

Prince Kyrith watched him with a furrowed brow, leaning against a weapons rack with as casual a stance as he could muster. It was the most relaxed Sol had ever seen him, at least. He had on a simple black tunic and breeches, but his twin Kashadon blades were also strapped to his back. He was startled out of his thoughts when he realized Sol opened his eyes but straightened within a blink. Sol rose into a kneel with a bowed head.

"Prince Kyrith," he said.

"Kyrith." Sol glanced up. The Prince clenched his jaw. "Just Kyrith... or Kyr, if preferred. You don't have to kneel."

Sol sank down once again, laying *Chylus* across his lap. The sword was content for the moment, leaving him be at long last. The Prince looked down at it and pressed his lips together, fighting himself in that subtle way which showed at the edges of his features alone.

"Is everything alright?" Sol asked. Kyrith's intense gaze lifted to his. He came a few steps closer and folded his hands behind him.

"Yes, I..." He had a habit of trailing off, Sol noticed, especially when he seemed to think he shouldn't have spoken at all. He'd never met a Prince who was so cautious with his words. "I came to train."

"With your swords?" Sol questioned, a bit puzzled. Due to the nature and power of the Kashadon weapons, most had a partner when they trained, so they didn't waste targets. Lady Enryn wasn't anywhere Sol could see, though, and considering the common saber she fought the shade with, he didn't believe a weapon had chosen her yet.

"Yes," his Prince said. He lifted a hand to the red grip of one of his blades and looked away. "I... hunted with the Princes yesterday. We found a daemon. *Eokor* hasn't settled."

Sol raised his brows in surprise. They came across a daemon? This far north?

"I would imagine so. Fighting with daemons can unsettle a weapon if it's big enough." Sol rose to his feet. Kyrith blinked once and his lips twitched upwards in a fleeting moment of rebellion from his stoicism.

"It wasn't the size, but the lack of it," he said, his tone even and calm. Perhaps it was just Sol, but he thought there might have been a hint of amusement there, too. "*Eokor* is used to hunting bigger daemons than the one we found. It's also a bit more volatile than *Askef*... Demanding, almost. I thought I might be able to let it get out some energy here..."

Casting his gaze away, Kyrith closed his mouth and set

his jaw again, seeming to realize how much he was talking. Sol didn't mind, however. He liked the way Kyrith lit up when he talked about the swords, a slight bit of his true self seeping through. His low tones weren't hard to listen to, either. It wasn't quite like Prince Avis' calming cadence, but there was something pleasing in his voice, even with the Southern lilt.

"Why don't you calm it?" asked Sol. A line appeared between the Prince's brow, though he didn't look up. "Do you calm Kashadon weapons with meditation in South Akadon?"

"No," came Kyrith's uncertain response.

It was Sol's turn to be confused. He thought all Kashadon used that practice and couldn't imagine the upheaval *Chylus* would cause without it. He glanced at the red hilted sword on Kyrith's back, the one called *Eokor*, apparently. The blade didn't rattle like *Chylus*, but he could see its quiet shudder every so often, an irregular heartbeat in its simple scabbard.

"Would you like to learn?"

Kyrith looked at him and held there for a beat, searching his features for something. Sol nodded towards *Chylus* where it rested in his hand. "That's what I was just doing. I can show you, if you would like. That way you won't have to exhaust yourself to settle the sword."

Kyrith's lips parted a bit, his thoughts shifting behind his gaze. It seemed as if he expected him to lash out all of a sudden, like offering help was somehow a test or trick. His eyes flickered down, and when he took in *Chylus* again, Kyrith nodded slowly.

Sol moved to the side and offered up a mat beside him. Both of them sat down and Kyrith mirrored his posture, taking the swords off of his back. He set the black hilted one to the side and held the other in a delicate, scarred grip.

"Most of us hold up our weapons like this." Sol demonstrated, hovering his hands above his knees with the sword laying flat on his palms. Kyrith shifted to do the same. "The Captain and the Masters say to hold it aloft is a form of discipline, and discipline is part of the foundation for a strong, solid practice. This is one of the aspects they make you meditate on first, but that is more to set up for drawing energy when young Kashadon are still getting used to their magic."

His gaze locked with the Prince's as he laid *Chylus* back in his lap. Kyrith was attentive in a way that Sol hadn't seen often, absorbing every word he spoke. The scrutiny made nerves spark in his stomach as he cleared his throat before continuing.

Inspecting Prince Kyrith's grip again, he reached out to correct his hold. Despite the sharpness in the Prince's gaze when he did, Sol offered him an assuring smile and moved his hands into a proper position. His skin was rough, calloused, yet yielded with ease to the corrections. Sol assumed it was from years of training and hunting, knowing from experience that someone didn't get as skilled as the Prince without rigorous dedication.

"Close your eyes," he said. Prince Kyrith seemed uncertain, but a moment later his eyes shut. He turned his face forward and Sol noticed *Eokor* tremble in his grip. "In the beginning, it's best to ignore the sword. It will protest, trying to distract you.

"The marble around you should cleanse the energy, so let that slip from your mind as well. Focus on the ground beneath you instead. The solidness of it, the sturdy energy that lives in it. Draw it into your being with a breath. Allow it to enter your core. Next, feel the air surrounding you. Its energy is much lighter, and quick. It should feel clean and bright. Draw on it, feel it in your lungs, and allow it to enter your core as well. Finally, listen to the crack of the hearth fire. Notice its heat on your skin, the draw of warmth and light, and let it join the others.

"When you're ready to, let the energy rise within you. Let it soothe your spirit first. You should feel a sense of balance return to your spirit before you continue on."

Sol watched Prince Kyrith with careful study. He had a line creasing his forehead at first, either in concentration or frustration, he couldn't tell. It lessened as Sol talked, keeping his hands motionless as not to distract him. The line disappeared, leaving a youthful smoothness in its wake, marred only by the pale scar that cut through one of his brows and disappeared into his hairline. What Sol had thought to be another scar appeared to be but a continuation of it, slicing under his eye to give a slight cleft to his lips and ending along his sharp jaw. It left the last, a ragged stretch that banded over the bridge of his nose, and the host of questions that infected Sol at their existence.

Tension left Prince Kyrith's body slowly, as it was far too at home within him to vacate any faster. He once again returned to the relaxation he'd been in before Sol disturbed him. This time, his face was calm as well, losing the stoic indifference for genuine peace. He really did resemble Prince Kalin when he was in such a state.

"When you're settled, send the energy through you to *Eokor*. The sword might try to rebel against it at first. If it helps, imagine wrapping it around the blade, entering into its spirit until the balance returns."

Sol turned his gaze to the angered sword, still quivering in its leather scabbard as they both held it. Sigils scarred its face, though they lacked the red sheen of blood Sol began to expect when it came to South Akadon. He could almost feel their power calling out to him as his eyes traveled over it, some in warning, some in power...

He tore his gaze back to the Prince when *Eokor* began to still, raising a brow. It was quick work. Especially for one that had never done it before.

"Once the sword is settled, you can either keep the energy flowing through you both for a while and focus on it, or you can release it."

The Prince settled on the latter. Exhaling long and slow, he opened his eyes after a moment. Sol met his inquisitive gaze and realized he had been staring at his Prince practically the entire time. And he hadn't let him go, either.

Glancing away quickly, he retracted his hands and distracted himself by studying Kyrith's other sword, *Askef*. Sol searched for something to say, uncertain as those grey eyes considered him a while more.

"You're quick to learn," he said. "Does *Askef* need to be settled?"

"No." Prince Kyrith took both swords in hand and studied each with a fond look. "*Askef* isn't like *Eokor*. It's quite calm and balanced in comparison."

"Interesting. At least you don't have to manage two unsettled blades."

Kyrith nodded once, flicking his eyes over to the greatsword resting in Sol's lap. "And yours? You have to do this often?"

"Often enough. Blood and fire are an unusual combination, each volatile in their own right. *Chylus* seems to live up to the expectation of both." Kyrith froze beside him and his grip turned hard on his swords. Moving with a slow kind of caution, his gaze found Sol's again, and he swallowed once it did. "I never did thank you for healing me that day in the village."

"Yes, I... You... There's no need to thank me." Sol cocked his head to the side and took him in.

"Why did you hide your gift?" Sol asked with a bit of hesitance, prepared for the Prince to turn on him and remind him of his place. "Is such magic not welcome in South Akadon?"

Kyrith shook his head. "I don't like to flaunt such things."

There was some hidden weight in his words, a message Sol didn't quite understand. Still, it wasn't his place. He had overstepped already, but he had also let the Prince know someone here understood his gift. Blood magic wasn't as polarizing as spirit, but people tended to have their own opinions on it. With how out of sorts he must've been already, Sol thought it was his duty to let him know he wasn't completely alone.

"I can take care of those, if you wish," he said instead of pressing further. He glanced down at the fading bruises on Kyrith's face, practically gone by now. That was the downside of their shared affinity. They might have the power to heal wounds and stop hearts, but they could only do it to others. Their magic didn't work on themselves, and they also had to know the anatomy of something before they could heal or harm.

The Prince turned away, brushing a thumb across the scar on his lower lip. "Thank you, Ser Maisym, but I'm fine. I... It's best to let lessons heal on their own."

Sol once again wanted to press, but stopped himself. Nodding once, he cast his gaze down to the floor and searched for words. It was odd to him, having the need to say something. Never had he experienced this feeling with others, whether they be peers or charges, but something about Prince Kyrith made him unsettled in the silence. His presence in the room was weighted, dark, and Sol couldn't help his urge to battle it back. He was a guard, after all, and his duty to protect the royal family from any threat was something he held to the highest regard.

"Thank you," Prince Kyrith said before he could figure out anything himself. "For your help. I apologize for disturbing you."

"No apology needed, Prin—" Sol cut himself off as a wince crossed his face. Despite this, it still felt foreign to say his name without the title. "Kyrith."

Relief passed over Kyrith as he met Sol's gaze and nodded in parting. He got to his feet and within moments was gone, steps so light that once Kyrith's figure disappeared, Sol had to wonder if he'd even been there at all.

CHAPTER
TWENTY-ONE

"I hate this," Kal said.

Ezran rolled his eyes from the chair he was making improper use of and turned the page of his book. He wasn't actually reading, but instead he was looking at the drawings that accompanied each section. Famous Kashadon weaponry from either side of the Empire met his gaze, and he could practically recite the text that came with it by memory. Now, he was looking at Sera Sakari Kliess' trident *Vikai*, a legendary Southern weapon that disappeared with its master a few years after the Fracture War. Though the mystery remained about where they both ended up, the accepted theory was they perished on a hunt gone bad in the mountains.

"You do not hate this," Ezran said. "You love parties and socializing. You hate the fact that your mother will scrutinize your attire before you can get inside. And you're nervous about Kyrith being present this year."

"I hate this," Kal repeated pointedly. "Did he seem off to you? After the hunt and everything, I thought he'd be a bit more comfortable, but dinner yesterday..."

Ezran knew what he meant. The entire room had been tense, and yet everyone tried to keep up cheerful airs. Kyrith hadn't eaten a thing. Queen Nefion ignored both Ezran and Lady Enryn, who could at best be described as uncomfortable. King Thamas, Kal, and Avis on the other hand discussed the daemon in Sae Hyura. When the King tried to engage Kyrith in the conversation, seeing as he was the one to finish it off, he replied in a curt manner, using no more words than he had to.

"He needs time, Kal," Ezran replied with another flip of his page, meeting with Ser Pryam Koylin's Northern mace, *Utauan*. Both were lost in the Fracture War, never to be seen again. "How long did it take me to start talking and engaging like normal?"

"You were six." Kal held up a tunic, then a robe, never satisfied as he alternated through the choices. He wasn't tossing them around in a frantic fashion, however, for which Ezran was thankful. "I can't tell if he likes it here. If he's happy to be home. If he's happy at all. I can't figure out anything about him."

"I was six, and it still took me a while. He's spent thirteen years there. It has been what, a week at most? Give him time. Don the green. It looks good on you."

"I had on green when Kyrith arrived. Not everyone can wear the same thing to every formal function they go to." Ezran smiled, comfortable in his black and white coat. "I know he needs time. I just... He doesn't... He won't talk about anything. He barely looks me in the eye. What happened to him, Ez?"

Ezran blinked, letting the book fall onto his chest. He couldn't say. He had the faintest recollection of his homeland. What he did remember wasn't exactly pleasant. The memories were dark, in a literal sense. Hearth fires lit at noon couldn't dispel the murk, nor the cold that seemed to live in the stones of the Fortress. In fact, when he first came to North Akadon, he thought the palace was made from the actual sun with it being so bright and warm. He remembered a woman's skirts and gentle hands... a pair of dark, steady eyes that frightened him. Scraps of images that made no sense and blurred with time.

Kal held up a set of wine-colored robes and tilted his head at his reflection. Ezran turned to look at them better, but his brother had already decided against them. He disappeared back into his closet as he spoke. "I thought, in a naive way I will admit, that when we saw each other, something would miraculously click between us and we would be like we were before. I thought I would know him."

"You spent a lot of time apart."

Kal reappeared a moment later, draped with fabrics of dark gold, jade, and scarlet. He held up one after the other as he talked, dissatisfied with each.

"I know. It was like they severed some part of me when they took him away. The worst part is, I think I've gotten used to him being gone. And every time I see him... it all feels too foreign, and yet, I can't bear the thought of him leaving again either." Ezran sat up properly as Kal's voice grew soft. His arms slowly lowered the tunic he held. He glanced back at Ezran, grey eyes swimming, looking so unlike himself with his trembling frown. "What if it never changes? What if I never feel the same about him as I did?"

Ezran pressed his lips together and interlaced his fingers, bringing them to his mouth as his elbows came to rest on his knees. "I'm not sure you will ever get the bond back that you two had before, but it shouldn't stop you from trying. Who knows, maybe something stronger will come out of it. No matter what, though, it isn't going to happen in a day, or seven, or anything less than a hundred, I'm sure. Two hundred, even. You can't rush these things, Kal. Take it slow. He's home now, that's all that matters. Nothing more can happen to him."

A knock cut either of them off from saying more. A moment later, Genn entered carrying a tray of tea. Ezran leaned back and crossed his arms.

"I thought you were bringing food with you."

The retainer's tone was flat and even as he set the tray down. "If you are hungry, Master Ezran, there's a splendid ball that you will attend in a little more than a half hour. I heard a rumor that there will even be dishes available to satiate yourself with once it starts."

Ezran made a mocking face in his direction as he poured himself a cup.

"Which do you prefer?" Kal asked, holding up the options for them to inspect. Genn seemed to take the question extremely seriously, studying between the robes and Kal with intent. Ezran simply flicked a casual glance over them.

"The red one," he said offhandedly. "Or the jade, actually. Just not the gold."

"You are so helpful," Kal scoffed.

"I have more experience taking off clothes than choosing them, Kal."

His brother rolled his eyes skyward as Genn sighed audibly. The retainer pinched the bridge of his nose before he lowered his hand to his hip. Returning to his thoughtful studies of the Prince, he nodded once with his conclusion.

"The jade would suit."

Kal went with the verdict, tossing the others onto a chair. He began to wrap himself up in the layers, fitting shirts under robes and fixing belts in place until he was the epitome of elegant Prince. He slipped on charcoal colored bracers and laced them up without looking.

"Is there anything my mother could nitpick me for?"

"I'm sure she's bound to find something," Ezran muttered as he sipped on his tea.

"Nothing comes to the eye," said Genn, who shot a pointed stare toward Ezran that he was content to ignore. Kal ran a hand through his curls, turning this way and that before the mirror. The color really did suit him, with his bronze skin and light eyes.

Ezran looked away, his gaze settling on his own pale fingers as they wrapped around the onyx teacup. He drained it and set it down before he could give voice to the thoughts swirling in the back of his mind.

In the end, as Ezran knew it would be, the Queen found no fault in Kal's choice in dress. Avis, too, was approved of in his royal blue robes. It was Ezran that received a scowl and a remark about wearing the same coat over and over. He took it with silence and a smile, the thought of Ves in her usual lilac circling in his mind while she spoke. His sister didn't receive such a lecture. At least, not in front of the others.

Then, Kyrith materialized from the walls themselves, and she went silent. There wasn't really anything different about him. He still had the discolored shadows of his near healed bruises, his impassive stare that never raised from the ground, and his true black clothes. However, even Ezran could tell they were of a finer quality than his usual attire. They had a bit of flare, too, as much as plain black could, with a more Northern style to the cut and hem of it all. Yet, there was nothing else on his person. No accents of gold like Ves, or silver like Avis, or even a simple sigil pendant that they all wore.

Queen Nefion said nothing. She didn't ridicule him for wearing something so plain or dark. She glanced over him and seemed like she wanted to speak, but nothing came from her lips. It was King Thamas who beamed brightly from his place behind them all and ushered them inside the ballroom to begin the night.

The household was already gathered. Shining silver guards flanked the golden walls like decorations, servants bustled to and fro with frantic energy, and several of the court members attending the celebration were beginning to show. It had to be all of five seconds before Ezran wanted a drink.

It only got worse as the night began in earnest. The King and Queen stood by the doors to receive everyone who entered, an endless number of names booming throughout the room. Ves found her place with some younger members of court, along with many of the Ladies, while Avis flitted from group to group. Kal, however, was the center of his own retinue, flanked by a vast circle of people that was only growing by the minute. He smiled and laughed along with everyone. They all seemed enamored with him, the very sun that gave them endless blessings.

Ezran was not so fortunate in receiving his brother's attention tonight. So, he came and went, mainly to drink where the Queen wouldn't spot him, and flirted with the occasional stray Lady. Court wasn't like a good tavern, though. He knew these Ladies either all had husbands, were intended to be married, or wouldn't ruin their potential prospects with a simple "Master." Especially one with the reputation he boasted. To them, he was but a servant to the crown, though clearly a rich and somehow still well liked one. With the entirety of the gathering made up of high class Kashadon, he wasn't going to even try his luck with any of the men.

He hated these things.

Stealing another drink in a back corner, he let his gaze sweep to survey the crowd once he was sure Queen Nefion was occupied. He admired the dancing partners, all moving in time to the elegant Northern tunes. Ezran smirked to himself as he raised his glass once again. The structured, rigid steps were nice and all, but there was something about a wild tavern rollick that he preferred more.

His gaze drifted over his brothers and sister, but nothing had changed except for who Avis was speaking with. The merriment was high. Everything was exceptional. But Kyrith looked like he was in pain.

Ezran tilted his head when he found the Prince. He was a hard find, too, even though he was the darkest clothed thing in the room and should have been an even bigger attraction than Kal. He secured himself to a corner, almost like a guard or cornered animal with how his back pressed into it. His arms were folded over his chest as he stared out at the crowd like he thought someone might spring on him at any moment.

Before he knew what he was doing, Ezran moved through the sea of bodies. He blamed it on the drinks. He tended to act on whatever he felt he should do when alcohol was involved, with either little or no logical thought to the matter. Kyrith saw him coming and lowered his gaze to the floor, but at least he didn't attempt to sink into a kneel.

"Master Breckhym." Kyrith's voice was so low that Ezran almost lost it under the tumult of the ball.

"Prince Kyrith," he returned. Kyrith's grey eyes began to scan the scene, ever wary of the surrounding people. Ezran shared both sentiments of the dislike concerning the crowd and title, at least for this night. "Are you enjoying yourself?"

"It's loud."

Ezran followed his line of sight, raising a brow. He guessed he was right, but it wasn't like the ball had dissolved into something rowdy and blaring. If it did, he might have a better time.

"It is," Ezran said slowly. Turning back to the Prince, he gifted him a smile in an attempt to alleviate the ever increasing awkwardness. It was odd when Kyrith didn't return it, or even acknowledge it at all. "This must be quite different for you, no? Are South Akadon balls like this?"

"My attendance wasn't allowed," he replied, curt and something bordering on final. Ezran pressed his lips together with a nod and took a long drink. How was he supposed to respond to that? He was terrible at socializing when it didn't involve flirting or joking. He doubted Kyrith would appreciate him attempting either.

"Well, you can expect one of these about every month or so. The Queen uses every excuse she can to throw one." The Prince didn't say anything, nor did he look particularly thrilled at the prospect. It became clear to Ezran that this wasn't a topic he wanted to continue with. "So, your swords. They seem pretty powerful."

Kyrith's eyes shifted to him, quick and sudden, which made him feel as if he made some kind of terrible mistake. The stare was unnerving, to the point that Ezran took another deep drink. Most Kashadon would respond with something along the lines of "thank you, and yours as well," before they used it as an excuse to speak about their weapons and accomplishments. The Prince said nothing. Instead, he looked at Ezran like he threatened him, or his words confused him. It was hard to tell. The only features of his that spoke were his eyes and a line between his brows that could have belonged to either reaction.

He needed Kal. Or Avis. Or anyone to make this exchange pleasant.

By the Gods' mercy, someone seemed to notice Ezran's distress and took pity on him. A noble strolled over, dressed in robes of silver and muddy red with a thin ceremonial sword hanging by his side. Grey shot through his dark hair, the lines on his face numerous and well defined. Despite his rank, Ezran was surprised he didn't recognize him. Being in court, he'd met most of the Northern nobility, and yet this face was only a vague hint failing to claw something free from the abyss of his memories.

The mysterious man gave a proper bow to Kyrith before he even began to speak. "Prince Kyrith, Master Ezran, I hoped to run into you both. It is such a pleasure to see you after all these years."

Ezran wracked his mind as they both returned the bow, panicking as he tried to place the face with a name. Any name at all. Yet, it continued to elude him. He flicked a glance at Kyrith, but he looked the same as he had before. If he did know the person, he wasn't showing it. Clearly, the noble knew them though, enough to be comfortable using Ezran's first name.

"Yes," Ezran began, when it was clear the Prince wasn't going to say a word. "I'm afraid it's been too long, ser..."

"Duke Erji Ralith, of the Iudica District," he said with a smile. Ezran froze and his grip turned white on his glass. Kyrith went rigid beside him, muscles tensing before his gaze lowered to the ground. "Don't be troubled for misplacing the name. You both were quite young when we met."

Neither needed the reminder. It came to Ezran like something rising from the darkest depths of the ocean. He could see it, though still hazy. The same face that was before him now, but full of youth and set in determined anger. There wasn't a sword at his hip then, but in his hand, and it was not some ceremonial decorum but a real cutting blade. He stood in a doorway, light blazing behind him, and stared down what had to be King Auberon. Ezran remembered warmth, then. Arms holding him and skirts that he gripped hard. His mother, he thought, clinging to her son as they took him from his home, sobbing and screaming her anguished pleas. His palms burned with the ghosting echo of fabric being torn from him as he was hauled up and away.

It was the Ralith who took him. With their patron God being Endelion, and gifted with his Mace, their House was the justice in North Akadon. Back before the Empire fractured, they oversaw courts and trials in the whole of Akadon, with representatives in every city from the North Sea to the southernmost tip of the continent. The conflict between crowns tore the family apart, pitting blood against blood with the division of the Fracture War.

When the fighting settled, and dust covered a litter of corpses on both sides, the Ralith took to justice. They charged both royal lines with inciting war, causing disruption, chaos, giving life to countless unsettled shades and enough negative energies to conjure legions of daemons. It didn't matter who started it. Neither ended it. The Nefion and Auberon were two equally sized forces that kept colliding over and over, destroying everything in their wake, as they had with every dissension that came between the two throughout history.

The people sided with the Ralith because of their faith

in the family's reputation, and more than likely to find some semblance of revenge or closure for all they lost. It didn't matter who answered for it, someone had to pay. Weakened by the war and with their own people against them, the royals ceded to the Ralith. The price for fracturing the Empire was simple; each crown would hand over a child to be raised by the other.

The reasoning never really got through to Ezran. The Ralith hoped, somehow, that each child being raised by opposing monarchies would lead to them returning to their own with respect and knowledge for the other empire. They said it would promote peace. Ezran thought it was the cruelest justice they could settle on. There was no possible way the Ralith could call for royal blood to be spilled, nor overthrow them with the Sword and Shield they respectively kept. But to hand over their children for the enemy to raise... it would be like ripping one's heart out, he was sure.

All he knew for certain was that he feared the North when he arrived, but after a year passed, he began to fear the Ralith would come and drag him back more. These shapeless terrors would haunt him in the night. Countless times he woke sobbing in his younger years, trailing to Kal or Avis' rooms for comfort.

"I am beyond pleased you have finally returned, Prince Kyrith. At last, we can begin to truly mend the severed strands left by the war." The Duke continued to speak, but the one he addressed had not raised his gaze from the floor or moved since the introduction. Ezran kept his dark eyes locked on the noble with his lips parted, unable to look away. Ice replaced his blood and muscles, fixing him there as much as the statuesque Prince beside him. "And you, Master Ezran? When will you be returning home?"

Ezran blinked. The question caught him off guard,

knocking him loose from his frozen state and letting the drink flow freely through his veins again. Before he could register such actions, his tongue let the first words that rose tumble free.

"I am home."

The Duke's smile faltered and Kyrith's formidable gaze burned into him. Downing the rest of his drink, Ezran parted without so much as a courtesy nod to either. After abandoning his glass on a table, he fled out of the ballroom like someone was chasing him. He didn't stop until he found a darkened hallway, deserted of any other living soul.

Heat flared across his skin like someone had set fire where ice was moments before. He blamed the drink. His entire body trembled, from his skin to his very bones, as he swept a hand through his brown hair and tried to get them to cease by centering himself. He blamed the chill of the autumn wind, even though the fires kept it from entering a breath into the Sun Palace. Fear, sour and sickening in his gut, refused to let go of him despite how he rallied against it. He blamed it on the darkness around him, and not the darkness storming within, dragging free the shapeless terrors he thought long forgotten.

TWENTY-TWO

W hat Arra particularly liked about these kinds of celebrations was the fact that everyone remained gathered in one spot, for the most part. The servants and royal family were there, along with most of their guards, which left the rest of the palace deserted. It was the perfect time for her to continue her search for a discreet way in and out of the palace.

The Sun Palace was wildly different from the Fortress in ways beyond that. She could sense it in the metal of the place, in the marble stones and autumnal smell of it. The Fortress was much older than this palace of gold and beauty. The metal there was strong, unbending. Its mountain stone was soaked to the brim with the energy of the Ages it stood, both negative and balanced. Powerful blood sigils were the only things to hold it at bay, which stained the scent of the place with iron and power.

The Sun Palace, however, was yielding and the gold in it fluid, able to be molded with the gentlest suggestion. The stone wasn't heavy with energy, but full of a cleansing lightness that flowed through the air. Not thick, either, but a thin veil that smelled of warm fires, of comfort and safety. Arra never felt anything remotely like it in the Fortress, or South Akadon for that matter, at least since she left Enryn Manor.

There was no place to be safe there. King Auberon could reach her if Marek couldn't. Sharply, she reminded herself that he could reach her here, too. Northern comforts couldn't lull her into forgetting that.

Newer palace or not, every one of them had a way of getting around unseen. Servants needed faster, out of sight ways, and nobles needed escape routes or food tunnels in case of attack. All she had to do was find one.

Arra stayed away from the lower parts of the place for now, knowing the possibility of her being discovered there was far greater. Instead, she stole up the stairs and searched the higher floors near the apartments. If there was a secret way around the palace, it would be close to where the royals spent most of their time.

Their apartments were huge and luxurious as well. Even the guest one Arra had been given was filled to the brim with treasures and twice the size of her chambers back at the Fortress. The Princes' were even bigger. With only two or three doors along one wall, all of them connected to one apartment. Prince Kalin and Prince Ezran's rooms opposed each other, and Avis' lay a bit further down the bend of hallways. She knew Kyr's rooms were the opposite way, with the Princess' near them. But she couldn't find a sign of any hidden doors or passageways among them, or even a servant's route craftily tucked away. She bit at her lip as she tested the wall along one side.

What if the entrances weren't in the hall, but in their rooms?

Her heart picked up at the thought. She didn't like the

idea of marching South Akadon soldiers through the Princes' chambers. She knew it was inevitable, but to die surprised in their beds... How could she face Kyrith after that?

His face came to mind, grief and anger cutting plain across his features. The accusation in his iron grey eyes. Yet, he would be alive to hate her, and maybe that would be enough.

Her heart beat too loud, her thoughts spiraled too much. Both masked the sound of footsteps from her attention.

"Kyrith? Ez? Are you there?" a bright and ever so Northern tone called. Arra didn't have time to hide. She pulled herself off the wall just as the other two Nefion Princes came into view, along with a distinctly Southern retainer who carried a lantern to light the way. "Lady Enryn. What are you doing here?"

Arra turned to Prince Kalin and fought against her urge to fade into the shadows. Walking forward, she smoothed her muted skirts and let out a false noise of relief.

"Oh, thank the Gods." She dipped into a low curtsey. "Forgive me, Your Imperial Highnesses. I meant to go back to my chambers for something, but I must've gotten turned around somewhere. Your palace is a bit confusing."

Prince Avis smiled at her, amiable and warm. "There's nothing to forgive. It can be confusing if you don't know it."

She returned the smile, clenching her shaking hands in the folds of her skirts. "What brings you all back to your chambers? Did I miss the ball completely?"

"No, no," Prince Kalin said. "It's just now reaching its height. Though, Ezran and Kyrith both seemed to have disappeared. We decided to take the opportunity for some air and look for them. Have they passed by here?"

"I'm not sure." She glanced away and tried for embarrassment, hoping that would explain the heat in her face. "Honestly, I haven't seen a soul since I got turned around up here."

Prince Kalin let out a sigh and peered behind her. Prince Avis nodded once, his eyes skipping over his companions. She found it odd how Kyrith's gaze could be so sharp while his brother's could be so calm and inviting.

"Let us escort you, Lady Enryn, so you don't get turned around again," he said. Arra carved a smile across her lips while her stomach sank. Stepping forward, the Princes' both turned and flanked her as they abandoned their search.. The retainer, ever dutiful, walked a step ahead to keep their way lit, one hand behind his back the entire time. Arra studied him from the corner of her eye, wondering how an Oshcan had come to be in the Nefion's service.

"Thank you, Your Imperial Highnesses. I apologize for the trouble," she said, pushing her curiosities away for the moment.

"It's no trouble," Prince Avis repeated. A small smile seemed to perpetually twist at the corners of his mouth, another odd difference between the brothers. Each of the Nefion offspring seemed to smile with ease.

Now that Arra thought about it, she didn't think she had ever seen Kyrith smile in a proper way. Or even smirk. She guessed the way he would twitch his lip upwards on the briefest of occasions counted, at least for him. It took a while for him to relax and be comfortable enough to do that, however.

"Have you known Kyrith long?" Prince Kalin asked, pulling her from her thoughts suddenly. She breathed in and straightened her skirts as she walked.

"I've known him for a time," she said, her pleasant tone

masking her caution on the matter. "I came to Sankor when I was young, but he was already present."

Arra didn't know what else to say. Her relationship with Kyrith was always something to be guarded, monitored with heavy scrutiny by Marek and King Auberon through the eyes that grew on the walls of the Fortress. No matter how minuscule or platonic, Marek's jealousy was a violent thing. For his sake, and for hers, they always had to be careful with their friendship.

"It must've been pleasant for him to have someone there," Prince Avis commented.

Arra bit back a cruel laugh. Yes, pleasant enough to have someone who could wash the blood from his back after the King whipped it raw.

"It was mutual. The Fortress can be a tad lonely." She forced another brief smile, hoping the topic would drop.

"Has Kyrith always been so... quiet?" Prince Kalin asked.

Arra swallowed as she hesitated, turning to the other.

"Since I met him, yes, Your Imperial Highness. He takes a while to warm up to someone."

She didn't know if he heard it in her voice, or if he simply wanted to stop his brother from interrogating her, but Prince Avis finally moved on. "How are you settling into North Akadon, Lady Enryn?"

"Quite well, thank you." She checked her tone to remain polite. "It's different from home, but lovely."

"Yes, especially this time of year."

They trailed down the steps, the distant sounds of the ball echoing from the palace depths to greet them. The lantern became no longer necessary and was abandoned on a spare golden table. The light from the hanging torches proved sufficient to walk under, allowing them to make out a figure coming from another of the linear, branching halls.

"Ez," Prince Kalin said in surprise. Arra trembled at the sight of him, but she fought hard to keep it off her face. He looked too much like Marek for her taste. Not that either of the Southern Princes were particularly unattractive, but pain and fear twisted those features into a warning. "Where did you disappear to?"

She had a way of reading people. It was something she was quick to learn in the South, when her day began to depend on a shift in mood from those around her. Arra could see the shaking tension in his body that he was trying and failing to hide. It was his hands that betrayed him most, dancing on his thighs with frantic taps. His smile was a bit too bright, his eyes bloodshot.

"I can't exactly drink with the Queen glaring down my back, now can I?" He laughed as he approached. Flicking his gaze over every one of them, he settled on her for a moment more. He bowed and she curtseyed, but no titles slipped from either of them.

"Please don't chase a stolen herd of sheep into the courtyard again," the Prince said. Arra's brow furrowed, wondering if it was some kind of joke, but doubting it by the look on the Northerner's face. "Did Kyrith leave with you?"

"Kyrith? No, I thought he stayed back."

Arra's nape prickled. Normally, when Kyrith was nowhere to be found, it was Marek's doing. She knew that it wasn't possible here, but she couldn't help the trained nerves that jumped in her veins.

Prince Ezran ran a hand over his face, pressing hard at the corners of his eyes. As his facade dropped, he seemed to sag downward, weighted by whatever was bothering him.

"I wouldn't worry too much, Kal. Duke Ralith came and spoke to us."

Arra's eyes closed as she pressed her lips together. Kyrith wouldn't run. The only time she had ever seen him do such a thing was in the dining room on his first day here. He would bear it, as always, and wait until whoever it was to be done with him. Then, he would normally return to his chambers. But would he do the same here? She hadn't seen a candle flicker or hearth fire lighting up under his door.

"He spoke with you?" Prince Kalin said, the sharp note of protection bringing a bit of force to his voice. "He had the nerve to come, and then to speak with you both."

"It was nothing, Kal. Don't become Vyn on me now," the Southerner replied light heartedly, reaching out to ruffle the Nefion's hair. Prince Kalin slapped his hand away before it could ruin his gilded appearance. "I needed a drink and some air. I'm sure Kyrith would need the same. Let's go back, yeah?"

The Northern royal didn't seem to want to drop it, but he followed the other anyway. Nothing was said between the group as they made their way closer to the ball. They entered without ceremony, and Arra was almost blinded with the splendor of everything around her.

She was slowly getting accustomed to the gold and marble walls, though it still made her wonder how this palace hadn't been ransacked by now. Even the iridescent windows, illuminated with stolen moonlight, were the same as the ones in the training room. The rest of mere decor here would have put South Akadon's vaults to shame. Crystal hung from three monstrous chandeliers, casting colorful refractions of light to dance on the guests. Food and drink were piled high on golden tables, in golden dishes, and in golden lined flukes with precious stones set into their rims. Arra had never seen so much of the metal in one place before, and that included the Hedon mines she'd once visited. It called to her in a fluid song that had nothing to do with the jaunty, warm melodies playing for the dancers.

The people matched the decor with jewelry dangling off of them like an entire basin of such had been dumped over their figures. They wore clothes of vibrant colored fabrics, all of rich quality. The women wore their hair long, curled, or in stylish coils about their heads. None had intricate braids like hers, which were common fashion in the South. Perfumes attacked her nose more than any temple's incense ever could.

Never had she seen such an extravagant affair, or a gathering of such expensive people before. A heated blade ripped through her stomach at the sight of it all, but this time it curled upwards and buried itself into her chest. This is what they had the time and money for, while her people fought, scrouged, died...

And how plain she appeared to them in her grey skirts and Southern tunic. She ran her hands over their rough texture, hating how they betrayed her now by marking her out.The need to disappear choked her with its urgency.

"Are you alright, Lady Enryn?" someone asked. She glanced up to find Prince Avis looking at her, worry etched in his personable features. She fixed a sharp, false smile to her lips and nodded.

"This is very unlike home," she said. He returned the smile, though his was sympathetic in nature, and offered his hand.

Arra stared at it for a moment. She wasn't supposed to touch a Prince. No one did at formal functions, unless they were close relatives or intended to be married. At least, that was how it was done in South Akadon. Clearly, that wasn't the case here.

Arra took his hand after an awkward pause and allowed him to lead her into the room. People stared. She tried her best to keep the heat from her face, knowing how obvious it would be on her pale skin. Her ears filled with a roar that wasn't coming from the ball. She had never felt so on display before, even as Marek's intended, and desperately tried to think of a way to escape it.

Yet, that proved impossible as Prince Avis remained standing by her. He let her go at some point but never moved on, and the same trained instinct that often kept Arra at Marek's side rooted her in place then. Her nerves had rattled her so much that she fell into what she thought would keep her safe. Arra could be quiet, polite and gentle, nothing noteworthy. She could fade right in front of people until their interest waned, hostile or not. Marek had given her plenty of practice.

It almost worked, too. Once the people realized their Prince would not be abandoning his Southern guest, they began to warily trail up to them. Few asked for her name, and fewer still tried to engage with her after it was given. Arra swallowed down the need to bolt and made meaningless, vapid replies when required. They lost interest, until one didn't.

The man that approached had a sword on his hip. Arra's gaze snapped to it out of reflex since she hadn't seen anyone else with a weapon but the guards. It was a pretty thing, all polished silver and crowned with gold, etched with Northern sigils whose meanings evaded her. She forced herself to relax again when she noticed the lack of sheath, as well as the bluntest edge she had ever laid eyes on.

"My Prince," the stranger greeted with a slight bow of his head. He was a burly man with a dark complexion, his beard already greying. Dressed in robes of gold and black linings, he had an air as regal as any of the royalty there.

"Duke Somir, what a pleasure to see you again." Prince Avis smiled. The Duke flicked a gaze towards Arra, dragging his fiery yellow eyes up and down her form. No greeting or bow slipped from either of them.

"I was happy to find I could spare the time, though a sickness withheld Teryn from traveling. He asked me to relay his apologies to the crown and our dear Princes on this most blessed day."

"Oh, there is no need for such apologies. The same withheld Ynette from attending. I will be certain to pray for Lord Somir's hasty recovery. I'm pleased you were able to make it, Your Grace," Prince Avis replied.

The Duke made a noise of agreement. "Yes, yes, I as well. There have been a few too many wandering shades through Nixa Ignan this year, but there seems to be a lapse for now that's allowed me to attend. How have you been treating Sol?"

"Ser Maisym continues to impress. I do believe he will make a fine Captain of the Guard one day. Unfortunately, I lost him from my personal guard so he could retrieve Kyrith for us."

Duke Somir grinned with pride at first, but it faded when he looked toward her again. "And this?"

"Yes, he was also accompanying Lady Enryn to the Capital," Prince Avis said. Arra sensed the shift in the conversation. Her neck prickled again. *Disappear.*

"Enryn," Duke Somir tutted with evident disapproval. Her throat and spine tightened. "I knew it had to be Enryn. There's much of your father in you."

Arra didn't know what to say to that. There was only one reason why this Northerner would know her father. Prince Avis wasn't much help either, shifting his gaze in discomfort as he seemed to search for a way out.

But the Duke wasn't done. "I last saw him at the Battle of Ovin Tal. He did his country proud there, even as he was forced to retreat. Before the battle even began, he killed every prisoner he had by forcing them to kneel in the Southern fashion and impaled them with spikes. Most of which were formed from their very own breastplates."

The heat drained from her face. Never had Arra heard such a story. Her father was a war hero, a valiant General who put up the fight to a bitter end. It was said he had to be dragged from the battlefield by the King himself once the truce was called.

Prince Avis' discomfort bordered on pain as he glanced between them. She knew there was no real way for him to help her, and she didn't expect him to. She was a Southerner. An Enryn at that.

"My father never really spoke on the war," Arra said, trying for light and failing.

Duke Somir's eyes glittered.

"Well, we have plenty of stories to share, Lady Enryn. We all remember quite clearly, if you ever find yourself in the mood to listen."

Her throat tightened again to a painful extent. Pressing her lips together, she feigned a smile, then curtseyed to both. "If you'll excuse me, Your Imperial Highness. Your Grace."

She didn't give a proper excuse, but slipped away all the same. Arra could feel his eyes as they glared into her back, burning the verdict onto her body, her hair, clothes, blood.

But she always had a way of disappearing, even when someone was looking right at her.

Finally reaching a darkened hall after she slipped between clotted groups of flashy Northern silks and gilded doors, Arra found a wall to lean her back against. Panic was a wild thing in her veins, and yet she did her best to tame it. Her stomach pitched, her heart beat louder than any drum she'd ever heard. She breathed in, but the air was too warm. This whole place was too warm. Too gilded. Too unsafe, despite the falsities of feeling so.

Arra clenched her hands into fists and desperately wished Queen Endri was there. She would have known what to do, what to say to soothe the Duke while also alleviating her. It was an uncommon skill she was apt at— when it came to handling angered men. Arra, however, was not, unless threatening to stab them counted.

Thinking of her made Arra's chest loosen the slightest bit. Chasing that reprieve, she remembered the letter. She had yet to give it to Ezran. After checking over its contents to be sure the Queen wouldn't give her husband's plot away, she resealed it but hadn't found the right moment to slip it to him. She should have known that Queen Endri would never endanger her life by doing such a thing.

A noise startled Arra into drifting deeper into the shadows of the hall, half expecting to hear King Auberon's angered shout or Marek's cruel laughter. Instead, a grunt sounded over a metallic rattle.

"Damn tables... everywhere," someone slurred, thick with drink. "Boy! Get the horses ready. We head out from this fucking place. Insolent Princes... Kalin fucking Nefion dares to speak to *me* in such... front of all of these self-centered..."

Arra dared to peer out from the corner. A man in silver and auburn had clearly been too in his cups, stumbling around and cursing the royal family. If he would have done such a thing in the South, he would have had his tongue removed at best.

A servant boy, dressed in a different uniform than the Nefion House livery, attempted to steady him. The man reached down and yanked his sword free after a few tries, a dead copy of the one Duke Somir had. He waved it about, which only caused more disturbance to the decor as the boy ducked away from his tactless swings. The clattering of expensive finery was loud enough to reach the spirits in the Gods' Realm. Arra was surprised someone hadn't come rushing to investigate it yet.

"Are you deaf?! I said go!"

The boy scurried away from his master with a glare. However, he didn't head toward the front of the palace. The direction he took was toward the side, where Arra knew no public exits were placed.

Following a few paces behind, she slipped past the inebriated apparent Duke. The servant boy was too distracted with his thoughts. He rubbed his arm where the blade struck a bruise, oblivious to the ghost tailing him.

He led her through the halls of the palace with hurried steps. Eventually, he came to a stop before a normal looking door. It took her a moment to realize how plain it was. Where the rest of the doors in the palace bore the Nefion sun crest, this one had nothing but dark stained wood. After the servant boy disappeared inside, Arra waited a moment to follow.

She opened the door to find crude stone steps, which were a stark, unsightly grey compared to the white marble used everywhere else. The walls were a similar shock, supported with aging brown wood instead of gold. This was clearly a place never meant for the public eye.

The boy's quick descending scuffs echoed up the spiral staircase to meet her. She followed much lighter than he, the only noise coming from the brush of her skirts on the ground. A door opened and slammed closed beneath her, echoing like thunder through the quiet cylindrical space.

Another plain door without a golden sigil met her at the bottom. Arra opened it, slow in her movements, but found such caution unnecessary when faced with a dark, empty room. Moonlight lit the area to a silver dimness, streaming through plain glass instead of whatever iridescent material they used in the palace. Nothing but stacks of hay bales and stable equipment lay before her, scattered in with sacks of grain, corn, and spare pieces of tack.

Arra had made it to the stables.

CHAPTER
TWENTY-THREE

S ol took his job quite seriously, but even he had parts that he didn't particularly care for. Standing guard during celebrations was one of them. He knew it was important as well as his duty, but watching everyone enjoy themselves in splendor while he remained stiff, unbending in his silver plate... It wasn't exactly what he wanted to do with his time. Still, he stood unmoving. *Chylus* had been replaced with a regular sword at his hip, and it was lifeless compared to the constant thrum of energy that ran through his greatsword. It was lonesome to be without it.

He had only one moment of relief throughout the duration of his shift. He hadn't been on duty when the Duke arrived, but he sought Sol out the second he noticed the change in guard. In truth, Sol anticipated the reunion since Queen Nefion announced her plans.

Duke Somir was a proud, regal man, and had much better things to do than check up on some royal guard. Yet, he always went out of his way to see him whenever he was near Elysia. He wanted to check how he was doing, if he was living up to the family name. He also continuously asked if a suitable woman had caught his eye yet, to which the guard tried to laugh and play off his anxiety as embarrassment. Despite this, Sol looked forward to meeting with the Duke whenever there was a chance to, seeing as he was the closest thing he had left to a true, blooded family.

The Maisym line originated in Nixa Ignan, the northernmost District the Somir ran with the blessing of Kanah's Dagger. The trees became tangled the further one looked back, but it was certain that Sol's family sported a close connection to the Somir, enough to be an offshoot of the noble line. They shared their affinity for fire, given by the Goddess herself, but also boasted a prolific lineage of warriors.

Sol's father grew up with Duke Somir. Life had taken them in differing directions, but Avaryn had a way of linking its people together no matter how many leagues separated them. His father chased his dream of being a royal guard. Prominence led him to enjoy the rank of Captain at an impressive young age... and then the war broke out.

The crown would have taken care of Sol. After all, his father had been vital to them as a strategist, a Captain, and finally a General, but Duke Somir would hear none of it. He provided everything for Sol, encouraged him in his studies and practice, and showed up for every life event without fail. The Duke treated him like another child, though he boasted two of his own. Both Teryn and Elyna Somir took to him as well, as close to siblings as he could get with his brother gone.

Sol still had his job to do, and scanned the crowd as the

two of them talked. They spoke in a brief passing about the journey to South Akadon, but parted with an agreement to catch up properly when he wasn't on duty. Once again, Sol was left to fight his disinterest alone so it wouldn't hinder his concentration as he watched the ball from the sides.

Prince Avis and Prince Kal were performing their usual roles, nothing out of the ordinary when Sol sought them out. Similarly, their sister was up to her usual antics. Princess Veslyn favored more toward Prince Kal, though. She enthralled her own company, often leading them out to dance to her favorite songs.

The King and Queen sat on their thrones above it all, engaging in occasional conversation or a dance. The Queen seemed off as tension lit in her body, pooling in her fingers, which grasped the arms of her throne with a fierceness Sol could see from his vantage point. What had shifted her mood so early in the night, he had no idea.

Sol scanned the crowd again, finding the usual white and black coat of Master Ezran hidden amongst one of the more crowded areas of the room. The guard sighed when he saw the drink in his hand, but at least he hadn't set fire to anything yet or nearly drowned someone trying to show off. While his trick of setting water aflame was rather impressive, his list of victims only grew every time drunken antics drove him to demonstrate. Personally, Sol wasn't in the mood to heal and console some equally inebriated noble that night.

As he moved on, Sol noticed one important member of the family was missing. No matter where he scanned or searched, Kyrith was nowhere to be seen. He expected the Prince to be swarmed with nobles welcoming him, or at least glancing in his direction, but it wasn't possible.

He wasn't there.

Kyrith seemed like the type to slink off when no one was looking. He had snuck up on Sol twice. It led him to wonder if it was a learned trait. After all, Prince Kal could barely sneak off to drink, much less do it at will.

Still, he remained on the wall for the last of his three hour shift just as he was meant to. Nothing really changed except for Master Ezran's intoxication level, but at least he was keeping himself in line for once.

"Maisym," a voice said. He turned to see Ser Ullys, dressed in the same polished plate as him, standing close. "Shift's over."

Euphoric relief raced through his veins as he nodded once, forcing his stiff legs to move. The weight of his armor pressed down all over his form. His hand came to the hilt of the lifeless sword as he moved through the crowd's edges, eager to leave the people and their noise. Once in the hall, where someone had knocked over one of the Queen's decorative tables, Sol began to loosen some straps and release the white cloak from his shoulders. He made it to the guardroom before he could liberate himself from it properly and placed the plate in his storage chest, along with the plain sword. Sol redressed himself with the silver coat of the guard, used when they weren't in armor to differentiate their rank, and took up *Chylus*. Then, he made his way back out to the hall.

He didn't expect anyone to be in the small training room when he arrived. Yet, someone was there taking shuddering breaths that stilled Sol. His hand came to rest on *Chylus'* hilt, though he doubted it was anything more than a wayward guest, probably drunk and heartbroken by a poor turn of the night.

Following the sound, Sol found a figure curled up behind a rack of swords, his back pressed against the marble behind him. Though he covered his face with shaking hands, those black curls could only belong to four people in the palace. Paired with the dark, plain attire he favored, Sol fought to hide his shock.

"Pri... Kyrith?" Sol said gently.

A hand came free from Kyrith's face as if to defend himself and he cowered away in an instant of unmasked panic. Sol blinked, finding it hard to link his stoic Prince to the figure on the floor.

Sol was slow to lower himself into a crouch, set his sword down, and raise his hands in peace. "I'm not going to hurt you."

The Prince didn't look up. Those piercing eyes remained lowered and he returned his trembling hand to his temple before he closed them. His chest moved with rapid and shallow breaths, making his words sound rushed. "It was too loud. Everything is too loud. There's so many..."

Sol softened at the admission and sat down properly, crossing his legs in front of him. Keeping his movements cautious, he pushed *Chylus* further to the side.

"Too many people?"

The Prince took a minute to nod, his face contorting with the confession. He pressed a hand to the center of his chest, curled in with an improper fist. It was plain for Sol to see how hard Kyrith battled himself to gain control again, to stop the shaking, to return to that impassive manner. It seemed though that the more he fought, the more the panic would spread.

Sol held out his hands, moving as slow as he could manage. Even so, the Prince still flinched away. "I can help. Take my hands."

Kyrith stared at him like he was debating whether he

was telling the truth, scared of what might happen if he wasn't. Eventually, his hands joined Sol's.

Shutting his eyes, Sol tried to concentrate. He focused on himself before anything else, though trembling hands were far harder to ignore than *Chylus'* rattle. Agitation poured off of Kyrith, the magic in his blood singing of it.

Drawing on the surrounding marble, on the air and fire, Sol sought out more this time and even included some other energies clotted around them. He pulled in the soothing calm of water in the corner basin, quiet from lack of use. Calling on the energy of his own magic, he tuned in to the steady beat inside of himself and tried to focus on lowering Kyrith's to the same smooth rhythm.

Balanced energy charged from him to Kyrith with dizzying speed. It was like the spirit inside his core had been waiting to leap between them, racing like a wildfire toward fresh brush. Sol felt so drained in that instant that he almost lost focus, but he forced himself to continue. He drew more from the energies, just for them to rip through him like a sharpened sword in their excitement to get to the Prince.

After a moment, the massive amount of energy began to equalize between the two. Sol sucked in a breath as it returned to him. When balancing, he always thought of it as a pot of water with a small hole at the bottom. One could add liquid, do as they wished with it, but it would always slowly deplete and release back to where it came from. It would wash the spirit clean in its wake, settling it, but that action would cause some of the energy to flee.

Not with Kyrith.

If anything, the energy was purified, doubled, and infected with excitement. It raced from him to the Prince and back again, so clean and pure that it burned with a cold ferocity. It was like nothing Sol had ever experienced before.

Kyrith stilled in his hands and let out a long breath. Tension left him, fled with the balance, and seemed to burn up within it. It took everything in Sol to force his spirit and the energy back to him, before making the latter release outwards again. It was like his own magic didn't want to leave Kyrith. He had never experienced that either, no matter if he balanced energy with others gifted with the same affinities as him or not.

Once it was gone, the two released their grip on each other. Sol opened his eyes. His spirit was tranquil, perfect in its balance, burning like a campfire on a chilled autumn night. He lifted his gaze to Kyrith's, but the Prince was only taking slow breaths. His eyes hadn't even opened yet.

"Are you alright?" Sol asked.

Finally, the Prince looked up, the usual impassive stare absent from his face. In fact, if it weren't for the scars and shadows of near faded bruises, Kyrith would have seemed almost gentle. His intensity reduced to a sort of sharp openness that Sol wasn't prepared for.

"Thank you," Kyrith exhaled. His voice was its normal low tone again, if a bit exhausted, and twisted with the Southern accent it carried. Sol's face flared with heat and he shook his head.

"There's no need to thank me," he said. "How are you feeling?"

Sol blinked when he thought he saw the smallest jerk at the corner of Kyrith's lips. He couldn't be sure it actually happened, it was so quick. "Better."

"Does that often happen with crowds?" Sol tried to be gentle as he pressed. If so, it was something his guard needed to know. They couldn't have the Prince disappearing like this every time, especially if he attended a ball of another noble family. Kyrith glanced away, his openness dropping, and left Sol's stomach to sink with its absence.

"It happens occasionally. When... Yes."

Something told Sol that he had more to say on the matter, but he remained quiet. Now didn't seem like the proper time to push. "If you find yourself in such a state again, you can use the same technique as you did with the sword to settle yourself. That's what I did just a moment ago."

Kyrith glanced back up at him, his brows gaining a line between them. "Really? And it will do that every time?"

Sol shook his head. "No, I don't think so. I have no idea why the energy was so intense..."

Kyrith looked away a bit too quickly, eyes flicking between the colored veins of the floor in a repetitive fashion. His mouth gained a tightness until he spoke. "It could be the ball... Kashadon..."

"Perhaps," Sol said. He doubted it. While a gathering of many people with magical abilities could excite the energy, it had never reached such a peak as a moment ago. Still, he wasn't about to prod the Prince when his discomfort was so clear on the subject. "Would you like me to accompany you to your room? Or did you want to sit here a moment longer?"

"I can find my room on my own," he said, though it wasn't dismissive or unkind. He stated it softly, a fact. Sol nodded once and gave him a small smile.

"I have no doubt you could, but I would like to see you there, and be sure you're settled."

Kyrith looked up, distrust once again crossing his features. Those eyes cut through Sol like he could see everything about him, from the secrets he kept hidden deep to his very spirit itself. He'd never been stripped so bare by a gaze. Silence stretched between them for a moment too long.

"Why?"

The question startled him, along with how it was said. It was as if Kyrith didn't expect for a royal guard to care about his well being. Sol didn't exactly know what to respond with. "You are my charge. My duty is to you, to keep you safe and make sure you're well."

The Prince looked like Sol spoke in an old dialect, too ancient to translate. Kyrith shook his head a bit and shifted his stare away at last, relieving Sol from its gravity.

"You don't have to care for me."

Sol furrowed his brow, studying him. What had they done to him in South Akadon to make him like this?

"It's my duty." He got to his feet, being sure to still move as slow as possible and take up *Chylus* on his way. Kyrith followed suit before he could even offer his hand. He stepped back, allowing the Prince a clear exit. "Let me see you to your chambers."

Kyrith considered him again. Sol didn't back down from his gaze, no matter how intimidating it was. The Prince seemed confused by something, though he didn't speak on it. Instead, he muttered, "Okay."

They walked together in silence through the palace. Its familiar yet tense presence remained as they made their way back through to the main hall, then up the staircase, and toward the royal chambers without a word spared. Just as before, that quiet weighed on Sol in a way that it never had previously. They made it to his chambers soon enough and Kyrith left the door open after him in what Sol took as his version of an invitation.

He blinked at his surroundings, surprised. Queen Nefion furnished the room with the same flourish as the rest of the palace, of course, providing the finest of amenities. Anything a Prince could ever want, really. However, most of the room appeared untouched. The only things Kyrith seemed to have utilized were a kettle and a few books. Aside from that, a pile of ragged looking blankets sat near the hearth, nothing between them and the hard marble floor. The bed hadn't been used at all. As fine as the upholstered chairs were, they now served as barricades against several doors to his other rooms, keeping them from opening without a hard screech.

Sol took in the scene slowly, unaware of Kyrith gazing at him and his reaction until the last moment. The two settled on each other, and he swallowed. He bowed his head to his Prince once. "Would you like me to stay?"

The question seemed to catch him off guard. Kyrith slipped his hands behind him, much like Prince Avis had been known to do, but in a less relaxed form. "I... You can stay if you wish... I'm sure you had something more important to do before I took up your time."

Sol shook his head. "You didn't take up my time. If you're well, then I will leave you to your peace. If you feel unsettled, though, I can stay."

"I'm better," Kyrith said. He paused, and his mask slipped a bit once again. "Thank you."

Sol bowed properly, which seemed to make Kyrith's discomfort return. "It was my duty. There's no need to thank me. Goodnight, Kyrith."

"Goodnight, Ser Maisym."

He didn't know what made him say it. Later, he rationalized that it made the Prince more comfortable. Perhaps, if he relaxed, then Kyrith wouldn't be so cautious or uneasy.

Whatever the reasoning, it slipped from his lips all the same.

"Solris. Or Sol, if you prefer, if I am to call you Kyrith."

The Prince blinked, something unreadable crossing his features. He bowed once as well, making Sol realize how uncomfortable it really was when one didn't expect it. "Goodnight, Solris."

PART FOUR:
KASHADON'S CHARGE

TWENTY-FOUR

S ol blocked the young trainee's advances repeatedly, barely straining in the process. Their regular swords were far lighter than *Chylus* was, and it allowed him even more strength when he switched blades. The poor fresh faced boy, Yuris, was on the cusp of his seventeenth year and still lean with his growing. Though he'd built up some muscle over the months since starting his path, he was far from a match for Sol's absolute dedication. He was learning, though, and proving to be one of their most promising yet.

Yuris tried his best to get the better of him, and Sol had to admit he was quite skilled for his level of training and age. Yet, he couldn't let him off easy. Someday, the royal family's lives could be in his hands, and then Yuris wouldn't have such a forgiving opponent.

The boy dropped his guard when he advanced, allowing Sol to block the blade before driving the weight of his shoulder into him. Yuris stumbled back and before he could recover, Sol disarmed him with two great swings of the sword, pinning him to the ground with a third. His hands raised in a sweaty yield and swept his honeyed brown locks from his face.

"Don't drop your guard," Sol said. Yuris took it in stride, accepting a hand to help him up.

"Sorry," he exhaled, still somehow keeping up a bright tone. "I'll try harder, Ser Sol."

"You should be trying your hardest already," he replied. "It's not a matter of trying, but learning and applying."

Yuris nodded and set his blue eyes with determination. He watched Sol's sword, waiting for it to move. When it did, he was quick to counter, filling the air with harsh clangs of metal. It was a symphony of guards training, noises of battle and yet not quite as fierce. It was a sound that Sol had grown up to.

"Royal Guard!"

Everyone ceased all movements as the voice echoed around the chamber. They stood tall, swords pinned to their sides with flashes of light. Each and every one of them sucked in air, responding with a collective shout of, "Captain!"

Captain Talvys wasn't a pleasant man, but he was good at his job. His flat expression glanced over everyone gathered as if they had all regarded him dismissively. "All hunt qualified guards are to report to the ballroom. Those on the roster for personal guard should report to the throne room."

Sol wiped his forehead with the back of his hand, exhaling. The younger guards and trainees, not yet qualified for either, stood with dejection as their sparring partners all began to trail out.

"You're improving," Sol said. He sheathed the sword and handed it off to Yuris, who flushed with a worn out grin. "Keep up your training and you'll be able to join us soon."

"Thank you, Ser Sol!"

Sol shook his head, a smile pulling on his mouth as he stepped away. He collected his silver coat from the rack he'd placed it on, eyes skipping over Ryslyn briefly as the guard took up his own clothing. He'd gone so far as to shed his shirt, sweat and muscle bared along with his usual grin. It stayed along his lips, keeping Sol's attention as he responded to something Ullys said while he shook out his brown, wavy hair.

Stop it. You're a Maisym. You have a duty, Sol reminded himself as he slipped knots into their keeps at his side and shoulder. Within a few moments, he was once again the picturesque guard that everyone thought him to be.

The throne room wasn't that crowded, but having all of the royals' personal guards in one space was quite uncommon. They all grouped together depending on who they were assigned to. The King had those weathered members who fought alongside him years before, while the Queen preferred the capable women in the ranks. It left the younger guards who tended to shift between their royal children in drifting clumps, dependent solely on the amount of trouble Princess Veslyn, Prince Kal, and Master Ezran were getting into.

Sol found his place next to Vyn, standing with his hands folded where the older guard's crossed his chest. Even though he had been in the service since Sol's father was Captain, he still managed to look uncomfortable any time he wore their silver uniform. They traded glances as a greeting and Vyn nodded once, raking hazel eyes down his form.

"Pulled you from sparring, then?" he asked. Sol nodded.

"Do you know what this is about?"

Vyn kept his arms crossed as he thought, shifting his weight as he muttered, "I have an idea."

Before he could elaborate, the door near the side of the thrones opened. The collective of guards all dropped to their knees as the King and Queen entered, followed by their sons and Master Ezran. The monarchs climbed up to their golden seats and settled in a swish of soft cloth.

"Rise," King Nefion said. In perfect unison, the guards did.

Sol cast his gaze over the royal family, searching for any sign of what could be going on. Prince Kal and Master Ezran seemed to vibrate with excitement. It wasn't much of a comforting sight. Kyrith appeared like he was trying his hardest to fade into the background. He looked better than he had a few nights ago, though, which was a relief.

"Thank you for all gathering before me today," the King said, pulling the focus. "I have decided to hold a small banquet tonight and invited local Kashadon to attend. I plan to address the increasing reports of large shades around North Akadon, along with announcing a hunt in Sae Hyura. I'm sure some of you have heard the rumors of daemons in the forest. I would have this investigated by every capable member of our Northern Kashadon, including you all. For this reason, I will allow half the guard to go. I request that half of you stay along for your duties, though I wish I could allow for you all. Captain Talvys will have the final say on the roster, but I'd hope you would settle it amongst yourselves."

The room buzzed with quiet excitement, a heavy portion of it coming from the younger of the gathered guards. Even Sol had to admit that some part of himself was interested in the idea, but he knew he would stay. It would be better to let one of his fellows go while he remained with the family.

Captain Talvys' hard glare silenced any of the soft whispers that began. If it was up to him, none of the personal guards would have gone, Sol knew. He detested "idle hands" and thought the best use of spare time was studying or furthering their practice in some way. Perhaps that was why he enjoyed Sol so much.

"Return to the ballroom with your comrades to sort out the details and then Captain Talvys will give you your shifts for the banquet. As always, thank you for your service to my family and North Akadon."

The guards all knelt again with a uniform, "Our duty, our honor, our King." They rose, conversation bursting out behind Sol the instant they could get away with it. Guards began to file out in clumps of excited groupings, much in the same order they stood around in. Allowing the King's personnel to go first, he hung back to wait with the others.

"Ser Maisym, Ser Vynlier, Ser Drestas, please hold back for a moment." Sol turned to his King, a respectful nod of acknowledgement coming a tad late out of surprise. None of the other guards really seemed concerned or curious as the three slipped away, standing before their King in similar stances of attention. He smiled at them, warm and inviting. "I have a request of you all. I would like for the Princes to go along on this hunt, and I would have each of you guard them personally. It wouldn't be a rotational shift, but a continuous one, so I understand if any of you would prefer to stay. I'd have Ser Drestas with Avis, Ser Vynlier with Kal, of course, and I would have Kyrith in your charge, Ser Maisym."

Sol honestly hadn't expected that to come from his King. Traveling South and accompanying the Prince home was one thing, but to be given a continuous, permanent place as his guard was another entirely. Despite his time within their order and his accomplishments, Sol was still young. He hardly expected to be trusted with Kyrith over a more seasoned, prolific guard.

He bowed his head in acceptance just as Queen Nefion made a noise. It was a cross between a laugh and a snort, something Sol heard many times before. Tension seemed to enter the room as the monarchs traded glances. "Kyrith won't be going."

Sol shifted his weight, and Vyn let out an almost inaudible sigh beside him. It wasn't uncommon for the crown to be at odds, at least since he joined the guard. In fact, if they ever agreed on anything, it was surely a gift from the Gods.

From what Sol had gathered from the older members of their order, it hadn't always been so. Once, they worked quite well together. King Nefion walked away from his arranged union to the late Princess Ettiane Auberon for her, after all, right in the middle of his intention trial. There had to have been something that once united them. The Queen always disagreed with her husband, but never so frequently as her challenges now. It was Kyrith's leave that caused the rift in their marriage, which only seemed to grow wider every year that he was gone. The pair would argue so often that sometimes King Nefion attempted to avoid it by keeping his Queen in the dark on his decisions, at least until he was publicly presenting them like this. Not that doing so curbed her at all.

"Illynthia," the King began with a low tone. Queen Nefion held her head aloft and raised her brow.

"I just got him back, Thamas. I won't have him running around away from home, where Gods know what can happen to him. I won't allow it."

Though the King tried to keep it hushed and between them, Prince Avis stepped forward with his hands behind his back and nodded at his parents. "Mother, I think you should reconsider. It would be an excellent way for us all to reconnect, and the Kashadon surely need our help if daemons—"

"Exactly," Queen Nefion interrupted. "Daemons are in the forests. It's dangerous, not only for Kyrith, but for all of you. I want you to stay and reconnect in the palace. Let the guard handle the problem themselves."

Prince Avis looked lost, his mouth closing slowly as his features shifted. It was clear he hadn't expected his place to be questioned. As he searched for the words to speak, Sol found he had them. Before he could lose his nerve, he stepped forward and bowed his head. "My Queen, if you will permit me."

The room was silent as they waited for her verdict. While it wasn't uncommon for a seasoned guard to give their advice to the crown, Sol had never done so.

"Speak, Ser Maisym."

"Forgive me, but Prince Kyrith is the most qualified in this palace to handle such beasts," he said, trying to pick his words with care. Lifting his gaze, he kept it on Queen Nefion alone, though he could see Kyrith drifting towards the back corner of the room in his periphery. "He has more experience with them than many of the royal guard. His training as a Kashadon is impeccable. It would be good for the hunters and guards to fight beside him."

Sol stepped back with a small bow to show he finished. He burned with all the gazes locked on him. The Queen's was knifelike while the guards studied him relentlessly. One gaze in particular, however, came from the corner and shot through him like an arrow, leaving no place to hide. Heat came to Sol's face as he fought the urge to fidget.

"Excellent point, Ser Maisym." Master Ezran's voice pulled the room's attention after a beat too long, and he stepped forward to accept the burden of such. Prince Kal tried to grab his arm, but he avoided it in a practiced way. Queen Nefion's face soured as soon as he spoke. Unperturbed, Master Ezran came before her with a bow. "Kyrith was the one to masterfully dispatch with the daemon we found. He can help and most likely save the hunters from terrible wounds in the process. Save their lives, even. We will all be with him, along with the outstandingly capable guard King Nefion has assigned to the Princes. And with the Kashadon alongside us, we will be the safest hunters out there. What a wonderful way for Kyrith to make an impression on the people and solidify his return as another accomplished, caring Prince for them to rely on. Don't you agree?"

The Queen didn't seem to appreciate the entire room turning against her. She pursed her lips and cut her sweeping gaze over all of them. "Kyrith?"

The Prince didn't come forward at first. He stood frozen, as if he hadn't expected to be acknowledged in this debate about himself. With inaudible steps, he crept forward like he thought one of them would spring at him and bowed stiffly. "Your Imperial Majesty."

"What do you think? Do you want to join them?"

Kyrith's mouth tightened, the lock in his jaw brief but present, and his gaze never rose from the floor. He seemed a statue in that moment, still and perfect. "I..."

A subtle look crossed his face, sweeping in his eyes and

the edges of his features. He seemed like he couldn't figure something out. It wasn't that hard of a question to answer, but it was apparent that he struggled all the same.

"I can be useful to the Princes," Kyrith said at last. Queen Nefion's perfect brow furrowed under her golden adornments. Seeing this in a brief glance up, he forced himself to continue. "I have experience with daemons. It's no trouble."

"But is it what you—"

"Illynthia," King Nefion cut in again. They shared a look, the King giving an almost nonexistent shake of his head. "Is it settled, then?"

Queen Nefion didn't answer him for a moment. She wore her disapproval as she looked among her sons, settling on Kyrith at the end. He didn't move or sway at all, even under her hard gaze. "Fine. If something happens out there, however, know that I will be very displeased."

TWENTY-FIVE

"I cannot believe you opened your mouth," Kal said for what had to be the thousandth time. It had been a full day and yet he was still stuck on it.

"Is it really that out of character for me, Kal? She relented in the end," Ezran replied as he tightened the breastplate on his horse. The chestnut snorted, shaking itself out in the dusky autumn morning that surrounded them.

"Yes, but if one of us gets so much as a scratch now, she'll be baying for your head."

"Let us not be so dramatic," Genn said. He checked over a cart full of their belongings, from chests to food to medicine, anything they would ever need on a hunt. "The Queen is reasonable."

"Not when it comes to me," Ezran said in quiet confession to his horse.

"Everything ready, then?" Avis' calm tone broke over them. Ezran turned with a smile.

"Just about. Is Kyrith ready? And those guards of yours?"

"Prince Kyrith has been ready since breakfast," Vyn said, slinging his own small chest into the cart. Ezran scoffed, but Avis raised a brow and gestured behind him. Sure enough, the Prince was helping Lady Enryn prepare her own steed, while his black horse stood with a hoof cocked and ready to go.

It was mid-morning by now. Had he really been ready since then?

"The guards are ready as well. You two are the stragglers." Avis smiled. Ezran made a face at his horse, petting Taevis' velvet nose.

"Well, one must wait for perfection."

Kal burst into a laugh as he secured *Sion* to his back. "You? Perfect?"

Ezran shot him a gesture that dragged free another round of laughter. Before either could speak, a youthfully high voice forced Ezran to hide his hand behind his back. "That's not nice, Ez!"

Ves came bustling through the entourage of guards and servants, who dashed to get out of her way at risk of being run over. Stopping short before her brothers, a few strands of her dark hair fell free around her face and framed her gap-toothed smile.

"You are completely right, my fair Princess. I shall never use such a gesture again," Ezran said. Kal flipped him off behind the Princess' back, to which Ezran narrowed his eyes and leaned down to her. He wrapped her up in a hug she didn't return while he once again stuck his middle finger up to Kal, shielding her from the exchange. "I'm going to miss you."

"You wouldn't miss me so much if you didn't keep taking these trips," came the muffled accusation into his chest. His hands rested on her shoulders as he let her go.

"I know, but this one won't nearly be as long."

"I don't believe you."

With arms folded in front of her and silver eyes growing distrustful, it was clear this was a deeply held thought.

"Do you believe me?" Kal asked. She shot a look at him over her shoulder.

"No."

"What of me, then, hm? Am I not to be believed either?" asked Avis. She cracked a bit for him, a smile tugging her lips upward even as she tried to fight it.

"Maybe..." She lost her battle as he brought her in for an embrace, grin spreading unhindered. Kal strode over and gave a gentle tug to one of her loose curls.

"It will only be a few days. A week at most. And then we will all be back for you to pester," he said. She disentangled herself from Avis to hug him instead, squeezing like he was about to disappear.

"You better." Her features shifted into something solemn as they pressed into Kal's dark green robes. "Is... is Kyrith returning with you? Or will he be gone again?"

The brothers all traded glances. Even Vyn and Genn seemed a little uncomfortable. The guard surveyed the scenery and the retainer busied himself with things he already checked.

Avis gave the tactful answer as Kal shot a helpless look at him. "Of course, Ves. Kyrith doesn't have to go back to the place he was at anymore. He's staying home with us."

Ves pulled away from him, but she didn't seem quite convinced. Ezran's hands tapped a rhythm with the uncomfortable shift of the air, which doubled when the Nefions all looked toward their stoic brother and his guard.

"And why didn't I get a hug like that?" Ezran said. Kal

broke out a grateful smile as the Princess crossed her arms again.

"Cause you are the one that said it wouldn't be so long last time."

Did he? Probably. He would say anything if she was upset. "So, I can't get a good hug?"

"No," she said, as haughty and refined as her mother. "Not until you come back. That way I know you will keep your word this time."

Ezran smiled at her as he shook his head. Her gaze drifted again as she glanced at Kyrith, unsure.

"Do you want to say goodbye to him?" Avis asked. Ves nodded while she bit at her lip. He escorted her over with his hands behind his back, interrupting as Kyrith tugged on the horse's girth.

"Do you think this hunt will really help us reconnect?" Kal questioned as they watched. Kyrith gave a slight bow to Ves, who fidgeted in place as Avis spoke. Eventually, it seemed her self control had reached its limit. She threw herself at Kyrith, who caught her almost as if he expected such an action, or perhaps it was a simple matter of uncannily good reflexes on his part.

"I think so. He's a good hunter. You don't get that good at your practice if you hate it. It's something you all can bond with." Ezran thought he saw a flicker of a wince cross Kyrith's face, but it disappeared with an awkward pat.

"Right," Kal said. He twisted a ring on the middle finger of his right hand absently, a black band with a white sun spinning around and around as it went. "Right. Hunting. He did open up a little at our last hunt."

Ezran pressed his lips together before he could say something stupid. Kyrith spoke three, maybe four times on that hunt, and his longest sentence had been about explaining what the daemon favored for its habitat. Perhaps to Kal, getting him to speak at all was a kind of victory.

Ves finally released Kyrith and dashed off like a sudden energetic gale. The Prince looked a bit lost, trading a word or two with Avis before he bowed. His brother caught his shoulder, smiling around the words of his reply.

Ezran didn't have to be close to know what he said, or how those words sounded coming from him. He remembered them on his own. Avis' warmth in telling him he didn't have to after catching him mid kneel or bow. To see it play out in front of him, without him, made something like a sickened ache drop into his stomach. Pressing his lips together, he glanced away before his thoughts could shift darker.

"Ready?"

"Absolutely," Kal replied, as if he too were searching for a distraction. They both moved toward their horses and mounted, causing Vyn and the other guards accompanying them to do the same. Avis, Kyrith, and Lady Enryn mounted soon after, with the first taking the lead at the column. Next came his brothers and the nobility, then the guards themselves in tight ranks. Only Vyn, Ser Maisym, and Ser Drestas were allowed up by their group, dressed in silver coats.

Lady Enryn stuck close to Kyrith's side. She spoke to him every few moments, too low for Ezran to catch. The Prince didn't reply all that often, but she still talked. He seemed relaxed with her.

"You're staring," Vyn said. Ezran cut his gaze back to him.

"I'm observing," he replied.

"You're staring. Ladies don't tend to take kindly to someone that *observes* them so intently, not to mention without blinking."

Ezran made a face at the guard. "I think I have a bit more experience in that area than you."

"Don't be so confident." Ezran whipped around in his saddle, a grin settling on him like a well-worn coat.

"Ser Vynlier! Do tell," he gasped, interest turning with ease. Vyn stared straight ahead as a flat look crossed his features.

"No. Face forward. You never know when your horse might spook or stumble."

"I'm sure the cobbled streets are safe enough," he retorted. "You never share any of your good stories."

He didn't answer and Ezran huffed at his silence, boredom creeping up on him already. This procession was infinitely faster than the one they'd had coming home, at least thus far. Elysians were used to seeing the guard, Princes, and parades, but he knew it would only slow as they made their way to Mo Byun.

Kal and Avis chattered at the head of the column, and he wished with increasing desperation that he could join them. He was once again in the position of Master Breckhym, not their brother. Even the foreign Lady was above him in North Akadon hierarchy. He was left with Vyn, Sol, and Ser Drestas, seeing as Genn was in the cart behind. Or he could try to pester Kyrith and the Lady, but he wasn't sure if he should, much less what would become of it if he did.

It took all of his self control to remain where he was as they left the Capital behind. With each pace of Taevis underneath him, his boredom grew, silence allowing his thoughts to spiral. He couldn't help it. Not with Kal and Avis separated from him by Kyrith and the Lady. It was harder for him to keep himself from that dark mindset when they were right in front of him, dressed in the fashion of South Akadon. He didn't mean to make them barriers from his brothers, either. It had been little over a year where Ezran hadn't felt the strings of his placement, riding freely with just Kal, Genn, and Vyn like any other hunting party. Even before that, he had to ride behind them, sure, yet never so separated like this. The distance, small as it was, held a vastness he didn't like to sit with.

Fueled by that discomfort, he reached the end of his admittedly short patience, which became exacerbated as their pace slowed to a crawl. He moved Taevis along a little faster, coming behind the Southern pair and keeping pace with them. Though the act was a small break in protocol, he felt much better having done it.

"Excuse my interruption," he said more out of custom than genuine sentimentality, "I have a question for you, Lady Enryn. Is this your first proper hunt?"

Her features struck him, so unlike the Northern people around her. They were sharp, unyielding, even when she glanced away from him far too quickly. "No, Master Breckhym."

"Please. Ezran will do. I'm not one for much ceremony."

That seemed to startle her, for whatever reason. She blinked at him like he sprouted a daemon's head from his own.

Unnerved by her gaze, he continued on. "So, do you attend lots of hunts like this in South Akadon?"

"When permitted," she answered cautiously. "Every Kashadon is required to hunt for the crown. Those studying to become Kashadon are encouraged to attend as many as possible for experience. There's no shortage of daemons and large shades down there, so they must be regularly maintained."

"That sounds exciting." Ezran leaned forward on his horse, like he could see it on the horizon. "You must be able to hunt every day. It's a Kashadon's dream."

The Lady and Kyrith shared a look. "It... Perhaps. Hunting there is very different from the North."

"How so?"

She looked forward again, her mouth pressing into a neat line. "You Northerners seem to think of it much more as sport. In the South, it's a necessity. It is protection and safety. If there are no hunts, then daemons and shades overrun the people. Villages, towns, cities, it doesn't matter. Hunting keeps us safe. It's a sacred duty."

Avis and Kal had gone quiet at some point, listening in. The guards behind them even seem interested. The Lady cast her gaze about and flushed, her pale skin giving little cover for her to hide it. In payment for putting the attention on her, Ezran shifted it back to him as he adjusted his seat in the saddle.

"Well, it's a sacred duty here, too. We don't have many daemons, and our shades are a bit less unsettled, but it's still our duty to keep the common people safe. I guess it becomes more enjoyable when it isn't so dire. What about you, Prince Kyrith? Did you go on these Southern hunts often?"

Kyrith jumped at the title, and Ezran wondered if he would ever get used to hearing it. He didn't respond for a moment, swallowing before he spoke. "Every hunt I was ordered."

Ezran's stomach turned. He knew he was in troubled waters, but he didn't know how to navigate out of it. "Oh. How... how many was that?"

"All official hunts. Occasionally others," he said, as if it explained everything. Ezran's brow furrowed.

Lady Enryn took pity on him. "There are two official hunts every month. They mainly have the largest prey, the ones hunting parties couldn't handle on their own."

Ezran's mouth went dry. Two large hunts per month? Topped by the fact that they were hunting daemons on the regular. Considering the thing they took down was common to Kyrith... what was a large daemon to them, that Kashadon couldn't handle individually or in small hunting parties? Did they find themselves meeting something like the legendary beast Rikaeviktis twice a month?

Ezran wasn't sure he wanted to know. He didn't even know what answer to scramble together, either. Avis had to beat him to it as usual, casting the words over his shoulder. "You both must be quite experienced, then."

"Sure, if looking at it from a Northern perspective," Lady Enryn replied.

Ezran was close enough to catch the soft "Arra" that came from Kyrith, as well as the small smile she tried and failed to repress at his look. Kyrith shook his head slightly before casting his gaze back to the forest around them.

Ezran had the distinct feeling that he missed something between the interaction, which stirred his discomfort again. Another thing putting him just out of place, reminding him he didn't belong in spaces he should have. If fate had been different, he wouldn't look at things from such a Northern perspective, as he apparently did. He wouldn't have to view the pair before him as a barrier because he never would have seen Avis or Kal as his brothers.

In a rare moment for him, Ezran kept silent. He let Taevis drop back, flicking a look over Kyrith again as his discomfort grew, tugging and trapping him back into place at Vyn's side.

TWENTY-SIX

Mo Byun, Pentral District, North Akadon

Mo Byun was supposed to be small. That's what Arra remembered one of the Nefion Princes saying. It was a small outpost that mainly hosted Kashadon, seeing as it was the closest habitable place to Sae Hyura.

What met her eye was not what she considered small. Everywhere she looked, she could see Kashadon strolling, laughing, shopping. Commoners didn't cower before them, didn't bow or stumble out of their way as fast as they could. Kashadon didn't walk with arrogant pride, as if the cobbles were graced by the simple touch of their muddy boots.

It was an odd sight to see them not only mixing casually with the common populace, but treating them with respect. They moved out of the way for children, or expectant mothers, even those carrying heavy loads. Smiled when people dared to greet them and often stopped them from bowing. Their magic wasn't brandished like a status, marking them better than those without. Kyrith didn't seem as shocked by these differences, but then again, he had gone out on that hunt with his brothers before.

The streets were littered with stalls and shops catering to every need of the Kashadon. Arra found herself drawn to the elegant weapons, the foreign sigils that didn't have blood coating them, the tunics and robes that were supposedly resistant to dirt, debris, and tearing. If she hadn't been on a horse in a royal procession, she would have spent hours going through everything. Lavish or not, Kashadon items were a practicality Arra could allow herself the indulgence for.

"How do they seal their sigils without blood? How do they make the magic stay?" she asked Kyrith as they passed a stall laden with pendants, carved from things as simple as wood to elaborate jade and gold. He looked them over with a brief, disinterested glance.

"Don't know," he said, ever helpful. "Perhaps the item itself holds it."

They had to be weak, then. Magic came from the spirit inside a living being, so without sealing it with a bit of themselves, how could the energy be expected to last? The item could be infused itself, but it was so much stronger when bound in blood. Unless spirit users were behind it, of course, but she doubted that. Then again, this was North Akadon. Perhaps they did waste their spirit users' time and energy on trivial things like jewelry.

"The Kashadon..." She trailed off as one stopped to help a woman who spilled her groceries. His sword glittered on his back and the metal sang with its power. "They..."

"I know," he said.

"This is all quite different from home."

She marveled at the profusion of people watching them march through, excited to see their crown Princes. They waved, yelling some type of blessing in an old dialect Arra hadn't heard before, and bowed at the last moment. Prince Avis and Prince Kalin took it all in stride, returning waves and blessings, smiling...

She tried to imagine Marek doing such a thing. The only image that came to mind was him grinning as he trampled someone with his beast of a horse. The Nefions certainly had a persona that they upheld well, even with those they spent so much time around.

The crowd seemed to still as eyes landed on her and Kyrith. The Northerners weren't full of contempt like she expected, but instead held an uncertain curiosity. She could almost see the questions in their minds.

Arra watched out of the corner of her eye when a few recognized Kyrith for who he was. Or, perhaps more truthfully, saw how eerie the similarity was between him and Prince Kalin. It took people a moment to remember and brush off the dust from his name after so long.

For his part, he didn't flinch or jump like he had every time the title came unexpectedly. His mouth set, though, a subtle thing that spoke volumes. Kyrith clenched his reins a little tighter and stared straight ahead like he was afraid of meeting anyone's gaze. In this study, she also found that he was taking deep, long breaths, and continued to do so all the way up to the tavern.

King Nefion paid for the entirety of the place, so the only people housed there were the guards and their Princes. The taverns surrounding it all seemed to be full to the brim with Kashadon and those trying to monopolize on the royal hunt. The dying afternoon light filled with sounds of life, music, conversation. Everything carried a sort of merriment with it that would have been hard pressed to find in the South.

Arra stretched gratefully after she dismounted the brown beast they'd lent her. She hated riding. Everything ached after the journey, and the animals didn't smell all that great. Their stink clung to her skin until she could scrub it to a vicious clean. She knew she wouldn't get the chance to, at least not for a while. The retainers that accompanied them rushed about to unload things, the guards moving to get settled, and their Princes decided to grab drinks. Seeing as her own room would probably be the last to be prepared, and the fact that she was in sore need of one, she stayed for a round.

"Go easy, Ez. It's still daylight out," Prince Avis said as Arra settled in at their table. Somehow, her Prince had been designated to pour, though he was the youngest in their current company. He handled the black jar of liquor like a familiar lover, filling cups faster than she could blink. Prince Avis accepted his, sipping at it like a cup of tea, while Prince Kalin knocked his back with a grimace and pushed the empty glass toward Ezran once more.

None of the guards gathered joined in their party's drinking. Ser Drestas, who sat next to Prince Avis on the end, stared out at the room like one of the royal guards would get the sudden idea to attack his charge. The one that accompanied her and Kyrith to the North took a seat across from him, watching Ezran pour like he was monitoring the intake. And the last, the tallest out of the three, didn't sit at all. He lorded above them with crossed arms and a beautiful Kashadon ax on his back.

Like every guard she'd come across since stepping foot into North Akadon, he was watching her as much as protecting the royal family. Arra knew when people were monitoring her moves. The Southern guards were much better at hiding it than their Northern counterparts, too. It left her to wonder if it was the Captain's orders or the King's.

"Lady Enryn?"

Her attention returned to the table. Ezran held out a cup, offering it with a raised brow of question. She cast her wary gaze about and caught a few cutting glares from around the room. Accepting, Arra downed it quickly to chase away her nerves, the liquor smooth and mellow on her tongue. She glanced up when she felt eyes on her and found near every gaze of the surrounding men studying for a reaction.

"Yes?" she asked, the word sharpened by her discomfort. Prince Kalin broke out into a smile as Ezran sat back, an impressed look coming across his features.

"This is strong liquor for someone not used to it," Ezran responded. "We didn't expect you to be able to drink it so easily."

Arra knitted her brow. This was strong liquor for them? "You clearly haven't had Southern spirits." Kyrith let out a short breath next to her, which counted as a laugh. A half smile crept onto her lips and she shot it his way.

"Kyrith, then?" Ezran asked. He held out another cup, but Kyr made no move toward it.

"I don't."

The Princes once again seemed shocked, but this time it was paired by a sparing glance from Ser Vynlier and Ser Drestas. Seeing as every Nefion at the table had a drink besides him, which also included the Southern Prince, she didn't think that abstaining from alcohol was exactly a family trait.

"Alright." Ezran downed the cup himself. "I'm glad I talked the Queen into letting us go."

"You?" Prince Kalin scoffed as he accepted another drink. "Sol was the one that convinced her. You nearly made her solidify her decision to keep us home."

"I admit, good Sol, your introductory speech did help. But I firmly believe that it was my ingenious oratory that got us where we are today!" Ezran said with dramatic, emphasizing taps of his finger along the table. The guard seemed unperturbed, almost used to such behavior.

So like Marek in looks, and yet so unlike him in personality. It confounded her every time. She couldn't imagine him acting like this in South Akadon. How had one Prince come out so cruel, so vicious, and his brother so... different?

At that, her mind drifted to the letter. Arra cursed herself, realizing she'd left it back in her room at the Sun Palace. After never finding a moment when Ezran was parted from Prince Kalin, she'd let it drop to the back of her mind. Here would have been a perfect place to get him alone. She'd find some time, she vowed, before her two months were up.

"Now that we are here," Arra interrupted, taking an offered cup and examining it as she spoke, "what do we do? How do Northern hunts work, exactly?"

"Well, first, we drink," Ezran said, tipping another cup back. Ser Vynlier grabbed the jar from him after and settled it down with a pointed thunk.

"Most of the time we would already have an idea of what to look for," Prince Avis took up, "but we are to hunt Sae Hyura, so we won't have much information. Some will go in blindly and hope for the best, since there are so many hunting parties here. However, we have a duty to the people, so we will ask around for signs of unsettled shades or daemons that have managed to get free of the forest's borders first, before we go in ourselves."

Ezran made a noise, laying the side of his head on the table and lifting his lip in disapproval. "All the good hunting will be done if we ask around."

"Then it will be perfect for you when we get there! You can be a big Kashadon and settle some shades all by yourself!" Prince Kalin said, getting a playful glare from Ezran.

"I'm not the one that needs help settling shades, you pompous ass—"

"Enough," said Prince Avis, shaking his head. "Please, forgive them, Lady Enryn. If you spend enough time with the pair, you will eventually get used to their antics."

Arra shifted in her seat as she noticed a few seasoned guards cast glances in her direction, including Ser Vynlier. None of them were amiable or curious, either.

Enryn. Never had her name made her feel so unsafe. In South Akadon, it was a prideful title, something like a shield, especially when it came to Marek. But here? It seemed like a punishable offense just to bear it.

"Arra," she heard herself say. Everyone glanced at her with questions in their eyes, but she only cared for one. Locking gazes with Kyrith, she sought security in his understanding. "Lady Enryn is a bit too formal, especially if we are to hunt together. Arra will do."

"Arra, then." Prince Avis smiled and she nodded in return, lowering her attention to her cup. "I suppose it is a bit inconvenient to keep referring to everyone's titles when addressing them. Should we forego them for the hunt?"

"Why not?" Ezran said. Prince Kalin nodded as well, finishing his third cup of liquor by that point. Everyone turned their expectant gazes to Kyrith.

He stared at the table, completely lost in thought even

though he had been present only moments before. Arra wanted to give him a flat look, but refrained. Something had to be bothering him.

"Kyr?"

He jerked upward and glanced at her before anyone else. Flicking his gaze quickly between the gathered, he clenched his hands under the table. "My apologies."

"There's no need to apologize," Avis said. "We thought it would be to everyone's benefit if we dropped our titles. Are you alright with it?"

Kyrith looked almost relieved and the barest hint of it colored his tone. "Yes."

"Excellent!" Ezran declared. Arra turned back to him as his fingers drummed against the table, energy infecting him. Another sharp difference. Ezran seemed to need constant motion, constant change, where Marek used his stillness like a threat. "Anyone care to stroll the streets? Might as well, if we are going to spend all our time gathering information. Get the lay of the land and all."

"I will be turning in for the night." Avis chuckled at the barb. "Make sure you all get some rest if you do decide to go out."

"Kal?" He turned and the Prince shrugged.

"It was a long ride. I think I'll stay back, too."

Ezran made a desperate noise in the back of his throat. "Kyrith? You aren't going to turn me down now, are you? Lad—Arra?"

She traded a look with Kyr, something passing between them without words needed. They reached an agreement and, like always, she was designated to speak. "Alright. Sounds fun."

Without a word, Kyrith got up and pushed his chair back into place. She really did have to work with him on conversing in royal company. Then again, she reminded herself, he was a Prince. He could do as he pleased in the North.

They left the other Nefion Princes, accompanied only by Ser Maisym as they wandered through the streets. People stared as they passed. It made her nervous at first, but then she noticed very few were actually acknowledging *her*—instead, they were staring at Kyrith. Mainly, his twin swords, and then his face, looking at him like something wasn't quite right. Did they even know they had a living third Prince?

"This way," Ezran said, pulling her from her thoughts. She followed him through the busy streets, getting hopelessly lost in the throng. Yet, he seemed like he was born on these particular cobbles, treading with confidence and a smile that wasn't cruel.

Kyrith fell back behind her, walking along with the guard like it was where he belonged. Arra didn't drag him forward, even though she itched to have his familiar presence by her side. If it made him more comfortable to stay back, she wouldn't pressure him. Not here, at least.

The markets came up suddenly, bursting forth into avenues dressed with color and vibrant people. Arra smiled despite herself, allowing Ezran to lead her forward through the wares and packed crowd. They passed shop after shop of everything one could ever need on a hunt. She found herself getting lost once the commonplace things began to crop up. She couldn't glean the meaning of the sigils carved into the things around her, from combs, to bracelets, to random stones. It didn't make sense to her why such trivial items bore the sacred symbols in the first place. The North was very odd.

"What do you all use this for?" she asked, picking up a

tablet carved with Northern runes. Ezran glanced at it and shrugged.

"Some give them as gifts, others find some use for them. That there is a concentration stone. It helps you focus, especially when you run your thumb over the sigil. Sol actually makes them if you find yourself interested. Could save you a few escs."

Daring to cast a glance back, she caught the look that came over the guard as he stood with a tense Kyrith a pace away. She figured the son of General Maisym was more likely to shatter his greatsword than do anything kind for the likes of her. Especially after the confrontation with Duke Somir.

Running from those thoughts, Arra set the stone down and picked up a fine bristle hairbrush, studying a golden symbol carved on its back. "And this? Do you settle the shades here by brushing their hair?"

Ezran laughed, full and loud. It surprised her to hear it and almost startled her into a smile.

"No. These are usually given by Kashadon to their lovers, as a sign of their affection. This symbol invokes protection. It's commonly put on gifts or everyday things. Do you not do the same in South Akadon?"

"There's no need." She put the brush down. Moving on, Arra took in the endless array of white stone pendants that hung from the rack above her head, plucking a few from their space to inspect their foreign symbols. "We paint blood sigils on the posts of our houses, doors, and a repelling circle in the center room that wards off negative energies. We don't need protection symbols on everything we own."

Ezran paused before he picked up some different hairpins, studying the gold and then the jade. "Blood sigils?"

"Yes." Arra tilted the pendant toward him, showing off the runes and lines inside. "Like these, but ours have more... edges, I guess. There are more lines, shapes, and characters. There are few round edges in them, unless they're circles instead of sigils. You draw them in blood or you cut them into skin to bind the magic to purpose. They're powerful, and last for a few weeks, or until the body heals."

Ezran looked from the pendant to her, glancing away. He pressed his lips together and settled on a hairpin, paying for it without another word.

They trailed down the streets a bit more, stopping here and there to admire something. Despite answering all her remaining questions, Ezran didn't further ask her about South Akadon. He pointed out some of the more recurring sigils, including clarity, strength, and protection. Ezran spoke, too, of the ones for the elements, resilience, healing. Above all, the most popular had to be the inter-locking circles and lines meant for balance. It was dizzying to gaze at for too long, endless connections and interruptions, but it did carry a sort of equilibrium to the makeup of it all.

Eventually, they reached the end of the streets, with Ezran being the only one to purchase anything among the group. Not that Arra didn't want to. Several of the items for sale were both beautiful and intriguing, but she doubted Marek would take kindly to her returning with a trunk full of Northern things.

Her stomach twisted sickeningly with the reminder. Looking for any sort of distraction to keep her mind off her task, she glanced around the tail end of the market. More stalls than shops seemed to reside there. Large common weaponry met her eye, along with giant slabs of stone, carved cobbles, and crude hunks of metal yet to be forged. "Let's walk a bit farther. I would like to see your metals."

Ezran lifted a brow at her, but he didn't protest as he led them through the street to the proper stalls. "Most of these are for people looking to expand their homes and such. They can buy cobbles and stones carved with symbols of their choosing, for a bit of added protection. If they have coin for it."

Arra nodded, her eyes glancing over the stones before her. Some of the stalls even offered large hunks of precious gems, glittering in the lantern light as the sun faded. She stopped her head from shaking but couldn't keep her features from betraying her thoughts. Did they really have such things out in the open? Did people really buy them for their homes, to shine and show off? Exuding wealth was a quick way to die in South Akadon, unless one had the strength and power to defend it. Even then, how long could someone hold out?

Kyrith was impassive when he walked by the stalls, only casting sparing glances. But as he drifted closer to one laden with crude, shining metals and precious stones, something caught his eye. Arra followed to inspect all the wares. Some were polished and carved already, going from bricks to thin pendants meant to fit in someone's palm. Kyr came close to one, a whitish looking thing that had an iridescent sheen to it and a stark black sigil carved in its center.

"Ah, yes!" The merchant appeared in an instant, smelling the opportunity for a sale. The metals drew Arra in, ranging from black to solid grey to a near white. "This is a spirit stone! Blessed and made by a genuine spirit wielder in the Temple of Aescian, a rare find. It helps give you an extra boost in magic! Long lasting, too, I swear by the Gods."

Kyrith stepped back so quickly that it seemed the merchant had threatened him in some way. Arra lifted her head with worry, flicking her gaze between the two. He really was that fearful of people, wasn't he?

"Kyrith, what do you think about this?" she asked, giving him an out. Both Kyrith and the confused merchant turned to her as she pointed to a chunk of white silver. The metal shimmered in the dim light of the lanterns, the call of magic much stronger than any around it.

"Ah, Cynian silver! Excellent choice, my Lady. It was pulled from the Asba Mountains and transported straight from Caeles! Strongest there is for Kashadon weaponry, but it makes a fine crafting metal as well," the merchant said. She didn't spare him a glance. Her attention was strictly on Kyrith as he looked it over, turning it this way and that with careful hands.

"It'll hold," he murmured. A smile spilled across Arra's face as she turned to the merchant.

"I'll take it."

CHAPTER
TWENTY-SEVEN

K yrith counted the chairs. It was the only thing he could allow himself to focus on as Ezran, Kalin, and Avis tried to get information. There were so many people around them. Everywhere he turned there were hunters with weapons strapped on their hips and backs, their spirits all so varied. He could sense their disparate magics, and their emotions that came with it, from nervous, to wary, arrogant, even excited. It was all so loud, so confusing.

He counted tables. Glasses. Heartbeats. He whispered numbers, fixing his gaze to the floor.

They had been at this for the better part of the morning, traveling from tavern to tavern and shop to shop to speak with locals, hunters, and everything in between. So far, the Princes found nothing substantial enough to get them to head out yet.

"I can't believe they have to actively search out hunts," Arra muttered to him. He lifted his gaze for the briefest moment, but her attention was on Ezran as he let out an easy laugh at the bar. A group of Kashadon surrounded him, all chuckling and smiling along with him. Kyrith looked down once again. He counted cracks in the table, in the floor. One by one, two by two, three by three...

He didn't know how long they stood there, but it was too long for his comfort. By midday, Ezran was the only one to find anything worthwhile.

Somewhere to the northeast, there was a particular valley in the woods that had caused some distress to the locals. People reported hearing strange noises, mainly in the night, along with a persistent and unseasonable fog. Regular forest animals fled from the place. Yet, when local Kashadon went to investigate, they found nothing but a cave. No bodies. Just a few shades that were handled quickly, so they thought the problem settled. However, commoners still reported the noises and fog.

Seeing as it was probably a collection of small shades causing trouble, Avis stayed back to search for other incidents that might require their attention. Ezran and Kalin decided to go. Kyrith went along too, eager to escape from the crowds.

He settled more when they got into the forest, accompanied by Arra, Solris, Ser Vynlier, and a retainer Kyrith heard them call Genn. He let his black horse trail behind them for the most part. Arra stuck by his side, like usual, and Solris took up the space by his other flank as they traveled on.

Despite not knowing him all too well, Kyrith was grateful for it. He had a particular spirit that came as a comfort. It was strong like Arra's, but not so inflexible. More peaceful, calm like Avis', but not as quiet, in a way. It burned, bright and true, a soothing kind of light like a hearth fire in a dark Southern winter. It always seemed balanced, steady, unwavering. It anchored him when his own spirit had been a storm, a chaotic wildfire that threatened to tear through him completely. Despite the shame of Solris finding him in such an unsettled state, and the danger that came along with it, he couldn't help but be thankful for what he did after. He'd never had someone help him like that before, besides Arra.

The wood they rode through was content, colorful, and didn't have a heavy energy hanging over the trees. While the autumn wind wasn't exactly warm, it was far from the chill that swept perpetually through the South from the moment summer ended to when it began again. It settled his spirit further, so that the longer they rode, the more Kyrith relaxed.

They almost turned back, certain they'd received misinformation. Just when Kalin began to suggest such a thing, a shade flickered in and out through the trees, almost as if it were beckoning them. They fell to the bait, the group slipping off their horses and tying them up till the job was done.

The shade wasn't a powerful one at all. It was barely a troublesome thing, and it wouldn't have been able to do serious harm to a living being for a long time. It could break things, like bowls or glass, rattle window panes, slam doors, but it was rather innocuous besides. *Askef* didn't even grant a warning to him. Kalin banished it with a single lazy sweep of his glaive.

"If that was the only thing causing all these rumors to spread, I'm going to be very disappointed," Ezran said. He walked with his hand on the hilt of his sword, a giant thing that was clearly quite powerful. With caution left behind, he stalked forward with determined steps and Kalin came to his side in a way born of familiarity. Kyrith set his jaw against the aching sense of something lost.

"If these are what normal Northern hunts consist of, I will be too," Arra whispered to him. His lip twitched upwards for a brief moment as he followed his twin, eyes ever wary for any sign of danger.

They met three more shades of the same threat level, taken care of by Ezran or Kalin with casual swipes of their weapons. By that time, the sun warned of oncoming night by sinking low in the sky, and it didn't seem like anything bigger was going to show up.

Yet, Kyrith sensed something was off. Nothing unusual met his eye, but it was like a scent in the air, subtle and unassuming. His neck prickled. Something wasn't right about this place. Something, somewhere, was calling, an echo on the wind...

Askef's power began to swell just as the fog they'd been told about rolled in on the same breeze. It filled the valley and settled between the two slopes of jagged hills. Kyrith pulled his sword free as Solris put his hand on his own weapon.

"Finally," Ezran said. Unafraid, he moved forward and pulled the rest of the party with him.

Kalin spun his glaive in his hand with a lazy motion. "Think Avis is going to be sore about missing out on this?"

"Not unless we find something big," Ezran replied. "Even if we don't, we should say we did, just to make him jealous."

Kalin laughed, a sound that pulled on Kyrith's memory so sharply that his chest ached. He remembered that boyish sound. Sometimes, he'd hear it in his dreams, a distant place he could never return to again. But now it was before him and was dragging something from the depths of his mind, where he stored away all the things that once made him happy.

A story told on gentle lips, though he couldn't remember if it was their mother or a governess. Still, he listened intently beside Kalin as she wove the tale of the inseparable first twins, Nirat and Aonai, his shadow made flesh. The Gods themselves gave such a gift and always blessed twins in such ways. Enthralled, he turned to his brother, so bright and shining even at that age.

"I'm your shadow, Kal."

Kyrith pushed away the memories before anything else could come of them. He focused instead on *Askef*, who was getting more unsettled the further they went. The blade began to shine out in a dull fashion, a red glow coloring the surrounding mist. The fog was thick, yet nothing came through it. Still, blue light lit Ezran's blade as well, and both *Chylus* and Ser Vynlier's ax shook in their owners' grips.

The cave loomed up from the fog like a giant, gaping mouth. Though he was a few paces from it, the terrible, opaque darkness echoed with tenebrous energy. He hadn't expected to find something with such intensity in the North.

A shade hovered in front of the cave like a guardian. It didn't move as they approached, keeping its head and limbs hanging down, which covered its face with a wispy curtain of hair. *Askef* flared with light and flickered with its fire.

"Here we go," Ezran said with a smile, lifting his own azure blade up as it burned. Kalin took up his other side, shifting his form back and forth as he waited.

The shade raised its head slowly, revealing pits where its eyes should have been. Pale, colorless skin stretched over what appeared to be a skeleton, though it left its corporeal body behind long ago. The mouth spilled open as it moved, too wide for a human, as if the shade didn't have the ability to close it. A swollen, black tongue swung out like a long whip and Kyrith's grip tightened on his sword. His breath caught, aching on his ribcage.

Quick as lightning, the shade lashed out, flinging its tongue as a weapon at them. Kyrith dodged out of the way and cut his sword downward. *Askef's* flame caught on the blow meant for him. It sliced through, severing the tongue in half to let the fallen portion burn away. The shade wailed as it brought the charred stump back. Thick, black tears fell from the pits of its eyes. Its features twisted, pain and wrath taking up equal measures. Clawed hands disappeared inside its unhinged mouth, pawing at its tongue to stifle the burned remains.

Ezran swung his sword through the air. Blue fire caught the shade around its midsection and sent it tumbling back into the darkness. Their prey screamed out an unearthly noise, scraping into the ears of all that would listen.

The shade folded in on itself, still screaming, as most of its body caught fire in the cave's mouth. Members of the group winced at the sounds, and even Kyrith's face twitched.

"Someone kill it, please, by the Gods," Kalin begged, pressing his hands over his ears. Ser Vynlier stepped forward.

He didn't get far. As soon as he was away from the group, the burning shade flung itself outward. It spun, a mass of fire and mist and claws, throwing itself at them as a collective. Ser Vynlier caught the ferocious ball with his ax. It sunk onto the blade, down to the shoulder even, but it didn't seem to matter. The shade's arms shot out from its misty mass, launching for Kalin on one side and Kyrith on the other.

Kyrith didn't get to see how his brother reacted as his chest tightened. He caught the clawed hand on his sword and dodged once again, fire blazing up the arm. It reached for him as it burned, then for Arra, who dealt her own blow. The cut leaked dark mist into the air, which was the best it was going to do.

Solris was there a moment later, bringing *Chylus* down in a calculated, violent attack. The arm severed at the elbow, white fire joining the red and blue. With all three burning through it, the shade was gone in a cloud of smoke mere moments later. Kyrith snapped his gaze around to see his brother unharmed, his short black curls spilling over his forehead as he smiled. He exhaled his relief.

"Avis is going to be ridiculously jealous if we find any more of those. Let's go." Kalin dashed towards the mouth of the cave with Ezran, which made Ser Vynlier run after them with a sigh. The rest of the party followed, though at a much more manageable jog, until they caught up.

Inside, the first opponent they encountered was the cave's unyielding tenebrosity. It was only the light radiating off of the three swords that even allowed them to move forward, red and blue and white clashing together on the stone walls.

"Convenient," Arra said, walking closely beside him, "to have three of you."

"Kal could do better. He simply doesn't enjoy showing off," Ezran replied, his voice echoing off the dark stone as they ventured forward.

Kalin let out an embarrassed chuckle. "Ez, it's not that much better."

"Really? What's not that much better?" Arra asked. Kyrith only half listened. Something about the stone was off and it kept pulling at his attention the further they went. It was smooth, and so was the rock at their feet. It wasn't exactly what he imagined a natural cave to be.

"Go on. Show 'em," Ezran said. A sigh followed, and a moment later Kyrith was blinking as light blinded him.

His lips parted as his eyes were slow to adjust. Golden rays spilled everywhere, bathing everything in radiance. The light came from his brother's glaive. Its blades flared a brilliant white, burning like the sun on a summer solstice. He blinked at Kalin in surprise.

"I'm impressed. I've never seen magic like that," said Arra.

"It runs only in the Nefion line," Kalin responded, sheepish. "A gift from Aescian himself, to show his favor. That's what they say, anyway."

Kyrith glanced away from the group. He didn't know that. A Nefion himself, and he didn't know that about his own family's heritage. Careful to keep his emotions off his face, he strode forward as Arra and the others continued to converse about it. Light. The magic was light. A fitting gift from the Sunbringer.

The tunnel they found themselves in was utterly smooth, too much so to be a natural occurrence. There weren't even rocks on the floor, or formations anywhere. Everything was a pristine, uniform grey, without water pooling, or plants, or indentations of any kind.

Kyrith turned his head as the tunnel widened into a small chamber, Kalin's magic casting long shadows on the walls. *Eokor* throbbed, so sudden and insistent that he pulled it from its sheath as he glanced around. Solris was there in an instant, following along. Both of them examined the darkness of the room, turning in slow, opposite circles. Nothing came out to attack them. But, as he turned with his swords in either hand, *Askef's* fire lit up one of the chamber's corners. A pile of reeking shed laid there, its scales an oily black.

Kyrith pressed his lips together. "Arra..."

His low tones echoed around the stone, amplifying until they reached the rest of the group. They came forward and Kalin's magic banished any shadows from the chamber. Arra wrinkled her nose at the sight. "Wonderful."

"What is it?" Ezran asked, poking at the skin with his sword. Fire from it caught on the scales, singeing them.

"Haubast daemon. They appear like giant snakes, but they have fins that fan out and rattle when they attack. They can shoot barbs from them, and spit acid, along with being exceptionally quick," she said.

"Excellent," Ezran grimaced. "How dangerous are they?"

"Depends on size," Kyrith said, "number..."

He cast his gaze about the chamber, eyes catching on a darkened path on the far end. Something... was pulling at him. Whispering to him from the shadow. The echo on the wind.

"This one isn't that big," Arra took up, "but it could be part of a nest, which means there will be more mature ones."

"Where are their hearts?" asked Solris. Kyrith dared to flick his gaze to him for a fleeting moment. A sort of determination settled on his fine features, a clear goal blazing in his green eyes. Kyrith looked toward the path again and took a few steps away from everyone else, needing the space.

Arra went on to answer. "In the center of their bodies. Cutting them in half is the best way to kill them. The older they are, though, the larger they become, and the tougher their scales. Some of the ancient ones have to be flipped on their stomachs to be disposed of."

"Perhaps we should return," Master Genn said. "Gather some more hunters to take care of this."

Ezran argued, "We have seven Kashadon. We should be able to handle it. Right, Kal?"

Kyrith stepped closer to the path, peering into the dark. *Eokor* trembled softly in his hand, but it was rapidly increasing its urgency. The energy in the air began to shift, pitching like a fall from a cliff's face. It called to him. Something in the tunnels overflowed with negativity in its spirit, and it was powerful. A headache spiked through his temple as its acrimony rippled over him.

"What do you think, Arra? Kyrith?"

His brother's voice pulled him back from the overwhelming wave, lapping at his core as it tried to turn its balance. He put *Askef's* hilt to his temple, taking a breath and cursing. The sigil wasn't working. They all needed to leave, but Kyrith's churning spirit made it far more pressing for him.

"There's no way to tell how many there are in a nest until you find it. The more hunters you have, the better," Arra said. Kyrith couldn't respond over his temple's throb.

"Are you alright?" a soft voice asked. Kyrith glanced up to find that Solris had wandered over to him. He asked so low that none of the rest of the group had heard.

"Headache," he said. "We should—"

Pain seared through his head as something screeched. Weapons rattled, *Eokor* included, and the sibilance of scales on stone joined in the symphony a second later. He whipped around to see two eyes growing larger, reflecting the light of Kalin's magic as it came down the path. Those slit pupils were hallmarks of a Haubast, but they were far, far bigger than whatever had shed the skin earlier.

"Go," he said. Everyone but Arra remained frozen.

"Go!" she echoed, loud enough to snap everyone out of their daze. They started for the exit, Ser Vynlier pushing the other Princes ahead of him, but it was too late. The beast was upon them.

It screeched again as Kyrith and Solris dashed for the group. The energy coming off of it was vile. He didn't know what agitated it, exactly, until it attacked. The snakelike head struck with a lightning quick movement, jaws snapping together with a deafening crack. It aimed for Kalin, but caught the stone of the tunnel instead.

It didn't like his magic.

Kyrith and Solris were nearly under the beast by the time it struck. The rest of their party made it into the tunnel, including Arra. The daemon reared back with a hiss, shaking dust from its snout as it tried to find the light source again. It fanned out the red fins on either side of its head and body, a distinct rattle filling the chamber.

Under it, the sharp crack of stone filled Kyrith's ears. His eyes snapped up to the impact, where smooth grey fissured far too quickly. They wouldn't make it. Instinct alone drove him then, tackling Solris back as rock fell and plunged them into darkness.

CHAPTER

TWENTY-EIGHT

S ol's breath left him as his back slammed into the ground, darkness plunging around them as suddenly as Prince Kal's light chased it away. Under the clatter of rock, the daemon's rattle rose to fill his ears, along with Kyrith's ragged panting.

His Prince saved his life. He expected something like this situation to happen, eventually, but he always thought it would be him saving one of the Nefions. Not the other way around.

As the dust settled, the little light they had in the chamber now flickered red and white from their Kashadon swords. It cast an eerie contrast on Kyrith's face as he forced himself up, settling over Sol. What breath was left in his lungs caught and held. Those Nefion features contorted into concern and were so close that Sol could see every detail of his dust covered scars.

"Are you okay?" he asked, voice thick with the debris in the air.

Sol didn't trust his own just yet, so he nodded. His

Prince was quick to get to his feet and stood, swaying a bit as he faced the daemon.

Sol rolled onto his side and forced in air, only to find his lungs full of dust. He heaved in and out, trying to recover quickly. How Kyrith wasn't coughing he didn't know. Getting onto his hands and knees, he spit the grit from his mouth and reached a hand out, searching without looking for his sword. In response, almost as if it were calling to guide him, *Chylus* rattled against the floor and flared ever brighter with its blessed fire.

If Kyrith looked sinister, the daemon was a nightmare gifted by Nakre. The sight made Sol mutter a prayer of protection to Kanah as his hand found his weapon's hilt. The scarlet glow of the Prince's sword was closer, making the beast seem like it bathed in blood. Its stark underbelly became a tempting target as it reared back, eyes flashing in the light, and shook out its vermilion fins as a warning. Gaping jaws opened to reveal black fangs, not like a snake's at all. No, it had rows of teeth, sticking out at every angle and all sharpened to a razor's edge. Sol was sure that if they caught even the edge of skin, it would leave a vicious wound in its wake.

He lurched to his feet beside Kyrith. His mind worked to remember everything Lady Arra said about the beast. Clearly, it was an old daemon, large with its years. Sol guessed they'd have to get it on its back to get at the heart.

But where was the center? The thing was gigantic, curled in on itself much like a defensive serpent would. How big was its heart? How were they going to get it on its back?

"Down!" Kyrith ordered and Sol dropped. Barbs flew past his head and hit the rock behind him. No, not just hit, but *buried* themselves inside of it.

What did it have? Barbs and acid?

And speed. That was clear. It had only taken the beast seconds to slither down the tunnel and cause the collapse.

Kyrith was on his feet again before Sol could blink. He sent cut after cut of fire towards the daemon, illuminating the tight space in a bloody glow. Magic burst on the daemon's underbelly, but broke apart like water over rock. It barely left a scorch mark in its wake.

It dawned on Sol, then. He'd seen *Askef* burn a shade before. *Eokor* must've been the blade that dealt with daemons, yet it only had blood magic fused within it, and thus couldn't send out arcs of power like the other Kashadon gifts could. *Askef* had fire, but it dealt with shades alone. Still, a blessed weapon was far better than a regular one in their current situation.

Chylus was a blade that could burn through both. Sol sent his own magic out in wide arcs, mimicking Kyrith's quick movements as best he could with his heavier sword. White fire slammed into the daemon and cut deep, charring its soft underbelly.

The serpentine thing screeched loud enough to deafen. It slammed its body down, slithering the length of the chamber to get behind them. Sol slashed as it passed. He could only get a few hits in before the thing splayed its fins, catching him in the leg.

He hissed and drew back as Kyrith came close. The Prince's blade glanced off scale and ripped down one fin. Barbs broke against the sword with harsh cracks. As the daemon slithered, it tore *Eokor* down further and further along the stretches of ruddy membrane. Sol came up beside the fetid wound and tried his best to aim for the streak of black blood.

Some of the fire landed and burned through the

daemon, causing it to contort its body with a sharp motion.
Both Sol and Kyrith dodged to opposite sides, narrowly
avoiding teeth. It reared back, hissing as it aimed for him
alone, content to ignore the other for now. Instead of dodg-
ing, he carved *Chylus* up at the last second before stepping
out of its path.

The blade caught under its jaw with a solid crack,
burning flesh and slamming teeth together hard enough to
shatter. Its head snapped backward and the body followed,
rolling once. Sol's heart seized.

Kyrith descended from nowhere. *Eokor* slammed into
the red flash of its underbelly and jerked viciously through
it. Sol expected a spray of blood from such a violent motion,
but none came. However, he had no time to dwell on the
oddly bloodless affair. The creature rolled free a heartbeat
later with a screech that vibrated in Sol's teeth.

Kyrith hadn't hit the heart.

The daemon dove for the Prince. Sol slung an arc of fire
towards it, catching its eye before it caused any harm to
him. It burned, a flare of bright white that ate through soft
tissue insatiably. All that was left was a charred ember. An
eerie dim glow in the darkness when compared to its reflective pairing.

A gurgling made Sol's stomach turn. He didn't need
Kyrith to warn him. His feet moved before he realized it.
Trying to throw off the daemon, he ran for its blind side.

A stream of putrid acid followed, sizzling as it made
contact with rock. Drops landed on his legs. Ate through his
clothes and skin before he could take the breath to cry out.
It burned like magma. Searing. Ceaseless. It took everything
inside him to choke down his scream and keep moving,
keep pushing on, as the spray continued to follow.

Kyrith lit up the chamber with bloody slashes. The

daemon turned toward him with the last of its acid dribbling free, rattling a warning with what fins were left, a patchwork of what had been in the beginning. Sol dropped to the ground and forced himself not to grab at his wounds. If he got any of the acid on his hands, he wouldn't be able to hold *Chylus*. As skilled as Kyrith was, he doubted he could take on this beast alone.

After the rain of barbs, Sol staggered to his feet. The daemon, focused on the Prince, left its flank ripe and open for attack. He rushed forward and mimicked Kyrith's moves as much as he could. *Chylus* cut through the fin as he quickly staggered down the length of the beast. Snaps of shattered barbs accompanied hissing flames as they burned up the thin membrane, until it reached the hardened scales of its body and guttered out.

The daemon whipped around, frantic as it slithered. The only fins it had left were by its head and the great ridge along its back, which kept flaring and retracting like a sail. He realized too late that the daemon was masking the sound of its rattle by scraping its scales along the stone wall. It halted as quickly as it had begun the erratic motion and whipped its head around with a force that should have broken its neck. Barbs tore through the air. He ducked, but not soon enough. One lodged itself into his abdomen as he screamed, hitting stone.

"Solris!"

Pushing himself up with his elbow, he placed a shaking hand around the barb and pressed his lips together against the vile ache. It was deep, but it hadn't hit anything important. He had to get up.

It took all of his will to force himself onto his knees, but he did so, and used *Chylus'* shuddering blade to get to his feet. Kyrith tried his best to keep the daemon focused on him. He sent arcs of flame toward its face, then slashed with *Eokor* every time it lunged for him. The blades, as powerful as they were, weren't heavy like *Chylus*. They wouldn't be strong enough to get the beast to roll again.

The daemon gurgled once more. Kyrith gave up the offensive and began a mad dash around the chamber, barely ahead of the acid's jet as it splashed the walls behind him. The beast followed, slithering quickly after the Prince.

Sol cut *Chylus* upward and hissed at a vicious lance of pain. Magic shot out and caught the daemon's side, slamming it back. It screeched as the vulnerable side of its neck burned. The force of the blow caused it to reveal only part of its underbelly, but it was all Sol needed.

He sent arc after arc of fire at the thing, keeping it pinned, burning and writhing all the while. Kyrith dashed forward with *Eokor*, slamming it down to the hilt a fraction higher than he had before. He carved the blade through the beast and gutted it as much as he could with a sharp motion of precise violence.

The daemon writhed. Screamed. Then finally, it relaxed.

Sol let out an exhale at the same time the daemon gave a death rattle. The prayer of thanks that left him was filled with relief. He dropped to his knee again as *Chylus* settled enough to stop shaking.

Glaring at the blade like it could see such a thing, he whispered, "Still not satisfied? Or are there more?"

The sword didn't answer, as expected, but he still sighed as if it had. Kyrith appeared by his side, kneeling and searching over him for the extent of the damage. He was a mess. Cuts covered his face from close calls, and one side had splashes of daemon blood adding another layer to the muck. Yet, even that couldn't hide the concern which etched itself across his face. His brow furrowed, face open and unmasked, almost gentle.

"Are you alright?" he asked.

Chylus' light battled with *Askef's* on his face, flickering over the sharp planes of his cheekbones and jaw. Sol glanced down at the barb in his abdomen and gave a weak, pained laugh.

"I'm fine," Sol said as he laid back. The Prince was careful but firm as he pulled Sol's hand away from the wound. "Just a prick, that's all. Some burns. Some scratches."

Kyrith took a deep, even breath. Worry left him and was replaced with that intense observation he was so prone to. He assessed each wound one by one despite Sol's trembling, deciding to start with the barb.

"I need you to hold *Chylus* here," Kyrith directed. Sol shifted so that the white light of his sword spilled over him. Kyrith's hands didn't shake at all when one wrapped around the barb and the other pushed down on his muscle, making him bite back a groan. In his normal low timbre, he continued, "It's hooked on the end. Normally, it's best to push the whole thing through if you can, but where it is..."

"You'll hit something if you do," Sol finished for him as he glanced down, teeth clenched. He could practically see the anatomy under his skin and winced at the prospect. It was better to focus on that than how cold he was becoming. Kyrith may be able to heal him, but not fast enough to stop something from leaking and causing more problems than they could deal with in their current situation. The only solution was to rip the hook out.

Sol fished out his pendant with his free hand, the metal insignia of the royal guard on one side, a strength sigil on the other. He bit down on it and laid back, nodding at Kyrith.

He was quick and strong, that was certain. One moment the barb was there, and then it was gone with a rough jerk. Sol choked out a cry, teeth nearly breaking on the metal as Kyrith hurried to lift his coat and expose it to the air. Blood wept over his side in thick rivulets as his wound ached, sharp and unrelenting. He forced himself to breathe slowly and deeply as his body shook. Kyrith pressed his hand over the gaping hole, closing his eyes.

Blood magic hurt with healing. A wound went through every stage in mere moments, accompanied with the pain of such a thing. It was like he had been punctured by the barb again, which then dulled to a horrid ache, and finally a vicious itch that marked the nearing end. By the time he finished, it was nothing but an echoing rawness of what once was.

Kyrith healed his leg next, which wasn't nearly as agonizing. The Prince let him have a brief break before he had him roll onto his side. The burns were by far the worst of it. Sol strangled another cry by biting down hard on his pendant, hands shaking into fists as *Chylus* flared brighter with his anguish. Gasping once it faded from the burning violence, Sol tried to get his pulse down to a reasonable pace and whispered another prayer. It was over, for now.

Exhausted, Sol forced himself to sit up and face Kyrith. Grey eyes studied him in the twin light, like he thought Sol might collapse at any moment. "Better?"

"Better," he said. "What about you? Are you hurt beyond..." He gestured to his face. The Prince turned to the side and shook his head.

"I'm fine." Kyrith didn't look at Sol again.

"I can heal those."

Kyrith's mask drifted back into place and he set his jaw. "It's alright. Best to let lessons heal on their own. Thank you, Solris."

"I should be the one thanking you." Sol laughed, though his exhaustion and pain made it soft. Kyrith shook his head again, but he caught the glance he cheated his way.

"There's no need."

Silence spilled around them once more. Sol flicked his eyes towards the daemon as *Chylus* pulsed. "We should move. I'm guessing that thing wasn't the one to leave such a small skin behind. We should see if there's another exit, or at least a place to wait out for the hunters. Whatever else is in here will probably come to investigate the smell of blood."

Kyrith got to his feet without saying anything, but he held out his hand to help Sol up. He hesitated for a second. Princes didn't offer guards...

But, then again, when had Kyrith ever acted like a Prince around him?

He took his hand and again found a surprise in his strength. It was the barest strain to haul Sol up, though he was more muscular and only a fraction shorter.

"This way."

CHAPTER
TWENTY-NINE

The dust settled slowly. Only when the rock's tumbling ceased did Arra dare move, knowing the tunnel around them could still collapse at any point.

There was still light. That was an excellent sign. She raised a hand to block it and saw Kalin splayed out, a fine layer of debris turning his colorful robes to a muted grey. His glaive lit the swirling dust and his shallow breaths, but at least both wielder and weapon still functioned.

Ezran was next to him, already trying to get to his feet. His sword had skittered off down the tunnel and blazed blue further toward the entrance. His movements were slow as he retrieved it, putting a shaky hand on the wall to guide him.

Two others of their party, Ser Vynlier and Master Genn, scrambled for their bearings as they coughed up dust from their lungs. The guard surged toward his Prince, rolling him onto his back as he began to wheeze as well.

But she didn't see Kyrith. Or the one that was supposed to protect him.

Arra didn't want to turn around. She didn't want to see a hand poking out from the rock, bleeding slowly through its cracks. Yet, her panic didn't allow for hesitation.

There was no hand. No blood staining the new wall of fractured stone. There wasn't Kyrith, either. She couldn't breathe. Scrambling toward the collapse, she placed her hands on it and croaked, "Kyr! Kyrith!"

Her voice was weak as she coughed again, but her hands scrabbled over rock anyway. They tumbled down around her feet, echoing like thunder in the silence.

"Arra, stop," someone wheezed. She didn't care who. They didn't understand.

Someone crawled to her side. Kalin, heaving in heavy air, joined her frantic digging. His voice was much weaker than hers as he said his brother's name repeatedly.

"Stop!"

This time, she recognized the voice as Ezran's.

"Both of you, stop!"

Hands grabbed her. Ser Vynlier pulled Kalin back, securing him even as he fought.

"Kyrith—" He coughed sharply. "He's still—"

"I know," Ezran's voice said next to her ear, laced with the hassle of fighting against her. "That rock is unstable. You move the wrong one and the tunnel could collapse further. You have to stop."

"I can't leave him!" she cried out.

Her training kicked in before she could really think it through, driving a blow into Ezran's side before throwing her weight against him. He cursed and dropped her as he fell back. She raced to the rock again, but Master Genn was there to catch her.

"Listen to me!" Ezran snapped as loud as he dared to. "Kyrith is the most capable out of us, and I'm sure everyone here would agree. Sol is with him. Collapsing the tunnel on top of us is only going to make things worse. If you want to help him, then we have to get back to town and get Avis. Probably more guards, too. But if we keep wasting time, Kyrith might not be able to hold out. Alright?"

Kalin stopped struggling, but he looked at the rock pile with desperation clear in his features. He ripped free of Vyn's grip and grabbed his glaive, stalking toward the entrance before any of them could get another word out. His guard went scrambling after him.

Forced to calm down, Arra realized what she'd done.

She struck an Auberon.

All the color left her face as Ezran's night dark gaze turned to her. She dropped into a full kneel, causing Master Genn to startle and step away from her. "I didn't mean to— I—Please, Prince—"

"Don't worry about it. I've been hit harder and survived," Ezran said as he rubbed his side. "We really can't waste time."

Arra rose, confusion and panic making her head spin. She took a step, and then another, leaving Kyrith behind. Just like she had time and time again to face Marek alone. She couldn't help the tears that spilled over her face.

They quickly made their way out of the cave, following the fading light of Kalin's magic. He was moving at an impressive pace. Ezran kept up beside her, almost like he was worried she was going to take off back down the tunnel.

"The Queen is going to kill me if we get out of this," he muttered. Cutting her gaze to the side, she saw his was set ahead of him. Dirt dusted the side of his worried features. He was talking to himself.

When they reached the forest again, the light faded to a slant that set its trees ablaze. The fog, too, was tinted with gold, and it would have been beautiful if the situation hadn't been so dire. Sunset was a threat to her, knowledge of daemons pulsing in her head. Every Southern Kashadon alive knew that night only increased their powers, as Aescian's Light was reduced to only the Moon he gave his lover. Even that was dependent on how close Odeion held it to her chest.

Kalin came across some low level shades again, drifting along their path. He cut them out of the way with a powerful slash, paired with shouts of frustration. They faded, nothing left of them in a blink. The magic kept going, gouging huge wounds into the trunks of several trees until Arra was sure some would topple.

They had to run to catch up to him fully. His glaive radiated power, trembling in the Prince's tight grip. Ezran grabbed Kalin's shoulder and forced him to slow.

"Kal, you need to calm yourself down," he said, and Arra winced. Those words never did quite work the way they were supposed to.

"My brother is trapped in a daemon infested cave, Ez! I can't calm down! He's just returned and I—I—" Kalin's weapon shook and lashed out, causing the entire party to duck. The Prince dropped the polearm as if it burned him. It singed the surrounding earth. The metal of its blades sang with it, thrumming like a steady forge.

Arra slowly rose. Ezran had both hands on the Prince's shoulders, which made her want to scream at them. They didn't have time for this.

"Take a deep breath and center yourself. Panicking isn't going to help him," Ezran said, then mimicked his suggestion. Kalin was forced to comply. It seemed to take an eternity, yet the magic dimmed in the weapon, its rattle stopping.

"Is everyone okay to ride?" Ezran asked after a moment of tense, too long silence. She nodded along with the other two. "Is anyone hurt?"

"No," Arra answered as she shifted her weight from foot to foot, casting her gaze about the fog. Everything inside her was screaming to go back, to dig a way through and help him. How many times was she going to leave him to the horrors?

They moved through the forest quickly, but they didn't run. Ezran kept the pace. She wanted to push it, to sprint to the horses, but she knew it would only deplete her energy. Arra used every bit of control to force herself to remain at a fast walk with them. She began to pray, even though she knew the Gods' mercy was something so rare that she doubted its existence.

Please, she begged, *please keep him safe. Keep him alive. I owe him.*

The horses were right where they left them. She made for the brown one, but Ezran stopped her with a gentle hand on her shoulder. It still made her flinch, but he didn't seem to catch it.

"Arra, take this one." Ezran held out the reins of the black beast Kyrith had ridden on. She took them with a questioning brow as he hurried to run up her stirrups. "Evaxas is faster than Brasna. You're a faster rider, too. You and Genn will go on ahead of us. Follow him."

"I'm faster?" she asked, allowing him to throw her into the saddle. She settled into it as he checked her stirrups.

"You're the lightest out of us. Less weight on the horse makes it go faster," he said. She fought herself from rolling her eyes skyward.

Nudging the beast forward toward Master Genn, she made to follow as he turned his expertly and spurred it on. She grabbed a fistful of dark mane and drove her heels into the horse's ribs.

The thing took off like she burned its hind end. It charged after the grey horse, legs eating up the ground as if it were flying. She clung on with everything in her, squeezing her legs around its barrel and leaning forward. The horse snorted and tossed its head, but it kept going without doing much else. That was all she needed it to do.

Ezran was right. She and Master Genn were the faster riders, at least on these beasts. She dared to glance back only once and almost lost her balance in the process. She didn't even see the Princes or their guard.

Still, every pounding hoofbeat on the forest ground reminded her that she was going farther from Kyrith. That he was trapped in that cave alone with Gods knew how many Haubasts. The one that caused the collapse itself had to be over four times Kyrith's height. Could he kill it with Ser Maisym, who was untrained at best when it came to daemons? What if there were others in the nest? What if they attacked?

She couldn't let herself think like that. She had been to plenty of hunts with Kyrith and had seen him train. Arra knew him. He was probably one of the most skilled Kashadon she'd met and could handle himself. All Southern Kashadon knew the principle motto of their practice; *the fight isn't over. It never is.* Instead of praying, she said that repeatedly. Gods were too cruel and uncaring. She put her faith in his skill, in her need to get back to him, and in Kyrith's own ability to survive. All he needed to do was hang on, and if he was capable of anything, it was that.

CHAPTER
THIRTY

Sol and Kyrith walked together, side by side with their weapons ready. The tunnel was blanketed in utter darkness, its walls their smooth guides. Too smooth. It must've been fashioned by someone, but who would make a cave near Mo Byun? Much less have the power and time to do so?

It didn't split or fracture off, either. The tunnel was linear and wide enough for the beast to slither through without problem. It echoed with a hollowness that made Sol uneasy. There was no sound at all, not even a wind's whistle. He tried to console himself with the fact that rescue would come far before a lack of air became a problem.

The tunnel widened, slow and surely, until they found themselves in another large chamber. The space ached in its emptiness, three branching paths like gaping mouths before them. Sol swallowed and glanced at each. No wind came from any of them, even as he approached. All went on in endless darkness, no matter how far he reached *Chylus* into it.

Though, only one had that familiar scrape of scales.

They dashed to enter another tunnel's mouth, shoving their blades into their scabbards to stifle the light as their backs pressed to the stone. The noise grew louder in the dark, and Sol forced himself to concentrate on keeping his spirit steady. With one hand on *Chylus* to silence it, all they could do was wait and pray.

Kyrith didn't make a sound, but he trembled, brushing their shoulders together. Without really thinking about it, Sol took his hand, making Kyrith jump from the sudden contact. Sol inhaled as he sent his spirit to soothe him, prepared for its eagerness this time. Kyrith took in his own breath as he settled with it, stilling, hand warm and calloused in Sol's own.

Eventually, the hiss of scales faded down the tunnel. They remained in the dark, unmoving for several moments, until they were sure the beast was gone for good. Only then did Sol release his hand. He took *Chylus* out again, caution making his movements slow.

The chamber was empty. No eyes flashed at them, no screech, no rattle. The daemon had come from the middle tunnel. Now, it was only a choice between the other two.

Kyrith seemed to make up his mind already. He pulled *Askef* free and stared down the tunnel they'd hidden in.

"This way."

Sol didn't question him. They walked down another dark, linear path for what seemed like an endless amount of time. Sol would have stopped if it had been him alone, waiting out where he was, but something drove Kyrith forward. The determination lay bare in his eyes and made his brow furrow every now and again. That look wasn't exactly a comforting thing.

Sol's focus was pulled forward when a noise drifted in

from the black before them. Soft at first, but growing with every step. It sounded like fire, wind, and water, all wrapped into one. Cracked like flame, but had air's hollow whistle through crisp leaves, a river's babbling music, a stone dropping into a deep cavern. It had an undertone of something dark about it, too, like a shade's song. Beautiful and off-putting. *Chylus* rattled in his hand, far more violent than it had ever done so before.

Kyrith sucked in a sharp gasp and put a hilt to his temple. Sol cut a glance to him, ever wary of a serpentine head coming out of the darkness from either end.

"Another headache?"

Kyrith nodded. He took a moment to compose himself, but nothing came out of the shadows to attack them as he did. They kept on, pushing further into the dark.

Chylus' upset increased the more they moved. The energy in it kept palpitating, angered by some unseen foe. His own apprehension grew the closer they got to the noise.

Light spilled in the tunnel, soft at first but growing in strength the closer they came. Rounding a bend, Sol found himself blinded by it. A pale, bleaching illumination, moonlight in the dead of winter. It came out of a pit, one that seemed to be filled with every element there was in a dizzying array. Black stones circled in colorless, roiling water. Silver fire engulfed both. All of it churned on a cushion of air around the edges, a continuous streak of lightning cracking beneath. The cover over it consisted of a pane of rough glass and metal, painted with a red sigil that was definitely not Northern in origin. It wasn't one he faced before, but the edges in it, the lines and symbols—he had seen plenty similar in South Akadon.

Kyrith gasped in pain at the sight. A shaking hand

pressed to his temple as he fell back against the wall. He shuddered, trembling like he had a fever.

"Kyrith?"

"You... That's—ah." He swallowed and gritted his teeth as both of his swords dropped to the ground. His fingers laced through his curls. "That's a daemon... daemon pit. You have to... break the sigil. Break it. *Please.*"

Sol allowed himself only a small hesitation, his concern over the Prince's sudden affliction and the shock of a daemon pit appearing in the North forcing him to. His gaze swung back to the pit's glow as he raised *Chylus*, negative energy ebbing and flowing like a tide. Even so, it wasn't that overwhelming to him.

Sol entered further into the widening cavern, taking his sword up with two hands as he approached. The wall sheared off from him, exposing another portion of the room that had been hidden, as well as the flash of the awaiting blade using such to their advantage.

Sol's heart spiked as he jerked *Chylus* up, a breath away from being too late. Even his sword's flames couldn't fully illuminate the figure, swallowed in a brown hood. There was just the silver of their blade, pale hands, and the blur of their fast counter to Sol's block. Their swords clanged together again as the guard barely landed his parry.

The person fought like Kyrith. Technical yet fluid, powerful, flexible in a way that Sol didn't quite know how to counter. He wielded *Chylus* with skill, but the blade relied on more strength than speed, and his adversary seemed to count on it. Desperately, Sol tried to find some way to attack, but he was forced to keep up his defensive stances as he was pushed toward the pit. That dangerous song grew louder at his back, taunting and threatening him.

Sol's arms burned as he forced his heavier sword to move quickly, metal clanging together over and over again. His breath came to him in gasps as he blocked. He couldn't even think of an advance fast enough before the person forced him to cede ground again. The stone at his feet was washed in white. He had to do something, push sideways, attack—

The assailant's blade whirled in the light, soaring up for an overhead blow. Sol braced, crying out as his searing arms snapped *Chylus* up to meet it. It never did. That split moment of vulnerability was enough for a sword to burst through the figure's chest. Red flames spat in anger at the blood they burned away.

The figure collapsed, making Sol stumble to the side to avoid them. He heaved in air as he stared, the scent of charred flesh stinking up the space as *Askef* continued to burn its victim. Sol snapped his gaze from the guttering red flame to the pit, a terrifying distance closer than he liked. He took his sword in hand again and stepped over the body, raising *Chylus* one last time. With another steadying breath, he drove it down with as much force as he could muster.

Glass cracked around his blade as he slammed it to the hilt. *Chylus* flared as if it were trying to contend with Aescian's Sun, and shattered the pane into an impossible number of shards. Sol stared in awe as they cut through the elements, shredding water, fire, and stone alike, before the magic expelled with a loud clap. The subsequent shock-wave sent him sprawling onto his back for the second time that day.

Sol allowed himself a moment to lay there. His body ached as he closed his eyes and settled himself. Once he was steady again, he shifted onto his knees, taking in the aftermath. *Chylus* finally calmed down and returned to its normal disgruntled state. As its fire dimmed, the darkness infected the chamber and draped them once more in its disconcerting embrace. Sitting back, Sol lifted his greatsword towards the body. He maneuvered around *Askef* with care and used *Chylus* to lift the hood from the person's face, whispering a prayer for their peace as he did. Blond hair spilled out over pale skin, the healing remains of a sigil carved into his neck.

He was from South Akadon.

"Kyrith," Sol said. He received no answer.

Alarmed, he lifted his blade up and dashed to where the Prince had been moments before. He lay there, collapsed on the ground, unmoving. Sol knelt by his side, checking his pulse. Concern strangled his own heartbeat into something painful and fierce. The rhythm of Kyrith's heart was strong and his skin warm. He wasn't injured or bleeding in any way that would cause him to faint, at least that Sol could see.

He sat back and bit at his lip. If it wasn't physical, then it had to be...

Sol put a hand to his core, drawing in energy to his spirit again. Using considerable effort to ignore the residual influence of the daemon pit and his nerves, he managed to draw in balanced energy with a few calming breaths. Once he was sure it was stable, he urged it on to Kyrith's familiar spirit, hoping to find some clue of what was wrong.

And he did. A shock speared through Sol as his eyes snapped open, staring down at his unconscious Prince. There, in his core, the same negative trace of chaos that had radiated from the pit. It would explain his symptoms, the weakness and fainting. But that didn't explain how he had managed to use his sword.

Sol dragged his gaze back to where *Askef* was still

hissing away. Kashadon with chaos-infected spirits would never be able to use their weapons. Not unless...

His mind railed against it, telling him it was a ridiculous notion. Still, the thoughts planted and took root. *Askef* was right there in front of him. Also, hadn't Kyrith troubles worsened around large groups of people, especially when they were Kashadon or magically inclined? His headaches came just before the daemon, or around the pit. Sol's own power left him with betraying ease for Kyrith, and the energies afterward...

Sol raked a hand over his dark hair as he sighed. There was no way he could deny it.

Kyrith was gifted with spirit.

THIRTY-ONE

K yrith thought he could hear Queen Endri singing like she used to. Her lullabies soothed him to sleep during those first few years, when he still cried at the beatings and whippings. She had been the one to wash the blood and bruises at first. Singing to him as she did, she wove tales of heroes and hunters who overcame monsters, who claimed victory in the end. Valiant people who suffered in silence, who bore the burden until the Gods repaid them in kind.

Kyrith had long since discovered they were simply lullabies. The Gods never granted mercy, much less compensation for suffering endured.

He was wrong, though. It wasn't Queen Endri singing. Nobody was singing. There was only a crackle of fire to wake him from his nightmares, the flickering light illuminating the unfamiliar stone of the dim tunnel. A silver coat he didn't recognize served as a pillow for his head.

Solris watched the flames nearby with *Chylus* balanced precariously on his knees. His coat was gone, leaving him in only a thin tunic that showed off his dark, even skin. The muscle under it was taut, veined and shaped distinctly by his profession's rigorous training. No scars marred him. No sigils ripped into the flesh for power or control or protection. He was safe and strong enough without them.

Solris must've felt Kyrith's gaze because his eyes drifted away from the fire, though it still flickered in those green depths. A relieved exhale spilled from his lips. "You're awake."

Kyrith sat up slowly and put a hand to his aching temple. "Where did the wood come from?"

"The guardian of that daemon pit. He was camping in here. I figured he doesn't really need these logs anymore, and the smoke should keep the other daemons from coming to investigate his body."

Kyrith furrowed his brow as he tried to think. Guardian? There had been someone there... a hooded figure. Yes. He had thrown *Askef* at them, because he needed Solris to break the pit. The acrimony and wrath of it had been too much, and his protection sigil was far too healed to keep it at bay. It festered, amplifying through him. Threatened to consume him entirely. It had been inside him, inside his mind, threatening to turn his spirit.

"They wouldn't anyway. The one we killed will be a bigger draw, especially for the other adult," he said as he looked around, finding both Kashadon swords by his side. Letting out a breath himself, he took them up.

"Other adult?"

"Based on the tunnels, there should be another," Kyrith replied, checking over his swords.

Solris nodded before he spoke with his gentle low tone. "I had to become pretty inventive to get that sword free and back in its scabbard. You missed out on an entertaining sight."

"Thank you," Kyrith said. He checked the twin blades over. Both were unharmed and settled, for once.

"Powerful swords," he said. Kyrith flicked a glance at him then set them down. "They'd have to be... to serve a Kashadon with three gifts."

The words froze him, heart leaping into his throat as his mind became ice. He knew. Of course he knew. He probably had it guessed when they meditated together. Kyrith didn't know that was going to happen, but it was clearly unusual by Solris' reaction. And the pit...

He swallowed and looked down. Solris would tell his family, the King, everyone. At best, he would be sent to a Temple and locked up. Thrown away again. They might have him killed if he refused, or shun him for the same. He would have to run. Fending for himself in the shadowed corners of the empire, waiting alone for that inevitable dark fate.

You can always return to me.

A shudder tore through him. He would not willingly return to the Fortress, no matter what befell him in the North.

"You and Prince Kalin are quite blessed. One with the rare Nefion talent, and the other with two of the rarest forms of magic. Some say twins are always blessed, that the Gods smile on them."

Kyrith looked away into the shadow of the tunnels. "The Gods smile on few, and I doubt I'm one." The silence between them was thick. He set his jaw once, preparing himself for the verdict. "Will you tell Avis, or wait for King Nefion?"

"Do you want me to tell either?"

His gaze ripped back to the guard. Certainly, he would...

"You could order me to keep silent, if you wished. If it doesn't threaten the King, then I'm not obligated to let him know."

"I..." Kyrith swallowed and lowered his eyes to the fire. He tried to search for the proper words, but found them all jumbling in his throat. "I would never... order you... You should do as you think is proper."

Solris considered him, and he sat in perfect stillness for the observation. Kyrith counted the logs as they burned, embers glowing orange as they smoldered. How long had he been out for? How long did he have until the others came?

"What do they do to those like you in South Akadon?"

The question wasn't expected, so its answer came slowly to his numbed thoughts. "Lucky ones make it to the Temple of Odeion in Sankor, to make weapons. Others are killed, especially if found by lower class Kashadon."

Solris looked down at his sword and ran his fingers along its clean blade. "They aren't killed here."

"They're shunned," Kyrith answered for him. He knew this. He knew it because he hoped for so long that he might have a place in his homeland, and then he scoured a book on those gifted with spirit. Not much was known about the power. The tome was filled with all they did, on either side of the Fractured Empire, and the actions they took with such knowledge. Even blessed Master Lyrana was over-shadowed by the atrocities and massacres of those like Benras the Cruel. If they weren't the only ones able to make Kashadon weapons, they would have been eradicated long ago.

Silence slipped between them for a moment longer before Solris said, "I won't tell them."

Once more, Kyrith froze. Raising his eyes cautiously to

find clear green ones, he tried to silence the hopeful thunder of his heart. Solris put a fist over his chest, against the pendant that dangled there.

"You have my word as your guard. I won't betray your trust, as long as it doesn't bring harm to the rest of the royal family or the North."

Never before had someone made such a vow to him, or done him such a kindness without knowing him. Part of him thought it was a trick. His brows came together a bit and he swallowed against the knot of words in his throat, pulling two free. "Thank you."

Solris nodded once. "It's my duty."

Kyrith didn't quite believe that. He didn't know why Solris was so bound and determined to help him, and he didn't know why he was doing so now. Yet, Kyrith didn't dare question it. Perhaps it was Solris' nature, or he wanted something in return. Either way, he didn't want to anger him into changing his mind.

But was Solris really the type of person to do that?

His spirit wasn't. The magic in his core was balanced, true, enduring. It lacked the shadow of Marek's, or King Auberon's, or the royal guards that descended on him under orders. Kyrith couldn't exactly explain it, but he knew Solris was an honorable person. He was like Arra. Safe.

Solris shifted under Kyrith's gaze and poked at the fire with his sword, sending up a cloud of cinders. "I know you said to leave your wounds, but I healed them for you. I apologize for going against your wishes. I didn't know if it would help bring you back around."

Kyrith lifted a hand to his face again, feeling around for fresh scars. None met his touch besides the ones long since suffered and healed. Solris was quite skilled.

"That's alright."

Casting his eyes downward, he caught sight of the silver coat, this time recognizing it as the guard's. He brushed as much debris from the cloth as he could and inspected it for any more signs of wear. It was of fine quality, surprisingly soft to the touch, but ruined with holes and spots of blood. Unable to fix that in the current moment, he handed it back to Solris.

"You... How long have you been a guard?"

Solris seemed surprised. He slipped the coat back on, fastening the knots into place as he spoke. "Six years under the oath, ten if you count when I started training. I began my path at twelve, the youngest they allow with certain circumstances, to follow in my father's footsteps."

Kyrith studied him, his face etched into determination. "Your father was Captain of the Guard?"

"During the war," Solris said, nodding. He leaned back against the stone tunnel and once again ran his fingers over his blade. Now that it was unsheathed and so close, Kyrith could see the Northern symbols running down its length in an intense spread of knotwork. It was beautiful, lethal, and even without knowing what the sigils meant, he could sense the power radiating from it. "He died on the battlefield with his men and the rest of my family at Ovin Tal."

Kyrith had heard of that battle, or perhaps more correctly been punished for it, repeatedly. It was King Auberon's biggest failure, his last mistake that led to the truce shortly after. Many left their lives on that field from both sides. People said it remained so unsettled that not even the bravest of Kashadon went to them. The shades there were vicious, violent with bloodlust and battle rage, known even to the Southerners who didn't have to worry about them.

It was also where Arra's father left many Northern prisoners to die, kneeling towards Sankor with spikes through their hearts made from their own armor and weapons. King Auberon was fond of that part of the story when giving Kyrith his gifts. He was only thankful it was never a proper punishment, or Arra would have been forced to witness it.

"That must've been hard for you," he said. Solris twitched the edge of his lip, a false action.

"I was young. I didn't understand what it all meant. All I knew was my family went off to war and not one of them came back. Not my father, my mother, my brother..." His eyes grew distant as he glanced away, running a hand over his short, dark hair. "The war cost many."

"Yes," Kyrith agreed, but he couldn't help but notice the differences between prices. He still had his family, whole and intact for the most part. Solris had lost everyone he'd ever loved. "I'm sorry for what it cost you."

A look passed between them. Solris seemed taken aback, unsure. Kyrith, for once, wasn't. The guard nodded slowly. "Thank you for your sympathies, Kyrith... and I am sorry for what it cost you, as well."

Kyrith blinked. What it cost him? A price he was willing to pay, he had to admit, if it came down to him or his brothers. The reason why he had to pay it, however, was something he couldn't let himself think about. It was a thought he never let cross his mind. He was afraid of the answer, of the feelings that came with it.

"It cost me less than most."

"Did it?" Solris asked. Kyrith fixed his eyes on his swords. The words rang around his head, over and over again.

Did it?

CHAPTER
THIRTY-TWO

Arra knew it took far too long to gather a group of Kashadon and get back to the forest. Those with gifts of fire lit their path, along with Kalin blazing a trail in the front, and the few shades that did wander too close were taken care of within moments. After all, there was an abundance of them trekking through on this rescue mission.

The Northern hunters remained in tight groups. They were silently alert, like in the South, but something still felt too odd to her. Even when setting out to rescue one of their own, they carried an excitement she wasn't used to. Energy crackled through them all, palpable and infectious, like this was some kind of sport.

The fog grew thicker and ever more eerie as Odeion's Moon claimed the sky from her lover, held close enough that they were left with a first quarter. The different hues of various magics around her stained the misty tide as it roiled. Formless shapes danced just out of sight. A screech ripped from its depths, startling many of the hunters around her. It wasn't a Haubast's call, for which she was thankful considering the bleak cover, but something was in there.

She pressed forward, flanked by Kalin and Ezran. Fog wrapped around them so thickly that she would have lost them had it not been for their glowing weapons. Even Kalin's glaive was doing little to burn it away. It set her on edge, knowing the negative energies surrounding them certainly caused the gloom. If it grew so much in mere hours...

Another screech made some of the hunters behind them jump again. Arra hoped that whatever it was stayed deep in the murk and didn't further delay them. She should have known that the Gods would hear such a wish and decide to slaughter it.

The shade screamed once more, close enough that even Arra flinched. Peering about, she tried to get a glimpse of whatever it was, but it was hopeless. She could barely see her own hands.

The shade selected its victim, who cried out behind her. A moment later, dozens of glowing arcs of magic lit up the night. The fog swirled with the activity. There were more cries, more screeches that cut through her eardrums, and so much magic being tossed around that she put up her hand to shield her eyes. It was a wonder a stray blow didn't hit one of the other Kashadon.

Had they never fought in conditions like these before? Or was everyone so eager to get in their shot while they could? Either way, their overuse of magic combatted the energy responsible for the fog. It cleared enough for her to see the shade disappear in a ball of green fire. Ezran glanced its way as well, but Kalin was staring straight ahead in shock. She turned to see what surprised him and almost took a step back.

The cave was right in front of them. She tried to think back, counting steps, sure they were nowhere near it. But there it was, and if she took only a few more confident strides, she would have slammed into the side of its gaping mouth.

"This way!" Kalin ordered with all the authority of a Prince. He charged forward with Arra and the rest on his heels, plunging into the dark without hesitation.

His magic really was quite useful. Especially now, when the tunnel seemed an impossible shade darker than it had before. There was no banter this time, no jokes shared among the Northerners, even with Avis' presence. Kalin's golden light banished every shadow, and soon enough, it spilled onto the wall of fallen rock. Nothing about it had changed. She didn't know whether to be hopeful or despairing about the fact. Almost in unison, the two Nefion Princes and their guard stepped forward. A handful of hunters came up to join them, putting away their weapons as they went.

"Hold the tunnel up and secure it as best you can. Vyn will direct you. The rest of us will move the rock," Kalin commanded, dividing up hunters as he set his own weapon down by his feet. Ser Vynlier's group prepared themselves, raising their arms up almost in unison, and mimicked the stance of holding the tunnel arch physically. A crackle of power seared through the air. Balanced strength filled the entire tunnel.

The Princes and those that joined them all faced the fractured wall. The rest of their hunting party, Arra included, took several steps back. Lifting their hands, palms outward, the group pushed without touching the rock at all. The wall trembled with their efforts, slow at first, as all earth magic tended to be. The Kashadon strained with the effort of getting it to move. Yet, it began to buckle against their will. Dust drifted into the air as a rock fell, then another, and another, until it was an onslaught of stone tumbling backwards into the dark chamber beyond.

Ser Vynlier's group seemed to be having issues as the wall fell. A hunter broke away from their ranks, and those who remained winced with taking up her portion. She coaxed the roots of a tree to break through the ceiling and stitch themselves into a supportive archway.

It was agonizingly slow work. Though Arra wouldn't admit it to anyone, she was a little impressed all the same. Pushing past them before they could even begin to drop their hands, she raised her blade and entered the chamber. The only sound came from the beat of her own panicked heart in her ears, unsure of what she would face beyond.

Light from the other Kashadon filled the space from behind her, casting long shadows. The length of a giant serpent was revealed, burnt and stinking from several wounds. The Haubast which caused this whole mess. It pressed against one wall and rested on its back, the smell of rot heavy in the air. Two gashes bisected the exact middle of its body, one on top of the other, deep and yet oddly bloodless. It gave her hope.

Fragile hope that plummeted a second later. Kalin and the rest finally entered the chamber, illuminating the barbs that pierced the walls and holes where acid ate divots in the grey rock. There were bloodstains everywhere, more black than red, but she couldn't help but swallow at their presence.

She didn't have much time to dwell. The second Kalin's magic lit the entirety of the chamber, it filled with the sounds of dozens of rattles. Snakelike heads rose from their hiding place behind the dead Haubast, red fins flaring and shaking. She counted four of them. All juveniles. The adult was most likely their mother, and her bloody scent had enticed the offspring there.

But Kyrith? Where was he?

"Aim for the middle of their bodies. Try to cut them in half if you can!" Arra called out as she ran forward. Two of the beasts dared to slither out from cover, the bigger ones of the litter. They had to be the females. Male Haubasts were smaller, less aggressive. These two were not being so shy.

The hunters all spread out in the large space, splitting into four groups for each of the daemons. Arra found herself facing one of the females, the one closest to another tunnel she hoped led to Kyrith, alive.

She admitted it was much easier to take these things down with seven to a group. She slashed through one side of the juvenile's fin before she could even throw out her barbs, and Ezran followed her lead on the other side. Avis and Ser Vynlier kept her busy by attacking her face with arcs of magic, and Kalin himself cut through her midsection before Arra could even recover for another blow.

The Haubast died with a scream. Arra glanced back at the others, who were being swarmed by Kashadon from every side. The ones behind the dead mother were giving the most trouble. They spat short streams of acid every time one of the hunters tried to get over the body. When magic flew in their direction, they ducked behind it for cover.

Hunters cleaved the second female in half as Arra made her way forward and shouted, "Ezran! Flush them out from that side with fire. Drive them away from the body."

Ezran ran in the direction she pointed, joined by several similarly gifted. Together, they sent arc after arc of burning magic at the males. They hissed and screamed, spitting acid when they could, but there were too many hunters.

They tried to escape instead. Slithering out like cracks of lightning, they made for the dark tunnel near their fallen sister, but the Kashadon were waiting. Weapons of all kinds slammed down on their bodies, shredding them into an unidentifiable mess. Arra swallowed down her disgust and stepped over a pool of black blood. Kalin didn't have such control and staggered away with a gag.

"You Northerners are rather thorough."

"It's not every day we get to hunt daemons," Ezran said as he jogged to keep up with her. "They all want the honor of saying they killed it."

"It was a baby Haubast. I wouldn't be that excited," she muttered. Her eyes scanned the new tunnel walls like Kyrith would appear out of one of them, stoic and brushing off his injuries like normal.

"The big one," Kalin broke in beside her, now recovered for the most part, "Kyrith killed it, right? Him and Sol? They had to. So, they should be fine?"

She didn't say anything as Ezran clapped the Prince's shoulder, relating something encouraging along with Avis. Not that she doubted Kyrith's skill, but an adult female like that was a hard kill for a hunting party. If he had killed it, it would be the Gods' mercy if he made it out without a scratch.

She shook the thoughts from her head and focused on moving. "We will find him."

Nothing more passed between them except tension, knitting over them all, threading them together in the pattern. Even Avis seemed to let it get to him. The tunnel kept going on, endlessly dark. They had to be going deep under the hills of the forest at this rate, and the weight of that pressed down on her. The forest above them, the earth, all held up by mere rock with no escape but the linear tunnels... It wasn't her ideal situation to be in, that was certain.

Eventually the path opened up into a large chamber, but when she spotted three different tunnels, she almost let out a cry of frustration. Three birth hollows, and no sign of which one Kyrith would have dared to take. The only blessing at that point was that the other adult Haubasts must've been full, as they hadn't come for the body in the main chamber. Their entire group came to a halt before their choices and stared ahead with nothing to sway them into making a clear decision.

"Which would he choose?" Ezran asked, and it took her a minute to realize it was an actual question. One pointed at her, too.

"I..." She stared at the three gaping archways in desperation. Which would he choose?

There was no wind coming from any of them. Each seemed like equal pathways to death. They were identical in shape, all disappearing into a void.

"We could split up," said one of the hunters.

Arra shook her head.

"Not unless you all know how to handle adult Haubasts," she replied. Panic clawed at her throat, insistent and growing. She knew Kyrith better than anyone else here. She should have been able to figure it out.

"Let's try this one," Kalin broke in, pulling her from her thoughts. He was peering down the far right tunnel, thrusting his glaive as far into it as he could.

"Why that one?" Ezran asked.

The Prince took a step forward as his brow wrinkled.

"We have to start somewhere. And I just... I have a feeling we should go down this one."

"It's worth a try," Avis said and followed the other Prince. "It would be better than standing around."

She admitted he had a point there. Dashing forward to catch up with them, she found nothing but the same plain grey stone and yawning darkness ahead. Whatever feeling drove Kalin, it was clear it hadn't been from some subtle sign. It was an endless plunge into black and her frustration was only mounting the longer they went without a change.

"Do you smell that?" Ezran asked after what seemed like an eternity of silent, tense walking. His voice startled many members of their group and made Arra inhale deeply. "Smells like fire."

It wasn't just fire. It smelled like woodsmoke.

Arra ran. The Princes called out for her, their boots echoing like a rock slide down a mountain, but she was quick. Her own steps were barely audible, even with her speed. She kept a hand out and brushed her fingers on the wall to keep herself from running into something, tracing the bends and turns in the tunnel.

The source of the smell lay farther down the path. A fresh smoldering fire. The barest coax could have returned it to life. Someone had just been down there. She prayed it was Kyrith. With only one way to go, she sprinted through the darkness again.

Bends in the tunnel became her guide as footsteps of the others followed close behind. There, at the end, she saw a flash of light that gave her hope. Red and white flickers illuminated the stone, urging her to keep going. Her pace never slowed.

Arra entered the chamber with featherlike steps. Two

forms were bent over a shape on the ground. They didn't even seem to notice her.

"Hello, little ghost."

One of the forms rose to his full height, taller than she by a significant amount, and turned to face her. His sword cast an eerie red shade across his bloodstained face. The black blood didn't bother her, but the scarlet hue that seemed to coat one side of his temples did.

She didn't know what possessed her at that moment. Throwing herself at him, Arra dropped her saber with a clatter and wrapped her arms around his neck. He caught her and stiffened, but his capable arms held her all the same.

"I'm sorry for leaving you," she mumbled into his shoulder.

"The entrance collapsed," he said, tone as monotonous as ever. She shook her head and held him tighter. The chamber filled with the echoes of running feet, and a mere moment later, light banished every shadow from the space. Still, Arra didn't let him go.

"I left you with the Haubast—"

"It's dead," he replied. Slowly, he set her on her feet again and pulled her arms from around him with a gentle coax. Only then did she realize she was crying.

"It could have killed you." She sniffled. Kyrith flicked his gaze to each of her eyes and raised his hand. It froze, brief but there, before he touched Arra's cheek and wiped her tears from her face.

"It's dead."

He glanced around at the group behind her. She composed herself in an instant, swiping at her eyes and picking up her fallen saber.

"You look like shit," Ezran said. Kalin punched his shoulder as Kyrith glanced down at his dusty clothes.

"I apologize," he replied. Ezran rubbed his arm, throwing a dirty look at the one who harmed him. Kyrith's impassive state came back to him and settled, at home on his features. Despite it, Kalin stepped forward and looked over his brother.

"Are you alright? Are you hurt?"

"Ser Maisym saw to me. Are you?"

It was the first time Arra heard Kyrith place any inflection in his words when addressing his family members. Kalin nodded. The twins both assessed each other with doubtful glances, like they didn't trust the other to tell them the truth.

"Thank you, Sol, for looking after him. Are you alright?" Avis cut in from beside Ezran, and Arra finally turned to take in the guard. Immediately, her eye fell to the large hole in his silver coat and the blood that surrounded it.

"It's my duty, Prince Avis. I'm fine, thank you. We saw to each other's wounds."

"What of the Haubasts?" Kyrith asked, a little too hurried in Arra's opinion, though he was still eyeing Kalin. He was hiding something. She could tell by the subtleties in his features, the clench of his jaw, the line of his mouth...

"We killed a few on the way in. Arra said they were babies," Ezran said.

Kyrith nodded once. "And the other female?"

The group all glanced at each other, nerves cracking where excitement had once been. Ezran flicked his black eyes from Kyrith to Arra, an anxious laugh parting from his mouth. "There's another o-of..."

"Of the big one?" Arra finished for him. "It would be strange if there weren't. I told you we shouldn't split off back there. They have many family units made up in nests like this. There should be two more females with juveniles."

"One," Kyrith said.

She raised a brow. Stepping back, he flicked his gaze around the room.

"This wasn't a birth hollow."

Arra's lips parted when she finally took in the room itself instead of just Kyrith. It was grey stone, like everything else, but what appeared to be a large pit was off to the side in the back. She could tell by the pooled elements, the shattered remains of a glasslike substance, the blood...

"A daemon pit," she exhaled. Her fingers found her protection sigil under her clothes, healed but a comfort all the same. The hunters around them shifted with unease. All except the one, who dashed forward and peered over the edge like an excited child.

"No way!" Ezran exclaimed, gaping at the ruins. "I've never seen one of these!"

"Please, *please* do not fall in there. I cannot bear having to save someone else today," said Kalin.

His oldest brother flicked a glance over to him, as if he had stolen his words. Ser Vynlier stepped forward, stopping at Ezran's side. When he leaned over further, the guard seized the collar of his robes and kept him from tumbling in.

"What is one of these doing so far north?" Avis asked as he, too, went to examine it, though at a much safer distance. It was a valid question. The pits were naturally occurring in South Akadon, places where the animosity, violence, and grief wore at the wards between Realms, allowing daemons to cross from the Gods' to theirs. The energy was abundant enough for them there, especially the closer and closer one got to Kiles Tann. But the North didn't have enough negative energy to sustain them, unless it was located on a battlefield. Mo Byun certainly wasn't one. Which left only one option...

"It was made, purposefully," Ser Maisym said and gestured to the thing on the floor. Arra's heart almost stopped beating in her chest.

"That's..."

"But..."

"How did he get here?"

"He's from..."

"South Akadon," Arra whispered. She glanced up at Kyrith and held his gaze.

His pale skin, fair hair, and carved sigils were enough to draw the conclusion, but he also had a seal dangling from his neck. A simple thing carved from onyx, depicting the red moon and sigil crest of House Auberon bisected by a black sword.

He was a member of the Royal Guard.

PART FIVE: A KINGDOM SHADOWED

CHAPTER
THIRTY-THREE

Elysia, Pentral District, North Akadon

Ezran begged and pleaded with him, offering up anything under the sun to keep Avis from sending a letter to the palace. He just wanted him to wait until the week was out and the hunt was over. Apparently, Avis' honor wouldn't allow for such a delay.

He had three days. Three days of hunting in Sae Hyura and Mo Byun before Queen Nefion demanded their return. It was not enough.

He rode dejectedly as they approached Elysia, paired with a much smaller procession this time. The Sun Palace loomed like a warning over the streets of Elysia, and each clop of Taevis' hooves made him want to turn the mount right around to gallop away. The Queen's anger was almost palpable from where he was.

"I bet she hauls us right into the throne room, Vyn. What do you say? Five escs if she doesn't?"

"I don't take bets I'm bound to lose," the guard said, plummeting his mood even further.

"How bad do you think it'll be?" he asked, but it was Kal who turned to answer.

"For you? I would probably say she'll have your head. You were the one to push for the excursion."

"Enough," Avis broke in, his voice somewhat of a comfort to Ezran's dread. "She cannot blame you for what happened. She'll be reasonable."

He doubted it. Kal was right—in her gaze, he pushed for the trip. He was the one who had to answer for what happened, no matter if he directly caused it or not. She might be reasonable with others, but he had always been the villain in her mind, especially when her children had been unintentionally put in danger. After all, it had been his drunkenly constructed knots that gave way and let Kal fall over the side of the stairs in front of another District's delegation. Not to mention the fire of his making that once destroyed Avis' silk tapestries before it could be controlled. And his knife that somehow made it into Ves' four year old hands when he left it lying around.

Even with these rather understandable circumstances this time, his record didn't give him much room to work with. And Kyrith being involved? There was no telling how she might react to that. Kal was her golden child, she was always protective of him, but Kyrith...

Ezran winced as his mind spiraled. In reality, there would be no way to gauge her reaction until he was before her.

They rode through the gates of the Sun Palace as a solemn collective. Ezran's stomach turned over and over again, especially when Captain Talvys came striding to greet them instead of Ves.

"Your Imperial Highnesses." He knelt, then rose

following a gesture from Avis. "The Queen requests your presence in the throne room immediately."

Kal locked their gazes together as Ezran swallowed.

"Are we not permitted to make ourselves presentable first?" Avis asked, amiable as ever. The guard's frosted exterior melted a fraction as he took in the Northern Princes. He shook his head.

"Afraid not, my Prince."

"Surely, King Thamas would understand and keep her preoccupied while we cleaned up. We've been riding for a good amount of the day," Ezran said.

He only gained a glare of ice and a clipped answer. "The King is away, Master Breckhym. He's gone to meet Duke Ferron to discuss the daemonic increase among the mountains."

Ezran had to force himself not to flee. Without King Thamas, there was no real buffer between them. The Queen wouldn't temper herself. The punishments had always been worse when it was her alone deciding them. It was as if Queen Nefion had to prove herself and her control to the household and court. Perhaps she did, being of lower birth than even some of the servants. Years spent as a monarch hadn't lessened this need for her, and often Ezran was the one forced to endure it.

The Captain led them through the palace doors and straight to the gilded room. Sure enough, she sat tall, imposing, and alone, her silver gaze cutting into him the entire time. The group came to a halt in front of her and bowed or knelt as proper, muttering formalities.

She didn't say anything for a moment as her anger seemed to heat the surrounding air.

"Rise."

Ezran didn't meet her gaze when he did so. Instead, he

let his eyes follow the golden decor, the elegant moldings of the room, the white marble posts, and the shining Shield behind her even though it practically burned his eyes.

"Ser Maisym," she spoke slowly, her voice like cracking ice in spring. "Thank you for protecting my son from the dangers he faced in Mo Byun."

The guard bowed his head. "It was my honor, Your Imperial Majesty."

"Of course. It's nice to see that someone can keep their word." Ezran pressed his lips together, fighting an anxious smile, and braced himself. "But it seems others can't. Do you remember what you said to me before you left, Master Breckhym?"

He didn't quite recall. It had to have been one of his regular bouts of words meant to convince her to let them go. As for the details of such, he wasn't so sure.

"You said you all would remain together. You would be safe together. Did you not?"

He bit the inside of his cheek before he spoke. "We were, Your Imperial Majesty, until the collapse cut us off from one another—"

"What happened isn't important. You broke your word," she said.

Ezran sighed, though he had the sense to keep it inaudible. Reasoning was clearly not going to be present for this lecture.

"Mother, certainly these circumstances are important in examining the events. Ezran is no more responsible for what happened than Kal or myself." Avis stepped in. "I remember both Ser Maisym and I implored you to let us go on the hunt as well."

"Don't think that my anger is only for Master Breckhym, Atavis." The Queen finally ripped her gaze away from

Ezran, letting him take a full breath once more. "Unlike you, he was not seeing to his other duties. Ser Maisym was the only one of you that kept his word. How was it that he could, but not him?"

"The daemon was quick, Mother. We were together, but it separated us. There was no way for us to all remain. If you blame Ezran for such a thing, then you must blame me, too," Kal said.

"Be silent!" Queen Nefion's voice trilled across the room. "It was not you who spoke out, Kalin! It wasn't you who promised no harm would come to my sons!"

"He made no such promise, Your Imperial Majesty." Though the tone was low and soft, it silenced the room with its Southern patterns. Ezran turned to Kyrith, but his gaze remained firmly rooted on the floor. A muscle jerked in his jaw before he spoke again. "He said my presence would save wounds, but never promised they wouldn't be incurred. Besides, I'm unharmed."

The Queen looked like she was fighting herself. She couldn't keep the hardness or anger from coloring her voice, even addressing him. "You were found with blood on you."

"But no wounds, Queen Nefion," he replied without inflection.

Ezran chewed on his cheek, daring to bounce his dark eyes between the two. The Queen pressed her trembling lips together.

"Wounds?" she said, her voice strangled. "You came back to me wounded. Look at you. You can't look at your own mother, or even call me such."

Ezran almost winced himself. Kyrith remained impassive. He didn't look up, didn't flinch or even clench his jaw again. The only thing that seemed to change about him was a few slow blinks.

"Mother..." Avis began, but she cut him off with a raised hand.

"I sent a son to South Akadon. A loving boy, quiet but caring. It tore my heart to pieces to do it but I did, because it was my duty. And when I received a Southern boy in his place, I let him into my home, my family, and treated him as fair as I could." She flicked a dismissive hand in Ezran's direction, glaring briefly as she met his gaze. "He was brought up like a Northern Prince. But you? How did those Southerners treat my son, with the same grace and respect as I did theirs? Look at you. They took my son and broke him into..." She stopped herself before another word could pour forth. Ezran couldn't look at her or Kyrith, or anyone for that matter. He bit through his cheek until blood finally coated his tongue. "Just when you return to me, when I know you're safe again, this Southern boy almost lets you get killed. Perhaps he meant for it to happen. Perhaps he's just like his father and plans to continue his work."

It hurt more than it should have, a knife that cut through his skin, muscle, and bone to get to his heart. Pain pricked tears in his eyes that he welcomed with a broken, cynical smile. It was what he was good at most of the time. Smiling through it, brushing off the seriousness of his hurt. But it was too hard to fight the Queen's words as they rang around his head.

"Ezran wasn't in South Akadon." Kyrith once again spoke in his monotonous, factual way, but there was something lurking in its depths. A hardness that refused to bend, break, or bow to the Queen. "He's been here, Queen Nefion, longer than he's been with his blood family. He isn't at fault for what happened there, nor did he purposefully plot this."

Ezran cheated a glance toward Kyrith, who stood the same as before. His chest felt odd, contracting sharply like he'd received a blow to the sternum. He hadn't expected him to stick up for him. Much less go against Queen Nefion in such a way.

"It was an accident, Mother," Avis said. "It could have happened to anyone. We are all safe and unharmed, and home, now. That is all that matters."

Queen Nefion raised her head and glared down at them all with bright eyes. Still, her tone lost its power and sharp quality. "Yes. You are home now. And you won't be going anywhere else."

It seemed like every pair of eyes besides Kyrith's flicked up to her in various forms of despair. Even Ezran stared at her in shock, his stomach and chest twisting more than it already had. She couldn't mean it.

"All of you are to stay in the palace. That includes you, Lady Enryn, until I can be sure of your role in all this. You will not go farther than the gates, no matter what. Am I clear?"

"Mother, please—" Kal tried, but her icy gaze silenced him.

"The palace gates, and no farther. Be grateful I don't keep you in your rooms," she snapped and lifted her head regally. Her eyes were slow to descend and stare down at him again. "You, Master Breckhym, should be very grateful. Though, you never quite learn from Northern punishment, do you?"

He swallowed, but he didn't dare look away from her now. She turned her gaze away before she spoke again, looking toward Captain Talvys instead.

"If any of you are caught sneaking from the palace or disobeying me in any way, you will meet my extreme displeasure. I promise you will learn a lesson from it, too. Leave me."

Everyone dipped into bows and kneels, the silence thick around them all. They didn't break it, even in the hall, but stood around in its arms for a long moment.

"I'm sorry, Ez. She shouldn't have said that to you." Kal was the first to break. Ezran shook his head and played with a clasp on his coat.

"She was upset, that's all. She didn't mean it," Avis said. He was grateful, and he knew they were trying to be caring, but he didn't want to hear it. Not now, at least. Ezran smiled at them and glanced away.

Kyrith was gone. He hadn't noticed him leave from their sides. Startled, he searched and found his dark form drifting towards the stairs. "Kyrith, wait!"

He jogged up to him as the Prince turned, looking down. He didn't look upset. He didn't look like anything but Kyrith.

"Thank you," Ezran said. Only then did his gaze lift, freezing him in place. "I know it must've been hard for you to speak against the Queen. So... thank you. You didn't have to do that for me."

Kyrith blinked, as if he were processing his words. When he spoke then, his own were measured, but his tone was the same as when he'd addressed the Queen. Flat. Factual. "We both paid for our fathers' sins. There's no need for you to do it again."

Once more, the words cut deep into his chest, but Ezran couldn't exactly tell if it was a sharp pain or an ache of understanding. Kyrith bowed before turning to retreat up the stairs with soft steps.

CHAPTER
THIRTY-FOUR

After she returned, it didn't take Arra long to realize there was extra attention trained toward her. Upon entering her chambers, she noticed someone had gone through what little things she'd left behind during the hunt. They had been meticulous in trying to place everything back the way it was, but she'd learned to pick out those subtle differences long ago. One of Marek's first acts of crossing boundaries had been to rifle through her things. Since then, she'd learned to hide what she needed to and track the traces someone left behind.

She found nothing of importance missing at first. In fact, it seemed like they had put everything back where it should have been, until Arra opened her copy of *Benras the Cruel and Other Tales of Caution,* thinking a complete history of terrible spirit users was enough of a deterrent to be safe.

The mistake had cost her.

Queen Endri's letter was gone, and with it, Arra knew the target on her was only growing. Eyes were always on her anyway, so she played the part of noble, of unassuming Lady, of intended partner sent away to pretend like her role would matter someday in the South with Marek at her side. When everyone's attention was already trained, it was best to give them something utterly ordinary, and let their boredom become its own kind of hiding place. Thus, she fell into Lady Enryn, diplomat, and made sure to spend as much time as she could spare with Avis, working out some minor trade agreements that would never see fruition.

Still, if she had to play this role much longer, her nerves were going to come apart. Especially in the palace. It had only been a few days, but she felt trapped. The Fortress had been a nightmare, but this was a prison. A fancy, golden, tiny prison.

Arra took to pacing the halls like a wild animal, keeping the notes for her saber and its metal on hand in case someone felt the need to invade her privacy again. Every little noise set her on edge. Every appearance of a person sent her scampering for cover. It pressed down on her as much as the cave had.

No escape.

No space.

At least in the Fortress, she knew the places to hide. There were entire sections she could lose herself in when Marek hunted her through the halls, and while he might've found her in the end, there was still space to try. Here, every inch of the palace seemed to have a guard, or a servant, a noble, a royal that filled it. Even the back gardens were haunted mostly by the Princess, no matter the biting autumn wind and rain, or the sun giving way to the stars in the sky.

Perhaps it wasn't the people. Perhaps it was the job, the one she was so graciously reminded of in the cave. King Auberon hadn't said anything about daemons or letting them loose in the North. But the body had the pendant of a royal guard.

How did that all factor into his plans? If Arra killed King Thamas and the guards took care of the rest of the family, Kyrith would be heir to the throne. He would be able to make trade agreements and open the fruits of the North to the starving South once again. People could be fed, and more importantly, safe from the very scourge those pits raised. It didn't make sense.

Nothing connected as she slipped from hall to hall, quiet as a ghost. It was certain to her that the King or someone with control of the guard had plans that she wasn't privy to. Her head ached, going around and around with it all. Acknowledging it only made it harder to escape the other thoughts nagging in the back of her mind.

Kyrith's brothers had been so worried for him, willing to rush into battle without knowing a thing about daemons. Kalin risked collapsing a tunnel on himself and those with him in his desperation. All without knowing Kyr like she did. As much as she tried not to, Arra dared to entertain the inkling that perhaps they could keep him safe. The North was much better for him than the South. Maybe, if she let them prepare, King Auberon might not be able to hurt him. She wouldn't have to kill the King.

And then what? Become the Nefion's prisoner for the rest of her life? Let her homeland suffer and starve for one man? Disappoint her parents, force them to give up all they gained and bear the wrath that was meant for her?

He would be alive, Arra told herself, even as her gut twisted into sickened knots. King Auberon would keep him breathing to have control over the North. He'd hate her, but he would live, and her people would be better off. Her parents would be safe. She had to think of her country.

After all, she would be Queen one day. Sacrifices had to be made. Yet, that did nothing to stop a biting dagger from slicing apart her insides at the future before her.

As much as she was preoccupied by her thoughts, she managed to find her way through the halls, passing by a familiar table. It had been righted, put back in order, the Duke's upset left only to the memories of her and the walls. Drifting down the marble floors, it was easy to follow her path from a fortnight before.

The plain door was much easier to pick out now that she knew to look for it and found silence when she pressed her ear to its wood. Nobody was coming, either up the staircase or through the hall. With only a faint rustle of her skirts, she slipped through and shut it as quietly as she could behind her.

In the daylight, the stark difference of the servant's stairs compared to the rest of the Sun Palace was much more prominent. Arra kept her steps quiet on the plain, grey stone, boots scuffing the stained but ordinary wood. Soon, she found herself in the storage room of the stables. The smell of sweet hay, grain dust, and leather filled her nose as she shut the door properly behind her. A pile of hay bales served as her vantage point, securing her boot in place before she dared to raise herself up to the window, lest she make an ungracious acquaintance with the dirty floor below her.

Sure enough, she saw the rest of the stables from her perch. The storage room was positioned between two long lines of stalls and faced out into the courtyard to another open barn. How the horses kept warm in the winter with those stalls, completely exposed to the air, Arra wasn't sure.

She lowered herself down with slow caution and

searched the storage room for an excuse. Spotting a bag of apples, she grabbed one and made her way out. The horses pricked their ears as she appeared, a sudden specter before them. One noticed the apple in her hand and stretched towards it, lipping the air as Arra sidestepped the beast and its teeth.

The stables were located inside the gates of the Sun Palace itself, but skewed off to the side so as not to interfere with the main courtyard. It seemed like the Nefions only received guests through the main gate, or welcomed their own family home. Arra had seen nothing else come and go through the ruddy gold things, not even a rotation of palace guards.

There had to be a back gate for supplies and deliveries, perhaps another for guards and servants to head out to the Capital. It was another flaw in the Nefion exuberance. The Queen would never tolerate servants of her home entering through the same place as her esteemed noble guests.

The back gate ended up being on the tail end of the stables, made of plain iron. The two halves came together in the iconic Nefion sun, but no other hint of extravagance hindered their function. Arra tossed her apple and caught it as she studied the scene. A pair of guards manned the gate in full silver armor, lounging against them without care. She grimaced at the dark conclusions that slipped through her mind.

"Lady Enryn, what brings you down here?"

To her credit, Arra did not stiffen or jump, though her heart had no such control. She turned to face the person as calm as she could manage, slipping a smile onto her face.

"Captain Talvys," she said and tossed her apple again. "I've just been wandering about the palace. There isn't much else to do. Besides, I thought I would stop by and see the horses for a bit of fresh air."

The Captain's stare was sharp, his face an open book of hostility and distrust. "Are you fond of horses then, my Lady?"

Arra forced her smile wider as she drifted over to a brown beast. It lipped toward the apple in her hand, which she held out for it to bite. She willed herself not to reel backwards from the flash of teeth.

"I am." She tried for warmth and affection. "Sadly, I don't get much time around them in the South."

"Ladies aren't allowed?" he asked.

Arra swallowed her scoff as her mouth tightened. Like her country would have such arbitrary rules for women, or could even afford to have such. To be sure she didn't respond to the insult, she let her wandering take up time as she moved to the other side of the animal. She tried to remain enamored with it in her face, but kept a vigilant watch on its mouth and eyes all the while.

"They are," she said and blunted the edge from her tone. It was especially hard for her, as her normal speech came as if words were sharpened knives thrown by the tongue. "But as Prince Marek's intended, there's not really time."

"Right."

He wasn't exactly buying the lie, but she didn't know if the Captain would brave calling her out for it here. It made her heart pound all the same.

Disappear.

"I hope you know my Queen is not easy handed. If she makes a declaration, the punishment will be dealt out. Even to guests and foreign dignitaries."

Relief made her knees weaken and her head spin. Either

he didn't have the spine or the evidence to challenge her just yet. "I have no doubt your Queen is true to her word."

The Captain studied her as she forced herself to stroke the horse's silken fur. It snorted with what Arra considered to be displeasure and hostility, so she patted it once before stepping a healthy distance away.

"Let me accompany you back, Lady Enryn. The autumn air can be quite chilling. It would be a pity if you caught something."

She nodded, keeping her manner pleasant, though her hands clenched behind her back. The Captain didn't seem the conversational type as they went from the open air to the warmed golden cage, never once uttering a sound as he escorted her all the way to her rooms. Arra feigned opening her doors, smiling at him as she put a hand to the knob. Only when she opened it wide enough did he leave her with a curt bow and a pointed stare.

Arra let her smile go at the same time as the door. It slammed back into place just as the Captain disappeared down the hall. She folded her arms across her chest, unsure of what to do now. She couldn't stay in those rooms, sitting idly by, letting that target grow. Her old habits were ironclad and refused to break. Marek might not be here, but remaining in one place would never feel safe to her. And besides, she was driving herself insane with how circular her thoughts were becoming. She needed a distraction.

Her hand fell to her pouch, where she pressed the leather against the metal inside. Arra carefully pulled it free along with her notes, caving to her only other pressing matter.

She checked the time before heading back down through the halls. Kyrith, too, had his habits, though they were more ingrained in him than adapted. At this hour in the South, he would have been forced to drill.

And she did find him in the training room, drilling, as expected. However, she did not consider the fact that he wouldn't be alone. Arra stepped through the doorway and stopped short, staring at the scene before her in surprise.

Ser Maisym studied Kyrith off to the side as he went through a series of Southern training poses, meant to strengthen the body and calm the mind. They were the first thing taught to Kashadon, foundations meant to be built upon. Kyrith had long since advanced beyond these basic poses, and could perform the more complex and demanding ones if he wanted to.

He straightened from the floor, where he'd been supporting himself by his forearms and tips of his boots. Looking barely winded, he ran a hand through his black curls to get them out of his face. His hair was getting long again, even for Southern tastes. She'd have to cut it for him soon.

"Hello, little ghost," he said. Kyrith didn't turn to look at her, but Ser Maisym did, and seemed surprised to find her there. He bowed his head.

"Lady Arra."

Arra crossed the room and stood before them. "What were you doing?"

"Prince Kyrith was showing me some South Akadon training methods. I was interested," the guard said. Kyrith didn't flinch at the title, but turned away and glanced at the metal in her hands.

"Finish the last sketches?" he asked.

She let the other subject drop, though she was dying to prod him for answers. Kyrith was too shy to ask Ser Maisym to train, so he had to have asked himself. But did Kyr offer to show him their training, or did the guard brave the subject?

"I have." She held out the ink blotted parchment for his inspection. A simple saber was rendered there with her chosen sigils, just waiting to be forged and brought to life.

"If you can shape it, I'll handle the rest."

Arra paused and tore her eyes up from the page. "And what, miraculously find a spirit user skilled in Southern sigils?"

Shrugging, he took the paper from her and looked it over with a serious study. "I can walk them through it. Unless you'd prefer to wait."

Arra stilled. She didn't want to wait. Many Kashadon didn't get their weapons until later in life, and she knew it wasn't odd that one hadn't chosen her yet, but she had waited this long already. The thought of the metal warm in her hands was enough to make her realize that she couldn't put it off any longer, but she still wanted it done right. Arra trusted Kyr to see it through.

"You'd bring a spirit user here and work with them for me?"

He nodded, as if it were the simplest request. Her chest contracted. He'd push himself like that for her, because she wanted this, and in return, Arra would kill his entire family to keep him alive in a place he couldn't get far enough away from.

Even though she swallowed, her voice was still rough when she asked, "Are you sure?"

Kyrith glanced at the metal and then looked back at her, his brow quirking the slightest bit as her eyes began to brim. Arra hoped he mistook it for sentimentality while her stomach twisted apart. "Form it how you want. I'll take care of the rest."

CHAPTER
THIRTY-FIVE

Arra's saber was a simple, lethal thing, which complemented her well. She forged it with a slight amount of Kyrith's fire to help, to save her some spiritual energy, and left the blade in his care. All it needed now was a spirit user to hammer in the sigils, give life to it, until it became a proper Kashadon weapon. After, Arra would be able to pour a bit of her own magic in to give it access to her gifts and bind them together, at last paired with a worthy arm. He took the job seriously and wasn't about to let just anyone handle her saber.

He needed a balanced spirit and a clear head before he did anything. The weapon forging tomes had stressed that each was essential. However, both were proving to elude him that night.

No matter what he did, or how he tried, he couldn't shake the feelings darkening all aspects of him. Kyrith couldn't tell what it was, whether residual energy from the daemon pit, the Queen's deep rooted anger, or the upset it caused a few days prior. Whatever it was, whether it be all, or one, or somewhere in between, it was making it impossible for him to be balanced enough to do anything.

Kyrith tried to meditate, to call on the energies around him like Sol had shown, but his mind was too scattered for it to be effective. He was remembering things he shouldn't. Memories were surfacing and plaguing him. Faded ones, covered in a thick layer of cobwebs, and fresh ones, sharp as a knife's cut.

Kyrith hadn't settled since the pit.

Eventually, he gave up and put Arra's saber next to his own swords. They didn't seem to have any trouble remaining settled, even in *Eokor's* regard. He envied them.

It still didn't feel like home here. Everything was too unfamiliar and brought about too much insecurity. There were too many doors to his room. Too many rooms for him. Too many ways for guards or a Prince to get in and catch him unaware.

Those guards and that Prince aren't here, he reminded himself. But still, the feeling didn't leave him. The ache in his back, the prickle in his neck. Kyrith hadn't slept well since he came to this place. He hadn't eaten well, either. The food was too rich, and there was too much of it to go around.

Perhaps Queen Nefion was right. The Auberon had broken him into something irreversible, something twisted and fractured that didn't belong in such a fine, opulent place. King Auberon would be right, then, too. He was too Southern for them now. Scarred. Different.

Kyrith couldn't let himself sit and wallow in these feelings. They would only grow and fester if he focused on them, allowed them to stay. If meditation didn't work, then more training could. After all, between Sol and Arra, he didn't have the chance to push himself like he should have.

The darkened halls were lit only by dim lamps when he stepped out into them. Kyrith walked with silent footfalls, his head down and his hands clasped behind his straightened back, as proper. In the South. For servants. He shook his head like it would dislodge the thoughts, just as a familiar laugh broke out from the hall's bend.

"Shh, Kal, Gods. You're going to get us caught already."

Kyrith rounded the corner to find Ezran, Kalin, and Arra all trying to sneak down to the Prince's room. He raised a brow. Kalin, face flushed and eyes bright, was trying to open his door as quietly as he could, but seemed to be having some kind of issue.

"Kyr," Arra said with a smile. It startled Ezran enough to hide the black jars behind his back.

"Kyrith! What a surprise to run into you out here! Did we disturb you?"

His gaze flicked between the group as Kalin mistakenly leaned on the door, attempting what he thought was casual. It gave way into his room and made the Prince stumble inside, where it sounded like the floor caught him. He laughed again.

"You're drinking?" Kyrith asked. Arra and Ezran traded a glance before the latter took out the jars, his grin turning sheepish.

"Perhaps. There's nothing better to do. We even caught poor Arra here wandering about trying to disrupt the boredom. I couldn't have that, but since Queen Nefion forbade us from going out anywhere..."

"She also forbade us from drinking, as I recall, sometime back," Kalin called from his room.

Ezran glanced around with cautious, darting eyes.

"Stop being so loud. That rule is an old one. I doubt she'll do anything terrible if we're caught drinking. It's practically expected by now. But I would like to have a decent time before we find out. Kyrith, would you care to have this conversation in Kal's room?"

He didn't say anything. Arra slipped inside with her usual quiet grace and Ezran followed, hugging the jars like they were precious jewels. Letting out a breath, Kyrith found himself following suit.

Kalin's rooms were lavish. The one he entered seemed to be a parlor and dressing chamber, filled to the brim with jade, gold, and dark wood. They all gathered around the warmth of the hearth, which lit the room, and settled into upholstered seats. Kyrith wandered over, taking in everything on his way, and cautiously sat down on the settee with his brother.

Ezran was already pouring drinks while Kalin studied him. Kyrith could tell he was eager for another round as a lazy smile drifted onto Kalin's lips. Ezran slowly lifted each white cup and gifted them to the gathered.

"Do you want some, Kyr?" Kalin asked and shifted beside him. He eyed the glass carefully, almost full with clear liquid. He shook his head as he lowered his gaze.

"Did they not let you drink in the South?" Ezran asked before tossing his back.

Kyrith blinked slowly, once, fighting against a memory as it tried to surface. It wasn't him who answered.

"Oh, they let us drink," Arra said and set her cup down pointedly. "Kyrith just doesn't tend to partake."

He locked his gaze on her, watching as her pale cheeks flushed and her eyes went glassy. They both knew why he didn't drink. It was hard to keep your guard up when you were intoxicated. Something Marek had made sure to ingrain in him.

Kyrith clenched his jaw. Did he need to keep his guard

up here? Did Marek really have such control over him from leagues away?

They took my son and broke him into...

He swallowed as it crawled up on him again, turning his spirit and mind. Kyrith counted the things on the table. One by one. Two by two. It wasn't helping.

Pressing his lips together against his anger, he held out his hand. Ezran, Kalin, and Arra all stared at him for a brief second of shock. The dark eyed Prince was the first to get over it, breaking out in a smile as he pulled another white cup from the tray made for tea.

"Excellent! We're corrupting the honorable, innocent gentleman that is Kyrith Nefion. I, for one, am exceedingly proud." Ezran handed the drink over. He didn't allow himself to stall or think about it too much.

"I'm not that innocent," Kyrith muttered before downing the entire thing. It was a mellow liquor, smooth as it went. Even as it burned a trail down his throat, Kyrith kept it from his face with ease. A far cry from the fiery liquid he'd been subjected to before. The difference was enough to soothe him and keep those memories from surfacing as anything more than vague shadows.

"Gods, you two. What do they drink in the South? Vinegar?" Ezran asked as the glasses all shuffled back towards him. Arra snorted and reclined in her chair with an arrogant grin. "One day, Kal, we have to find a way to try their alcohol."

"Ah, ah. That will have to be an endeavor you pursue on your own. I'll settle with our mild brews, thank you." Kalin laughed. He put a hand against his temple as he sat back. Kyrith studied him for a moment longer than he should have. As if he felt the weighted gaze, he turned to catch him and raised a brow. "Everything alright, Kyrith?"

He nodded and turned away. Lacing his hands together, he watched Ezran pour another round and pushed any more painful thoughts from his mind.

"So, do you two often get up to this kind of debauchery?" their barkeep for the night asked. Arra's dark amber gaze cut to Kyrith, a solid sweep like the saber she was so fond of.

"I do," she said. The rest of her meaning hung in the air, visible between the two of them alone. "I'm quite fond of settling in with a few drinks, especially on hunts."

She left out the fact that she only ever did drink on hunts Marek hadn't joined, which were few and far between. Her intended would allow her to indulge, of course, but within arm's reach only. Arra had better sense than to do that.

"Mm, that's another thing. You must take me on a Southern hunt with you someday, Arra."

She snorted again and accepted her cup. "You will need more training before that could happen."

"Oh, that he would be happy to take part in. All he ever wants to do is hunt, train, or drink," Kalin said and tipped back his own offered cup. After accepting his, Kyrith studied the liquor before he followed suit and reveled in the burn. At least it felt like something other than unease.

"You're missing one key interest of mine, Kal," Ezran said. The two smiled at each other as Kalin gestured towards Arra.

"Sparing the Lady your charm, Ez."

"Spare me nothing." Arra's smirk was a cynical one. "I'm spoken for."

Kyrith stilled and lifted his gaze up to her in the brief pause. There it was. He was too focused on himself to really pay attention, but something was clouding up her spirit. It was too strong, too unbending to be affected like his, but a darkened layer still flowed over it like mist on metal. Something had upset her, and he could tell that it wasn't simply the thought of Marek.

"Right," Ezran said, though a hint of temperance came to his tone. "You are... you are to be Queen, then?"

"Eventually."

The silence was a choking heat that came over them. Arra's gaze gained a far off look, and she seemed to get lost in a cloud of thoughts that brought more darkness over her spirit. Her fingers worked against each other in an absent, repetitive motion.

Then, her head snapped up while her gaze focused on Ezran, staring at him in a way that Kyrith knew too well. Arra looked at her opponents in the same manner.

"You look like him, you know. Your brother."

"Arra," he said softly, low compared to the rest of them. Her gaze tore away from Ezran and shot to him instead, shaking her head as if to clear it.

"Do I, really?" asked Ezran. His voice grew quiet as well, but it held no hints of hurt. Instead, he had a careful sort of curiosity.

"A bit smaller," she said, dropping the edge in her words, "and he's taller than you. But the resemblance is striking."

He was quiet for a moment. Then, he began to pour, and spoke with false merriment. "I don't really remember him all that well."

"Be thankful you don't."

Kyrith sighed as he accepted another cup and downed it before Ezran could pass out the next one. Warmth spread through his entire being, relaxation beginning to take him, slow and sure.

"Is it... really so terrible there?" Kalin asked. Considering her cup before she spoke, Arra's words came free and unhindered, the drink relieving her typical guard.

"More so for others. Marek is really the only terror for me. Some find them everywhere in the Fortress."

Eyes fell on him. Kyrith clenched his jaw and kept everything neutral as their questions hung in the air, waiting to be given solid life among the group. He didn't know what he would do if they did, though.

He couldn't speak on it. He wouldn't.

Perhaps Kalin could sense his discomfort, or he was still too cautious of him to ask, but he decided to grant mercy for the time being. "I'm sorry for your experiences. Perhaps we should move on to a lighter topic?"

"Yes, we're drinking. Everyone should be enjoying themselves," Ezran chimed in.

"Gladly," Arra said before finishing her cup. "What does one do for enjoyment around the North?"

"Depends on the person," Ezran replied. All sense of anything other than contentment slipped from him with a sly smile. "If you're like Avis, you spend all your time doing your duties and furthering yourself as a gentleman. And tea. He loves to make up tea concoctions."

"Kyr loves tea," Arra said. He shot her a look and dropped it back down to his cup. Alcohol apparently made her the sharing type, and he didn't quite know if he appreciated it in their current company.

"Really?" Kalin broke in. "I do, sometimes. When I'm in the mood."

"I'm indifferent." Ezran reached for all of their cups again, and Kyrith slid his own across the table. "Ves hates it, though."

"Ves is also nine. She hates anything that doesn't have at least three spoonfuls of sugar in it."

Kyrith ran his fingers over his scarred knuckles, an absent gesture that didn't make his next question any easier. "When... when was she born, exactly?"

Ezran flicked a dark glance toward his brother and began to pour. Kalin's tone was gentle. "Mid spring. She was actually born on Aethradon."

The Day of Life. Fitting for someone like her. Kyrith nodded once and willed it to memory. Kalin was still looking at him, so he raised his gaze and found a smile there. A small one, but meant for him all the same, and something in his chest loosened.

"I'm sorry about what Mother said."

Kyrith froze, wanting to look away but forcing himself to remain as he was. Her words echoed around and around, acknowledgment only making them louder.

"She was upset," he replied.

"She still shouldn't have said it, to either of you," said Kalin as he turned toward Ezran. He shrugged in a way that hid what he was really feeling, passing out the drinks with a smile. His storming spirit told a different story.

"I thought we were moving on to lighter topics." Ezran tried to laugh. Kalin raked a hand through his dark curls, lightened a few shades from Kyrith's by the abundant Northern sun.

"She was wrong about you two, I hope you know. You both belong here. And..." Kalin paused, catching his lip with his teeth before continuing. "What I'm trying to say, badly, is I care about you both. I'm glad you're home, Kyrith. And I'm glad you're here, Ez. I don't want her to make either of you think you don't belong or something's wrong with you."

Kyrith couldn't keep looking at his twin, or any of them. The cup became the subject of his attention instead. His jaw tightened once more, a guard that kept his feelings from running free over his features.

He wanted to believe Kalin, and his words did get through to him slightly, but the Queen's were more persistent. They muddied up his head and made everything unclear, more so than the alcohol, or the tears that were sudden threats, pricking the corners of his eyes. Taking a deep breath, he refused to let them fall.

Arra was looking at him. The weight of her study only added to his discomfort. Ezran's spirit stirred, the same shift that was inside of Kyrith, and he could tell that the Southern Prince was desperately clinging to his own form of mask when he spoke. "Gods, Kal, I'm going to have to cut you off if you continue to get emotional on us."

"Alright, alright. I apologize. I had to say it, and that seemed as good a time as any. Give me my cup."

Everyone took up their drinks in an identical fashion. As one, they all took sips, but both Kyrith and Ezran finished theirs in one go. Kyrith closed his eyes against the burn, feeling the tension leave, the echoes of his memories growing fainter.

CHAPTER
THIRTY-SIX

Sol was still Kyrith's guard, and so, he had the job of being sure the Prince remained in the palace. The past few days, it hadn't been that challenging of a task. While he was on duty, Kyrith would train for impressive stretches of time. If he wasn't training, he was content to stay in his room. He hardly ever went anywhere besides those two places. When Sol would do his last check on the Prince, being sure the night guards had gotten to their posts as well, he would always find him in one of the two.

Tonight, that was not the case.

He checked the training room and the Prince's chambers to find him in neither. When he asked the night guards if they had seen him, all he received were shrugs. Considering they only patrolled through the halls and weren't stationed with any of the royal siblings, it would have been easy for him to slip by.

Sol cursed himself for not checking in on him at some point. He should have, even if it wasn't required of him. Now, he would have to go searching through every nook and cranny of the palace.

And of course, it had to be Kyrith, too. Sol wasn't familiar enough with him to know where he might hide out or sneak off to. If it had been Prince Kal or Master Ezran, he would have at least known where to start.

He checked with Prince Avis, but he was alone with his tea and a book. The Prince hadn't seen any of his siblings that evening. Checking with Lady Arra brought him to more empty chambers. Had both of them snuck out? Neither seemed the type, but then again, Sol didn't know them well enough to be sure.

Sol walked back through the palace and knocked on the Master's chambers. Again, he was met with a dim, empty room, and sighed. It looked like it was shaping up to be a night scouring through Elysia, but still, he had to check with Prince Kal to be sure. Perhaps he would find Vyn there, and at least have help in tracking the four of them down without getting the Captain involved.

He didn't expect to turn to the Prince's chambers and see light within. Chastising himself for leaping to conclusions, he knocked on the door with relief. However, his ear was met with scuffling and something crashing to the ground, followed by laughter. All in rather quick succession, too. His gaze grew flat before he even entered.

"Come in!" Prince Kal's call came. He opened the door and found all four of them sitting there, trying to act casual. Sol could tell what they were up to by the flush across Lady Arra's pale cheekbones, the red eyes on Prince Kal, and the lazy smile on Master Ezran. Kyrith was the only one out of the group that appeared in any way sober.

"The Queen doesn't want you drinking in the palace, Your Imperial Highness." Sol knelt as he was supposed to, but rose without prompt. In situations like these, he didn't have to wait for the command.

"Drinking? Who said anything about drinking?" Ezran said, casting a hand over the back of his chair. "We were just having a lovely conversation with one another. Bonding."

"Just bonding," Prince Kal took up with a bright smile. "No drinking."

Sol wandered closer, catching the smell of expensive alcohol wafting obtrusively in the air, like it wasn't obvious enough in their movements and speech. He took up a teacup and lifted it to his nose, raising a brow.

Ezran smiled in a bashful way, trying a different tactic. "Awe, come now! Kal's twenty-one. Why can't he have a drink or two if he wishes? It's not as if we went out to do it. We stayed in the safety of the palace. Doesn't that garner us some favor?"

"The Queen doesn't want any of the royal family drinking," Sol reminded him, "and you, Master Ezran, are younger than the Princes."

"I'm nineteen. If I can buy the liquor in taverns, surely I can drink it here, too. Besides, this isn't the worst we've done. Spare us, please, gracious and benevolent Sol. Mercy, I beg!"

Sol debated himself on what to do as he lowered the cup to the tray. It was a rather minor infraction for them, considering they had been cooped up in the palace for so long. Still, it was Queen Nefion's orders.

"Sol. What brings you here?"

He glanced up to find Vyn entering the Prince's chamber, flanked by two other guards Queen Nefion had ordered to check on the Lady and the Master. He nodded at Ullys and Ryslyn, earning the same greeting in return. Dropping his gaze to the party, he found all of them avoided his eyes.

"I was looking for Prince Kyrith," he said.

"And you uncovered a party instead," Vyn concluded. He came to stand between the pair that most likely orchestrated this and folded his arms. "Would it kill you two to behave for a single day?"

"If we are considering me, then yes," Ezran replied, smiling. "Kal, he could probably go a day or two. But as I was saying to our dear and wondrous Sol, here—"

"Save it. I think it would be wise for you all to go to bed."

A collective groan came from three of the sitting members, and protests came from two. Vyn raised a brow until they were silent.

Dejected, Ezran rose from his chair and bowed low.

"It has been a wonderful evening, my Lady, my Princes, but alas, our time must come to an end. Good night to you all! May your dreams be gentle, your spirits balanced, your minds clear! May we meet once more under Aescian's everlasting Sun!" He trailed out of the room as he recited the dramatic goodbye, tailed by Ullys.

A rather unladylike snort came from the Southern woman next to Sol.

"He's rather... flamboyant at times."

"This is tame for him, believe me," Prince Kal said. "But he's right. Our time has come to an end for tonight."

The Prince stumbled up from his chair and brushed off Vyn when he reached out a steadying hand. Shuffling away, he disappeared into the bedroom of his apartments and left the rest to find their way out on their own. The Lady rose without a problem. She traded a glance with Kyrith, but nothing was said between them, and then she was gone like the rest. Ryslyn followed, looking tired.

Kyrith got to his feet, but he stumbled as soon as he attempted to walk. Sol caught him, more out of reflex than anything, and helped steady him. He glared at the floor like it betrayed some kind of sacred pact.

"The ground shifted," he mumbled in quiet accusation. He didn't let go of Sol but didn't move forward, either, as if he didn't want to chance it.

"I think it's more due to you being drunk than the ground," Sol said. He fought to keep the amusement from his voice as he coaxed the Prince forward. "I'll help you."

"You don't have to. I can walk on my own."

Yet, he still didn't brush him off. Sol took his arm in a gentle grip and slung it around his shoulders.

"Come on. Let's get you to bed."

They made their way through the halls of the palace, slow and careful. It was a quick trip, but the Prince leaned on him the entire time. When they came upon his chambers, Sol kicked the door open and together they staggered inside. It was a wonder, with Kyrith's weight and current lack of balance, that they didn't end up toppling onto the floor.

"To the bed," Sol said. He dragged his Prince over to the large canopied thing and only then did he let him go. He dropped onto the mattress with a heavy collapse and groaned.

Sol shook his head as he went over to the hearth, stoking the fire back to life with a flick of his fingers. Kyrith shifted and tossed on his sheets behind him, but Sol didn't pay it much mind. Often, he'd helped Prince Kalin in similar situations, and endured the fits he threw due to being put to bed for the night. He had long since become accustomed to the drunken antics of the Nefion brood. Even Prince Avis had his moments, though he'd never admit to them.

"It's... it's too... soft." Kyrith's slurred tones were almost inaudible. Sol was still trying to piece together what he said when the accompanying loud thud came.

Turning, he found that the Prince had rolled to the floor. In a flash, he went over to him and knelt. Kyrith seemed far more content to lay on the cool marble, his dark curls spilling around him in a tangle. It left most of his face uncovered, his scars and those piercing eyes. Even drunk, they were intense, if not a slight bit bloodshot and hooded.

"You need to sleep, Kyrith," Sol said as he helped him sit up. He hauled him to his feet once more and caught him when he swayed. Kyrith looked up and patted his chest, as if he were testing the muscle underneath. Sol raised a brow. This was a fresh experience he hadn't encountered with any of the other Princes before. He became very aware of how close they were and tried to ignore the heat that crept along his face.

"You're strong," Kyrith said, his gaze lifting to Sol's before drifting around the room again. He caught sight of the blankets in front of the hearth and reached out for them, clasping the air. "Bed."

"I'm not letting you sleep on the floor. Why not your bed? Does it not suit?"

"Too soft," he grumbled. Somehow, his voice dropped even lower. "Don't want blood on things that can ruin."

"Blood?" Sol asked, alarmed, but the Prince was already focused on moving. He tried to walk forward towards the hearth, but the guard held him. Kyrith looked down at the arms around him and patted Sol's hands with surprising gentleness, like that would loosen their grip.

"Strong," he said and looked back. "Bed."

"How about the settee? That's firmer, and you won't be sleeping on the ground."

Kyrith's attention swiveled to it, and he stood there,

considering. It took him a long while to shuffle forward with Sol's help and drop onto it.

"Bed."

"Bed," Sol repeated with an amused shake of his curls. He didn't pull the blankets from the floor, but instead stripped them from the actual bed in the room and brought them over. The Prince hadn't removed his boots or even shed his coat, but remained curled on his side. His spine pressed tightly against the back of the settee and he stared out at the room with bright eyes, ever alert, even with drink in his veins.

Once he was taken care of, Sol turned to go. He wouldn't leave until the Prince was asleep, but he would at least give him space and settle at the doorway.

"Wait."

He turned back to Kyrith and paused. Kyrith's cheeks colored a bit, though his skin was doing it's best to hide it, and he buried half his face in his arms.

"Can... you..."

"What do you need of me?" Sol asked softly.

"I... Stay?" He muffled his voice with his arm. Sol lifted both brows in surprise. "Please."

The Prince raised his head a bit to watch Sol make his way back and kneel by the settee. "If you wish, Kyrith. I'll stay."

"How long?"

"Until the dawn's light, if that's what you need me to do."

Kyrith seemed to seriously consider this before he blinked and laid his head back down.

"Close," Kyrith said. Sol lifted the corner of his mouth. He shifted, putting his back against the settee's arm as he sat on the ground.

"Close enough?"

The Prince nodded, obscuring the rest of his face with loose curls and arms.

"Safe now," he whispered, barely loud enough for Sol to hear. "Strong. I can sense your spirit."

Sol rested his head back against the upholstered arm and looked out at the rest of the room. The blocked doors, the untouched items. His chest ached. "What is my spirit like, then?"

Kyrith didn't answer right away. Sol almost thought he'd slipped off, and yet he spoke after a long pause. His words were slow when he did, slurred and laced with exhaustion. "Calm. Bright. Strong. Safe."

Sol let that sink in. Turning to ask another question, he was met with the gentle rise and fall of Kyrith's chest, and Sol knew he'd surrendered to Nakre's hold. As he rested, every bit of tension left him, more so than it did during meditation. Sleeping, he was just like his brothers, though handsome in a far rougher way. Not so perfect around the edges, nor so out of reach to one of Sol's lesser rank.

Don't think about him like that, he reprimanded himself and forced his gaze back around the room. Kyrith was a Prince, Sol a royal guard, and they were both noble Kashadon to varying degrees. There were expectations and besides, he doubted that a Nefion held the same suffocating secret as him. Forcing it from mind, he leaned back against the settee's arm and entreated the mysterious Goddess to bless the Prince with gentle dreams.

THIRTY-SEVEN

L ightning was beginning to become a permanent resident in Ezran's veins as the days slipped by. There was no place he could let it ground, as training lost its attractiveness once it became the only one of his interests he could entertain. He hated this constriction. Ezran had to get out, do something. He couldn't be left with his spiraling thoughts and shaking hands anymore.

Ezran hardly had time to register his decision before he was on his feet and racing out the door. If they were to do this, they'd have to be quick. Vyn and Genn only had an hour where both of them were off, and they would have to be back to the palace before one of them returned. For once, he was grateful for the difference between him and Kal. Since Ezran wasn't worthy of a full time guard, he didn't have to worry about slipping them.

Dashing from his room, Ezran hadn't expected people to be in the hall. He accidentally barreled toward both of the twins right outside Kal's door and slid to a stop just short of colliding with Kyrith. The Prince flinched a step back all the same.

"Gods, Ez. What's got you in such a hurry?" Kal was the one to ask. Ezran flicked his gaze between the two.

"I need to get out of this place. I'm going to start crawling on the walls." He tapped his fingers against his leg without registering the action. "Come with me?"

Kal looked at Kyrith's impassive face. For once, he hadn't dropped his eyes to the ground. Instead, he studied Ezran with the same intense yet utterly unreadable look he always had.

"What of the Queen?" Kyrith asked.

"What of her?" Ezran said with much more bravery than he felt. "She's done this before. The punishment is always the same. I will be restricted to my room for longer, or I'll have to copy some old text, or clean part of the stables. It's worth it if I can stop feeling like I'm going to come out of my skin at any moment. Please, Kal? Just a jaunt through Elysia. We can even be back before the hour's up. We won't get caught."

"Get caught doing what?"

Ezran whirled on his heel to find Arra standing mere feet from him. She'd been silent climbing up the steps, a real talent of hers that he didn't appreciate at that moment. Though, he was grateful it wasn't a guard. His heart hammered away as he let out a chuckle of nerves.

"Ez wants to get out of the palace for a bit. I'm not sure we should. Mother's been a bit more on edge lately, and after the way she received us... I don't think it would be a simple matter if we were to get caught."

Ezran stepped up to Kal, trying his best to remain still as he put his hands on his shoulders. "Kalin. Half an hour. In and out. A brief moment of time. Five minutes, even. Please? I cannot stay in this palace another moment without coming apart at the seams."

His brother's grey eyes studied him as he pressed his lips together. His face crumbled along with his misgivings as he caved to the urge. Ezran had to stop himself from exclaiming in joy.

"A half hour. That's it."

Clapping once with his minor victory, Ezran whirled again and dashed back into his room. Within moments, he'd slipped on a simple grey coat and grabbed *Atka*. He scampered out into the hall to wait for the other Princes, impatience stirring up more energy within him.

Arra, surprisingly, was the first to return. She'd thrown on a muted blue outer robe, one that looked warm enough for winter. Her hair spilled over her shoulders in intricate pale braids and, once again, he was struck by how vibrant her dark eyes became due to the lack of color about her aspect.

Kyrith arrived later in his standard black and Kal came soon after him, dressed in a dashing shade of dark blue he hardly ever wore. He glanced at Ezran and his face fell, even as he grabbed both the Northern Princes' wrists and hauled them forward.

"Why do you have *Atka*? Ez, half an hour—"

"I just want it! Let's go!"

He dragged both twins down the stairs, checking for guards and servants with a quick scan of his eyes. He knew this palace like he knew his magic, and that meant he knew how it worked. The servants and guards were like a river's tide. One only had to time the turn of the current if they sought a clean escape.

Dashing down a few hallways, they finally came to an unmarked door in a tucked away corner, obscured from view. Ezran led them through, urging them to move quickly, as they flew down the steps and came out to the stables. Of all the routes he and Kal had discovered to get around, this had always been their most reliable.

"Wait, what of the guards?" Arra asked as he peeked out the window of the storage room, lifting himself to the balls of his feet. "The ones that hang around the stables and such."

"They only do that after they patrol through the city, which is in intervals of roughly half an hour or so. What's going to be hard is the gate guards. Ready?"

"As I'll ever be," Kal replied, voice full of resignation.

Ezran grinned and threw open the door, ushering all of his fellow escapees out to take the lead once again. They stuck to the far side of the stables, ever wary of the guards posted at the gate and the regular stablehands that dashed around, performing their tasks. He walked with them, forcing the pace to remain calm and leisurely, until they reached the back end of the stables. There, he found the crates, still in the perfect place to climb.

Kal went first, scrambling up the wall as Arra gaped. "You want us to scale the wall? And then what, leap to our doom?"

"You'll see," Ezran said with a smile. "Don't you trust me?"

She huffed. "Not in the slightest."

Laughing, he clambered up after his brother and hauled himself onto the wall, staying low to keep watch. Nobody cared to look back this far, not when they had to shovel horse shit and clean leather for the fifth time that day. This let them go unnoticed as Ezran helped the Lady up, taking her hand and pulling her alongside him. The strength in her grip surprised him, along with the ease of how she supported her own weight once she could properly reach the edge.

As she brushed herself off, Arra caught his stare. "What?"

"Nothing," Ezran said with an impressed undertone to his voice. She turned away from him and glanced down at the ground below, swallowing her evident unease.

Ezran meant to reach down and help Kyrith, seeing as it could be an awkward climb if one wasn't used to it. Yet, the Prince had no problem getting up as he jumped and grabbed the lip, then hauled himself over it in a fluid, easy movement. Ezran blinked at the two of them and tried not to wear his awe too conspicuously. By Anbast's Judgment, what training did they do in the South?

"Now what?" Arra asked.

He gestured to Kal and grinned.

"Follow us."

His brother crouched low and moved a bit farther down the wall, to the point that the Sun Palace itself became a shield for them. Kal stopped and turned to the street below. Facing the shops and buildings on the other side, he prepared himself, then jumped.

Arra rushed forward to see what became of Kal. Ezran smiled, counted to five in his head, and launched after him.

The shop's old awning creaked when it caught him, but it remained whole until he rolled off. A harsh slap of leather soles on the cobbles echoed as he landed, accompanying the grin he tossed up at the two left on the wall. A second later, Arra's slight form came tumbling down, and Kyrith's after a moment more.

The Lady brushed herself off again and turned to him, a flush already spreading over her fair skin. "How do we get back in, then?"

"I'll show you when we get there. There are a dozen ways in and out of the palace, and I've used every single one," he said, taking the lead once again. "Now, my good friends, we must escape the general vicinity of the palace and its watchful guards. To the Kashadon quarter!"

He seized Kal and Kyrith's wrists again, seeing as it was improper for him to do such a thing to Arra, and hauled them through the streets. Still, he caught the roll of Kal's eyes.

"You brought *Atka* just so you could get into a tavern and drink again!"

"I would do no such thing! Drinking is the best route to an unsettled spirit, I tell you!" he shot back, mimicking the disproving tone of a priest. He couldn't keep from grinning, however.

Sure enough, once they hit the Kashadon quarter, Ezran hauled them into the nearest tavern he knew the guards hated and finally released the Princes. They grabbed a table in the back, just in case a few off-duty guards did decide to give it another chance, and Ezran grabbed a jar of liquor from the bar. Once he settled into a chair with his spoils, he reveled in the way his heart beat with rebellion and satisfaction.

"Kal, Arra, and me." Ezran chuckled like a young child as he divided the drinks.

The look on Kyrith's face, eyes darting and mouth stiffened into a hard line, told Ezran he wasn't going to accept anything offered.

"You said half an hour," Kal reminded him again. Ezran downed his drink and took a minute to let it settle before he answered.

"Three quarters of an hour. We will be back in time before they can possibly notice us missing. And if they do, so what? I've long since gotten used to her punishment."

"I'm pretty sure that's exactly what she lectured you

about the last time," Kal said. Still, he tipped back his drink and handed the emptied cup over for another.

"She lectures me a lot. It all blurs together after a while."

Pouring them all another round, Ezran willed that statement into being. It wasn't exactly true. The last lecture was a fresh thorn that still prodded his side, but he didn't let it dampen his mood.

Freedom.

Even if it was simply defying a rule in a little way, Ezran felt better after he had done it. Nothing could secure him or tie him down. He had control of his own actions. At least, in this small amount.

They sat for roughly fifteen minutes, downing liquor and chatting amongst themselves on light topics. Arra's guard was back up, so she only spoke on trivial matters instead of her true thoughts. Ezran didn't know whether to be disappointed or grateful. He liked it when she did open up, but then again...

"You look like him, you know. Your brother."

It wasn't exactly a compliment, but was far from an insult. Perhaps it was better that those kinds of deeper conversations remained silent for now. He was just beginning to relax, too. The energy was alleviating and he didn't feel so trapped anymore, either in the palace or his skin. He settled with it.

Then the door was thrown open.

Ezran thought it was the royal guard coming to search every tavern until they found them. He even ducked with the thought as Kal and Arra snapped around, like that would save them. Instead, a Kashadon hunting party stumbled in. They seemed exhausted, beaten to the Gods' Realm and back, sporting wounds and covered from top to bottom in a layer of dirt.

"What happened to you lot?" another hunter called out. The room's chatter dampened, intrigue of the newcomers piquing.

"You wouldn't believe it if we told you," one of them said, a greatsword strapped to his back and a fresh cut lancing through his cauliflower ear. Ezran winced. What had they found that beat them so, and this close to the Capital as well?

"We got word a small outskirt village was having an issue. Livestock dying, noises in the night, normal shade behavior. We get there, poke around for a bit, can't find this damn thing, and then a fucking giant daemon pops out of the ground like a fucking rabbit."

Some scoffed, some gasped, but Ezran turned back to his group. They all traded solemn gazes as the hunters kept talking around them.

"Right. And Kanah came to my bed last night."

"Where's the proof of it? The body?"

"Are there more?"

"Which village?"

The greatsword hunter downed a full mug of ale before he continued. One of his companions, who looked like she had been dragged through the dirt, dropped a tied roll onto a table while he did.

"Your proof," she snapped and flung the ties open. The room gathered around, obscuring it from view, so it took a moment for Ezran or anyone still seated to see what she had presented.

Finally, a gap came in the mass as people stepped back, pressing fists to their mouths. Ezran caught a glance of what appeared to be spider's legs, larger than a horse's, covered with thick, spiny fur. He swallowed as his imagination pieced together the beast that previously owned those.

"What is that?" Kal gasped.

It was Kyrith's low tone that said, "Arachnis."

"Makes sense the livestock died. They bury themselves in the ground during the day for the most part, hunt anything that moves at night," Arra continued, pouring herself another drink with disinterest. "Tricky bastards to kill at times."

"And do they come in nests?" asked Ezran, his lip curling. The images his mind came up with were only getting worse.

"Depends," she said and he found little comfort in it. Her cup hit the table a second later. "If it was female, it could have a sac of eggs buried out there. But normally they're pretty solitary. The babies devour the mother right after they hatch and go their separate ways."

"Daemons... are such loving creatures," Ezran tried to joke. He couldn't take his eyes off the legs, and no one moved to cover them either. They were all too invested in the details of the kill that the hunter launched into. "Anyone care to go back to the palace?"

"Yes," Kal said eagerly. They left a few escs for the jar and made their way out to the streets, two shaken and two indifferent.

"What'll the hunters do?" Kyrith asked from behind him. Ezran startled out of his thoughts by the question, thankful to be ripped away from the images of giant spiders ripping apart their mother after they burst free from an egg sac.

"Report it to the city guard, or the Kashadon ambassadors. Either way, they will probably call on the crown for support. We'll have to go out there," he said and swallowed, his stomach turning sour at the realization.

"*We* probably won't. Avis might, the top of the guard, sure, but I highly doubt Mother will let us go take care of it," Kal countered. Ezran wouldn't ever admit to it, but relief coursed through him at missing out on such a thing.

"Really? Kyrith could probably go handle them right now," Arra said with a huff. "Would the Queen really not take advantage of that?"

"Arra."

"What? It's true. You and I have had to take care of those things every autumn."

"They're that common in South Akadon?" Kal asked with an overtone of alarm.

"Sort of. They aren't one of the more threatening daemons. More of a nuisance than anything. Scarier to look at than to fight. If they didn't kill livestock we can't afford to lose, then we probably wouldn't bother."

Ezran shook his head. He couldn't figure out how this woman could be the quintessential Lady one moment, polite and refined, and the next be talking about daemons as if they were no more than a common pest. He didn't believe her, either. A daemon that had spiny fur and looked like a spider in any capacity would haunt his dreams for weeks. Ves may enjoy those creatures, for some Gods' known reason, but they were living nightmares sent straight from Nakre to Ezran.

His thoughts remained clouded until they arrived back at the palace. The entrance they used was a crack in the wall, barely big enough to crawl through if one held their breath. Kyrith seemed to have the worst trouble, but he managed to scrape himself through after a bit of maneuvering. Ezran shoved the box that covered such a weakness back into place once they were done.

"Why didn't we use that to leave instead of flinging ourselves off a wall?" Arra asked, brushing the debris from her skirts. He gestured to the action and smiled.

"Dirt. Can't show up in a tavern looking like you crawled through a hole in the palace wall, now, can you?"

The Lady shook her head as Kal spoke. "Can we get going before we're caught out here? They will know if they see us in such a state."

"Alright, alright," Ezran said, leading the way. He rounded the bend to the stables. "We came back early. They probably haven't even gotten off break yet, much less noticed—"

A large group of guards turned at the sound of his voice, stopping Ezran dead in his tracks. He smiled, then faltered, then smiled again as Kal, Kyrith, and Arra all came to a halt behind him, his mind already trying to cycle through some kind of explanation of their appearances.

Sol, Vyn, and Captain Talvys all had displeased glares for the lot of them. The Captain especially seemed to narrow in on Ezran with his best frosted expression of distaste.

"Never mind. We've found them."

CHAPTER
THIRTY-EIGHT

He couldn't even come up with anything before Captain Talvys clapped a hand on his shoulder and shoved him forward. Ezran's mind spun faster with words, pleas, and flatteries that might get him out of the situation, but the Captain was never one he could sway. And with Vyn and Sol herding the rest of them as well, he knew they had already informed the Queen. Still, he had to try.

"Good friends! We were just—"

"Be quiet, Master Breckhym, if you know what's good for you." Captain Talvys hauled him forward by the bicep. Figuring the unpleasant man to be right for once, he shut his mouth, instead focusing on what he might say to smooth this over with the Queen.

Sure enough, they were brought before the throne with a small mass of witnesses made of court members. Ezran had been there many times to receive discipline, even without the King, but never had he done so with Queen Nefion looking so angry. Her gaze could have cut him in two. Red flushed her tan skin, her mouth pressed into a thin, hard line. All the flatteries he lined up for her died within a heartbeat on his tongue.

Perhaps Kal was right. They shouldn't have gone out.

"Master Breckhym. Do you want to tell me where you all went?"

He didn't know why, but Kyrith stiffened beside him. Swallowing, his heart picked up a rapid pace. His mind worked hard to come up with something, anything that might calm her. The true answer would only send her further into her anger.

Yet, he couldn't come up with anything remotely acceptable either. His stomach was turning over and over as his mind kept blanking, slowly freezing, getting caught up in his own head. The energy made his thoughts pass too quickly to focus on.

"Well? No witty words? Nothing? Speak, Master Breckhym. You have a tongue."

"I…"

"You? So, you went alone, and did not take my sons with you? The Lady Enryn just rolled in the dirt and joined you at the exact time you came back?" The Queen's voice was a lethal calm that frightened him more than anything. It wasn't helping him in trying to form sentences.

"Mother—"

"You will be silent, Kalin Nefion!"

Both Ezran and Kal jumped from her tone, but Kyrith was a sturdy wall beside him. Swallowing once again, he tried to make his leadened tongue work.

"I convinced them to go, Queen Nefion. We went to the Kashadon district," he answered slowly, hoping it would be enough. Her glare told him that it wasn't.

"Captain Talvys?" she asked, her voice returning to the frightening calm. The Captain stepped forward and bowed.

"They've been to a tavern, Your Imperial Majesty. They smell of it."

Ezran sent the man a thousand curses as he avoided the Queen's gaze. Did he always have to be such an ass?

"Drinking. Leaving the palace. Is there any other rule you broke?"

"It was me, Queen Nefion, I convinced them—"

"That's very clear, Master Breckhym." Her fingers curled on her throne until they paled. He clamped his mouth shut. "It is always you, isn't it? You influence Kalin. You can't obey a single rule. You don't learn, no matter how many times you're punished."

He took a note from Kyrith and kept his eyes lowered. His stomach turned again as he cursed himself repeatedly for not listening to Kal, for needing the freedom, the control. Worse, he dragged them all into this because of his selfish urges.

"Step forward, then. Take responsibility for once." He did as the Queen commanded of him. "Do you remember what I said to you just days ago?"

Like he could forget. He simply didn't know which part she wanted to hear. "I do, Your Imperial Majesty."

"Really? Good to know you can remember and yet still chose to go against me." Ezran winced and bit at his cheek. "What did I say would happen if you were caught sneaking out?"

He racked his brain for the proper wording and forced his lips to move. "I'd displease you greatly. And there would be punishment involved."

"I said you will meet my extreme displeasure, and I promised that you would learn a lesson from it," she said.

Pausing, she looked off to Captain Talvys, and the air shifted like wind before a storm. His heart raced, a warning ringing sharply around his head. Ezran chewed his cheek raw as he waited for it all to break. It was probably going to be awhile before he saw the light of day again.

"You never seem to learn from Northern punishment, Master Breckhym. No matter what kind we give you. Seclusion, meditation, studies, work. None of it sinks in. What am I supposed to do?"

The Captain shifted in his periphery, disappearing around the side of the throne. Ezran tasted blood. "I will learn, Queen Nefion, I—"

"Yes, I think you will this time."

The Captain came around the throne again and stood before his Queen. She nodded to the side at something new in the throne room, something Ezran had missed in his initial panic. It was another golden contraption, lost among the others. Thin, imitating a sawhorse in structure, made out of poles instead of solid wood or anything substantial.

"Maybe the method of punishment wasn't right for a Southern blooded boy like you. Do you know what that is?"

He didn't dare trust his mouth, so he answered with a shake of his head while he eyed the innocuous looking thing. The whole of court seemed to be waiting, holding its breath along with him.

"A rack. You will stand there and take your punishment of five lashes, like in the Southern way for going against the Queen."

Ezran's heart plunged into his stomach as he stared up at her, unable to keep his mouth from parting.

She couldn't.

She wouldn't dare.

"Mother, that is completely out of line." Kal tried to step forward, but a pair of guards were on him with a wave from the Queen.

The court was silent on the matter, with no one else willing to speak out. Either way, it was Queen Nefion's decision, and Ezran had been in too much trouble over the years for someone to defend him now. Her mouth somehow pulled tighter, her gaze becoming more icy.

"Out of line? Was it out of line for them to hurt my son before sending him back? Clearly, this is the only way to teach someone from such a place."

"Please, Queen Nefion—" Ezran began to plead along with Kal's objections. The Queen turned her head away.

"Captain Talvys."

The sharpest crack filled Ezran's ears, as if Genn released one of his arrows right next to him. A harsh sting cut over his arm, his side, his stomach, and he fell back with a painful cry. Instinct drove him to curl up as an ache invaded his whirling mind, hearing Kal's scream of protest.

He'd really done it. She actually ordered him to be whipped, and the Captain followed through. Only his brother seemed dissident to it as well, the silence of the court its own kind of whip to wound him.

Another crack made him flinch, but no sting came after. Instead, a sharp gasp spilled from the crowd, and Kal ceased shouting. The room grew deathly silent, nothing but the heavy beat of his heart pounding in his ears. Ezran dared to peek out from the safety of his arms and his chest seized.

Kyrith stood before him. Forearm lifted, he had caught the blow and held the whip as it wrapped around his wrist. In a fluid, decisive motion, he tugged the weapon away from the frozen Captain and wound it up calmly.

"Southern tradition for disobeying the crown is lashing," Kyrith spoke slowly, quiet as normal, and yet his tone was enrapturing. "If five is the number you've settled on, then five lashings it'll be, for every person who disobeyed you. That means Lady Enryn, Kalin, and I will receive the same punishment, unless your plan was simply to single Master Breckhym out and harm him for your own satisfaction."

The Queen became statuesque, staring at her son with wide eyes. She clenched her hands on the throne. Kyrith's tone wasn't accusatory, or even angry. It was factual and placid.

"Do you know of Kven Endelio?" Kyrith stared up at her, waiting for an answer that never came. After a moment he glanced down at the whip again and explained, "Southern tradition allows for a replacement, a volunteer to bear the punishment for all. The crown cannot refuse this and has no choice in the matter. It's known as Kven Endelio. I claim that right and will take the punishment. Twenty lashes for us all."

"Kyrith," someone protested, but he kept his gaze on his mother. Ezran's stomach turned in sickened understanding.

She couldn't go back now. If she changed the punishment, if she denied him, then she would admit to singling him out in front of the small bit of court she'd gathered. Then, the punishment wouldn't be legal in either empire. She couldn't pardon him, either, because the Captain already struck Ezran. But she couldn't possibly agree to whipping her son.

Not for him.

He should have listened to Kal.

The Queen didn't move or speak for a long time, and neither did her son. He did not look at the floor. Kyrith stared right at her, unbending, challenging. Nothing about him even quivered.

Ezran looked between them as his arm and side ached. He would definitely bear the bruise of that for a while. The single blow was harsh enough to cut through a part of his coat, and he couldn't imagine bearing it on skin alone.

Finally, Queen Nefion fractured. She looked toward the Captain, who stared right back at her and could give no escape. He nodded, confirming Kyrith's words, Ezran suspected. Her lip trembled and tears began to streak down her face. Turning back to her son, her tone lost every bit of its prowess. "Captain Talvys."

"No," Ezran said, scrambling forward as Kyrith handed back the whip. "Don't. I'll take it. It's my fault."

"Quiet," the Queen tried to snap, but her voice broke. She lifted a hand and guards descended on him, restraining him.

"No!" Kal joined in on his cries of protest. Arra remained silent, but her face was certainly not one of contentment. She stared at Kyrith with what Ezran could only describe as pain.

The Nefion Prince didn't acknowledge them. He removed his coat in a way that was far too practiced, hauling his shirt over his head, and let them both drop to the floor beside the rack.

Kal and Ezran both went silent at the sight of his bared form. Kyrith didn't look up. Oddly enough, his impassive state made him seem almost bored with the events. Yet, his skin told a wildly different tale.

Sigils, too straight and full of edges to be Northern, littered his chest, his shoulders, arms, waist. He bore marks from cuts, burns, and things Ezran couldn't even begin to classify. His back was a wreckage of scars. Some were thin, some thick, some pale, some raised. The most horrifying thing, to him at least, was the exuberant amount of red and purple scars, fresh from healing. They covered nearly every inch of his back and were displayed perfectly as the Prince braced against the rack.

Ezran couldn't say anything. The sight of what Kyrith endured choked him from protest and simple breath. Not only endured, but suffered in his place. He couldn't think. He couldn't do anything but stare.

Captain Talvys cracked the whip. A thick, angry red line appeared, raising old scars and new. He cracked it again. And again. Not once did Kyrith move or wince.

"Don't spare me because you think me your Prince, Captain Talvys, especially if you didn't intend to spare him."

The Captain paused. When the whip cracked again, it split the skin, and blood began to weep in a slow, scarlet track from the wound.

Ezran couldn't tear his eyes away. Over, and over, and over, he was struck. Not once did he wince. Not once did he do anything except tense, the corded muscles of his back flexing as the only sign of his pain. He didn't scream or whimper. The entirety of the punishment was borne in complete silence, even as the whip crossed over a previous lash, or the ever increasing amount of blood dribbled down his back.

Twenty lashes, all met with indifference, and then the whip stilled. He didn't even take a moment to compose himself. The Prince pushed off from the rack and slipped his shirt back on, put his arms in his coat but didn't fix the clasps. Instead, he strode forward and stopped at the foot of the dais.

He sank to his knee, leaving the other one to press against his chest. Kyrith touched his knuckles to the ground and bent his head. "Your Imperial Majesty."

The silence around them grew thick and weighted. The Queen stared at her son, and her voice came out choked when she finally found the courage to speak. "You can go, Kyrith."

He rose to his feet without buckling or swaying, bowing deeply to his mother, before he turned around and strode out of the throne room.

Ezran was numb. Arra broke out of the trance first. She curtseyed to Queen Nefion in a rather rushed manner and took off after Kyrith, running steps quiet as falling snow in the silent room. Sol moved next with a proper bow, a hand keeping his sword quiet, and was almost immediately followed by Kal. He didn't follow the court protocol. He jerked free from the guards' grips that held him and stalked away, with nothing but a hurt, accusing glare given in farewell to his mother.

Ezran shook himself free of them as well. He spared a glance toward the Queen, who's gaze was still locked on the place where her son knelt. A few stark drops of blood were left in his wake, scarlet and bright against the veined marble.

He didn't bow either. Turning his gaze away, Ezran walked out of the throne room and put a hand to his aching side.

CHAPTER
THIRTY-NINE

K yrith took a step. Then another. And then another. Because he would always keep moving forward.

Kyrith's back protested, but it was a far cry from King Auberon's work. He gritted his teeth against the burn of the lashes and tried to get up the stairs. They were a new challenge, something he never had to climb after an encounter with the King, and his lack of experience caused him to stumble. He caught himself, choking down a grunt as it tugged on the wounds. Shutting his eyes, he took a breath and counted.

Twenty-four stairs. There were only twenty-four more stairs.

He sensed her before he saw her, that unbending spirit washing over him with its strength. Kyrith didn't open his eyes. "Hello, little ghost."

Her arm snaked around his as she helped him up. A hand shot to the wall as a steadying anchor, head swimming as he shook it. It hadn't been that many lashes, nor had they been gifted that hard. Why was it troubling him so?

"Kyr."

"I can walk on my own," he said through his teeth.

"Clearly," she returned and tightened her hold on him. "Why did you do it?"

He looked at her then, sensing the others approaching fast. A strong, bright spirit. Another that flickered with anger, but had a gentle disposition under it. Like sunlight through summer branches, he thought, and his head swam again.

"Because it wasn't about Ezran," he said.

Her brow furrowed, but nothing else was muttered between them, mainly because Solris came up to his other side.

"Here," Solris murmured, calm and seeming unbothered by the situation. His lack of a reaction was a comfort to Kyrith as he took up his other arm, lending his strength.

"My room," Kalin said. Kyrith shook his head and ground his teeth together as they began the climb. Twenty-three steps. Twenty-two.

"I don't... want to get blood on your things," he managed to say.

"I don't care about things, Kyrith. Take him to my room, it's the closest. Vyn, go get Avis. And tell Genn to get some water on the way."

The guard dashed past. Kyrith stared up at him, noting how calm his spirit was. It was like Solris', but sturdier. More like an old oak tree, one that stood through several Ages. Still, there was a flickering of something within, a kernel of anger he hid well.

A headache was coming on to him as they moved. He

hated this. Hated the fuss of it. He wanted, needed, to be alone.

Eleven steps. Ten. Nine. Eight.

Their spirits tugged at him, plagued him, all in disarray. Kalin's clouded with his anger, Arra's with concern. A dark twist of feelings came from behind him, and the unique blend of spirit could have only belonged to Ezran. His blazed with passion, like a roaring fire or a rapid river on normal occasions. The two elements that he could control usually kept each other in balance, for the most part, though they were energetic inside of him from what Kyrith experienced. Now, it was like he was in a raging storm or a vicious wildfire, uncontrolled, struggling for equilibrium between the extremes.

Two. One. Solid floor.

Though he wanted to brush them off then, Solris' strength and balance was the only thing keeping him grounded. Kyrith clung to him a little tighter than he did Arra and hated the weakness of it. That was unacceptable, showing it like this, and yet he didn't have time to gather the courage to let go.

They brought him into Kal's room, and despite his twin's insistence to settle onto the couch, Kyrith collapsed onto the floor. Shrugging off his coat, he winced as he hauled off his shirt and refused help from any of them.

The door burst open moments later. Avis rushed forward and halted at the sight of him, putting a hand to his mouth. Kyrith sighed. At least his spirit was relatively steady compared to the others, but it was still cracking with his concern and outrage.

Kyrith didn't understand why he would be outraged, but he didn't have much time to dwell on it. Pain invaded his thoughts, and if it wasn't the pain, then it was the tumultuous energy in the room, growing ever more frenzied.

"What prompted this?" Avis asked, the usual temperance of his voice threaded with something that trembled. Behind him, Vyn shut the doors left open by his hasty entrance. "Why..."

"It was me," Ezran said. As he claimed a seat on the arm of a chair, the only things he looked at were Kyrith's back, his chest, his sigils. He didn't like the attention. It made him want to throw his shirt back on and hide from them all. "I made everyone go out and we got caught coming back in. I didn't think she'd... I..."

Kyrith closed his eyes as Ezran's spirit battled within him. It was almost overwhelming, spiraling, two elements spinning as they tried to win out against each other, growing and growing and growing—

Kyrith snapped out of his head when the door opened yet again. He took a deep breath and focused only on himself, or Solris, who knelt behind him to examine each lash with care. Genn entered, armed with a washbasin and a kettle of heated water.

"She decided Southern punishment was more in order for Ezran," Arra said. Kyrith didn't know if someone spoke between that. He was too preoccupied with his reeling mind, a battlefield for the overwhelming spirits. "But she didn't understand everything about it."

"I don't understand..." Avis murmured as Genn settled the basin near Solris. The retainer showed nothing on his face, whether he was shocked or disgusted or anything in between. His spirit, too, was an unchanging thrum of crackling energy, and betrayed nothing. Kyrith almost voiced his relief.

"It was out of line. I don't know what's gotten into her," Kalin said, his anger flaring in him once again.

Kyrith winced, but seeing as Solris was now attempting his best to wipe the blood away, no one really found it strange. At least his twin wasn't looking at him, likely due to his squeamish reaction to wounds.

"She blames me for what happened. She's always found me to be a replacement for Kyrith, a poor one at that, and now..." Ezran didn't have to speak more. All of their gazes ran over Kyrith again and he clenched his jaw to keep himself from attempting to leave. Doing so wouldn't allow him the peace of solitude and a break from the energy, as they'd only follow. Yet, fighting that urge was fast becoming a harder battle to win.

"She doesn't blame you," he pried from his teeth. "She wanted an outlet."

He knew, because he saw it. Like with King Auberon, and the darkness that twisted through his spirit. Unlike his, the Queen's had a lightness to it beyond the momentary shadow, but it wasn't enough to keep it in line. King Auberon never did truly think he was to blame, but he wanted, *needed* something to beat on. That darkness in him drove him to it. As long as he bore the name Nefion, it was good enough. Paired with Captain Talvys' innately darkened spirit, the whole event had been far too familiar for Kyrith to let it play out.

"You took the punishment for him?" Avis asked as Ezran finally looked away. Kalin flicked his own grey gaze back to the Southern Prince, but it seemed like he resigned to speak with him later.

"Kven Endelio," was all Kyrith managed to say as an explanation.

"It's a respected tradition mainly used by generals and

leaders to protect their men during times of war, before the Empire united..." Arra stared at the guard behind him with a frown and a furrowed brow.

Kyrith clenched his jaw as he fished around his belt, pulling free his athame with a bit of difficulty. He held it out. "Arra."

She snapped out of her reverie and took it, more out of reflex than actually recognizing what it was. Pulling the blade free and biting her lip, she swiped her other hand over his shoulder. The knife pressed to his skin and she began to cut with precise, practiced lines.

"What are you doing?" Kalin exclaimed, rushing forward only to stop short. Kyrith couldn't answer. The second the blade touched his skin, it was as if Arra drove it deep into his muscle. It took everything in him not to scream.

"It's a protection sigil. It keeps negative energies from entering the weakened body," she said and kept on. Kyrith tried to endure it, but every slight nick of the blade was like she was dragging it through him completely, cutting to the bone. It became too much despite how much he fought, and he let out a gasp that stopped her hand.

"It's hurting you?"

Kyrith couldn't answer. He clenched his fists tightly as the pain refused to ebb, even as she pulled the blade away.

"Of course it's hurting him, you're carving into his skin," Kalin snapped.

"No," Arra replied. "It shouldn't hurt him. He's used to it, normally, but even if not, it shouldn't be like this."

A cry clawed itself free again. His arm burned, and that burning was spreading fast, slithering under his skin and veins and core. Hands gripped him and he couldn't even flinch away from the touch, as he was too caught up in his sudden agony.

"Kyrith," someone said. It was a low voice, soothing compared to the others. "Kyrith, breathe. Breathe in."

He sucked in air as he sensed the spirit closest to him. It flared brightly, unyielding.

Safe.

Energy whirled between the two of them, and as the clean, balanced light entered into him, it overwhelmed everything else in a better manner than the sigil. The Southern technique tried to cut free the unsettled part of his spirit to give way for the balance, but the meditation simply flushed his core with energy to carry it away. The tension left him so quick that his head dropped back against something secure, solid.

"Breathe out," he heard in his ear.

He did, and the energy left him. It wasn't gone, though. He could sense it returning to Solris, taking all the infecting darkness with it. Somehow, the balance of the forces between them was too great for negativity to remain, and it left completely.

They did this a few more times, breathing in as the energy transferred to Kyrith, growing in strength each time, and left to Solris when they exhaled. Only when he was sure there was nothing left, when Kyrith held only perfect balance within, did they both let the energy go.

When it did, a lot of his strength went with it, yet pain no longer tore Kyrith apart from the inside. His spirit was once again settled and at peace with itself. Slowly, he blinked his eyes open.

Solris embraced him, arms secure as they wrapped around him, and let his head rest on his shoulder. His coat had to be soaked through with blood from his back. Getting up gingerly, he winced from the tugging at his wounds and ignored the heat that came to his face.

"Your coats keep getting ruined around me," Kyrith muttered. The guard laughed slightly and freed the knots from their place, shrugging the clothing off.

"As long as you're alright, a coat doesn't matter."

Kyrith paused, but he didn't have time to dwell on it. Instead, six pairs of eyes questioned him. The words were in their gazes, on their lips, but Arra was the only one brave enough to ask. "What was that about?"

Kyrith grimaced as Solris brushed his fingers along his back, beginning to heal the wounds. He didn't even have enough energy to protest. "I should've had you carve the sigil after the pit."

"Why?" Arra questioned.

Kyrith dropped his gaze from her and counted the cracks in the marble beneath him.

"It's a protection sigil that banishes negative energies," Ezran broke in, his tone thoughtful. "And he'd need it to balance and protect his spirit again."

"But you weren't around the daemon pit for that long," she said. "You weren't even injured when we found you."

"You were injured at the time, though, weren't you?" Ezran asked. Kyrith looked off to the side, but it was all the confirmation he needed. They had all seen the red blood on his temple when they found him. "You would only need to have a slight wound and spend a little time near a pit for it to affect you, if you were a spirit user."

Arra rocked back on her heels, his athame dangling from her fingers. She stared at him. Everyone was staring at him. All except for Solris, whose fingers brushed against his back and healed the lashes with skill. It felt like he was being whipped again at first, the pain of it threading through his muscles and jaw, then it ebbed to a sting, and then a soreness.

Kalin sat down on the floor with slow movements and faced him. He was the only one Kyrith dared to look at as he asked, "Is it true?"

Running his fingers over his knuckles, he counted each dip and rise as he went before dropping his gaze to the floor again. Kyrith nodded slowly, because he couldn't say it out loud, couldn't bear to face their reactions, the rejection surely coming for him. Avis sank into a seat. No one seemed to know what to say after the admission, and Kyrith waited for the verdict, resolution heavy on his brow.

"You never told me."

The accusation in the tone of Arra's voice surprised him. He glanced at her, wincing as Solris moved on to another lash.

"I couldn't," he said. Something seemed to dawn on her, spreading over her sharp features and making her gaze shift away. Whatever it was, it stirred up her spirit and scared her enough to let it show openly.

His heart stuttered, sure it was fear of him. Kyrith hated to see that look on her face. It wasn't as if she was vulnerable—Arra never was anything remotely close to the word—but more as if she were a wild animal, hurt and cornered, ready to lash out with whatever she could. He'd seen that look pass over her features too many times when Marek lost the little sense of control he had.

Her amber gaze cut to his and he came to the abrupt realization the fear wasn't for herself. "Arra?"

"He will kill you," she whispered, but the room seemed

to still with the weight of those words, at least for the two of them. He could sense it, not only from her spirit, but also from her features and the way she shook. "He'll never let you near him with spirit. It'd be an excuse to kill you after..."

"After what? Who's trying to kill Kyrith?" Avis asked, and Kalin shifted closer. Even Solris paused in his magic, which led Kyrith to lock his jaw when he started again.

Arra trembled. Tears spilled over her cheeks as she finally looked away from him. Fixing her gaze on the ground, she paused to steel herself over.

"I have something to tell you. About why I came here... About why King Auberon set you free."

Kyrith stared at her as Arra gathered her words. Even still, he didn't miss the way Avis slowly rose from his chair, crossing the room to face her. Vyn moved to place himself between Arra and the Princes, a subtle shift that made Kyrith's heart beat harder against his sternum. Arra didn't miss it either, the panic clear in her eyes when she looked up at him again.

"There's..." Arra began, visibly swallowing, "there's a plan for a party of royal guards to gain entrance to the Sun Palace. Their orders are to eliminate the Northern royals except for one, and to retrieve Ezran, then to take them both to Sankor. Kyrith would be the one they spared if..."

Silence held the room in a tense grip as Arra looked to the floor again. Kyrith could hardly breathe from how tight his chest became. Behind him, Solris rose to his feet, moving to stand with Vyn as both guards sought their daggers. Arra remained perfectly still. In Kyrith's periphery, he could make out the shock that Ezran wore plainly and the hand Kalin pressed over his mouth.

"If what, Lady Enryn?" Avis asked, the icy politeness

doing nothing to hide his anger. Arra took a moment more to look up at him, unyielding.

"If I found the way into the palace," she said. "And if I killed your father myself."

END

ACKNOWLEDGMENTS

This is a story that I needed to write. It came to life during a very transitional period of my life when I had to reroute a bit of my path and figure out what a lot of things meant for me. I moved from one coast to another, then a little farther than that, and this story followed me along the way. Yet, as every writer knows, *The Traded Prince* would not be what it is today without the help of some incredible people.

First off, I have to thank my sister, Megan, for always championing my writing. It was she who led me to Nymeria Publishing and ultimately gave this novel the chance it needed. A poet and writer herself, she inspires me every day to keep pursuing my passions.

Next, I have to thank Kennedy Champitto and Sarah Caro for all the hard work they've put into breathing life into this novel, both as publishers and editors. I couldn't have asked for better people to work with, and their investment in this story has always been astoundingly touching. In that same vein, I have to thank my editor Rachael Lord, whose amazing work brought this thing to its final stages.

I would also like to thank the talented artists and brilliant beta readers that were involved in the making of this book. To Sarah and Victoria, I especially give my gratitude for your feedback and love for these characters of mine. To Sam, thanks for lending your spectacular talents for the beautiful cover, and to Kyle, so much gratitude for turning a scribbled idea into a map of my dreams.

In closing, I want to say thanks to every writer and teacher who has shaped my craft along the way. I couldn't have made it this far without you. And lastly, my gratitude goes out to every reader who takes a chance on this story. I hope you find your way home.

ABOUT THE AUTHOR

JL Kayson is a trans author and poet with a Bachelor's in English, as well as a Certificate in Queer Studies, from the University of Hawai'i at Mānoa. When not spending copious amounts of energy on fictional worlds, he tends to enjoy the company of horses, his cats, and the rain. Known as someone who comes from a little bit of all over, he's waiting to see where the wind will take him next, and what tales he'll write along the way.

Printed in July 2023
by Rotomail Italia S.p.A., Vignate (MI) - Italy